KNIGHT IN SHINING CAR

Before Tori could think through the stupidity of her actions, she kissed him. She set her lips against his, a thrill shooting through her at the touch of his mouth, even if he wasn't actively kissing her back. His body jolted, going rigid, but he didn't pull away. He remained still. She wasn't even sure if he breathed.

Kissing him might not have been her best plan, but at least she got to scratch that off her want-to list. Heat rose to her cheeks and what she wouldn't have given to be able to crawl under the Tesla and hide.

A part of her withered, dying at the evidence that he just didn't feel the same about her. That had always been a big risk. They were different people, with nothing in common, and it wasn't like they knew much about each other. Still, she wanted him with an unreasonable desire—and he didn't return it.

She pulled back and pushed at Emery's chest. He shifted away from her, but she hooked her leg between his, tripping him as he put more space between them. His eyes widened in shock the instant before he rolled backward, into a controlled fall. He was much more of a fighter than she'd ever realized. The brawls Aiden and Emery had must be something to watch.

The part of her that wanted to win the fight said to jump on the opportunity to pin him. The rest of her said to run away, fast, before he called her to task on her dirty move.

"Careful, twinkle toes. Even tough guys can get distracted." It wasn't a dignified retreat. It wasn't even a smooth exit, but it was her way out. Mortification gave her speed. She wanted a phone, she wanted to call her sister, but she couldn't.

She'd kissed Emery. And she wanted to do it again.

Books by Sidney Bristol

Drive

Shift

Chase
(coming in December)

Published by Kensington Publishing Corporation

SHIFT

SIDNEY BRISTOL

ZEBRA BOOKS
KENSINGTON PUBLISHING CORP.
http://www.kensingtonbooks.com

To Nicole & Peter
You make dreams come true

Chapter One

Some operations he could see unfold before the first move ever happened.

Emery Martin watched the little drama go down across the street where two Iranian jewel thieves were no doubt pissing their pants, surrounded by six federal agents. Emery sipped his martini, but he couldn't enjoy the taste. He hadn't been able to think about anything since his last conversation with the frightened thieves.

The Russians are sending someone to Miami for a hit. It's not us. Word is it's because of some old grudge, but we don't want to be anywhere nearby when that goes down. You can get us out of here, right? They said you were the man to talk to if we could pay the price.

There were only two people in Miami the Russian mob might want to take out badly enough to send a hit team after them instead of hiring some local dime-bag thug.

The Chazov twins.

Tori.

Emery fired off a quick text to the arresting agent. He'd struck a deal when the case agent came to him with a gig outside of Emery's current operation. Emery would work his regular, high-end document-forgery angle, keeping the thieves stateside long enough to get a warrant, and the Feds would allow Emery first crack at them. Undercover, he could only ask so many questions before the thieves got suspicious. It was time for the suit to live up to his part of the bargain and for Emery to get answers.

Though Emery was employed by the FBI as an agent and field tech, his role was much more elaborate. Deep cover. He leveraged his ruined reputation and embellished criminal past to create a persona that fit the FBI's needs, while he got to work for the good guys and pull in a paycheck that didn't leave him hating the air he breathed. It was a deal that worked.

His phone buzzed with an incoming text.

Alley.

It wasn't an ideal location, but he needed to know for sure why an assassin team was coming to Miami.

Emery kept his head down, slipping out the back door of the club and into the alley. No one would comment about him making a clandestine exit. After all, everyone knew Emery was a money launderer and go-to guy when the needs were high tech. Too bad the majority of his customers wound up in jail or passing on merchandise that was bugged by Uncle Sam.

An unmarked van idled at the end of the alleyway. He kept close to the brick wall, eyeing the van. A man stepped out of it, closing the door quickly behind him. The yellow FBI letters were emblazoned across the back of his bulletproof vest.

"Seriously? Are you trying to make me?" Emery glanced from the vest to the arresting agent. The last thing he needed was for someone to link him to the FBI.

The agent ignored his protest. "They said someone's coming to do a hit on some girls. That's all they know."

"They—who? He mentioned a hit team." Emery jerked his head toward the van. He'd learned a few things while stalling the thieves. Like all the lowlifes in Miami were suddenly finding somewhere else to be for the foreseeable future.

"Doesn't know who. Just that it's the Russians sending them. Got to get them to lock-up." The agent thumbed toward the van with one hand and held out the other.

Emery shook it, trying not to grimace.

"Thanks again."

"Don't mention it," Emery replied. He stepped back, keeping to the shadows and put as much distance between him and the van as he could.

Assassins in Miami.

That was the last thing he needed.

He paused at the end of the alley and watched the van pull out onto the street. It merged with the evening traffic, blending in seamlessly. He was already mentally sorting the who's who of the Russian mafia in the States. He'd made it his business to know each and every face, their record and family vendettas. The FBI wouldn't appreciate his recreational uses of their intelligence, but he couldn't find it in him to care. Not where she was concerned.

Tori Chazov was his every temptation. The one bright spot in dark days strung together in a blur of surveillance and counterintelligence. Emery's life was a twisted mess, but hers made his appear to have been a cakewalk. Tori and her twin, Roni, were the daughters of a KGB spy turned American informant almost thirty years ago. Their old man was dead, but the girls were still kicking. They were also part of Emery's undercover FBI team, pretending to be nothing more than talented mechanics at Classic Rides, a garage that specialized in muscle-car restoration. Though Emery had never been tasked to keep an eye out for those who still had a beef with the Chazov family, he did it for Tori. Not that she knew, or would even appreciate his vigilance, but it made it easier for him to sleep—when he could manage to close his eyes, which wasn't very often lately.

He turned the corner and strode through the alley, heading toward the valet lot where he'd left his ride. If something bad, of the Russian variety, was coming to town, it couldn't be good for Tori or her twin sister, even if they weren't the intended targets, which he found unlikely. There was no connection between the Russian mob and the criminal organization their crew was stalking. None at all. There wasn't even a Russian presence in Miami to speak of. So why now? What were they after?

He needed to set scans to run all TSA screenings against his database, which was on top of his current mammoth workload.

Three months ago, he'd thought the team was finally in the clear, that their primary objective was completed and the job done. The whole purpose of their team setting up in Miami was to take down the kingpin of the biggest drug ring in South Florida, which they'd done without harming a single civilian. Except their target, Michael Evers, was still in police custody. Not rotting in a federal penitentiary. And there were no new marching orders. Add to it a rival street racing gang who wanted to see Emery's crew dead, and he'd spent more time lately watching his rearview mirror than the road ahead of him.

"Shit," he muttered.

He hovered in the alley as two patrol officers and a man in a polo shirt and slacks walked around Emery's Tesla Roadster. The hundred-thousand-dollar car was a hand-me-down from a government bust, meant to bolster his street cred. Too bad it also made him stick out at the least opportune times.

Emery sucked in a deep breath. He wasn't a people person, preferring his bank of computer monitors to actually dealing with the living. The last person he wanted to interface with was Detective Matt Smith. The cop had kept his distance after Aiden brought him in to make the arrest on Michael Evers. What was more, Matt knew their secret and hadn't shared it, to Emery's knowledge. At least he hadn't e-mailed, texted, or chatted about it. To cover their asses, Emery had hacked the good detective's accounts and set up a program to record every keystroke. Matt hadn't so much as run a search on any of them.

That was a lie.

Matt had looked up Roni's record once, but nothing came of it. Emery had ensured the girls had nothing out of the ordinary in their public files. Still, it was curious.

Emery pulled out his phone and activated the app that connected to the car. The electric vehicle had almost a full charge and it didn't appear that the detective had attempted to tamper with the vehicle. Good for both of them. Emery had somewhere to be. Too bad it didn't appear as though Matt was going anywhere.

"Can I help you, Officers?" Emery strolled toward the trio and one nervous valet, hands at his sides.

Detective Smith stood at the front of the car, hands on his hips. He'd pushed his sunglasses up on his brow, messing up his perfectly gelled blond hair. Aiden, the coleader of their crew and Classic Rides, their operation's front business, had nicknamed the cop Golden Boy, which was fitting. To Emery's knowledge, Matt colored inside the lines.

"You wear something besides your grandpa's clothes?" Detective Smith smirked.

Emery stared at the detective. He'd heard every variety of insult in his life. Picking on his clothes was about as boring as it got. Besides, the clothes were designer—some name brand all the South Beach hotshots were wearing. Yeah, it looked ridiculous, but it also helped his high-rolling, go-to-guy image.

"What do you want?" he asked.

"Checking on a stolen car report. Running serial numbers, that's all."

Was this some kind of code? Did Smith want to talk? Then why bring the uniforms? Only an idiot would think the Tesla was stolen.

"Where's DeHart?" Smith asked.

"I believe he has a date tonight, so you'll have to get in line for your good-night kiss." For a couple months, before their crew got involved, Matt had tried to shield a woman named Madison Haughton from her ex-husband, one of Michael Evers's fall guys. Emery, like many others, had suspected the detective of being sweet on Madison, but Smith wasn't her type. She'd moved in with Aiden DeHart and had all but taken his last name in the intervening three months.

Matt stalked around the car and got up in Emery's face. The detective was about the same height, but Emery was willing to bet the good ol' cop would go down easy. That was the problem. Cops had to fight fair, while Emery fought to survive. He'd had plenty of practice and had managed to keep most of his skin, while he was willing to bet Matt had only ever suffered scraped knuckles and a black eye.

"I need to talk to DeHart," Matt said, pitching his voice low.

That was it?

Something had to be up if the detective couldn't just ring the Classic Rides garage, but this wasn't the place to talk about it. First the Feds, now the cops—there was far too much brass in this part of Miami tonight for Emery's taste.

"We'll be in touch." Emery pitched his voice louder so the uniforms heard. "Unless you have something of worth to say to me, get away from my car."

Matt glanced down. "That knee of yours is looking a little tight. Bothering you?"

Fuck you.

Emery didn't say it, but he sure as hell tightened his right hand into a fist. Matt had to be snooping on a device that Emery hadn't hacked yet if he knew about Emery's knee injury. Instead, he gestured to the valet, who produced his key fob.

"Don't let me catch you sniffing around my car again, Detective. You won't like the consequences." Emery would have to dig around on the detective a bit more. Truth was, they could use him. Especially if Smith could tell them why Evers wasn't in federal custody.

Something wasn't right, and Emery had to get to the bottom of it all before shit hit the fan. His team relied on him to head off or warn them about possible threats.

He dropped into the Tesla and slid his phone onto the cradle. The engine hummed to life, barely noticeable compared to the noise other cars made. The suit jacket and button-up shirt were stifling, but he didn't have time to shed them. The cruiser backed off, giving Emery enough room to burn a little rubber as he left the lot. The cops didn't make any move to tail him, but he still kept an eye on his six.

Unlike the rest of Emery's crew, he worked away from the garage and cars, in a fortress of solitude and servers. Not many knew he was connected to the mechanics at

Classic Rides, and he liked it that way. It gave him the
freedom to perform tasks the others couldn't. Which meant
it was probably easier for Matt to approach him, rather
than the others, without drawing notice.

The on-board computer muted the music as the clatter
of an old-timey phone rang through the speakers.

"Incoming call from Tori," the mechanical voice announced.

His pulse jumped. Were the Russians here already?

"Answer," Emery said.

The car's system beeped, activating the call. He tapped
the steering wheel and consciously decreased the pressure
on the accelerator.

"Tori?"

"Hey, are you at home?" Grease. Laughter. Mint gum.
Torn coveralls. A hundred little details about her he'd
catalogued flitted through his brain. There was a new one
to add to his list. Strain. Her voice didn't contain any of the
sunshine it usually did.

"No. I'm headed there. What's up?" Screw it. He accelerated, cutting in front of an eighteen-wheeler and turning
onto a side street, then onto another two-lane road, zigzagging
his way through the heart of Miami.

"I just . . ." She sighed. "Roni's going to the Orlando
Race Battle with the others."

"Oh."

He scrambled to recall the discussion they'd had about
the merits of the trip to Orlando in their last get-together at
the Shop, a warehouse they'd outfitted for their less-than-
legal operations.

On one hand, the crew had a lot of targets on their back,
and dividing the team for an upstate race was leaving them
handicapped in Miami. Their line of work attracted adrenaline junkies, and the best way to blow off some steam on

this operation was to engage in a little illegal street racing. Staying active on the race scene kept them up to date on all the shady dealings in Miami. The downside was that they'd gained some notable enemies. Like the Eleventh Street gang who the crew had gotten involved in a shoot-out with just a few months ago. The Eleventh Street's leader, Raibel Canales, was still deep underground, running from the cops and Emery's crew. There was a small chance Canales could show up, which would give them an excellent opportunity to bust his ass.

A serious point of contention was Roni, Tori's sister. Not only did the Eleventh and Evers want her dead on principle, but she'd bled all over a crime scene. The cops hadn't connected her to it—yet—but they would eventually. Having Smith in their corner would be handy to know what was rolling down the hill at them, but until tonight all members of their crew had kept their distance. Add to it there might be some extra heat from the Russians, and he wasn't sure the race was a good place for Tori's sister.

"What do you want me to do?" Short of murder, there wasn't much he wouldn't do for Tori. It was a new, sad state of his obsession that he realized just how far he was willing to go.

"Can you keep a tracker on her?"

"I already track everyone through cell phones and the GPS in your cars." Did Tori know? His other sad, sick fascination was pulling up her location on an auxiliary screen while he worked, watching her red dot blink, teasing him with all the things she might be doing.

"No, I mean, something she wouldn't take off or intentionally disengage."

So Tori knew. Had she given him the shake before?

Emery checked his rearview mirror. He'd hit a quieter side street and the only lights behind him were overhead.

Coast was clear. He pressed the accelerator, kicking up his speed.

"What do you have in mind?" Tori had a way of leading people into her plans. Smart, because she wasn't seen as the instigator. The others never noticed, and truth was, Tori had a sharp mind for strategy, but she wouldn't play those tricks on him.

"Roni broke the clasp on her necklace. I picked it up and was thinking . . . could you do something with it?"

"Not sure. I'd need to see it." He could picture the necklace in detail—both twins wore them. Gold chain, nothing too fancy, with a locket smaller than a dime and a charm featuring one of her saints. He'd never figured out which one of the Russian Orthodox figures it was because he rarely allowed himself to get that close.

It was one thing to admire Tori, to be conscious of her movements, but he'd drawn the line at seeking her out. Being in close proximity to her. Girls like her didn't exactly date the resident geek.

"Well . . . that's what I called about. I was kind of hoping you were home, but I guess you're out tonight."

"Where are you, Tori?"

"Your house."

He glanced at the phone, itching to pull up her location via the tracking app he'd created for their team. She was at his house? Tori knew where he lived? The only team members who'd been inside his house were CJ, Kathy, Julian, and Adrian. The rest more or less ignored him unless something was broken or they needed a bit of tech.

"I'll be there in fifteen. There's a gate to the left of the house. Go through it and wait on the patio."

"Yes, sir." She chuckled and he could hear the squeak of the gate. "I knew you lived in a nice area, but I don't think I realized how fancy it was."

The house was another government seizure they'd handed down to him. From the paint to the knickknacks, even some of the photographs, it wasn't his. He might sleep and eat there, but the house would never bear his thumbprint.

"Man, we need to have pool parties at your place."

"Anytime." The pool and the converted shed were the only features he made regular use of. What would it be like to take a break from work, go out by the pool, and find Tori sunbathing?

It was temptation, the likes of which he didn't need.

Chapter Two

Tori Chazov peered through the rear windows into the large den, dining area, and kitchen that made up the back of the first floor of Emery's home. She'd been in the house once, maybe a year ago, when Emery had taken his security off-line for some massive overhaul. He'd informed them, like the good Fed he was, and she hadn't been able to help herself from sneaking inside for a little look around. That was probably when her fascination with the Walking Brain had begun. She'd wanted a glimpse of who he was, and for some silly reason she'd thought being in his house would tell her more about him, but it said nothing. His Tesla had more personality than his home.

She tiptoed down the flagstone path toward the shed. From things Emery had said, she'd picked up that his computer stuff was housed out here. The two windows on either side of the white door were shuttered and blacked out from the inside. She eyed the keypad, tempted to try her hand at bypassing it.

Emery would know it was her. She could guess that there were several cameras aimed at her right now, but it was the challenge of it.

Could she do it?

She glanced over her shoulder and slipped her hand into her pocket and pulled out a flashlight. Some girls didn't leave home without lip gloss; Tori was more of a tools girl. She examined the keypad and the exterior casing. It was a fairly common model, which made it easy to customize. The question was, what had Emery done to it? There was no doubt in her mind it was tricked out more than her racing Lancer.

Tori might soup up cars and push them to their limits, but what Emery did was so much more fascinating. If she made the wrong move, what would happen? Was there a bomb inside?

"Two-six-seven-nine-five-seven-five-nine."

She froze, her whole body going on alert. She hadn't even heard him.

Tori tilted her head to the side, enough so she could see Emery's big frame silhouetted against the evening sky. With the moonlight to his back, she couldn't make out his expression, but her mind supplied the details. Strong features, hazel eyes, light stubble, brown hair. He had a brooding, hottie-next-door look that drove her crazy. All she wanted was for him to see her, notice her, but she doubted he did, apart from his checklist of responsibilities. This fascination had to go.

She blew out a breath and punched in the numbers as Emery strode slowly toward her, hands in his pockets. He wore a light gray suit and a green-and-silver striped shirt. It was a drastic change from his typical jeans and pearl-snap shirts, but she dug it. Another facet of Emery's personality to file away for her fantasies, of which there were many.

The door beeped and the locks disengaged. Emery reached past her and grasped the handle, whisking it open.

She stood in the doorway for a moment, taking it all in. Music played softly in the background and a couple of lamps gave the room a low glow that was completely invisible from the outside.

"Go in." Emery pressed his hand to her lower back, ushering her inside.

Tori stepped over the threshold, trying her best to not stare.

"Reinforced and soundproofed?" The shrubbery hid just how big the shed really was. It had to be at least twenty-five feet long and twelve feet across.

"Yup. Had to or else the neighbors would complain." Emery strode ahead of her, through the racks of—whatever they were, and into the back half of his domain, out of view.

She turned in a circle, noting the futon that appeared much more slept in than the bed inside. There was a mini fridge, microwave, and hotplate that certainly weren't for show like the big chef's kitchen. If she had to guess, Emery didn't see the inside of the house very often, because everything was right here, down to a rolling rack of pearl-snap shirts and jeans, with a laundry basket stowed on the bottom. She inhaled, drawing in a hint of his scent and—bananas? A basket of brown fruit sat on top of the microwave under a stack of napkins. Emery was brilliant, but sometimes the normal things flew over his head.

Tori plucked the ruined fruit from the basket and dropped them in the wastebasket.

This had to stop.

"Do you have the necklace with you?" Emery called from the back of the shed.

"Yeah." She passed the racks of humming electronics and pulled up short. Emery was tugging a pair of blue jeans up to his hips. She stopped breathing as her brain screeched to a halt. The man had an ass she could bounce a quarter off, and those shoulders . . .

She'd often wondered what he'd look like shirtless. Scars had never been part of the vision.

Puckered skin crossed his back, drawing lines over his shoulders and sides. She couldn't begin to imagine how painful those wounds must have been. It made her stomach twist in knots at the thought. No one deserved that kind of treatment.

Emery grabbed a T-shirt and pulled it on, his scowl deepening.

"Sorry, I didn't realize you were changing."

"The necklace?" He fastened his jeans and tugged the zipper up, presenting once again the face she always saw: unreadable, with a bit of a permanent scowl she suspected was more a sign of his deep thoughts.

"Here." She pulled the necklace out of her pocket. The jeweler had put it in a plastic bag for pickup.

"What saint is this?" Emery plucked it from her fingertips and carried it over to the lamp in the corner to examine.

Tori followed, watching him pour the necklace out into his palm and pry the locket open. She resisted the urge to snatch it back, to keep the locket's secrets private. He was doing her a favor, she reminded herself.

"I don't know."

He glanced at her, his brows drawn down in a line. She could practically hear his unspoken question: *What do you mean, you don't know?* Emery had a tendency toward silence. At some point she'd begun to imagine him speaking. It made these moments less awkward. For her at least. She'd never really gotten a feel for what he thought about her. If he liked her, tolerated her, or hated her. He was simply there. A silent, ever-present shadow and partner in this crazy mess of an operation.

"They were family heirlooms. Roni and I both got one, but we were never told which saints they're supposed to be.

And really, when they're this small, what can you tell about them? It could be Baba Yaga for all I know."

"The Russian witch? Unlikely."

"Hey, you never know." She blinked, surprised he'd caught that reference.

He prodded the tiny photographs inside the locket. "If I can pull the picture out, I can put a chip in the space behind it. I'll need to set up the tracking. It'll take a few minutes."

"So it's possible?"

He blinked at her. *Yes, it is. Make yourself comfortable.*

Emery turned and walked to a worktable that bisected the rear half of the workshop. Against the wall, a bank of monitors formed almost a semicircle. A few on the side displayed security-camera feeds from outside, some from Classic Rides, the Shop, three from Aiden's house. There were even two that showed her front door and the parking lot outside the apartment she shared with her sister.

She knew he kept an eye on all of them, sort of like their personal protector, but she never knew how or where to look for him. These cameras and microphones were nearly invisible. The monitor showing her apartment didn't switch to another image. It just sat there; nothing interesting going on. Maybe she should be disturbed by the breach of privacy, but she wasn't. Actually, it was kind of comforting.

"Do you really watch those all the time?" She leaned over the desk, pointing at the feeds.

He glanced up from the table to the monitors.

"Yes." *Someone has to make sure you're safe, and that's my job.*

If Emery could hear her mental conversations with him, he'd probably have some nice men with white jackets come keep her company in a padded room. She had to get this obsession under control. Maybe what she needed was a night out where she could find some big, buff guy with dark hair and hazel eyes like Emery's. Yeah, that was a bad idea. Sure, Emery was attractive, but that wasn't what had drawn her initially. It was the way he handled himself.

It was the first flip job they'd done as a crew—and Tori's first ever. Sure, she'd stolen a car a time or two when she was really in a bind, but she didn't make illegal activities a pastime, at least not until coming to Miami.

That night, Aiden had everyone running a tight shift, barking orders. The Feds had denied them backup, so their plan had been to steal the cars, remove the drugs, then clean and flip the cars for profit they could put back into their operation. She'd gotten through stripping the car of identifying features, but she'd been nervous about the car's internal computer. They were different make to make, model to model, and if they didn't do everything just right—their flip job on the car would flop.

Maybe it was nerves, but she hadn't noticed Emery's arrival, at least not until CJ, their FBI handler, tapped her on the shoulder and introduced her to tall, dark, and wordless. Emery had nodded to her. That was it. No greeting, banter, or get-to-know-you. Just a stoic nod and down to business. Emery had handled the job with confidence that impressed her, and from there she couldn't soak up enough of his presence.

"I tried to talk Roni out of going to Orlando." She sank into a worn-out armchair and turned to face him, curling her legs under her.

Yeah?

"She thinks they'll find Canales, and she's bored." Tori rolled her eyes. "I'm worried about her."

Totally understandable.

Emery bent over the table, miniature tools between his fingers. He was such a big man, and yet he operated with such finesse. She propped her chin in her palm and watched him, enjoying the rare opportunity to simply observe Emery in action.

He extracted the small photograph with a pair of rubber-grip tweezers. The images were so small and blurry they were hardly legible. It was partly by design on her and Roni's part. After all, if the images couldn't be scanned for facial recognition, they were safer. At one point, Roni had suggested getting rid of the keepsakes, which was probably the safest thing to do, and yet when it came down to it, neither of them could make that move.

They'd lost so much of who they were and where they'd come from over the course of the years since the hit on their father. The necklaces were all they had left. They didn't bear the darkness of his touch. The heirlooms were from their mother, though Tori wouldn't put it past their father to have lied about that, too.

"If she's so set on going, why worry?" Emery glanced up from his work.

It took her a moment to realize it wasn't his voice in her head she was hearing.

"Because she's my sister."

Emery shrugged and flashed the tiny portrait at her. "Who's this?"

Our mother.

"No one. Done yet?"

Family was one thing she couldn't talk about. Not even to the people on their crew. The best thing for Tori and her sister was if all knowledge of their past and their family died with them someday, hopefully a long time away. It would make the world a better place.

Emery studied Tori. Her auburn hair gleamed in the low light and her skin had a slight glittery sheen to it, as if she'd applied some sort of lotion or powder. She smelled of soap and citrus. Was that the lotion? Or her body wash? Did she wear perfume?

It was rare to see her without a smudge of grease or dirt on her skin. The first time he'd met her she'd worn dirty, torn coveralls. She'd glanced up at him and there under her eye, slashed across her cheekbone, was a bit of grease. His fingers curled at the memory. He'd had to hold himself back to keep from wiping it away, not that she cared. Tori was a capable woman, which was one of the things he liked about her. She never hesitated when it came to tackling a problem.

He inhaled again, parsing out what her scent was supposed to be.

Grapefruit.

She smelled of grapefruit.

There weren't grapefruit-scented perfumes, were there? Then it had to be soap. Which meant she must have showered before coming to his place.

Soapsuds, the spray of water on her—

No. Not going there.

Tori stared at him. He had the vague notion that he'd heard her voice while lost in the memory.

He replayed the moment, aware the silence was moving into the territory of awkward.

"Almost," he replied at last and bent once more.

He applied a bit of adhesive to the inside of the locket and placed a tiny chip, no bigger than the head of a pin, to the sticky stuff.

"This won't track in real time," he said.

"What does that mean?"

"Every thirty minutes this will transmit a location."

"But what happens during that thirty-minute window? What if we need to find her?"

He could picture the answer as a process flow inside his head, but that didn't necessarily translate to words. The only people he talked to on a regular basis didn't do all that much talking. CJ handed over what needed to be done and Aiden showed up whenever he wanted an even fight. Even the criminal clients he interfaced with didn't want to talk that much.

"If I need to force the transmission I can for a one-time-only location. After that, the chip is dead." He slid the picture back in place, nudging it with his nail until it fit perfectly back into the locket.

Emery didn't want to hand the finished product over to Tori, not yet. Who was the woman in the picture? The two babies had to be Roni and Tori. He'd never heard them speak of a mother or any female family figure.

"That will have to do. Thanks." She held out her hand. "I'll get out of your hair. Have a good night."

Emery didn't want her to leave, but there was no reason for her to stay. He liked how she spoke without prompting and didn't always need him to reply. Often, especially with fine detail work, he couldn't spare the focus to carry on a conversation, but with Tori he didn't need to. Which was why, on the off chance they wound up in a garage together, he worked closely with her if he could. The guys talked, made plans and bantered, expecting him to participate, except his work took his full concentration.

He reluctantly handed over the necklace.

"Are you going to Orlando?" he asked. If she was, perhaps he needed to apply the same tracking methods to her, especially if there were unknown Russians in the picture.

"Oh hell, no. I'm smart—and someone has to get work done. It's just going to be me and Gabriel in the Shop with CJ. That's a disaster waiting to happen, in case you didn't know." Her smile lit up her eyes as she stood, pocketing the jewelry.

"If you need anything, let me know." And by anything, he really meant *anything*.

Tori patted her pocket. "You just gave me peace of mind. Thanks."

She turned and walked between the server racks toward the front of his workshop. A dozen excuses to keep her there flew through his mind, but each one would delay his search for the Russian threat. In the scheme of things, keeping her safe was more important than keeping her near. He watched until she slipped through the front door and by the time the locks reengaged he'd turned, bringing the images from his external cameras onto his main screens.

Tori strolled past the pool, glancing away from the camera. Was she aware of the move? As often as he'd observed her, he'd noted the seemingly ingrained reaction to avoid cameras, keep her head down. The old spy must have passed along some of his tricks to the girls, which was a good thing. For their sakes. Still, he treasured these glimpses of her.

He continued to stare at the monitors until she reversed out of the drive and pulled onto the street. Even then he could pivot the camera on the fence to watch her all the way to the four-way stop sign at the end of the street. More importantly, it told him there wasn't a soul lying in wait for her.

Who was the blond woman in the photograph? He hadn't been able to copy the image, with her watching him so closely, but he could recall the features and pose enough to do a quick sketch.

Emery had each team member's files on hand. He was tasked with keeping them up-to-date, but even then they only went so far. Each file covered the highlights of a person's history, but there were holes big enough to drive a '67 Chevy Impala through. Tori and Roni's files in particular were missing chunks of information. He was reasonably certain the FBI had it but wasn't sharing.

Did he dare to hack the system to find out more?

What if the key to the new threat was buried in her history?

Before he could think better of the urge, he spun to the monitor set as his FBI terminal. His security clearance could get him a lot of things, but his record kept his hands tied in some areas. In a time of need, well, he didn't have many qualms about hacking the government's systems.

After a precursory search on Tori's name provided no further information, he switched to a different monitor. While he might be sitting in Miami, Florida, a handy piece of code made it appear as though he were accessing the systems via the Quantico offices. A direct search for the information would set off red flags, so he set a program to crawl the database for entries with a list of key words. Those key words would serve as doorstops to areas he wasn't granted permission to see, allowing him to then access the files associated with his search.

He wanted to watch the results as they slowly dropped into his queue, but he had a Russian to find and one to protect.

Tori pulled into the parking lot at her apartment complex. From the security feed at Emery's, she estimated she was on the very edge of the monitor. Was he watching? Did he notice her comings and goings? It took every bit of her control not to wave when she got out of her Lancer and strolled to her front door. He probably wouldn't appreciate her pointing out their security measures, on the off chance someone from the Eleventh or Evers's operation was watching. It was a sobering reminder that they weren't safe. They were just waiting for the other shoe to drop.

The lights in her unit were on, leaking around the blackout curtains. No doubt Roni was inside packing for her trip. Tori hated that she was going. There were too many uncertainties and potential threats to divide their team. If their father were still around, he'd tell them it was time to split. Make a clean start. God, they'd run so many times it was her first instinct.

It literally made her sick to her stomach to think that Roni would be away, where Tori couldn't watch her back. They'd always been close, maybe because they had to be or because that was just how twins were. It wasn't like they could trust anyone else. Except these last few years had given them a respite. A team who actually cared about them.

She slid her key into the lock and tapped the door twice with her knuckles before twisting the dead bolt.

"It's just me," Tori said, stepping quickly into the apartment.

Miami might be the place they'd been able to live in peace the longest, but it didn't mean it would last. They lived with the constant knowledge that someday the knock on the door wouldn't be a friend, and they'd have to hit the road again. Just the two of them.

"Where have you been?" Roni stood in the doorway to her bedroom, several shirts thrown over her arm.

"I had a few errands to run and I stopped by Emery's." She wanted to stuff that little detail back into her mouth.

"Seriously?" Roni rolled her eyes and stepped into her room.

Tori followed, trying not to bristle. She would not take the bait. Wasn't happening.

"What were you doing at Emery's? Tell him you want his hot bod yet?" Roni tossed the shirts onto her bed in separate piles that appeared to be outfits. She glanced over her shoulder and winked at Tori.

She wasn't going to engage. It was just the smart way to go.

"I had some questions about how to rewire the Lancer and wanted to get his opinion on an idea." Okay, so she hadn't actually asked him—yet. She was saving that for a really low point when she needed an Emery fix and didn't have a better reason.

"Really? You'll have to tell me about it. I could do with some tweaking on my car. I think the acceleration is off a bit. Think we could speed that up?"

"Before tomorrow?"

"Nah, it's still fast enough to win."

"Okay." Tori shrugged. She might not agree with her sister's every decision, but that was why Roni was the driver and Tori the mechanic. There wasn't anything that said they couldn't flip their roles, they simply chose not to.

"How was Emery?" Roni purred his name. Tori wanted to punch her. Why had she ever confided in her sister? Worst idea ever.

"Fine."

"Come on, give me more than that. What was he wearing?"

Tori could recall every detail of each outfit—and the span of moments in between where he'd only been halfway dressed.

"Shut up," she said, refusing to fall victim to her sister's seemingly innocent question.

"You could just tell him you like him, *lapochka*. Or get him drunk and fuck him. Might be better that way. You could tell him it was all a happy accident afterward and go on with it. I really think you need someone with a bit more spunk. I mean, I think I get why you like him. He's safe, part of the team, knows our history more or less." Roni shrugged. "You could do worse."

Tori squeezed her hands into fists. Emery wasn't safe. Still waters ran deep, and tonight she'd glimpsed a bit more of who he was. Those scars were a story she didn't know yet.

"Here. I picked up your necklace." Tori pulled the chain from her pocket and handed it to her sister.

"Thanks, I was going to pick it up in the morning." Roni studied the locket and saint for a moment before fastening the chain around her neck. "Julian's not going with us tomorrow. He's got a gig."

Tori's stomach fell. Again? So soon?

Julian and Aiden were the coleaders of their little operation. While the majority of the crew were contract employees of the FBI, Julian was basically the Hoover's bitch. They'd coined the term for their government overlords in the beginning because the red tape bullshit was a waste of time, and it had stuck. For Julian, though, whatever trash they needed cleaned up, whatever dirty job had to be done—the Feds sent him in to end things.

"Roni, I don't like this." Tori pushed the clothes aside and sat on the edge of the mattress. "You guys in Orlando, a couple of us here, and Julian—God knows where. We're too spread out. I mean, we don't know shit about why we're still here or what's going on. I have a bad feeling about this."

They were quiet for a moment, neither speaking while Roni went about her packing.

"I know, it's not ideal, but whatever." She folded a pair of pants and tossed them into her small suitcase.

Their contracts with the FBI for this gig should be over, except it wasn't. They'd nabbed Michael Evers like they were supposed to and now . . . No word. No orders. Not a peep.

"I think it's weird Evers's people are basically silent. It's like they just disappeared." Roni spoke staring at the wall.

"I'd have expected one of the mid-level bosses to try taking over or something." They'd gone through the list of things they expected and suspected a dozen times, and yet they never came closer to a real reason for the lack of traction on the case. They were stalled. Spinning out. Stuck in the mud. Something had to change.

"I need to drive." Roni tossed the rest of the clothes into her bag and turned to face Tori. "Want to ride shotgun?"

"Where we going?"

"What does it matter? Come on."

It was late and Tori would be doing the job of three people for the next few days—but it didn't matter. A drive always put things into focus, even if she was only focused on their lack of a plan.

Chapter Three

Emery rubbed his knuckles over his eyelids and silenced the incessant beeping of his phone as he rose to consciousness.

Fifteen minutes.

It would have to do.

Besides, the guy he needed to speak to would be sitting down at his desk in a matter of moments. At least this time Emery wouldn't have to pretend to be someone else.

He'd had several successful hits on his data crawling program, but he hadn't reviewed his list until it was so late some might call it early. To say it was a night of discovery was an understatement.

Emery knew Tori's history was a hall full of locked doors she couldn't talk about, but he'd never realized just how much she and Roni kept back from everyone. Now he had many of the keys and knew what was behind some of those doors. They were the things nightmares were made from. Like the time CPS was called out to their rural home in upstate New York because the girls bore marks from their father's weekend "training." Considering the Russians were known for making their special forces trainees wade through pools of blood while fighting off seasoned Spetsnaz, he could only guess at what Tori had survived.

To start with, Tori wasn't Tori's real name. It was Viktoriya. And this wasn't the first time she'd changed her name, but for some reason both she and Veronika had gone with derivatives of their birth names.

There were more questions where Tori's family was concerned, but now he knew who the blond woman was. Her mother. Olga. Emery also felt reasonably certain the Russian hit team was being called in on some sort of retaliation hit job against the girls' father, Alexander Iradokovia. Unless the spook had faked his death, he was long gone, but the mafia had an even longer memory. Emery also knew where the girls' new surname came from. Chazov was the maiden name of one of Olga's aunts.

The girls' lives had woven in and out of the FBI records since they were babies, first as footnotes to Alexander's files, then later because the girls were proving useful. The details about their early work were vague, usually pertaining to information they could provide, often missing chunks of time or reports that should have been filed, but the FBI had used Tori since she was a girl. And now she was a contracted employee. It was a miracle the girls hadn't been killed, considering all the FBI had asked of them.

Their history was fascinating, but it didn't give him the window into Tori's life he'd secretly wanted. It was merely a road map that told him the when and where, but never the why. Guilt gnawed at him. Though it was part of his job to know, he didn't have to pry. Would Tori be upset at him for digging around? He couldn't tell. The good thing was, he had a lead. Or at least a place to start.

Special Agent Tony Cardno was stationed in New York and worked on the FBI's mob task force. If the Russians were shifting people around, he was the one to ask. He was also the source of Emery's most informative data hits of the night.

What exactly was the agent searching that would return results that included Tori's history?

The last time he'd had to call an FBI source, Emery had made up a name and a bullshit reason to get the information he needed. At least this time he'd met Tony.

Emery grabbed a cup of instant coffee and settled in at his desk. It took him a few moments to route a call through Washington, D.C., for good measure. By the time he slid his headset on, the line rang.

"Pick up," Emery muttered.

"Cardno."

Emery almost sighed with relief.

"Tony, it's Emery down in Florida."

"Hey, what are you doing calling me?" Tony's tone brightened. Emery had almost expected the man to have forgotten him.

"Hey, man, is this your work I'm hearing all over the news?" Emery sipped his coffee and waited. For the last few days Emery had caught snatches here and there on all the major channels about the Russian spy ring and their method of passing information along in seemingly innocent items. Hats. Umbrellas. Sporting tickets. It was all very Cold War, and they'd been quite successful with it for a while.

"I can't talk about that, man."

"All right. Well, give my congrats to whoever is busting that spy ring. That's some crazy stuff."

"Isn't it?"

"Yeah, man, but that's not why I called. I was hoping I could ask you a few questions. I've got an asset I think some mob boys are about to target, and I was hoping you'd know a bit about the current Russian movements in and out of the state."

"That's not specific at all. Remind me, what op are you running?" A door closed, shutting out the ambient noise of an office in the morning.

The sounds of normalcy hit Emery in the stomach. He'd pretty much been on his own since his indoctrination into the FBI. Granted, he worked best without distractions, but there was something about being near enough to a buzz of human activity that was comforting.

"Did I lose you?" Tony asked.

"No, sorry, still drinking my coffee."

"I hear you. You caught me between my second and third."

"I'm in deep cover with a team here in Florida. Couple of field agents and assets working in a front business. It's a long-term type deal. We've got someone on our team with a family history of being on the wrong side of the mob. Picked up a couple of jewel thieves who were trying to scramble their way out of town before some badass Russian touched down. I'm hoping this won't impact my team, but . . ."

But he was afraid their luck was up and the walls were about to come crashing down.

"Damn." Tony sighed. "I was hoping word on the street was wrong. Give me a sec." Keys clicked on Tony's end and Emery turned his attention to his still active data aggregator. Tony's search results returned in real time on Emery's end.

He had a name.

"Matvei Kozlov is a sick son of a bitch. We know he's the big dog's go-to hit man, but we can't pin him for anything. He doesn't leave anything behind. No evidence, DNA, or bodies. The guy is a spook. His targets just disappear. The last job we think he did was the family of a mid-level boss who was about to turn informant. He wiped them clean off the face of the planet." Tony's tone changed once more, and Emery got it. There were times when the injustice of what they couldn't fix was depressing.

Emery had latched on to the FBI as a way to do the right thing. To fix his wrongs. But sometimes it felt like they couldn't do anything to change the downward spiral the world was in.

Tony continued speaking over Emery's momentary lapse. "I hadn't heard Matvei was on the move, only that one of his associates was, which usually means Matvei is about to be activated. He works with a team of three men, really bad guys."

"Figures."

"Who's he after?"

"Heard the name Chazov before?" Despite Emery's searching, he couldn't get a full list of the twins' prior aliases, but he'd seen them referred to by half a dozen different handles.

"No."

"What about Iradokovia?"

Silence.

"The twins?" Tony sounded surprised now.

"You know them?" Emery sat forward. Was that good or bad recognition?

"They're not my biggest fans. They're assets now?"

If Tony hadn't accessed the twins' records, who had? Of the hits Emery had seen on their info, a few were direct searches. As in someone out there was actively digging into their past. Emery had hoped it was Tony, but there was no way to tell without setting off alarms and bringing the wrath of the FBI down on his head.

"Yeah. They do a pretty good job."

"Good. I'm glad to hear they're still alive." His voice rang with sincerity. Whatever their history, Tony was genuinely glad they were breathing. "Last I saw them, they bolted after one of their dad's old buddies found them in protective custody. Can't say I blame them. It was a fucked-up job. They doing good?"

"Good enough."

"Good to hear. All right, so . . . I don't think you have clearance for this, but fuck it. I want Matvei's ass nailed to a wall and I don't care how it's done or who does it. I'm sending you some files and my notes. He's slippery, smart, and some god has given his blessing or else we'd have caught him by now."

Good thing for Tony, Emery's crew didn't have to follow the letter of the law.

"I really appreciate that, Tony."

Emery gave Tony a remote server to send the files to. Emery would have to remember to repay Tony in some fashion. Before they ended the call, the files hit Emery's end. He dug into Tony's gift immediately. The information was extensive, and more than he had time to go through, so he focused on the more recent reports, opening and scanning the documents before going to the next. One of the most recent included a set of telephone numbers recently associated with two of Matvei's associates.

Either Emery could undertake the long process of filing for permission to locate the cell phones based on GPS capability—or he could use the completely legal means of tracking their social media accounts. It was the same way Emery kept tabs on many of the Eleventh Street gang members.

He doubted Matvei had much of a digital footprint. The man was of an older era. Everything from how he operated to his complete loyalty screamed *archaic* in the ever-changing world of crime. His younger companions, they were expendable. According to a list of known associates, Matvei's companions didn't last more than five years before ending up dead, or disappearing, which meant his current team was a hodgepodge of younger men. People dependent on the Internet and all its conveniences.

It took some creative digging and a few unlikely leaps to connect several accounts to the three younger companions, but Emery did it. The names associated to the accounts differed, no doubt in a weak attempt to hide their identities, but it was almost impossible to remain completely anonymous online these days. Things like ISPs didn't lie. At least not without a lot of technical ability these street toughs didn't have. Plus, so many social media sites tagged posts with location data, it did the work for Emery. He had a real-time way to track the team's movements, and judging by the lack of activity and a check-in at a coffee chain in the Atlanta airport, they were probably in the air right now. Headed for Florida.

He checked the time—creeping past seven thirty. With most of the crew taking off for Orlando in a few hours, the garage would probably be open late. He brought up the security feeds to verify that Classic Rides was still closed.

Emery's knee-jerk reaction was to drive straight to Tori's house, bundle her up, and hit one of the safe houses. Proper procedure dictated that he speak to CJ first. As the case agent, he took lead on any threat to the team.

What was in Tori's best interest?

If there was a threat to their crew, CJ might override the Orlando trip. With everyone in Miami at the twins' back, maybe they wouldn't feel the need to bolt and go it alone. Besides, Tori wouldn't be up anytime soon after being out late with Roni. He'd seen their departure and arrival at their apartment.

Emery grabbed his cell phone and punched CJ's speed dial. It rang twice.

"What's on fire?" CJ's voice was gravelly, a little rough first thing in the morning.

"Nothing. Yet."

"Hit me."

"I have reason to suspect a Russian hit man is coming to Miami and the twins might be his primary target." Emery paused, holding his breath.

"Yeah, and?"

"And what should we do?"

"Nothing."

Had he heard CJ correctly?

"Excuse me?" CJ might be Emery's direct superior, but in the scheme of things, that didn't matter. They were not going to gamble with Tori's life.

"I thought this would have happened sooner, but I guess the Russian organization was busy. Don't do anything, and sure as hell don't tell Roni or Tori."

"Is that really the best plan?"

"Don't repeat this, but they haven't been the most reliable assets in the past. I'd like to keep us doing business as usual right now, at least until we know what's coming at us." The whole crew was in agreement something was up, but Emery didn't like the idea that Tori's life might be in danger to satisfy the status quo. "Got to go."

CJ hung up without bothering to get Emery's verbal compliance.

An uneasy sensation settled in Emery's stomach.

Julian was already headed out of town.

CJ and Kathy were pretty well insulated from the rest of the crew when they weren't on-site at Classic Rides. What if CJ were involved with whatever the FBI wasn't telling them? Emery had no illusion that the FBI would tell him the same things they told CJ. Though he'd worked for the FBI for years, he'd always had probationary standing because of his record. His black-sheep status didn't bother him usually, but now his lack of information might put Tori's life at risk, and that was unacceptable.

He punched in her number before he could think better

of it. The line rang and rang. Did Tori keep her cell phone close to her at night? Or was she one of those who turned it off?

"Damn it, pick up," he muttered.

"What?" Tori grumbled into the phone.

He closed his eyes, relief flooding him as a plan took root.

"Meet me for breakfast."

Silence.

Shit. Maybe he should have asked? He wasn't good at conversation.

"Okay," she said slowly. "Where?"

"The IHOP by Classic Rides."

"When?"

"Twenty minutes?"

"If I'm late, don't shoot me."

He wouldn't be late.

Emery grabbed his emergency bags and powered down his station, putting it in lock-down mode. It would be a while before he came back here, because like it or not, he wasn't about to let anything happen to Tori.

Chapter Four

God, I'm pathetic.

Tori peered at her reflection in her car's visor vanity mirror. At least she didn't look too sleep-deprived for her breakfast not-date with Emery. She hardly knew what to think about it, but she wasn't going to miss it. Yes, it made her more than a little sad that she jumped at the slightest invitation from her crush, but she was beyond caring about her pride, so long as he was there.

She took a deep breath and got out of her Lancer, glancing around out of habit, taking stock of the cars, people, entry and exit points. Though the area around Classic Rides wasn't as heavy on crime as some areas in Miami, the IHOP was squarely located in a not-so-great armpit of the city, but she got along well enough.

Emery's Tesla was parked in front of the restaurant. A couple of tree trimmers stood on the sidewalk, eyeing the car.

Good luck, guys.

The Tesla was a piece of fascinating work. Emery had let her kick the tires a bit a time or two, probably to get rid of her. Her fingers itched to lift the hood and get her hands dirty. Sure, it wasn't exactly a sexy obsession, but she'd long since accepted that what made her heart beat faster was far more important than who liked her.

She stepped inside the IHOP, visually scanning the premises. Emery sat in a corner booth, a baseball cap pulled low over his face, but not so low that she couldn't see his mouth. She'd had another dream about his lips, and the things he could do with them. Today's pearl-snap shirt was a light blue, white-and-maroon plaid pattern. She liked how it hugged his shoulders, the way the snaps seemed to strain just a bit. Her mind kept going back to what was underneath the shirt. She couldn't get the glimpse of him shirtless out of her mind. Yeah, she was obsessed.

Tori tried to mute her smile, but she was having breakfast with Emery. About the only thing better in her world would be waking up with Emery. Fat chance that would happen, so she'd settle for what she got.

Tori dropped into the booth, finally noticing the two travel cups of coffee with creamer and sugar. She'd been so fixed on him that she hadn't paid attention to the table. Stupid. So stupid.

Warning bells rang in her head.

Was it too much to hope the guy she had a crush on might actually want to hang out with her? That danger might not be involved?

Apparently so.

"What's up?" she asked, instead of bolting for the door.

"Morning," Emery said.

She lifted her gaze to his face. "What's going on?"

Why was it just the two of them? Where was everyone else?

"I'd intend—"

"I don't care what you intended. What is going on,

Emery?" She enunciated each word carefully, every fiber of her body vibrating with the urge to duck and run. There'd been a number of close calls in her life and she'd rather not have another anytime soon.

He sipped from one of the cups. The silence punctuated by the waitstaff calling to each other in Spanish only unnerved her further.

"Is your sister still at your apartment?" he asked.

"She shouldn't be."

"Good." He took a deep breath and stared straight at her. "I think Roni is safer in Orlando than we are here."

"Why?" Her pulse beat faster at the thought of her sister in danger so far away.

"I have reason to believe a hit team is on their way to Miami."

Those words, those concise, circumspect words terrified her.

"Tori." Emery reached across the table and wrapped his hand around hers. The contact shocked her almost as much as his statement. "I'm on your side in this."

She wanted to sprint out of the restaurant, get in her car and just go. Emery was right, Roni would be well protected with the crew in Orlando. It was her hide she needed to worry about.

"I have a safe house prepped. I'd like to take you there and set up a remote—"

"Yes. Let's go. Now." She stood, almost knocking over a teenage waitress. Tori rushed to steady the girl while Emery lifted two to-go boxes out of her hands.

"Keep the change." He pressed a few bills into the waitress's hands and passed Tori coffee and one box.

She glanced around, unable to shake the sudden sensation that someone was watching. Of course, people were watching the crazy white couple because she was on the verge of panic. It was in her accelerated breathing, the pounding of her heart, the fight-or-flight response kicking in.

Emery took a single step, almost barreling over her, but he pulled up so close they were only a few inches apart.

"They're not here yet. I am. I'm going to keep you safe."

Those words were not spoken in her head, but they were the same thing her imaginary friend Emery might have said. He sounded so confident, as if he knew all the potential outcomes and one had already been decided. She just hoped it was one wherein she got to stay breathing.

Emery stepped ahead of her, leading the way out of the restaurant. She peered through the glass windows, but nothing had changed. Not even the men around the Tesla. She eyed their tree-trimming equipment, the sharp blades. Her father had always taught her to see potential threats in everything.

"They're going to know what you drive. We should leave the Lancer here." Emery paused in the foyer to the restaurant, walled on all four sides in glass.

"What? No way. I am not leaving my baby here." She'd poured her blood, sweat, and tears into the car. No one would ask Aiden or Roni to leave their street rides anywhere unattended.

"It's daylight. The morning shift of cops are going to drop in soon. CJ and Kathy take this route to the garage. The cops will make sure no one touches it for a few hours because they'll be too busy running the tags on a car like yours. No tickets?"

"None."

"Good. CJ will notice it on the drive in. When you don't show up, he'll know something is wrong and come check it out—with the spare set of keys. He won't want the attention, so he'll move it. Probably stash it somewhere."

"You have this all planned out. How long have you known?"

"Since six this morning. I heard a tip yesterday and started digging."

That wasn't that long ago, only a couple of hours. And he must have started digging last night, right after she brought him the necklace. Knowing the way Emery worked, he'd researched all the factors until he had stacks of information. The threat was real. Very real. And she was in it without her sister.

Roni was safer in Orlando.

"Won't CJ pull the crew back when he realizes we're missing for no reason?"

A family of five passed through their glass fishbowl; all the while, Emery stared at her. Why was he being so strange? It wasn't a question that needed secrecy.

Of course he will. Damn it. Why didn't I think about that?

More silence.

The real Emery didn't echo the one in her head.

"We should go. I'd like to be settled before they land." He turned and pushed the door open, his head swinging from side to side, scanning the area.

She stood rooted to the spot, sifting through the implications. What wasn't Emery telling her? She watched him cross to the car and unlock it without a backward glance. Last night when she'd gone to him, he'd known, or had an inkling of an idea. He hadn't told her then. Why?

If she didn't follow him, she'd never learn what he

knew. She'd be running blind, probably get herself into trouble.

Tori stalked after Emery. The tree trimmers strolled back to their jobs, leaving them alone.

"I'm not getting in that car. Answer me." She glared at him. This was her life, her safety he was toying with and she didn't appreciate the lack of detail. What did he not want to tell her?

Emery straightened from having deposited his coffee and food in the car. He turned to face her, his lips compressed. Emery's expressions were a study in the tiniest variation. The difference was in how much he squinted. If one side of his mouth tilted up. Compressed lips could be him deep in thought, angry, irritated, suppressing a chuckle, any number of things.

CJ would pull everyone back to Miami, wouldn't he? She desperately wanted him to say yes.

"No, he won't. CJ wants it to be business as usual so we maintain the status quo of our operation. This hit team has nothing to do with the Evers investigation that I can tell. His objective is to keep us focused on that."

A phantom pain sliced her breast. She felt the stab all the way to her heart. CJ might be her handler and a Fed, but they had a friendship. He was like a father, always telling her and Roni to be careful. Kathy brought them food sometimes when things got so busy they forgot to eat. Tori's interactions with them were different from the others, because . . . well, she didn't know why, but Emery's words were a betrayal of the people she knew. And yet, CJ was the kind of person to make those tough choices.

"He knows, doesn't he?" She wasn't sure what CJ knew, but it was bad enough Emery was avoiding the truth.

"Get in the car and I'll tell you."

"No, you tell me here and now. I have to know I can trust you." Emery wasn't her sister. He didn't get a blanket pass. If Roni said it was time to go, Tori didn't ask where or when. She went. No one else got her unquestioning loyalty.

Emery stared at her, one corner of his mouth lifting slightly.

"I told CJ about the threat. You were still asleep, and it was the correct escalation of the situation. If you're threatened, so is the crew." She sensed frustration in his voice, but only a drop. He spread his hands and his shoulders dropped. "He knew before I did. He knew and didn't say anything."

CJ was willing to sacrifice her in order for the machine to keep running. But Emery wasn't. Emery was FBI. And he was essentially going against his boss's orders. To keep her safe. If that wasn't a vote in his favor she didn't know what was. It could also be a ploy to keep tabs on her, but she didn't think Emery's frustration was make-believe.

"Let's go." She strode to the passenger side of the car and slipped into the lap of luxury. The interior was black leather, silver and tech. It was a car perfect for Emery.

She strapped in and wrapped her hands around the coffee, soaking up its warmth while the rest of her felt numb. The safety she'd felt with the crew was gone. If CJ knew, wouldn't Aiden and Julian?

Emery reversed out of the parking spot and within moments they were headed toward the highway.

"How many know?" she asked. Was Roni really safe?

Emery glanced at her, but the voice in her head was silent. She couldn't take false words right now. She needed the real thing.

"CJ, probably Kathy, you and me."

"Not Julian or Aiden?"

"Julian would never leave if he thought we were

threatened, and Aiden wouldn't have gone to Orlando. He'd have everyone off the grid or somewhere defensible."

His words comforted her, but only a little.

It was just CJ then, and by extension Kathy. The two agents, husband and wife, did nothing without each other, though their roles were very different. CJ was ultimately in charge. Kathy was an odd mix of administrator, tech support, and communications hub. They'd also become family. But family didn't turn their backs on each other.

Tori drew in a breath and glanced at the road. The stoplight ahead of them flipped from yellow to red. It took everything inside of her to not scream at him to keep going.

"Why are you doing this?" she asked.

Emery was FBI. He should have stuck to CJ's plan.

Emery eased the Tesla to a stop and turned to face her. She shivered under his intense gaze.

"We're a team. Teams look after each other."

And I'm in love with you.

She wished.

"Thanks." The light turned green. The acceleration pressed her into the leather as he shot off the line. Oh, to race the Tesla . . . wouldn't that be fun? "Tell me about the hit team. Why me? What do they want?"

"That is unclear."

"What do you know?"

"I was undercover and received intel about Russians coming to Miami for a hit. They mentioned something about it being girls and a grudge. I'm making an educated guess based on information about Evers and the Russians. There's no sense in putting our team in danger."

She wanted to lean across the console and kiss him. Sure, he might be doing this for whatever logical reason made sense to him, but to her, he was a knight in a shiny car. It was better than any fairy tale she'd ever read. Now if the hero would just like her back.

"What next?" They needed a plan. And she needed to get her head out of the clouds.

"Dispose of our phones. Get supplies. Lay low. I tagged the hit team so TSA will check their bags. The cops will also receive a heads-up. Hopefully they don't like the attention and call the whole thing off."

"Why me?" And Roni, but for now Roni was safe.

"I don't know."

Tori had an idea, but she prayed she was wrong.

She sucked in a deep breath, the Florida skyline blurring in her vision. How long would this go on? How could she continue to live like this?

Emery stared at his screen, tapping keys at random. The gibberish on his screen couldn't pass for any known language. He couldn't focus past the noise of Tori moving through the house. Her presence felt like a constant pulse against his skin. He'd always been aware of her presence, but this was getting ridiculous. He could work under any circumstances, anywhere, anytime. Except right now.

Tori stepped out of the bathroom, a paper bag tucked under her arm. He watched her in his peripheral vision while he continued to pretend to work. She glanced left, then right before opting for one of the guest bedrooms for whatever task she was about to perform.

The Boca bungalow was a mostly open concept design. From the dining area he'd taken over as his workstation he could see into almost every room. More importantly, he had a clear view of the three entrances to the house, the street out front, and the driveway. The rear of the house was more or less protected by the neighbor, a canine cop for Miami-Dade, who kept several big German shepherds loose in his backyard. The neighbors on either side were an elderly couple and a white-collar jackass, respectively. All they needed to know was that Emery and Tori were another set of renters in a long line of faces.

The house wasn't an FBI asset, though.

It belonged to Emery. He'd taken it for payment for a side job and set it up as a vacation property for out-of-towners to rent, though he left it vacant more often than he let it out. One of the consequences of his deep cover was performing the duties he was renowned for. He'd accumulated a small wealth of assets, but right now the house was the most valuable of all. On paper, it was owned by an alias Emery had used on occasion. It was as untraceable as he could make it.

Tori paced from one bedroom into another, carrying the paper bag from the hardware store with her. He needed to get her clothes, toiletries besides what they'd scrounged together at a gas station, and more supplies. The stops were unavoidable. They couldn't go backward. Their homes were potentially compromised. They could only move on, but each time Tori showed her face created another opportunity for the hit team to find her, be that by their digital footprint or a sighting.

The thought spurred him to action. He brought up the sites where Matvei's flunkies had checked in and also the dispatch log of police officers at the Miami airport. According to flight records, Matvei Kozlov's plane had landed almost an hour ago. From the TSA logs he could see that the security agents had acted better than Emery hoped, and taken the Russians into custody. It wouldn't last. Chances were, they'd already been released, but it still meant Emery and Tori had a head start. He'd love to log into the NSA's tracking capabilities, and were he operating under the FBI's sanctioning he could. But he wasn't. They were on their own.

He had no way of tracking the Russians in real time unless one of them used their social media accounts. It was the best he could do without a tracking device or tricking the hit team into downloading a GPS app. Even they couldn't be that stupid. Last he'd been able to identify, the Russians were in the airport, on the road, or already hunting.

Emery brought up the app he used to keep tabs on the crew on his new phone. The image zoomed out until he could see most of Florida. There were several dots on the screen clustered to the north, which would be the group with Aiden. The others were in relative proximity to Miami. He zoomed in until he could see the spread of locations. CJ might not realize Emery's defection quite yet.

"Any developments?" Tori dropped into the chair across the table from him, one arm draped over the back, her legs crossed.

"Nothing."

"What do we do now?"

"Nothing."

"Is that the only word you know?"

"No." Emery inhaled. Growing up he'd been the un-wanted second child. His input was never wanted and the opportunity to be involved was rarely provided within their family unit. He knew his conversational skills left something to be desired, especially considering how chatty Tori could be. For her, he'd make an effort. "It looks like Roni and the others should be getting to their hotel soon."

"What about the necklace tracker? Is it working?" Tori leaned forward, her hand lifting to her neck.

"Yes."

"Good." She pushed to her feet and turned a circle. "I'm going to get a drink. Want something?"

"No, thanks."

She muttered something as she strode into the kitchen. He was acutely aware of her movements, the way she made almost no sound when she walked, the sway of her ponytail and how she avoided touching any surface, probably to avoid leaving fingerprints.

He had to snap out of this. They had a big problem on their hands and too few resources. If he couldn't solve the matter of the Russians, he could work on something else to clear his mind for a bit. Like figuring out what was going on with the rest of Michael Evers's operation.

Before he'd been tasked with the jewel thieves, he'd been following a new lead.

Michael Evers had dozens of front companies they hadn't known about. Many of them were completely separate operations from his primary drug trade, the people operating them totally cut off from the rest of the organization. It was how he'd hidden his import-export businesses from the FBI for so long. They could thank Madison for pointing them in a new direction to investigate how the drugs and goods came into the country. But how was Evers's operation still going without someone in charge?

The most reasonable thing to figure out was where the money was coming from. People wouldn't continue to do a job if they weren't getting a check. So who was running the show?

"Here. I made lemonade." Tori set a glass of yellow liquid with ice cubes swirling in it down on the table, inches from his laptop.

He plucked one of the napkins left over from their

breakfast order and set the glass on it, an arm's length away
from the valuable electronics.

"I guess there's nothing much I can do. I don't have
anything with me." Tori sipped from her glass and stared
out the front window.

Was he supposed to respond?

It was easier to admire her from afar so he didn't have
to puzzle through what to say or do, how to act, or worry
that he was out of line. Women spoke another language, as
far as he was concerned. Even Tori, who was a different
creature from other women, was a mystery to him.

"You know, if you don't talk to me I'm going to start
going stir-crazy." Tori stared at him, a slight wrinkle on her
brow.

Well, at least she was throwing him a bone.

"There might be some tools in the garage."

"What am I supposed to do with them?" She rolled her
eyes and sat across from him.

"I'm sure you could find something to tinker with.
Too bad we couldn't bring the Tesla here or you could
mess with that." The car was too recognizable to keep here.
Besides, they needed an escape car stashed somewhere in
case of an emergency.

She went very still, the only movement a slight widening
of her eyes.

"You'd let me mess with the Tesla?"

He shrugged. "Sure."

She was the best damn mechanic they had. Even Aiden,
who'd been under the hoods of cars since he was a kid,
couldn't match her with a wrench when it came to the cars
they built from rusted-out frames. It was a gift. She took
something ugly and worthy of a junkyard and made something beautiful.

"Man, I want to, but we can't risk our only ride being

SHIFT   49

out of commission." She lifted her hand to her face, tapping her fingers on her lips. "What are you doing? Anything I can help with?"

His knee-jerk reaction was a firm *no*. The laptop, his gadgets, they were his. Everything had a place, all things worked in an order, there was a process he followed.

"Maybe." He clicked through a few of the records he'd downloaded to leaf through. The data they'd confiscated from Evers's many machines before the cops started collecting evidence was extensive. The man liked his records to the point Emery was starting to suspect the real leads were buried in a thousand useless documents intentionally.

"What is it you're working on? Or is there a reason you're ignoring my question?"

"No, just concentrating." He sat up and met her gaze.

"Should I leave you alone?"

"You don't have to." He didn't normally shy away from conversation, but with Tori it was always a struggle to know what to say. She didn't fit into any neat box in his life. But she had told him to talk to her. He gestured at the screen. "I've categorized most of the data we took from Evers and I'm looking for the flow of money."

"Oh? Money talks?" Tori leaned forward, elbows on the table.

"Exactly." He paused, taking a second to organize his thoughts before he continued speaking. This was going to be work. Even CJ didn't expect him to converse more than necessary. "Most of the front companies are either false or haven't been used in so long there's no record of them. I'm trying to determine which ones are still in operation and where the funding is coming from."

"Dang. What about the company that was flying into Everglades Air?"

"Prestige Shipping. They closed shop the day after. Completely shut the operation down. Haven't been able to track them. Whoever is running the import-export business is good."

"That sucks. What do we know about the rest of these shell companies?"

"Almost nothing right now. There's too many of them." He grimaced.

"What do you think is going on?"

"Nothing for sure, but I'm starting to think it's intentional." And that worried him. What if this mountain of information was specially designed to slow down the Feds—him—while Evers implemented some kind of getaway plan?

"How long have you worked for them?" She turned her glass, drawing in the condensation.

"Seven, almost eight years."

She didn't reply immediately, and he was fine with that. It gave him the chance to simply look at her. She'd dressed for a day at the garage, wearing a charcoal-gray tank top and jeans over steel-toed boots. She'd let her hair down in the last ten minutes, which was unusual, but she had an elastic band around her wrist, ready to solve that problem. He liked her hair down. It had a gentle wave to it and framed her face in a manner that softened her features.

"Can I ask you a question?" She didn't look at him.

Christ, she could ask anything of him and he'd do it, but that was probably something best kept to himself.

"Depends."

Her gaze flicked to his face and she frowned. "You could speak in complete sentences."

"Ask me the question."

She opened her mouth and closed it.

What bomb did she have to drop on him now? He

waited, muscles tensing while she seemed to gather her thoughts.

"Why do you limp sometimes?"

His knee didn't hurt so much as ache in remembered pain. He shoved the memories down before they could whack him senseless.

Damn. He should have seen that coming.

Emery sat back in his seat. How much to tell her?

"I had an injury. There was substantial damage to the joint. The limp is more muscle memory than anything else." The shrink at Quantico had told him when he was ready to let go of his past, the limp would probably fade away. The only problem with the doctor's theory was that Emery had already let his past go.

She balled up a napkin and threw it at him.

"I can tell that, jackass. I mean, how did it happen?"

He'd deliberately misunderstood her question, postponing this answer. It wasn't a secret, but it was tied to his shame. The necessary people knew his history, but beyond that he didn't bother to share it, allowing people to come to their own conclusions. But this was Tori. For some crazy reason he wanted her to understand, even if he hated telling her. He propped his elbows on the armrests as he sifted through the threads of events that led up to his injuries, trying to pick the best place to begin.

He gathered his thoughts, busying his hands by flipping through several tabs, refreshing as he went. "You're aware we were all selected for this operation because we could fit the roles Julian wanted."

"Yeah."

Opening those memories was akin to slicing his wrist just for the fun of watching it bleed. He might tell himself he was over it, that it was all history, but it was a lie. The residual ache was gone, but the betrayal was still there.

"My brother got mixed up with some guys he met at South Beach and came to me for help. I helped him. And he skipped town after taking out a loan from the same guys, in my name. I couldn't repay them so they *took their due out of my hide*." Those were the exact words. They'd played on repeat in Emery's head all through the extensive recovery and rebuilding of his knee, not to mention how long it had taken all the other injuries to heal.

"Your brother?" Tori gaped at him, her mouth hanging slightly open.

"Not all siblings are like Roni."

She shook her head. He could feel her automatic denial, but it was the truth. His brother, the wanted child, was a scumbag.

"What . . . What was he doing? How did you get involved? Why?"

Though her questions didn't follow a logical order, he'd expected Tori to ask. Usually Emery didn't share the story at all, much less answer the first question, but it was Tori. And he'd just spent the morning ripping into her family history. It was only fair. He inhaled slowly and leaned back farther, glancing at the front of the house at the same moment a neighbor strolled by with her fluffy purse pooch on a leash. Thing looked more like a stuffed animal than a real dog.

"How could your brother do that to you?" Tori leaned forward, elbows on the table, hands in her hair.

She was truly distressed on his account. He hadn't expected that. The knowledge dislodged something within him that went knocking about in his chest while the muscles contracted slightly as warmth spread through his torso.

He pushed the emotions aside, refusing to feel anything when it came to his brother or family.

"My brother was always the favored child. He probably

thought I could handle whatever they threw at me, because up until then I had."

"What did he say after?"

Emery stared at her a moment. "He hasn't said anything."

"What? Is he . . . is he dead?"

"No, last I looked in on him he'd moved into our parents' garage out in Deerfield, so he's very much alive."

"Wait—so you're saying he's never spoken to you after all that went down? Even now?"

"Correct." Anger was a hot, dangerous thing that felt as though it wrapped around him, showering him with the toxic rage that had for a time threatened to make him go too far.

"Emery. Whole sentences. Please?"

It went against his nature to talk about himself. His parents had made sure to impart the knowledge to him, from a young age, that no one cared about his story, and though intellectually he knew that wasn't the case, the little boy inside of him still clammed up in moments like these, expecting nothing more than the sharp tongue of his mother or the backhand from his father. But Tori wasn't either of those people, and she was nothing like his brother.

"Helping my brother meant getting involved with some bad people. My brother skipped town, down to the Keys, holed up, and let me take the fall for the skimming he'd been doing. He knew he was about to get caught, so he got a loan in my name, to shift the blame, and left. These guys, they knew it was my brother, but they still held me responsible. They made sure to tell him what they did. I know the cops talked to him at some point, but that's it, really. I haven't spoken to my brother since then."

"What about your parents?"

"My parents called a couple of times. They believe it's

my fault, that I led him down a dark path. He was always their favorite. I was the accident." The echo of his mother's voice flitted through his mind. Her words had long since lost the ability to cut.

"Emery." Tori had one hand over her mouth and her eyes were wide. Maybe he'd spoken too much, shared more than he should have, but he wouldn't take the words back. They were the truth of his history. Someone might as well know.

Chapter Five

Tori wanted to jump across the table and wrap Emery in a tight hug. He wasn't exactly the hugging sort, so she remained in her seat, hands clasped tightly together.

Not only had his brother betrayed him—but his family blamed him? She couldn't fathom such an awful thing. Sure, it wasn't as if she'd had a perfect family. Her mother was out of the picture before Tori could remember, and her father had subjected Roni and her to a torturous upbringing that had left scars on her soul. But that was her weird life. Emery, the others, they should have what she didn't. Warm, loving families who worried about them.

"It was a long time ago," Emery said quietly.

"But still, that sucks."

He simply shrugged.

Her heart hurt for him, for what kind of life made him accept the betrayal so easily. Her father might have been a cold son of a bitch, but he'd provided for his daughters. Not always in the expected manner, but they'd had food, a home, and they hadn't died. He'd given them the tools to survive, and survive they had.

Emery's laptop chimed. He sat up, peering at the screen, and started clicking away. She let it go, not wanting to force him to talk. Though she might chat away with her imaginary Emery, the real one was far more closed off and silent. She couldn't imagine why he'd actually answered her, but she treasured the fact that he'd been willing to share.

"Something happen?" she asked.

"Not exactly." He sat back, frowning at the screen.

"Not exactly what?" She didn't think it could be anything to do with her sister, but her heart beat a little faster and she tugged on her hair. The sitting and doing nothing wasn't her style, but she didn't want to abandon the crew that had become her family.

Emery's gaze rose to her face, and though he didn't smile, there was a fleeting sense of humor in the way the corners of his eyes crinkled. "Whole sentences?"

"Yes, please."

"There's too much data to search through by hand. I set a search to work through it and return items that fit certain parameters. Most of the information is coming back on front companies we've already looked into. The chime means a new-to-the-search company has been flagged." He didn't look at her, but was already scanning away at his computer.

"Why haven't we looked at this one yet?"

"Because it hasn't been operational."

"What is it?"

"The company name is just Greenworks, no description or history. They don't even have an office or a telephone number. Or . . . they didn't." He spoke slowly, his brows a dark slash across his brow.

Tori didn't want to distract him, but she also wanted to know what the hell was going on. She got up and circled the table, peering over his shoulder as windows flashed across his screen so fast she couldn't tell what they were.

"Are you actually reading those?" she asked.

"Yes."

She perched on the windowsill, watching him more than the screen. On average, he spent three seconds on each page of information. Some appeared to be invoices, others scraps of paper or e-mails. Every couple of minutes he'd grab a bit of text and take it to a browser and run a search. The rate at which he processed everything was astonishing. He really was amazing.

After a while, her attention drifted from the screen to the man. How was it he'd been produced in an environment where he wasn't wanted—and still had turned into an incredible human being? She'd often thought it was the nature of her birth that led to her lifestyle of danger and fast cars, but with Emery, it was different. He'd turned from the natural path of his life to become something better.

Part of her wanted to look up his family and make sure they realized just how incredible their son was. It was her protective instincts kicking in. Sure, Emery was part of the crew and she'd take a bullet for him, but deep down she knew it was more. Her girlish crush on him was founded on more than just good looks. She respected him. Unlike her or the others, Emery fought many of their battles before the rest of them even knew there was danger. Technology and information were weapons far greater than she'd anticipated when she was younger and focused on guns and munitions. Maybe if she'd known the way the world would go, she'd have taken up computer science instead of mechanics.

Yeah, that would never have happened. She was too hands-on for what Emery did.

The image of a building filled his screen, grabbing her attention.

"What's that?" she asked.

"The Greenworks building. Purchased around the time Evers was arrested."

"That's a fortress." She leaned over his shoulder.

The mostly concrete building had few windows and was surrounded by a chain-link fence with razor wire over the top.

"Where is it?" she asked.

"North of Fort Lauderdale. It looks like the power and water were turned back on a little more than two months ago."

She didn't need to be a computer genius to see that connection.

They'd wondered where Evers's operation had moved to since his arrest. Had they just found the new hive?

"Is there security footage?" She hovered over his shoulder, watching as he pulled up aerial footage of the building and clicked through the frames.

"Probably."

"Can you hack it?"

"If the cameras are online I can hack them, but it might be faster . . ."

"Faster to?"

"Sorry." He shook his head. "A place like this, sometimes it's easier to hardwire into their system. It's got to be fairly sophisticated."

"We need to do a drive-by then. Do you have the stuff you'd need to wire in or whatever you're doing?" The team had been searching for the last two months for whatever Evers's people were up to. To finally have an answer for the crazy series of events would be fantastic.

"I'm not sure going by now is a good idea." He turned toward her, gaze narrowed in thought.

The hit team.

The little fact of their bolting.

But it was just a drive-by. Checking the location. Nothing major.

"If we don't jump on the opportunity while we have it, it may disappear. Like the import-export company. There's no guarantee this site will remain operational. Besides, what if there's another location we don't know about?" She gestured to the image on the laptop.

"I agree, but your safety is more important."

It felt as though a million tiny butterflies took wing in that moment. For a second, she didn't draw a breath. Emery was putting her above the operation. Her cheeks heated slightly before the guilt slammed into her. She was not more important than the work they did. Her safety wasn't grounds enough for compromising a solid lead, which was more than they'd had in months.

Tori shook her head. "If I stay in the car and be the lookout, there shouldn't be any issue. These Russians are looking for me, but they'll also want to steer clear of Evers's people. No one wants a turf war."

"I don't want to put you at risk. I could drive by on my own. Hardwiring into their system shouldn't be terribly difficult."

"Without me? Hell no."

His gaze narrowed. She was prepared to fight him on this, tooth and nail. They were crew. They had each other's backs. She wasn't about to let him save her and run off to put himself in danger. He might be used to working solo, but that was before today.

"We drive by the location. If I can hardwire in, we do it. If not, I'll find another way. We need a different ride though."

"I can borrow something." And by borrow, she meant steal. But only for a little while.

"Do it fast. I'd like to be locked in for the night by five."

"Let me see what I've got to work with."

It might be a little stupid, but she was excited about working with Emery. Seeing him in action. It was a great way to spend an afternoon.

They were doing too much.

Emery wanted to insulate Tori from the whole world, wrap her up in cotton and pack her away where no one would find her. And yet, here they were, rolling north on I-95 in a stolen three-year-old Camaro.

CJ was already trying to locate them. So far, Emery had blocked CJ's attempts through the network to track their location, but Emery would have to go off-line soon. He had bounced their connection through a dozen different countries through redirects, plus they'd burned their phones and he'd disabled the Tesla's GPS and other online capability. Hopefully it would be enough until they got off grid, where nothing could find them.

Emery had suspected the FBI of using their operation and leaving the crew in the dark before today, but now he was certain of it. What he feared was that CJ might have other methods of tracking them that Emery wasn't aware of. He'd always been something of an unwanted stepchild in the agency. He fit in far better with the questionable types they hired than the agents he'd trained with. Honor among thieves, it seemed.

"What's our plan?" Tori slid into the middle lane, passing the slower traffic.

"I'll look for a junction box. It's probably not going to be outside the fence."

"Then we have to get inside the fence."

"That's not a good idea. We're supposed to be lying low." It was completely crazy to still be working on the operation, especially when the FBI was possibly hanging them out to dry. Too bad Emery couldn't turn his back on the job he'd said he'd see through.

"I hate to break it to you, but we aren't exactly good at that." Tori glanced at him and grinned. Behind the wheel, she looked more like a troublesome pixie, ready to burn rubber and cause havoc.

Emery blew out a breath. He knew that, just as he knew locking Tori up for her own good would kill her. She was a free creature. So he needed to manage the situation delicately.

"We get close, then let me out. Drive down that main street along the front of the building, and wait for me at the corner. I think there's a little bodega there."

"What are you going to do?" She glanced at the toolbox on the floorboard.

"Wire us into their security."

"I don't want to leave you alone."

"I won't be. I need you to watch my back."

She frowned and merged into the far right lane, steering it toward their exit. The Camaro was a smooth enough ride, though too flashy for this little adventure. He'd have preferred a simple sedan or a work truck to blend into the surroundings, but Tori had wanted speed.

This far out, there was a little space between the buildings they passed instead of being built squished up next to each other. The area was mostly industrial, though a few street peddlers pushed their carts of ice cream and tamales around for the shift workers.

The Greenworks building sat on a couple acres of land with little traffic around it. They drove parallel to the compoundlike structure, observing it from a distance.

"Pull into this lot." Emery pointed at a nondescript office space with a parking lot that cut through to the street that ran alongside Greenworks.

"Need me, call me." Tori kept the car on the windowless blind side of the single-story office building.

Emery stepped out, hefting the toolbox.

"Bodega. Twenty minutes." He pulled a pair of sunglasses from his front pocket and slipped them on. Between the baseball cap, sunglasses, and nondescript workman's shirt, he could be anyone, which was the point.

Tori turned the car and eased back onto the street, continuing in the direction they'd been headed. She couldn't get too close in the car. Especially if the security system was up and running. The last thing he needed was Evers's idiots on her tail, too.

Emery strolled through the parking lot, across the street, and down the fence line of the Greenworks property. Most commercial businesses incorporated a little of the Florida color palette by way of flowers or some decoration. Greenworks had nothing. Not even a palm tree out by the road. It felt . . . wrong.

The street was completely deserted. No traffic, especially no one else on foot. It was as if the neighbors had a good idea who had moved in and they were keeping their distance. The back of Emery's neck itched, like he was being watched. And he was.

The security cameras were mounted on the side of the building, every twenty feet. There was no way to get close without coming up on at least one of the feeds. The trick was to appear as though he belonged there. Part of Emery's value to the team was being an autonomous entity. While Tori, Aiden, Julian, and the rest were easily identified at a glance, Emery was almost completely separate to them. It made for a solitary existence, but no one would be able to see him and connect the person on the camera to Classic Rides or their people.

Now, where was the junction box?

The main gate also serviced the loading docks. A dozen men loitered about the lot. Except normal loading dock employees didn't carry handguns. He was willing to bet the man in the guard shack was packing something of the automatic variety.

He stopped in the shade of a billboard and peered at the side of the building. From the way the cameras were positioned, he should be on the very edge of the frame.

There.

The junction box for the security cameras was mounted against the side of the building. He'd passed a bit of shoddily patched fence ten feet back, where he thought he could get through in a pinch, but there was no way he'd make it the dozen or so feet to the box before someone spotted him, if they hadn't already.

He needed a distraction. Something to pull the guard's attention away from this direction for a minute. A Dumpster and a stack of blue barrels would cover his position at the box—if he could get there.

He wanted to get a look inside the facility, but he couldn't risk Tori's safety. She was the priority. Nothing could change that. Not even an opportunity to figure out why the FBI might be hanging them out to dry could tempt him otherwise.

Emery turned and retraced his steps, but only got a few feet away before tires screeching on pavement broke the calm. The red Camaro slowed to a stop, just on the other side of the front gates, the hood billowing white smoke.

"Damn it, Tori," he muttered.

The guard at the gate stepped out, his hands empty as Tori jumped out of the driver's seat, a scarf wrapped around her head like some rich South Beach miss. At this distance he couldn't hear what she was saying, but he could make out the distressed tones of her voice.

Tori.

Distressed.

As if.

Her act had the desired result. The guards circled around the car, several working together to pop the hood.

This was it. Maybe his only chance.

Emery snatched a set of needle-nose pliers from his toolbox and snipped the wire woven between the broken links to keep the fence together. He shouldered through the hole, carrying his toolbox against his chest.

At most, he'd have a couple of minutes to do a ten-minute job. Good thing he was quick with his hands.

Emery ducked behind the Dumpster, listening for a shout or footsteps to let him know he'd been made. He lifted the lid of the junction box, torn between a groan and pumping his fist. The wiring was old, probably older than the cameras. It should have been swapped out when the system was upgraded, but someone had cut corners.

Their loss.

Emery's gain.

He pulled out a knife, cutting away the plastic casing on the wires until he could ensure a good enough connection. Instead of the government-issue toys he normally played with, he'd put together a simple transmitter for their purposes. All they needed was the footage. If he kept the receiver online and functional, they'd have everything.

The Camaro revved and the sound of an excited female voice drifted toward him. The men's voices were a jumble of bass tones that got lost in the rumble of the car. Whatever Tori had fucked up, he was pretty sure they were about to fix it.

He grabbed the transmitter and very carefully set the live ends against the exposed wires. It would be ideal to solder the metals together, but there wasn't time for that. In a pinch, electrical tape would have to work. He wound the black adhesive around the ends, securing the transmitter to the wires.

A man called out to the others in Spanish, just on the other side of the Dumpster. Emery ducked his head and peered out at the street. The skin on the back of his neck prickled. They were cutting this way too close.

Tori stood by the Camaro, smiling and talking to the guards while the car idled—no smoke streaming from the hood now.

He made the last connection and wrapped the whole thing in tape to keep the connection from slipping due to the weight of the transmitter. Taking an extra moment, he shifted the wires, turning and pulling them so his additional tech wasn't visible. He slid the lid closed, cringing at the rusty scrape of the metal, but no one paid him any mind.

Now, how did he get out of here?

Emery pressed his back to the Dumpster and edged to where he could see the street and a bit of the loading docks. Most of the dockhands had dispersed, meandering back to their stations, or to whatever they'd been doing before. Tori dropped into the driver's seat of the Camaro and the guard from the shack closed her door.

His distraction was gone. Unless she drove the car into the guard shack, he would have to get out of here on his own.

He shoved one hand in his pocket and strolled in the opposite direction of the gate, toolbox in hand. This was the part of the job he'd struggled with in the beginning. Pretending to act normal. Time, practice, and the memory of what he'd suffered had taught him better than his instructors at Quantico. Now, he had a range of practiced reasons to be anywhere for any reason.

"Who are you?" A young man wearing new kicks, saggy jeans, and a shirt so neon it hurt Emery's eyes to look at stepped out from behind a metal door. There was no handle on the outside, which meant it was some sort of emergency-only exit. Clearly not hooked up to a security system. Good to know.

"Hi, I'm from Gexa. I'm checking the amps on your meters. Any idea where the subsidiary meters are?" This kid wasn't one of the hired staff. He looked . . . like someone the Eleventh Street gang would have driving for them.

"What are you talking about, man?" He scowled at Emery. "I don't know where no meters are."

"Okay. I'm just going to look on the other side. I'm sure I'll find it." Emery kept walking, glancing at the fence line, looking for an out. He couldn't make it over the razor wire before one of the guards was alerted. Considering they were packing, he didn't want to take his chances getting hung up and shot. Tori was just crazy enough to drive in and save him, and he was supposed to be protecting her. Going over the fence was out. He hadn't seen another weakness in the chain link. That meant he'd have to get through one of the gates. The primary one was too well guarded, but the secondary entrance hadn't appeared as secure.

He glanced once over his shoulder, but the young thug wasn't anywhere to be seen. Hopefully he went back to whatever he'd been doing before Emery arrived.

Chapter Six

Fifteen feet to the corner of the facility.

Emery rounded the corner, keeping his arms and shoulders relaxed. Most of the time, if he just acted like he belonged somewhere, no one questioned him. Creeping around a place like he didn't want to be caught was the fastest way to blow his cover.

From their brief tour around the facility, it appeared most of the activity was centered behind him on the back side of the building, where the loading docks were located. The front had been almost deserted.

Emery cursed their luck. A cluster of workmen on their lunch break had taken over some wooden picnic tables. A few yards away a couple of people in business casual attire were on a smoke break. It was business as usual. Except it was Saturday. Didn't office workers tend to avoid weekend shifts?

The most alarming things were two new additions to the parking lot. They were not the kinds of vehicles purchased for commuting.

A souped-up Nissan GT-R with a spoiler and body kit that weren't stock, and a heavily modified Ford Mustang

GT 500. Those were racing cars. He was willing to bet he had their license plate numbers on file.

One of the external doors opened and a man wearing work boots, jeans, and a plaid shirt speared Emery with his gaze.

"Hey, you from the electric company?" The man stalked toward Emery, crunching the gravel underfoot.

Shit.

He hated interfacing with people.

"I am," he replied when the workman was close enough he didn't have to yell.

"Are you here about the combustion problem in—"

"No, sorry, that's above my pay grade. They sent me out to check the meter lines to make sure you're getting adequate power. Once I verify that, they can figure out what's wrong and who to send out."

"Damn it. We need those working." The man put his hands on his hips and shook his head.

"What are you making here?" Emery peered up at the building.

"Not sure yet. We're getting her up and ready to run."

"Oh, okay." Emery shrugged. "I'm going to go grab some things from my truck. Is there a better way around here?"

"Where'd you park?"

"On the street. I needed to see the meters over there." Emery turned and gestured at the line of smaller businesses. "Then the ones over here. I thought I'd just walk it, but that might have been a mistake."

"Yeah, man, that was a mistake." The workman chuckled. "Go around the back. I'll let them know you're on your way."

"Thanks, man. I'd appreciate that."

Emery resisted the urge to sprint for the gate. Someone in Evers's organization was bankrolling this building. Why? And why were there Eleventh drivers on-site?

The entire walk took less than ten minutes, but by the time he reached the bodega where he was supposed to meet Tori, he was sweating. No red Camaro was in sight.

The bodega was older. The gas pumps had more rust on them than paint. All of the windows were covered by metal bars. But no cameras. He decided to take his chances and ducked inside. It was almost as hot inside as it was outside. Several fans moved the air around, but it didn't alleviate the stifling temperature. Emery's stomach growled as the aroma of pulled pork and spices reached his nose.

The back of the shop sported a little Cuban deli, with heating lamps keeping today's offering warm. Emery grabbed a couple bottles of water and strolled to the back to inspect the food.

Tori loved a good pulled-pork sandwich.

The bells attached to the main entrance chimed and several loud people entered, speaking in a mix of English and Spanish.

Just his luck.

Emery tilted his head to the side. He wasn't surprised to see the flashy drivers for the Eleventh stroll in. With the way their day was going, this was about par for the course. These guys were more than a thorn in their side now. They were a problem.

The elderly man chopping what looked to be brisket wiped his hands on a towel hanging from his waist and turned his attention on Emery.

"*Dos tortas de carne de cerdo deshebrada, por favor.*" Emery gestured to the day's offering, labeled pork on a paper flag stuck into the meat. Chances were the old man didn't even speak English.

The thugs' presence was a dark shadow. The deli man glanced several times at the Eleventh Street crew carrying on, picking up candy or chips before putting them down. They were kids with no purpose other than causing trouble.

What kind of crap did they pull here? How much had they stolen simply because they could?

Emery couldn't stop today, but he would put an end to their nonsense.

The man handed over the food and Emery paid in cash. There would be no more plastic currency for him. Not until the threat to Tori was gone. He didn't know what kind of resources the hit team might have, but they weren't the only ones on their trail now. CJ probably had his accounts and aliases flagged.

"*Gracias.*" Emery nodded at the man and turned toward the door.

"Hey you, the electric company man." The same saggy pants–wearing kid chewed on a straw not five feet away. "You find what you lookin' for?"

"Yeah, just grabbing something to eat before getting back to work. Have a good day." Emery strolled toward the front door.

Easy does it. Act natural.

"What electric company you work for?" an older one of Saggy Pants's companions asked.

Emery paused at the door. "Gexa."

He had no idea if Gexa serviced this part of town, but it was a guess. His luck, the brains of this little group might actually know. He pushed out of the front door, scanning the street for the red Camaro.

Nothing.

Where the hell was Tori?

A van parked by the street honked its horn. He couldn't see the driver, but he could guess who it was.

Emery checked his six o' clock using the reflective lenses of his sunglasses. The brains of the little group watched him. Great.

He crossed the dusty parking lot to the van and pulled the passenger door open.

"Get in. Get in, now," Tori said, pitching her voice low.

He climbed into the passenger seat and she accelerated before he'd even closed the door.

"Where'd the other ride go?" he asked, strapping in.

"The Eleventh is here." She'd lost the headscarf, but her hair was up under a baseball hat she hadn't worn earlier, and half her face was obscured by sunglasses.

"I saw that." He buckled himself in before he got thrown out of the van, and checked the mirror. The Nissan and Mustang sat in front of the bodega.

"What are they doing here?"

"I don't know." But he intended to find out.

Tori was ready to be done with the day. Nearly two hours after they left the bodega they were strolling on foot toward the safe house. It wasn't that she'd done much, but the stress of it all wore her out.

Emery tapped at the screen of his phone doing God-only-knew what. He'd reported the car and van as abandoned, using a variety of apps to reroute the calls, all while walking. It was fascinating to think what he could do with something so simple as a phone. All she used hers for was to play games, take pictures, and text.

"Stop." He reached out, grabbed her arm and pulled her under the overgrown branches of a lemon tree heavy with fruit.

"What is it?" Tori glanced around. Nothing appeared out of place. The street was quiet; only the occasional car passed them by. They were still a block and a street over from the house.

"The webcam feed."

"The what?" She couldn't begin to make sense out of those three words.

His brows drew down into a dark slash and the frown was enough to make her anxious.

"What is it?" She pitched her voice lower, for his ears alone, keeping her gaze on the street while he stared at the webcam feed on his phone. What if one of the Eleventh had followed them? What then?

"Someone is in the house. I can't see their faces. The laptop must be tilted too low."

Damn it. That wasn't good. She peered over his shoulder, and sure enough, two men passed by the laptop. One had Emery's overnight bag in hand.

"Are they there now?" Did they chance a confrontation? Were they friendly? Or had the hit team found them already? Could they get away?

"Not sure. This is from an hour ago."

She said a quick prayer under her breath. If it hadn't been for their zigzagging path back to the safe house, they might have been there when these people came looking for them.

"Is it the Russians? Or FBI?" she asked.

"They aren't FBI."

Then the Russians had already found her. There was no doubt in her mind. If they needed confirmation she was in danger, this was it.

A cold sweat broke out along her hair line and down her spine. Despite the heat, she shivered.

"You must have a tracker on your things, or maybe on you." Emery's gaze traveled over her body before resting at the base of her neck. "We've got to change. Dump everything. What we can't dump we can mail to ourselves."

Her necklace. Could someone have done to her what she'd done to Roni? She pressed her fingertips against the charm. It hadn't been off her body except to take showers, and good luck to anyone stupid enough to come into their apartment. So not her necklace, but what? Trackers could be sewn into fabric. Her bag was a good target. She carried it with her everywhere.

"It has to be my bag. I don't keep money in it, so I leave it unattended a lot. Anyone could have slipped something into it." She dropped to a knee, digging through the canvas messenger bag.

"We've got to leave it."

"I want to know for sure." She dumped the plastic case of screwdrivers on the sidewalk, followed by her small flashlight.

Emery grabbed her arm and pulled her to her feet.

"Trackers can be tiny. So small you'll think it's a rock, a bit of nothing. We don't have time to look for it."

Tori nodded and took a deep breath. The bag held no sentimental value. It was just a tool to get her things from point A to point B. She scooped it up, walked to the nearest trash can out for pickup, and dumped it all inside. Her necklace, though, that she couldn't throw away.

"Keep it for now." Emery's voice was soft, kind, as if he understood her struggle. "Anyone who would tag it had to have gotten close to you. It's more likely it was your bag. We've got to move."

"What about the laptop?" she asked. It had value.

"It's compromised." Emery grasped her hand, lacing his fingers through hers, and pulled her across the street, away from the house.

Compromised? Had they just lost their leads? All the work Emery had done—was gone? Panic made it hard to breathe. She could deal with one thing, but two? Losing their edge and safe house? This was not good.

"But all the information?" she blurted.

"It's on my servers. I'll wipe the laptop remotely." He started poking at his phone with his thumb while they walked.

"Wait—what? But, Emery, what are we doing?" She

gripped his hand, tugging on his arm. His solution was so simple she should have seen it, but she was too amped up to see the forest for the trees. What did she do? What about his role in this? The last thing she wanted was for Emery to get hurt or in trouble on her account.

Emery paused on the sidewalk and turned to face her. They were so close she had to tip her chin up, way up, to look at him.

"We're going to walk casually to the nearest bus stop, hang out until we know we haven't been followed. Once we can confirm no one is on our tail, we make our way to the Tesla. It's not ideal, but I doubt they tracked us to this location through me. It means that we are leaving their means of tracking us behind. The Tesla is too flashy, but we can't risk getting caught with a stolen car. We're going to stop at a strip mall, get some new clothes, new supplies, and find somewhere to hide out. As soon as we can, I want to take a look at your necklace just to be certain."

With each sentence, the tightness around Tori's chest eased and she drew an easy breath. Emery had a plan. It took a lot to rattle her, but without her sister she felt vulnerable. Having Emery's support was priceless.

"I know a place," she said.

"You do?"

"Yeah. There's this guy, Leo, he races sometimes and he has a cabin out in the Everglades. He's in lock-up for a bit. No one will be there."

"What was he arrested for?"

"Too many speeding tickets." She grinned.

It was a plan. They had something to do.

She took a step, leading Emery down the walk. It would work. It had to work.

"What about my sister?" Tori glanced over her shoulder as Emery drew even with her.

"I'm still tracking Roni, but we can't communicate with her. It might put her in danger."

"But if the hit team is tracking me, they're tracking her." Who was tracking her? How?

"CJ will be trying to find us. Chances are he's a few steps behind the hit team. Once he finds the safe house he'll realize the threat is real and will warn the others. Roni will be protected. The crew won't hang her out to dry."

Hearing Emery say it was better than thinking it herself. Whatever was going on with the FBI, it was good to know their crew was solid.

"Why do you think CJ did it?" His betrayal stung. CJ and Kathy had become like family. She'd trusted him. Taught him how to work on a car, blend into the garage. To think that the person she'd shared hours of sweat and hard work with could betray her like that hurt more than she wanted to admit.

"Don't know. Computer is wiped." He shoved his phone into his pocket and glanced around.

"Guess." She wanted an answer, damn it.

Emery's thumb swiped over her knuckles and she stumbled. She'd almost forgotten the connection in her distress. Heat unfurled low in her belly. She always reacted to Emery. It was an uncontrollable response. Roni was right. Tori probably just needed to get laid, but she hadn't been interested in anyone else for . . . God, months.

They walked in silence for a few moments. She glanced at Emery's face every couple of steps. The little lines around his mouth were the first indicator she'd picked up on when he was thinking through a problem. They weren't frown lines. More like . . . thought lines.

"I don't see CJ keeping the hit-team intel from us maliciously. He's been concerned about the lack of federal involvement with Evers, just like us. In his position, being kept in the dark, I'd want to keep the crew together and unified."

"He didn't argue when Aiden and Julian said they were going to Orlando."

"CJ's treading very delicately around Aiden."

"He still thinks Aiden should have made Madison go into witness protection?"

"Yes."

Aiden's new girlfriend, Madison, was the star witness in the case against Evers. Even Tori thought the woman should be under lock and key, but she respected Madison's determination to fight for what she wanted, which was a chance at a life with Aiden.

Tori and Emery's stride relaxed and their joined hands swung in time with their steps. If she didn't know better, this stroll could be out of her daydreams. A romantic walk with the leading man in her fantasies. The houses were even cute, the scent of flowers mixed with the ever-present scent of salt, and trees shaded them from the early afternoon sun.

"I like Madison," Tori said.

The former housewife turned accountant-slash-roller derby queen wasn't as fragile as Tori had first assumed her to be. Madison didn't shrink from danger, especially when it threatened something she wanted. Like Aiden and the life she'd managed to put together following her messy divorce. It was hard not to like Madison, and that wasn't factoring in how she'd risked herself to save Roni's ass. In short, Tori owed her. But she didn't owe CJ a damn thing.

She shivered and glanced over her shoulder, but the street was quiet. If the hit team was following them, Tori knew she'd never see them coming. This wasn't the first time the Russian crime organization had tried to squeeze her or her sister for information. When their father had come to America to turn informant in exchange for their safety, he'd divulged many KGB secrets, but not all of them. Both the Americans and Russians had pressed Roni and her for the last bits. The Americans wanted to fill in what they didn't know. The Russians wanted to know what the Americans thought might be valuable. Truth was, their father hadn't confided a single thing to his daughters.

Tori just wanted the whole mess behind her. But it would never end. Her father's legacy would haunt her forever. It probably wasn't worth changing her name again, either. No matter how far she and Roni ran, where they went or how careful they were, eventually one side or the other latched onto them again. Working with the FBI was just the lesser of two evils.

"I'd be a lot more inclined to trust CJ if he were honest. Now . . . I don't know if we can trust him. Or anyone." She didn't like admitting the truth. Trust was hard-won in her world, and she'd trusted CJ. Maybe more than she should.

"Me?" Emery swung his head toward her, pinning her with his gaze.

"Of course I can trust you."

"Good." He squeezed her hand, and damn it if she didn't feel those stupid butterflies doing laps inside her again.

Chapter Seven

Emery gripped the Tesla's steering wheel with both hands, grinding his teeth. Just who the hell was Leo and why did Tori know all about his secluded cabin in the middle of nowhere?

It was jealousy, and he had no right to the possessiveness clawing at his insides. Where was Leo now, when she needed backup? In jail. Which was probably for the best. Emery would enjoy punching the bastard far too much.

"There it is." Tori stopped toying with her necklace and leaned forward, peering past the trees. She'd been relieved when he told her the necklace was clean.

The cabin was old, with peeling paint and a tin roof that was liberally patched.

"How exactly do you know Leo?" Emery asked.

"I told you. He races."

"What else does Leo do?"

"Come on. Leo's a good kid. He just had a rough start is all. Don't be that way."

Emery glanced at Tori and found her looking at him, mouth drawn down into a frown. He shrugged and studied the rickety shed and tin awning that probably served as the "kid's" shop, judging by the toolboxes.

"Leo's not a danger to us. He's all of twenty, no connections, no allegiances, no reputable enemies. There were some backwater neighbors that were giving him a hard time, but Roni and I took care of it. He just needs a break in life." Her tone softened, almost as though she were talking about something else. Had someone given her a break?

Damn it. He should not be jealous of a twenty-year-old kid who lived in something that looked like a hard wind might knock it over.

Emery pulled the Tesla through the makeshift garage and partially into the area behind the house.

"I bet there's a tarp around here somewhere we can use to hide the car. I haven't been here in a while. Leo's really cleaned this place up." Tori popped her seat belt and reached for the door.

Emery grabbed her wrist before she got it open.

"Let me look around first."

"Seriously? Which of us is the field agent? Besides, no one knows about this place." She pulled out of his grasp and pushed her door open.

Emery didn't correct her. He was field-rated, but unlike her, he worked alone.

He cut the engine and got out, sweeping the overgrown landscape for any signs of a human presence. There were too many places to lie in wait. He'd never been much for the outdoors, like Aiden, but he'd picked up enough skills in training and on the job to get by.

"You want to check the shed while I take the house?" Tori suggested.

"We'll do it together." He bent and pulled his Glock from under the front seat.

"Where's mine?" Tori put her hands on her hips, glancing from the gun to his face.

"Later."

"Fine."

He'd packed the Tesla with a variety of supplies before he'd left that morning. A set of four handguns and a rifle were in a custom stash he'd put under the trunk. But to get to them they'd have to pull out everything they'd purchased on the way to the cabin. A threat might pick them off while they armed themselves. He'd rather take any danger head-on before it had time to get a better position.

Tori sighed and strode to the garage awning. She went straight to a toolbox and flipped the lid open, picking out a set of keys from a bunch of nuts and bolts.

"You know Leo well."

"Well enough." Tori chuckled and straightened. "He got trashed a few times and Roni and I drove him home. Showed us this hiding spot the first time. Back door or front?"

"Back."

They stuck close to the side of the house. Tori slid the key into the lock and twisted it slowly. The bolt scraped as it slid free, announcing to anyone listening where they were.

Emery blew out a breath and nodded. Tori pushed the door open and he stepped into the open space, gun up. Leo might not be here, the hit team might not know where they were, but there were other threats. He wasn't about to walk into it blindly.

The kitchen was dingy. The white cabinets, counters, and floors were a beige color from all the gunk on the surfaces, and black grime clung to the joints and corners. Pots and dishes were stacked up in the sink, and a pan sat on the stove, full of something that had long since gone bad.

"Watch the door," Emery said, pitching his voice low.

He advanced through the open doorway into the main part of the house, a dining room and living space combination. It was sparsely furnished, but the TV and game consoles spoke of a younger inhabitant. The first bedroom was more of a stockroom of car parts, while the second one was clearly where Leo slept. There weren't any signs of recent activity, much less nefarious goings-on. By all appearances, Leo was what Tori said he was. A down-on-his-luck kid who liked his car and games a bit too much.

"Clear," Emery called to Tori.

"Good. Let's see what's in the shed. I'm starving. You should have gotten more of the pulled pork. That was so good." She rolled her eyes upward and smiled, crossing to the second structure.

He glanced around, wishing there weren't so much cover for someone to watch them from. On the other hand, the cabin was difficult to get to and far enough out it was unlikely anyone would purposely come here.

"Wow," Tori said.

"What?" He turned back to the shed and paused. "Shit."

Though the exterior of the shed was questionable, it was clear Leo—or someone—had reinforced the structure from the interior. It practically gleamed with new fixtures, fresh drywall, and polished concrete. There was space to park a single car on one side, and a mat with a hanging punching bag that had seen better days.

"He's done some work in here." Tori stepped on the slab.

Emery didn't have to wonder where she was headed. Tools were hung on the walls and the metal drawers no doubt held even more.

"We can park the Tesla in here. There's an outlet, so I can charge her."

"Good thinking. I'd hate to have a low battery when we need her to run fast." She turned in a circle.

Emery tossed the keys at Tori. She caught them with one hand.

"I'll carry the supplies inside. Can you park her?"

A wide grin spread across her face. "You bet I can."

Damn, but he liked to see her smile.

Emery wasn't as possessive of his ride as the others on their crew. And Tori wasn't the others. She was Tori, and he knew getting behind the wheel of the Tesla would make her happy. It was worth it.

He gathered the bags from their supply run and carried them into the cabin while Tori stashed the car and got it charging. He knew she'd pop the hood and get her hands a little dirty. They could both do with a distraction, but not at the same time.

What separated Emery from a regular field tech was ingenuity. His value was the knowledge and preparation he could bring to his team. Without a laptop, regular connection to the Net and its resources, his options were limited. That didn't mean he was useless. He was still a field-rated FBI agent with enough training to get them through this.

The house wasn't exactly what he'd call a prime defensive location. The exterior was old, many of the boards rotting out. If they were pinned inside, bullets would tear holes through it like Swiss cheese. He moved the sofa and other furniture against the exterior walls, even dragging the mattress from the bedroom out into the main room for a quick escape if need be. At some point he heard the squeak of the back door and Tori moving around inside. He liked being under the same roof with her, even if the circumstances weren't ideal.

Given that the Russians weren't native Floridians, they wouldn't be at home in the Everglades and the swampland. Their approach would most likely come from the south and east. Of course, he hoped he and Tori were left alone.

"Are we having a slumber party in the living room?" Tori leaned against the kitchen doorway, a slapped-together sandwich in hand.

"Windows are boarded up in the bedroom."

"Oh." Tori blinked and her shoulders slumped. She stared at the wall, but it wasn't the hideous wood paneling she was seeing.

"What is it?" He paused in putting the cleanest sheets he'd found on the mattress.

"I didn't even notice. I'm so out of it."

"It's okay." He shrugged.

"No, it's not. I should have noticed something like that." Under normal circumstances, he'd agree with her. They all went through the field training. One of the most important lessons was constant awareness of their surroundings. A fact like the bedroom being a kill chute should have registered, but Tori was under a great deal of stress.

Emery stepped over the corner of the mattress and crossed the floor to her until she had no choice but to look at him.

"You were in there for—what? A minute? You can't take it all in, not when you're still off balance. That's why I'm here. I've got your back. I'll keep you safe."

"Fine. You're right." Tori sighed and turned into the kitchen. "Want something to eat?"

"I'm good."

"Well, I'm bored. No, I'm not bored. I just—want something to do."

"Eat."

"I am." She glanced over her shoulder and took another bite, but it was lackluster and mechanical.

He followed her into the kitchen and leaned against the counter next to the refrigerator. The food and the clothes they'd picked up sat in bags on the table in the breakfast nook.

While Emery was used to sitting back and doing his thing alone, Tori was different. She was a creature of action, always in motion. He'd have to figure out how to keep her occupied. If she didn't have time to dwell on the danger to her life, things would go smoother. But how the hell would he accomplish that? All he had with him was a tablet, two phones, and a toolbox, besides a very small go-bag that had remained in the car. And guns. Couldn't forget the guns.

"Eat and we'll get the rest of the stuff."

He hadn't brought the guns inside the safe house because he'd thought Tori and he would be untraceable. Now that he'd learned his lesson, they wouldn't be without a firearm close by. It was his fault for underestimating the threat. He'd failed her once, but not again.

"This isn't all of it?" Tori shoved the last part of the sandwich in her mouth.

"It's everything we bought. Good grief, don't choke on that. Come on."

She fell into step behind him, following him out of the cabin.

"I like this new, more chatty you."

"Chatty?" He swung his head toward her.

"Okay, so you're still the silent wonder, but at least I've got you speaking complete sentences. There's hope for you yet." Her smile was bright, pleased.

He didn't talk much because what was he supposed to say to her? Everything that came to mind when she was around was completely inappropriate. He was guilty of single-minded thinking when she was around. Hell, if he did more talking she was likely to deck him for what he'd say.

They returned to the shed-turned-garage. It was clear from the setup this was a recent renovation. It was cleaner and the equipment much newer than anything else on the property. Tori crossed to the punching bag, took up a loose fighting stance and threw a few punches. He'd never seen her work out, only work on cars.

"We could spar. Don't you and Aiden box, or something?" Tori grasped the gently swinging bag and glanced at him.

The mental image of Tori covered in sweat, pressed up close as he pinned her arms and took her to the mat . . .

"No. Come here." He popped the trunk on the Tesla and circled to the back of the car.

"No, you don't want to spar? Or no, you and Aiden don't box?"

"Both."

"But . . . he's talked about you guys boxing."

"We don't box." No, the kind of fighting he and Aiden did had a lot less finesse. It was dirty and dangerous, especially for two disproportional people. Aiden he could toss to the ground and not worry about hurting. Tori, he'd crush her and not even mean to.

"There's nothing else in the trunk." Tori wandered closer, not paying him much attention.

That was fine by Emery. He wasn't accustomed to having an audience, much less a constant presence around him. That it was Tori as his companion just made it worse. He had to keep his mind on the job of keeping her safe, and off her sweet ass.

"What the—?"

Emery pulled the modified bottom of the trunk up and out. Underneath were several boxes that fit together to make a new floor. He pulled out a rectangular box and handed it to Tori. The second box was long and skinny.

"You have guns stashed in your car?" Tori's jaw hung slightly unhinged.

"Yeah."

"There goes the good computer-boy image. What else are you packing?"

He covered the rest of the boxes with the pull-out floor, smoothed the fabric in place and closed the trunk. There was no seam, no ripple in the upholstery to give away the secret cache. Just like he'd designed it. Truth be told, he was a little proud of this modification. Even Tori couldn't have done better work.

"Nice." That one-word compliment meant more than it should. She jabbed him with her elbow. "Come on, you can tell me."

"Nothing to tell." He frowned, unsettled at the sense of satisfaction spreading through him. It wasn't enough to know his work was top-notch? Mentally he recognized the human urge for acceptance. He'd never gotten it from his parents. Teachers had never mattered. Now, it was different. He knew he'd done a good job because they were both still alive. And yet, he liked knowing Tori approved.

Whatever.

He liked her. There were bound to be more nuances of the attraction that he didn't care for.

He set the rifle on the workbench and pressed his thumb to the sensor on the side of the case. It took the print reader a moment, but the locks disengaged with a click. He wasn't the best sniper. John, their resident redneck and veteran, could hit a quarter out of the air from fifty yards. Tori and Roni were close seconds. Equipping her with the distance weapon meant she'd be farther back from danger in a sticky situation. He'd never keep her locked up, safe and sound. She wouldn't stand for it and he was smart enough not to try. It was a compromise. Besides, she wouldn't be the Tori he coveted if she were a delicate flower.

"Keeping secrets?" Tori placed the smaller box on the workbench and leaned an arm on the surface, facing him.

"Being prepared is a secret?"

That word *secret* made his skin crawl. He'd dug into her past without her consent. Sure, he'd done it for her safety, but it still sat heavy in his mind. They all had secrets.

"Okay, Boy Scout." She rolled her eyes.

"I was never a scout. My brother was." Another activity his parents deemed him unfit for. Not that his brother had appreciated the scouts, or that Emery was particularly interested either, it was just another way in which his family differentiated between them. He pushed the rifle aside and pressed his thumb to the carrying case for the handguns.

"And here I thought all you did was spy on my front door." Tori flipped the lid up, one side of her mouth hiked up in a smile. "Didn't like group activities?"

"We should scout the area. Figure out where the best cover is. If someone comes for us, I'd like for you to have a sniper's perch somewhere while I distract them."

"Fine. I can take a hint. Don't talk about family." She sighed.

Emery scrubbed a hand over his face, the generous stubble on his jaw rasping over his skin.

"It's not that, it's just—I don't think about them. I don't wonder how they're doing. They don't give a fuck about me, so why should I care? Why should I remind myself that as a kid, Eric got everything, even when he didn't want it? So, yeah, he was a Boy Scout. I wasn't, because they weren't going to spend the money for me to tag along."

Tori stared at him, her lower jaw working silently.

"Sorry," she finally said.

Fuck. And now guilt gnawed at him—for what? Answering her question? Sharing something less than perfect about himself?

"Don't be. It's the past. I shouldn't have brought it up."

"Actually, that's my fault."

He blew out a breath. Great. Making things awkward seemed to be his secret power.

"Let's scout the area. Fifteen minutes, back here. You

take the east side, I'll be on the west." He handed her another Glock.

"Sounds good to me." Tori slid the gun into her waistband while looking at him kind of funny. It was because of the comments about his brother, wasn't it?

He closed the carrying cases and stowed them in the stash space under the workbench. By the time he straightened, Tori was gone. He shook his head and headed for the tree line on the west side of the property. Judging from the clouds of insects, there was water somewhere nearby.

Time apart would allow him to clear his head, get back on track. He should stick to silence, but he liked hearing Tori talk. The things she said, the stories, he could spend days just listening to her.

Yeah, he needed to get a grip. Maybe rub one out to alleviate some of his pent-up lust, but masturbating while thinking of Tori just made him feel pathetic. Some agent he was.

He paused under the shade of a tree and pressed the toe of his boot into the ground. The terrain farther away from the house was soggy, giving way to low-lying areas that would make for slow going on foot. If they got rain, many of those places would fill with water, a good, natural defense, but the sky was clear. Here in Florida that didn't mean anything. A storm could blow up in the blink of an eye.

By the time he'd completed a circuit on foot, he was sweating, dirty, and had a number of insect bites. The little cabin was a welcome sight, but more so was the woman standing in the open doorway of the shed. She didn't appear any worse for the journey on foot, unlike him.

"Anything?" he asked her as he drew closer.

"Nothing." She tossed him a bottle of cool water.

"Good." He twisted the cap off and drank deeply.

"Electricity is out in the house."

"Shit."

Which meant they were stuck with the little cooler they'd brought with them for keeping food and liquids cold. It wasn't ideal, especially since it meant a daily trip to a gas station, but it couldn't be helped. They had to eat.

"Find a perch?" he asked.

"There's an old tree house about fifteen yards that way. It's still sturdy. Has a good view of the house and the road."

"Good." He drained the rest of the bottle of water. They could make this work. All that was left now was settling in and lying low. Not much else to do.

"You sure you don't want to spar?" Tori asked.

His hands on her body? The sweat? Little grunts she'd make when he put her on the ground? Hell no. That sounded like the worst kind of torture.

"No." His voice came out too rough and low, but he couldn't help it. She affected him like that.

"No, you aren't sure? Or no, you don't want to spar?" Tori was all mischief, from the way she smiled to the way she brought her hands up and danced from foot to foot. She'd be fun to spar with. She might not be able to take him down by brute strength, but he had no doubt she'd use some pretty dirty tactics. Dirty with Tori? That was the stuff of fantasies.

"No." It had been a long day and his frustration was through the roof. With himself. With her for being so damn tempting. With the hit team. With CJ. With Aiden and Roni. With the FBI. With the whole damn world.

Besides, he still didn't know how the hit team found them so fast. Plus, they hadn't had a moment to sort out what the Eleventh at the facility Michael Evers owned meant. He needed to figure it out soon.

"Come on." She took a playful swipe at his arm. "Scared you'll get beat by a girl?"

Unlikely. He might choose to do his fighting behind a computer, but it didn't mean he was an easy target.

"Knock it off, Tori." He pulled his gun from his waistband and set it on the workbench.

"I'll go easy on you, I swear." She tapped his shoulder with her knuckles in a quick one-two punch.

He wouldn't go easy on her and that was half the problem. For some reason, his mind went to a whole other place when he fought. Which was why the only people he would go up against were Aiden, and on occasion Julian. He trusted them, and individually they were a pretty even match. Tori was a tough lady, but she didn't have the muscle mass to take a hit like one of the guys. If he hurt her . . . No. He wasn't going there. Wouldn't. She was too precious.

Then again, she would be a lot of fun to pin down. Tori favored the Russian sambo style, which was a mixed martial arts form that incorporated a lot of dirty fighting. Emery liked to fight dirty. It was real. It was useful. But that was feeding his obsession, and he knew there were lines he couldn't cross. Even now the lines between professional teamwork and personal interests were blurred.

"You aren't being fun, Emery." Tori threw a left punch, hitting him in the chest. She turned and followed it up with a swift tap of her foot to his left leg. The joint buckled, but he caught himself and straightened.

He grunted, not because it hurt, but the memory of pain was strong.

"Shit! I'm sorry."

He drew in a deep breath and mentally punched the memories back where they belonged, in the past.

"Emery, I'm really sorry. I didn't think . . ."

He hated the sudden change in the way she looked at him. As if he were broken. Fuck that. The doctors had put him back together and then he'd fixed himself.

One short round with Tori wouldn't kill him.

"Hands up." He backed up to the middle of the mat while Tori stared at him.

She was a lot faster than he was. His knee might slow him down a fraction of a second out of habit, but she was an agile fighter. The trick would be waiting her out. Make her come to him, fight on his terms.

Tori followed, wiping her palms on her pants before lifting her hands. She kept a couple of feet between them, her gaze wary.

"Don't go too easy on me," he said, partially in jest.

"I won't." The good humor was gone and she was all business now. Fighting kept them alive. This wasn't just for fun; it kept them sharp.

He kept his left leg slightly bent. She had years of conditioning to believe his limp was natural and not habit, so he'd lure her in with that as a target. He kept his gaze glued to her face, taking in the loose, easy way she held her body, and didn't miss the split-second glance at his leg.

Emery wouldn't pin her too hard. Just enough so she knew she'd been beat, and that would be that. She'd take her lumps and they'd be done.

They slowly began to circle each other. Tori stayed light on the balls of her feet, like a dancer. In comparison, Emery was a lumbering giant, but he knew his strengths. He had to be patient. He could wait her out. Tori was a creature of action. Around and around they went, neither making that first attack. He'd give her that honor. Besides, he wasn't likely to get this view of her again.

"I thought you were going to fight," Tori said.

"Ladies first."

"What lady?" She laughed, but there was no humor in it.

They went several more revolutions with neither making an attack. Emery had patience in spades, but he doubted Tori did.

And he was right.

She attacked first, moving in so fast he could only block the blow. Her punch glanced off his forearm when it was aimed at his shoulder. She retreated and quickly moved to flank him, but he circled with her.

"That's all you've got?" He didn't usually talk when he sparred, because what was the point? They were usually blowing off steam, looking to cause a little damage, but this was different. Tori might say she wanted to burn off her frustration, but she didn't fight like it.

"You're one to talk, big boy."

Her husky tone was a verbal stroke to his dick. Lust was not supposed to be part of this fight, but when did he not want Tori?

"Come closer, little girl." This needed to stop. He'd pin her, move off, and that would be that.

Her mouth was set in a hard line. She held her arms in, closer to her chest than he would have recommended, but what did he know about female fighters?

Tori must have sensed his distraction. She lunged, landing a solid blow to his kidney before spinning away. He grunted and moved with her, kicking out with his right leg and tripping her up slightly before she got enough distance between them.

"Good one," he said.

She did not reply.

Instead of circling, she moved in again.

Her mistake.

He didn't even try to block the punch to his chest. He dropped to a knee and shot in on her, wrapping an arm around her leg from the inside-out when she took her last stride toward him. He secured her thigh to his chest while Tori's momentum almost took her over his shoulder. He felt the jolt of her muscles. She began to shift tactics in an attempt to defend, but in close quarters he had the upper hand by sheer strength. Before she got her feet back under her, he swung out with his right arm, capturing both of her legs, and chopped at her thigh. Her leg buckled. He shoved her to the side, pushing up as he went, taking her legs with him.

He caught the shocked expression on Tori's face the second before her back hit the thick mat.

Not too hard. Not too hard.

Emery pinned her with his bulk, holding her body to the ground. If he were fighting Aiden, he'd go for a better position to keep the other man down, but he wasn't about to fight Tori on the mat. Her under him would go nowhere good.

He braced himself for her fight, but her body relaxed under his, turning soft. His head was just under her chin, her breasts rising and falling before his eyes.

Yeah, he needed to move. Now.

He pushed up to his knees, glancing away, blowing out a breath.

Chapter Eight

Tori stared at Emery, her entire perception of him shifting. That was not boxing.

"Wrestling?" she blurted. He'd taken her out with a basic wrestling takedown. And she hadn't even seen it coming because she expected him to box. His weight pressed her down, making it difficult to draw a deep breath. "That wasn't fair."

Okay, so it was, but damn it, that round hadn't lasted long enough.

"You never said there were rules." Emery pushed to his feet and offered her his hand.

Tori almost didn't want to take it, out of spite. She fared better sparring with Aiden than she had with Emery. He tugged her to her feet, and damn it, she couldn't be angry with him. He'd shot her leg so fast and easy, it was really her fault for not being on the defensive better.

"Fine. Again." She let go of his hand and backed up a few paces, trying to ignore the pesky awareness sweeping through her body. Yes, he was hot. Yes, his body was way more amazing than she'd realized. And yes, he'd just kicked her ass, but she wasn't done yet.

"Why?" Emery frowned.

"Because I can do better." And having Emery pin her wasn't all that bad. "Come on. Hands up."

He stared at her for a moment before lifting his hands.

"What styles do you study?" she asked as they danced around each other.

"All of them."

Was there anything Emery didn't do?

This time, she didn't wait. She moved in fast, punching and staying agile, moving left, right, ducking away from him. He kept pace with her, keeping on the defensive. She threw a right punch followed by a quick kick with her left foot. He deflected the punch and grabbed her thigh. She twisted, breaking his hold and spinning away, but not before his hand cracked across her ass.

Tori yelped, more in surprise than pain.

"Sorry. Going for your leg." Emery held his hands up and took a step back, grinning sheepishly. "My bad."

The heat in her cheeks was all due to the warm Florida weather, right? It had nothing to do with Emery touching her.

"Try harder next time," she said, somehow without stuttering.

Emery grasped his jeans at the thighs and tugged them up a bit before dropping into a lower stance. So far he'd defended with mostly wrestling maneuvers, but the way he moved was more like a boxer. Getting in close was her mistake. She'd expected him to be slow, relying on the weight of his punches; she hadn't expected him to be fast or agile.

She changed her stance and he mimicked her, rocking back and forth, foot to foot.

He rushed in suddenly, forcing her back almost to the wall before she sidestepped him. At the last second, Emery's arm clotheslined her waist. He spun her, tripping her with his feet, and took her to the mat face-first. She grunted and tried to wiggle free. His hold was tight, keeping her locked against his chest so only her hands and knees touched the ground. He supported both their weight on one arm.

The whole situation might be hot, except it was starting to piss her off that she couldn't get one up on him. She could damn well defend herself, and yet Emery was besting her without breaking a sweat.

She pushed up against him and he released her, sitting back on his heels.

"Again?" he asked.

"Yes." She stood and stalked across the mat. Having Emery on top of her was a fantasy, but not like this. Of course now she had firsthand experience to make those daydreams a little more realistic. Just what she needed.

She shoved hot, sweaty thoughts of Emery and the way he moved out of her mind and focused on her body. It didn't work. All she saw in her mind's eye was him shirtless, hot and bothered.

Tori turned to face Emery. She was more conscious of her body, of how his heat had soaked into her skin, the strength in his arms. It was not the kind of distraction she needed.

This time neither spoke. They also didn't dance around, waiting for the other to start. Beginning at opposite sides of the shed, they each took a step. By the second stride, they were face-to-face. She aimed a punch at his chest that he deflected with a quick side step, batting her fist away.

But she'd expected that.

She spun with him, kicking backward and catching him in the thigh. Emery grunted, but didn't even stumble. He made a wild swipe for her leg as she pulled it back and dropped into a fighting stance. She landed a fast double blow against his chest and kidney while his arms were dropped, but the truth was she didn't have enough physical strength to do more than annoy him.

If she met a mean Emery in an alley, she'd be sure to run—or use whatever was on hand.

Her shoulder bumped into the punching bag.

Whatever was on hand, right?

Tori backed up, grabbed the bag, and swung it at Emery. While his attention was on pushing the bag aside, she circled, flanking him, and attacked from the side, throwing all her frustration into her arms.

"Shit." Emery held his arm up and turned, dropping into a defensive position.

She backed off once he was ready for her.

"That was dirty," he said.

"It's just a punching bag." There were a lot of other dirty things she could think of.

"I'll remember that."

Emery lunged, but there was enough distance between them she was able to scramble sideways out of his reach. Or she thought she was. He grabbed her elbow and yanked her toward him, wrapping her in those big, strong arms—and fell.

She grunted as they landed, him on top of her. The first couple of takedowns were gentle by comparison. He supported most of his weight on his elbows, which was nice and thoughtful, while irritating the hell out of her. She was not some delicate flower that needed gentle handling. She kicked, trying to hit him with her knees. Her arms were completely useless, pinned by his grip.

Tori was more capable than this. He shouldn't have been able to best her so easily. That he had—more than once—grated on her nerves. If she couldn't protect herself from Emery, what about when she was face-to-face with an enemy? The hit team was bad fucking news, and she couldn't handle herself.

Emery chuckled, shifting until her legs were pinned under his. Damn it if she didn't feel the vibration of it against her nipples, crushed to his chest. He was so much bigger than her that he practically covered her. She pulled on her arm, still tight in his grasp, but she was completely immobile. His wasn't a perfect maneuver; it was rough, ugly, and got the job done. She couldn't fault him, only herself. She hadn't moved fast enough. She'd left herself open. And she was a hell of a lot better than this.

"Done yet?" he asked.

She let her body relax and met his gaze. Any other time and this would be an ideal position. If she weren't so frustrated, she might appreciate the way he almost smiled and the way his focus was entirely on her. Half the time she didn't think he actually saw her.

"Yes."

He rolled off her and she took an easy breath. Actually being on the floor with Emery wasn't so bad, except he wasn't kissing her. This was probably a bad idea. There was too much going on for them to be out here rubbing each other the wrong way. Granted, if Emery wanted to rub her the right way, she wouldn't protest.

She pushed to her feet before he could offer to help her up again and strode to the opposite side of the shed.

Okay, so sparring with Emery was a horrible thing to do. Especially that last round. If she'd ever wondered what he felt like, well, now she knew. There was no controlling the way she reacted to Emery. She'd accepted that months ago, but that didn't help her now when she was frustrated and turned on.

"Again?" Emery asked.

Hadn't he been the one dragging his feet about sparring?

She wasn't going to beat him, or even match his attack. If she was going to win even one round, she had to fight dirty. Really dirty. Hurting him wasn't the objective, but something to break his focus enough so that she'd get the upper hand.

"If you want to stop—"

"No." She turned, sweeping the shed with her gaze. There were only tools, things too hard to use against someone she didn't want to injure. The only thing she could use was the punching bag or herself.

"We can stop." Emery stood with the Tesla at his back, clear on the other side of the shed.

"Nope. Just getting warmed up."

She couldn't match him for strength. He had a greater reach than she did. She needed to be quick. The problem was Emery. He was faster than she'd expected a guy of his size to be. A lot faster. When he wasn't thinking about his knee, it didn't seem to hinder him at all.

"Ready," she said.

He took a step forward, arms up, knees bent, waiting for her to attack. They'd already played this game. He'd drawn her in with the fake-out, letting her assume his left side was weaker. She sidestepped to her left and he circled with her, putting the wall of the shed to his back.

In a game of patience, Emery would win, so she had to be sneaky.

Tori rushed forward. Two strides closed the distance and as she took the third step, she brought her left leg up and kicked. Emery grasped her foot, but he didn't twist it for a takedown. He'd been very careful with her, ignoring some opportunities another person might have exploited. This close, she struck out and punched his unprotected chest, getting in one solid blow. He dropped her leg to defend, but that was what she'd counted on. Before he could get his arms up, she hit him again. Her knuckles ached and she felt every impact all the way up her arms.

Emery made some sort of growling noise and lunged, completely dropping his guard. He grasped her by the shoulders, almost in a wrestling stance, and forcibly moved her, pivoting until he had her back up against the shed wall. This time, there was no gentleness in the way he immobilized her, and damn if it wasn't kind of hot. His body braced against hers, one leg pinning her lower body flat to the wall. There was no martial way to get out of the hold. But he hadn't quite pinned her. At least not to the ground.

This close, she could see the sharp focus of his gaze, the flecks of gold in his hazel eyes, the way the skin around his mouth crinkled when he frowned, the dots of sweat on his brow and the way the little dark hairs stuck to his forehead. She could also feel his erratic breathing.

"Done?" he asked.

Their faces were so close.

She'd never be done with her obsession with him. Not unless she did something about it.

Before Tori could think through the stupidity of her actions, she kissed him. She set her lips against his, a thrill shooting through her at the touch of his mouth, even if he wasn't actively kissing her back. His body jolted, going rigid, but he didn't pull away. He remained still. She wasn't even sure if he breathed.

Kissing him might not have been her best plan, but at least she got to scratch that off her want-to list. Heat rose to her cheeks and what she wouldn't have given to be able to crawl under the Tesla and hide.

A part of her withered, dying at the evidence that he just didn't feel the same about her. That had always been a big risk. They were different people, with nothing in common, and it wasn't like they knew much about each other. Still, she wanted him with an unreasonable desire—and he didn't return it.

She pulled back and pushed at Emery's chest. He shifted away from her, but she hooked her leg between his, tripping him as he put more space between them. His eyes widened in shock the instant before he rolled backward, into a controlled fall. He was much more of a fighter than she'd ever realized. The brawls Aiden and Emery had must be something to watch.

The part of her that wanted to win the fight said to jump on the opportunity to pin him. The rest of her said to run away, fast, before he called her to task on her dirty move.

"Careful, twinkle toes. Even tough guys can get distracted." It wasn't a dignified retreat. It wasn't even a smooth exit, but it was her way out. Mortification gave her speed. She wanted a phone, she wanted to call her sister, but she couldn't.

She'd kissed Emery. And she wanted to do it again.

Chapter Nine

What the hell just happened?

Emery didn't push to his feet. There wasn't time for that. Tori was trying to get away, and he couldn't allow that. He rolled himself almost into her path. He grabbed her ankle and rose to his knees in a messy, single-leg take-down that might not have worked were Tori ready for him. Instead, her arms windmilled, her eyes went large, and she tumbled backward onto the mat. He pounced on her, pinning her on her back with his body, acting more on instinct than anything else.

She'd kissed like a woman with passion, not one fighting dirty. He might not be well versed in women, but he knew the taste of a lover's kiss, had imagined what Tori's might taste like—and now he knew.

He didn't think. If he did he wouldn't react and she'd run from him.

Her hands on his biceps weren't pushing or grappling with him. This wasn't a dirty fight anymore, at least not of the variety they'd engaged in until now. This was something else entirely.

There was a split second when he held back. This moment would change everything. And he didn't care.

Emery dipped his head and kissed her. He just did it. He didn't think about it. Didn't worry about the consequences or if he should. He just did it.

He'd been too shocked to do more than let the experience wash over him for the split second Tori had kissed him. Now, he wanted to feel her mouth, taste her. It was a longing that couldn't be shoved down or pushed aside.

Tori's body bucked under his, but it wasn't a fighter's move. Her muscles had gone soft and she groaned. Her lips moved slightly against his.

She kissed him back.

He touched her face, his fingers tangling in the strands of her hair. She hooked one leg around his, as if she needed to keep him there. He swiped the seam of her lips with his tongue, not daring to hope for more. When she opened her mouth all the blood in his body rushed to his dick.

Her hands curled around his shoulders, pulling him closer until he thought he might crush her with his weight. God, she was amazing, and he didn't deserve her. He wrapped his arms around her and rolled until she was sprawled on top of him.

Their lips only parted for a moment before Tori was kissing him again. He hadn't imagined it. It wasn't something he'd made up. This was real. In this second, she wanted him just as much as he wanted her.

She used his shoulders to pull herself, sliding her body against his. He held the back of her head and thrust his tongue into her mouth, mimicking what he wanted to do to the rest of her. His hands nearly shook with the intensity of it. Months of pent-up desire couldn't be burned up in a kiss.

Tori moved against him, maybe intentionally or by accident. Her thigh rubbed his groin. Each stroke of her body against his was blissful torture. He cupped her ass, urging her on.

He sucked her lower lip, loving the little ways she gasped, making the most helpless noises while it was her driving him crazy. He could taste the hint of cherry lip balm, smell her fruity shower gel. She was softer than he'd anticipated. Sure, she had working hands, but the rest of her was supple, womanly. But was she soft everywhere?

Her hair fell over one shoulder, brushing him. That hair had spawned more than a few fantasies. He reached up and wrapped the thick tail of red hair around his hand, thrusting his fingers through it until he had a firm hold on her.

The rational part of him cited every reason this needed to stop. There were plenty. He'd even gone so far as to categorize the strikes against this sort of thing. But he was beyond listening to that voice. Right now, the way Tori kissed him spoke the loudest. And she wanted him.

Emery pulled on her hair, not too hard. Her body went limp, allowing him to bend her head back, exposing her neck. He kissed her jaw, along the tendon that led to her shoulder and nibbled at the last bit of exposed skin at the edge of her new T-shirt.

Tori made a frustrated sound in the back of her throat. She sat up, pulling out of his hold, and grabbed the hem of her shirt. She yanked it up and off. There was no mistaking her purpose or where this was going. They'd built up too much momentum to go back now.

He lay there, committing every detail to memory.

When he thought about what Tori wore under her clothes, it was always satin and lace. Soft, feminine garments that sparked lustful thoughts. They hadn't exactly gone to the fanciest of stores to outfit themselves, yet her plain gray sports bra was the best thing he'd ever seen. Especially because her nipples stuck out in hard relief. She grabbed his left hand and placed it over her breast. His big palm covered her and the hard points prodded him.

Her gaze was sharp, focused. Her intent was clear. And he was a willing participant.

She pitched forward, catching herself on her hands at either side of his shoulders. He lifted his head and met her mouth as it crashed down on his. She moved her hips, grinding against him. He could all too easily imagine doing this naked, with nothing between them. He squeezed her breast and groaned. She hit just the right spot, making his vision go hazy and light blossom behind his eyelids.

Christ, if this went much further he'd come in his pants like a boy.

He slid his free hand around her waist and lifted his pelvis, rubbing against her as she undulated. She moaned into the kiss, arching her back. Tori was the hottest thing he'd ever seen. He rubbed his palm over her hardened nipple and didn't miss the way her breath caught and her body shuddered.

Was she as turned on as he was? Was she close to climax?

She grabbed the front of his shirt, hauling it up in handfuls. The plastic mat rustled under them, reminding him of where they were.

Did he really want to do this out here? In a garage?

"Tori—"

She wrestled his shirt up under his arms.

"Hey, wait a second."

She deserved more than a dirty floor.

Tori sat up, scowling with her jaw thrust forward. He didn't want her angry, and the last thing he wanted to face off with was a pissed-off Chazov. Emery grabbed her shoulders and rolled with her, putting her back to the mat. He kissed her mouth, hating how the corners curled down.

"Slow down," he said between breaths.

"Why?" There was so much frustration in that one word. Frustration he understood.

"Do you even know what you're doing?" Did it matter to her that it was him and not someone else?

"I know exactly what I'm doing. Or was. Get off me." She shoved at his shoulders.

"I don't think you do." He should concede to her demand, but he didn't. He wasn't ready to lose her nearness.

"You want me. I want this. Do you really think we can go back?"

He stared down at her, shock slapping him in the face. How long had she known? Or was she going off the last few minutes? He sure as hell wanted her, but in a much more permanent sense than what she was alluding to. He wanted all of her. And not just right now.

"Emery," she snapped.

He licked his lips, his gaze drifting down to her mouth.

"No," he said.

"No, what?" She pushed at his shoulder, but it was lighter, as if she were prodding him for attention. Or a better answer.

"We can't act like this didn't happen." He couldn't. He was good at a lot of things, but these moments would stick in his brain forever.

Tori's body softened and she slid her hands over his shoulders.

"What are you going to do about it?" Her voice was husky, not quite like what she sounded like when she was sleepy. She was aroused.

Tori was aroused because of him.

The single fact brought all thought to a screeching halt.

She wanted him. Or this. Right now there wasn't a lot of distinction in his head.

Tori's fingers trailed down his chest and she grabbed the bunched up mess of his shirt once more. This time she worked it up over his shoulders. He let her pull it off him because really, it was just getting in the way. She pushed up and kissed him. He let his shirt drop to the floor. She curled her arms around his neck, pulling him down into the cradle of her body.

He wanted her, but they shouldn't do this. At least not out here.

Tori shifted under him. It took him a moment to grasp what exactly it was she was doing. She wiggled and with a little grunt, pulled the sports bra up and off.

He stared, vaguely aware he should do something, touch her maybe, but there was too much to take in.

The sports bra had left angry lines around her ribs and over her shoulders. Her necklace pooled at the base of her throat, leaving her chest bare of distraction. Tori's breasts were enough to fill his palms, but not too big. Just the right size. Her nipples were a dusky brown and drawn into tight peaks. He'd felt them through the fabric, but now, he needed a more intimate inspection.

"Emery." She groaned his name.

The notes of her voice hit on a pitch that telegraphed her frustration. He wanted her hot and bothered, not frustrated.

"What?" he asked when she didn't say anything else.

"Touch me, damn it."

"I will. I'm looking."

"I can't feel you looking."

"Then I must not be doing it right." Later. He'd do it right later. Right now, he really had to touch her.

Emery covered her left breast with his hand, rubbing it up and down. He bent his head and kissed her right breast. Tori wrapped her arms around his neck, pulling him closer and arching her back. He licked and sucked his way around the stiff peak.

"Emery, not nice!" Her nails raked over his shoulders.

He smiled. Driving Tori to frustration might be his new

favorite hobby. He wrapped his lips around her nipple, rubbing his tongue over the hard nub.

"Oh!"

He gently massaged her other breast, capturing the hard point between his fingers.

She wrapped her legs around his thighs and bucked.

He wanted hours to spend on her body, but not here.

"Tori, hold on a second." He pushed up, breaking her hold on him.

"What? What is it?" She practically growled at him.

"Let's go inside."

She laughed and splayed a hand over his chest.

"Babe, I'm way more comfortable in a garage. Besides, you, me, in a garage? That's hot."

Tori anywhere was hot.

This—her and him—it was happening.

Emery got to his feet, grabbing her hand and hauling her upright with him. Tori swayed a bit, but he had her. He twisted the tab of her jeans open with one hand and went to a knee, yanking the denim down her legs. While her sister wore shorts most of the time, he'd glimpsed Tori's legs on only a few occasions. Like the rest of her, they were long and lean. He pressed a reverent kiss to her hip bone, fingers coasting over the edge of the plain cotton panties.

His hands shook with the effort to go slow and treat her gently. She was tough, but he could still hurt her. He grabbed the waistband with his fingers and pulled. The fabric ripped down one side.

"Guess that's what you get when you buy cheap." Tori sputtered and laughed.

Emery ripped the rest of the seam, taking out the rough edge of his desire on the unfeeling material. He cupped her ass and sat back on his heels to take her all in.

Tori stood there in nothing but a pair of socks. Her

hands were on his shoulders and she swayed slightly. She was beautiful in a raw, primal way. Tori would always be a tough, hard woman, but her strength only made her more desirable. Her chest rose and fell with her accelerated breathing while a light sheen of perspiration made her glisten.

He was not about to do her on the floor of a garage, no matter what she said.

Emery stood, hoisting Tori up and over his shoulder. She yelped and laughed. He crossed the distance to the workbench in three strides. It was the only remotely clean surface besides the Tesla. He could bend her over the car, but then he wouldn't be able to see her face, and he wanted her to know who it was that was inside of her.

He set her down and gripped the edges of the red metal fixture. Part of him was still in denial. She couldn't possibly want him.

Tori reached for him, pulling him closer, kissing his mouth. He cupped her ass, grinding against her, and thrust his tongue in her mouth. He'd always figured her for a feisty lover, and he wasn't wrong. God, she was better than a dream or anything he'd ever thought of.

She clawed at the front of his jeans, getting the button through the slit and his zipper down. The last vestiges of coherent thought ceased as her hand wrapped around his cock and pumped him with a little added squeeze at the end.

"Oh fuck," he muttered against her mouth.

"You are going to feel so good." She kissed his jaw while she worked her hand up and down between their bodies.

Christ, he could come like this.

Emery cupped her mound, passing his fingers through her folds. She was wet. He could hardly believe it, no matter that she'd told him she wanted him. She could lie with her words, but her body couldn't. The evidence of her arousal nearly broke the strenuous hold on his control.

She groaned and her hands stilled.

Was she ready, though?

He eased a finger into her and her muscles tightened around him.

"Emery." She said his name like a plea, pulling him toward her by his cock.

"Condom," he choked out. Shit. There was one in his wallet, but how long had it been there? Was it even good?

"Hell yes," Tori replied, unaware of the sudden very important detail.

He pulled his wallet out of his pocket and flipped it open. The foil packet was folded in half around a couple of business cards. Tori grabbed it before he could find the expiration date. She ripped it open and the words of warning stuck in his throat while she rolled the latex down his cock. It didn't break.

Tori wrapped her leg around his thigh, canted her hips and guided his erection to her entrance. He let her dictate how fast he went, not wanting to harm her in his exuberance. He felt her heat through the thin rubber barrier first. She rolled her hips and the head of his cock slid into her. He sucked in a deep breath, his grip on her tightening. She cupped his cheek and kissed his lips in a tender gesture.

It was his move now.

Emery rocked into her, trying to be easy.

Her mouth opened on a silent groan. This close he could hear and feel everything about her. Her gaze was on his mouth and her hand hadn't moved from his cheek.

"Emery." She unwound her leg from his, perched her toes on the drawer handles and pushed against him, taking him deeper.

"Shit," he muttered as her internal muscles squeezed him. She was tighter than he'd anticipated.

"I want to feel you." She closed her eyes and let her head tip back.

He kissed her throat and thrust with more force than he intended. Had he hurt her?

"Oh yes!" Tori's hand went from his cheek to his shoulder.

Not too hard then.

He withdrew and thrust, watching her face, fascinated by the tiniest movements. Her eyes squeezed shut while her mouth worked silently. Nothing in her expression spoke of pain, only pleasure.

"Emery . . ."

In and out he moved, while his hands coasted over her body. He touched her, learning the way her muscles bunched and moved in a whole new way.

"Emery!"

"What is it?" Speaking was a chore, a task he didn't want to think about, but Tori needed words.

"God." Her nails scraped down his arms and her gaze went a little unfocused, staring off over his shoulder.

"You feel so good." Good was an understatement. How else did he communicate what she did to him though?

"Mm." She dropped her head back, exposing the long column of her throat.

He chuckled. Had he ever seen her at a loss for words?

Emery leaned forward and kissed her throat, up over her jaw and mouth. He had a serious hunger for her. If he had his way, he'd spend days doing just this, or better.

He pulled almost entirely out of her before thrusting back in, sinking his entire length into her pussy. Tori cried out, arching her back and lifting her hips off the table. He gripped her hips, transfixed by the pleasure on her face and the way her breasts swayed with each thrust, taunting him. He hadn't spent nearly enough time there.

"Harder." Tori panted, her eyes open and staring at him now.

Emery lifted her ass almost off the table, supporting her weight between his hands, and thrust. She moved with him, or tried to, but he was in control. He moved in and out of her body. The sound of flesh meeting flesh was the loudest sound in the garage next to the mix of gasps and groans. Tori muttered encouragements, things he couldn't hear. Not that he needed to. Her body was giving him all the right signals.

The skin at the base of his spine prickled. He was close, but damn it he would not come first.

"Come on," he muttered.

"Oh. Oh, Emery."

Tori ceased her attempt to move, allowing him freedom to rock into her body. Instead, she reached between them, her fingers grazing his cock. She began to rub her clit in hard strokes while he moved in and out. He very nearly blew his load then and there, but his resolve to see her pleasured first held firm.

"You are so damn hot." It was the hottest fucking thing next to the visual of himself buried deep inside of her.

Her breathing hitched and her spine bowed. The rhythm of her hand faltered. He felt the spasm all around him. The invisible iron bands around his chest broke free and he inhaled, letting go of his control, allowing her orgasm to spark something deep inside of him that connected them in this moment. He braced one hand on the bench for leverage as his climax rolled up from his toes. Her gaze sharpened, focusing on him in that last second. He shouted as he came, thrusting roughly while his vision blurred from the force of the orgasm.

He collapsed forward. Tori slumped against the bench and wall behind her, half sitting, half lounging. She cradled his head to her chest, her breasts taunting him with all the things he had yet to do.

Holy shit.

There were no words.

He wrapped his arms around her, squeezing her. How had his heart come to be wrapped up in one, bite-sized woman? And how did they proceed from this?

Chapter Ten

Tori towel-dried herself in the dim bathroom after a much-needed cold shower. A couple of candles were the only source of illumination since the sun had set. She strained to hear movement in the house, more worried about where Emery was than the threat of a Russian hit team. It was a weird shift in priorities, but chances were, Emery was a hell of a lot more dangerous to her right now than men with guns.

She didn't know what had come over her in the garage. Frustration? Pent-up sexual tension? She couldn't blame Emery for doing exactly what she'd told him to. He was a man, presented with a naked, willing woman. God, how could she face him? She'd wanted him so badly for so long she hadn't exactly thought about what they were doing. He wasn't someone she could fuck and leave. They worked together, for Christ's sake.

Given the circumstances, she needed to be up-front with him. Emery was a reasonable guy. She just hoped he didn't treat her like a piece of ass after this, not that she thought he would. He was more likely to go back to forgetting she existed, which was probably better in the long run, though it would hurt her. He'd continue to tinker with his electronics and she'd pine for him. It wasn't a great plan, but she'd lived with it for this long. Eventually she'd get over him and move on, or the job would end and they'd go their separate ways.

Armed with a flimsy plan, Tori got dressed in another pair of cotton panties, the same sports bra she'd worn earlier, a new tank top and jeans. It wasn't the most flattering outfit she'd ever worn, but it would do in a pinch. She gathered up her discarded clothing and exited the tiny bathroom. Almost immediately she was aware of the overwhelming sense of Emery's presence. He stepped into view at the end of the hall, his shadow stretching out toward her.

"Made sandwiches." *Thought you might be hungry after all the exercise.*

"Thanks." She clutched her clothes to her chest like some sort of shield.

He lingered a moment longer before stepping out of view. She could hear his footsteps creak as he retreated toward the kitchen, leaving her in peace.

So much for tackling the problem of their coupling head-on.

Tori went straight to her duffel bag of new clothing set against the wall and squished the dirties into a side pouch. If they had to run, she didn't want to leave much evidence behind of their presence. In a pinch, she could shoulder the bag and keep her hands free to shoot.

Emery had a few candles placed through the house to provide a little light. The windows were open to let the breeze in, and outside the bugs hummed a chorus of sounds. It was almost peaceful. Except for the impending awkward conversation. They couldn't let this rest between them. Not when she needed to count on him. Being distracted could cost them their lives.

She stood, pushing her shoulders back.

It was better to handle this like a Band-Aid. Rip it off all at once. The sting would abate and they could move the heck on. Or pretend to.

She strode into the kitchen and blinked in the light. A battery-powered lantern provided far more illumination than the candles. Emery stood leaning against the counter, sandwich in one hand. He blinked at her, which was infuriatingly cute. A man with that much hidden strength should not be sexy—and cute. His hair was still rucked up on one side and she could remember sliding her hands under that very shirt not too long ago.

"Turkey?" He held out a sandwich neatly divided into triangles.

"Thanks." She took the offered food and backed up until she could lean against the refrigerator. She bit into the bread and meat without tasting it. How did she begin? What did she say? She swallowed and stared at the floral print on the paper napkin.

"About earlier?" Yeah, what about it? How did she begin?

"Hm?"

Like a Band-Aid.

She lifted her gaze to his. If she was going to be honest with him, she'd do it with pride and own the truth.

"I shouldn't have kissed you or pressured you like that. I'm . . ." She took a deep breath to keep going. The unwavering quality of his gaze was a little unnerving. "It was my fault. To be honest, I've had a silly crush on you for a while. I don't know why I did what I did. It was stupid. I don't want it to change our working relationship."

Heat rose to her cheeks and her eyes pricked. There was nothing stupid about what she felt for Emery, it was just unrequited. She couldn't fault him for not feeling the same about her.

Emery stopped chewing. In fact, he didn't move except for the gentle rise and fall of his chest. He just stared at her.

You're crazy if things are going back to the way they were. I'm madly in love with you.

The imagined Emery voice almost made her smile. Wouldn't that be wild to hear?

He put his unfinished sandwich down on the counter and dusted his hands off. She wanted him to say something, but time had proven that she couldn't rush him. He'd speak in his own time.

"I thought we'd talk about that later," he said.

"Why not now?" Couldn't they just agree to move on?

Emery shrugged.

"Look, we can forget it happened. Cool?" She bit one of the triangles in half, still not hungry.

"No. That's not cool." His frown deepened.

"Then what do you want to do?" she said around the bite of sandwich.

"I don't think you're silly or at fault. No one is at fault here. We're adults. We can talk about this."

That was remarkably reasonable, and full of complete sentences. She nibbled on the rest of the triangle, a bit more interested in food now.

"I've been thinking while you were in the shower," he said.

"Hurt yourself?"

"No."

He paused, piquing her curiosity.

"What were you thinking about?" She wasn't sure if she wanted to know.

"That we've both been oblivious." He shoved his hands in his pockets and glanced at the floor before looking at her once more. "I think today was bound to happen. I'm attracted to you. Have been for a long time."

That sounded an awful lot like what her imaginary Emery said, minus the admission of love.

"Wait. I'm sorry. What?" Had she heard him right?

Emery crossed the kitchen in two strides until he loomed over her, filling her vision and blocking out the light. Just looking at him, the counter pressing against her back, she could almost feel him moving inside of her again and that brought heat crawling up her neck.

"If you've got a silly crush, I have an unwise obsession." He placed his palms on either side of her and leaned down until his face was mere inches from her own.

Was he serious? Her heart pounded against her ribs, the deep ache of desire throbbing alive. What if this was a joke? Was he being serious? Or telling her this to—what? Play along to keep her with him? That was silly. Emery hadn't lied to her or tried to control what she did. He'd presented the facts, just like he was doing now.

He was attracted to her.

"Say something," he said.

"What am I supposed to say?" She gripped the half of her sandwich so tight the pieces of turkey squished out of her grip and hit the floor.

"Whatever you're thinking. You always have something to say."

"I'm wondering if this is some kind of practical joke." There. Every opportunity to own up to his bad humor.

"I'm not kidding around." His brows drew down into the serious expression she was used to from him.

That was a relief to hear. She didn't dare hope for more, but she couldn't stop the yearning from bubbling up inside of her. She wanted him. And he wanted her, too?

"Why haven't you ever said anything?" she asked. How much time had they wasted?

"Why should I?" He shrugged. "I didn't see the point of it."

"How is it not completely obvious?" She pushed the napkin and what was left of her sandwich onto the counter to free up her hands. "I call you all the time."

"With work stuff."

"I do not." He'd fixed her laptop. Tricked out her sister's necklace with a tracker. And a dozen other things that had nothing to do with their job.

"I am guilty of being oblivious to what is otherwise obvious to other people. But I'm not about to forget what happened today. Not at all." His gaze dropped to her mouth, and damn it, she wanted him to kiss her.

"Then . . . what are we going to do?"

"I'm going to kiss you." He bent his head a little, and damn if she couldn't feel the memory of his lips. "But only on your mouth, and only once. Any more and I'll get distracted. We can't afford to be caught unaware."

"O-okay." She could appreciate his forethought, even if her body screamed at the unfairness of it. Her hormones were overriding her critical-thinking ability. The safety of her sister and the threat to her should be at the forefront of her mind, but all she could think about was Emery. This close, she could see the lighter flecks of gold in his hazel eyes.

"One kiss," he said.

Was he taunting her, or promising her?

Tori held her breath. Emery leaned toward her and bent his head a little more. His lips whispered over hers in a gentle glide.

"That doesn't count." She reached for him, but he grasped her wrists, holding her hands prisoner. In this setting, she didn't mind him pinning her hands.

"No." He pressed against her, trapping her body with his.

Emery sealed his mouth over hers. He licked the seam of her lips, demanding entrance. There was nothing of the shy lover she'd imagined him to be. She didn't have to coax him out of his shell. He thrust his tongue into her mouth and she curled her fingers into her palms. She wanted to hold on to him, and yet the way he took complete control was a major turn-on.

The pieces clinked together.

She'd never been attracted to a guy like what she'd imagined Emery to be. Her body had recognized the strength in him even when she hadn't. She melted into his hold, wishing they were skin to skin. Once wasn't enough. She wanted him again and again. But damn it, there wasn't time for that.

As if Emery heard her thoughts, he broke the kiss. He pressed his lips to her forehead, breathing deep. She closed her eyes, soaking in his strength, the quiet competence she'd taken for a single facet of his personality.

"I can't let you keep distracting me." His lips moved over her skin. Did it count as a kiss?

"You're right." Tori pulled her wrists from his grasp because he allowed it and hugged his waist. She'd never again make the mistake of thinking she could show him up, unless they were talking cars. "What are we going to do?"

"I can't think when you're touching me."

"Really?" The Walking Brain had a weakness?

"I'm thinking a lot about things that won't help us." He stared down at her, gaze narrowed.

"Like? Dirty, sweaty things?"

"Yes." He frowned.

"Want to tell me about them?"

"No." Yet he slowly brought his arms around her, as if he thought she might bolt if he moved too fast.

"It could be fun. We could compare notes."

Chapter Eleven

Emery strode toward the cabin in the early morning light. He peered at the windows, looking for some sign of life inside.

Tori had kissed him again this morning before crawling into bed. Just a quick peck, but there was nothing friendly about it.

He could still hear her voice, quietly rambling when he passed out. He couldn't remember a single thing she'd said, but her nearness and the sound of her were comforting.

He glanced through the windows, but couldn't make out more than deeper shadows. It would be good if Tori could sleep longer. It might help make the day shorter for her.

The back door squeaked as he pulled it open, but that was unavoidable. He stepped into the kitchen and blinked in the relative brightness of the LED lantern. Tori sat on the counter in a pair of running shorts and a tank top.

"Wondered where you were." Her voice was still husky from sleep.

"Just looking around."

"Anything out there?" She ripped open a package of powdered donuts and held it out to him, but it wasn't the donuts he wanted.

He plucked one from the package and lifted it to her lips. She didn't hesitate to open her mouth and bite it in half, leaving a smear of white sugar across her lips.

"Nothing." He shoved the other half donut into his own mouth, watching her tongue swipe the residue from her skin. He caught himself before he mimicked the action.

"What's our game plan?"

He leaned against the refrigerator and pondered their options. There were too many questions and not enough answers.

"Do you think the hit team is connected to Evers somehow?" Tori's voice was quieter, smaller.

"Unlikely." He'd thought about that long and hard before discarding the idea. It was too coincidental. Besides, the mob didn't play well with anyone, and Evers wasn't the kind of person to share turf with anyone, even on a temporary basis. He wasn't sure how the Eleventh factored into things yet, but he'd find answers.

What Emery wouldn't give for a laptop and a Wi-Fi connection. He was pretty sure he could uncover something now that Evers's organization appeared to be in bed with the Eleventh. He hadn't paid as much attention to the Eleventh's soldiers' activity on social media since they'd been focusing on Evers's dummy corporations. The two working together was the only explanation for the Eleventh to be openly hanging out at Greenworks. There was a good chance Emery could pick up something on the Internet, now that he knew what to look for. The Eleventh crew wasn't anywhere near as tight-lipped as Evers's people.

"Will you say something, please? I'm tired of listening to myself think."

"Things we know." Emery held up a finger and ticked off each item. "Someone is protecting Evers. Maybe even someone in the FBI or higher up. We can probably assume

Evers knows we are FBI and that we successfully infiltrated his organization through Dustin Ross before he died. It makes sense that the enemy of my enemy is my friend. With Evers in prison, he needs foot soldiers now that Dustin is gone. The Eleventh has a process that works for them, but they aren't the sophisticated machine that Evers had going. They're also expendable."

"I need coffee if you're going to talk this much."

"You said to talk." He grabbed a bottled latte from the cooler and handed it to her. They'd be without hot coffee until they got back to civilization.

"I know. Do you talk to Aiden like this?" She twisted the top off and drank deeply of the creamy liquid.

"When I have something to say." He watched her throat flex as she swallowed. He'd felt those same muscles constrict under his lips yesterday.

She breathed deeply, perking up a bit. "Okay, keep going."

"The hit team does not fit into their operation." Emery stared at the floor, rolling the question over in his head.

"What if Evers's organization is trying to pick us off? Divide us? It's not like we've raided any of his other operations. Fuck, we can't even get FBI backup to pull that off. I don't believe in coincidences. Someone in the FBI could be protecting him, but I'd guess whoever *they* are also can't hang us out to dry directly. That still doesn't totally explain the hit team."

Emery had gathered enough evidence to prove the nefarious activities of a couple of Evers's fringe companies over the course of the last few weeks. They'd still been denied operational authority to raid.

"The Russians have to be here on their own. For some other reason. Someone else wants you and your sister dead. I think it's time we made use of Detective Smith," Emery said.

"Really?"

"He wants the same thing we do. Fuck, he wanted to talk the other night. Said he had something to tell Aiden, but I forgot. I was too focused on you." It was a potentially dangerous mistake. What if Smith knew something? What if he'd been trying to warn them? Emery's single-minded obsession had him tripping up where he shouldn't.

"What did he want to talk about?" Tori asked.

"I don't know." Emery scrubbed the side of his face. This wasn't normal. He was usually on top of things, but the threat to Tori had overridden all priorities. "I've got to talk to Detective Smith."

"Now?"

"Yes."

"No way. Emery, we've got to stay off the grid, remember?"

He glanced at her, noting the lines of worry and wide eyes. She was awake now, and maybe even scared. He crossed the space between them in a single stride and gripped the edge of the counter on either side of her legs. There were a number of laws he'd broken to protect her, and he'd break more to keep her safe. These were truths he'd grown comfortable with.

"We can't contact Smith. It's not safe," she said.

He hated seeing this strong woman afraid. Not that he could blame her. In her shoes he'd probably be halfway across the country by now, and with good reason.

"Tori, if these guys are as good as they're supposed to be, they'll find us eventually. We need help. We need Smith to at least run interference with the Eleventh and keep them off our ass while we handle this mob mess. If we can't get it from CJ, maybe Smith will help us. We did him a solid calling him in for that arrest. He owes us." And Emery would call in the favor on Tori's account. When Aiden and Julian were debriefed on exactly what was going down, Emery did not expect things to go well. Shit was going to hit the fan, because he seriously doubted CJ would rock the boat right now with the crew. "Is there somewhere nearby we can go to use a pay phone? Something they can't link to us?"

"Let me think." She cradled her head in her hands.

He had to touch her. It had been over six hours since their last kiss, and nearly an hour and a half since he'd sat in the living room watching her sleep.

Emery wrapped an arm around her waist and pulled her to the edge of the counter, hugging her to his chest. She came willingly, resting her head against his shoulder and looping her arms around his neck. He felt her breath against his skin when she sighed. In his arms. He barely dared to breathe for fear of waking up and realizing this moment was a dream.

"There's a campground. We passed it on our way here." Her voice was slightly muffled, but he felt the vibrations down to his bones.

"Good." He wished they had a different ride. The Tesla was flashy. Perfect for his role in Miami, but out here it would stick out. If they could acquire another set of wheels, that would be ideal, but time-consuming and risky.

"We should go now, before it gets too much lighter and people are up and around."

"One of us should go—"

"No," Tori snapped and sat up straight. "We don't split up."

"Okay. Then the faster we go, the better." Did they pack everything up and take it with them? If Smith had something to tell them they might need to go fast.

Tori pulled him closer, squeezing his shoulders and burying her face against his neck. He gently hugged her, allowing his eyes to close and his senses to revel in the smell and touch of her body.

"We're going to be okay," he said.

She straightened, nodding, but made no other reply. For lack of anything better to say, he backed up a few steps, giving her space.

"I'll get the food packed up. Can you get the bags?" She gathered the prepackaged foods back into the plastic bags, moving with purpose. It appeared she was making the call. They were preparing for another run. Another place to hide. Hopefully this time and place would provide them with more security—and a little privacy.

Emery didn't know what to call this thing between them, but he wasn't about to let it go. He wanted her. The Russians couldn't have her.

Tori glanced at Emery's profile as he drove. The newly risen sun bathed his face in a golden light she itched to reach out and touch. He calmed the panic in her soul and made her heart beat fast for a whole other reason.

She'd often imagined what sex with Emery might be like. How it would feel. His quiet demeanor had led her to think of him as a strong, gentle giant. Boy, how wrong she'd been. He hadn't hurt her, but she'd been shocked and thrilled by his roughness and the barely contained power. But where did they go from here? What did it mean?

Last night she'd finally shoved her lust for Emery to the backseat and focused on the immediate needs—which did not include a stroll through her fantasies. Today, no matter how much she tried to focus on the dangers facing them and their crew, she couldn't ignore the way her nerves bunched and tied themselves into knots every time she looked at him.

"Emery?" She turned to face him, giving in to the desire to simply look at him.

"Hm?"

How did she ask him without sounding pathetic?

Deep breath.

"About yesterday . . ." *You know, when you fucked my lights out?*

"Which part?" His calm, even tone gave nothing away. The jerk. Couldn't he be as tightly wound as she?

"Is that going to change things?" She held her breath, praying he wouldn't be obtuse this time.

"I'm going to assume you aren't talking about the hit team or Greenworks or—"

"I mean between us, asshat."

He glanced at her, the little thought lines bracketing his mouth. What did that mean?

"Yes," he replied.

"Yes—what?"

"It changes everything."

Not even her imaginary version of Emery said more. She stared at his profile, trying to puzzle out his words. They didn't calm her or ease her mind. Change in a bad way? Or a good one?

"I want you safe. That's got to be my first priority, then the crew. I can't offer you more than that right now, but I have no intention of pretending like yesterday didn't happen."

Tori turned to look at the road, her mind abuzz with a hundred possibilities. She couldn't argue with his logic; she could even get behind it.

"Tori?"

"That's perfect. I don't think I could forget either."

She noticed the yellow-and-black KOA signs ahead of them. There were people moving around the RVs in the campground, but not much activity. It would have been better if they'd gotten up earlier to do this run, but it couldn't be helped.

"While I call Smith can you see about ice?" Emery asked.

"Of course."

He turned the Tesla into the campground, easing down the gravel path lined with palm trees. The first row of RVs sported container gardens and plastic pink flamingos. The residents clearly didn't intend on moving anytime soon. There were a few people out sipping their first cups of coffee and enjoying the morning sunshine, but not many.

"How's the car's charge?" she asked.

"Fine."

"What's fine?" She peered at the dash but Emery cut the engine before she could see how many bars of charge the electric car had under the hood.

"We could go a couple hundred miles still."

Emery parked the Tesla in front of what appeared to be the administration offices, general store, and hot dog stand all in one. A pay phone out front had wires hanging out from behind the unit. Not a good sign.

"I'll find a phone to use," he said.

"I'll get ice." Tori pulled out the handgun she'd stashed in the glove box and stuck it in her waistband at her back.

"Think you'll need that?" Emery asked.

"You never know."

She stepped out of the car and pulled the big, ugly aviators down to shield her face under the ball cap. Her hair was pinned to her scalp to hide her long, red hair.

The ground was damp with dew, and dust clung to everything. Her feet thumped on the wooden floorboards as she crossed to the double front doors of the general store. She glanced over her shoulder at Emery striding toward a group of older men, his cap pushed up and a smile she didn't recognize on his face. It looked plastic and wrong to her, but only because she knew him.

She'd never seen him at work in the field, only at the garage when he was in his element. It struck her again that there was more to him than she'd ever guessed. He wasn't just a tech, he was a dangerous field agent with the skill to mesh into any environment.

And he was on her side.

Tori pushed the doors of the store open and glanced around. There were a couple of dining tables on the far side where people were gathered for coffee and donuts. Several older women had their heads together, whispering furiously, their penciled brows arching at whatever was being discussed.

She smiled at the bored teen manning the register and glanced around for anything useful. Armed with a plastic basket, she grabbed a couple of packaged foods and a bunch of barely ripe bananas.

"I heard them. All night they were at it," one of the ladies said loud enough for Tori to hear. She chuckled, amused that despite her harrowing experiences, the world still went on as normal for others.

"What were they doing?" another woman asked the first.

"Racing is what my Jerry said. Buzzing those awful cars up and down the road all night long. Didn't get a wink of sleep."

Tori's blood turned to ice.

She didn't believe in coincidences. If someone happened to be drag racing on this strip of road, it had to be the Eleventh. What if they were outside right now? What about Emery?

She almost bolted for the door in a blind panic.

One . . .

She could panic for five seconds.

Two . . .

Her heart nearly beat itself silly against her ribs.

Three . . .

She couldn't have moved if she'd wanted to. She'd seen

rabbits freeze in front of her car before. Was this how they felt?

Four . . .

God, what about her sister?

Five . . .

Tori inhaled and grabbed something at random off the shelf in front of her, as if she'd been considering her options. She strolled past the women, but their conversation had moved on to where and when their relatives had served in the military.

She took her bounty to the register and handed it to the teen.

"Two bags of ice, please."

"It's outside on the left." The cashier rang up her purchases and she paid, but her mind was a couple hundred miles away in Orlando.

Had CJ told the others of her defection? What did Roni think? Did she know? Was she okay? If they were sending a hit team after her, what about her sister? Was the Eleventh hassling them, too? Were there others going after her?

She accepted her change and threw out a polite, "Thank you," before heading for the front doors. The beveled glass squares set into the wood made it difficult to discern more than blobs of movement outside. She took another deep breath and concentrated on the feel of the gun tucked into her waistband. The door swung open on well-oiled hinges. She swept her gaze over the campground, but didn't find any thugs or out-of-place cars waiting for her.

Emery was nowhere in sight, which concerned her. He might blow her mind with what he could do, but he was still only one man.

She left the bag of goods on the hood and walked the dozen or so steps to the freezers. The cold air was better than a shot of espresso to her system. She wished she knew when the Eleventh had been here, but asking would have drawn the wrong kind of attention. She got two bags of ice, bumped the door shut with her hip, and turned toward the car.

Emery strode toward her. His expression was grim, but she couldn't tell if it was normal grim or if he'd heard something similar to what she had.

"We need to leave," she said in a low voice.

He didn't reply, but the way he turned and swept the area, as if he was looking for something, told her all she needed to know. There was more danger than what she'd heard inside. They stashed their ice and food in the trunk, the tense silence drawing tight between them until the moment they dropped into the Tesla.

Emery didn't bother with a seat belt. He started the car and reversed, his motions controlled and precise.

"I think the Eleventh was here. There were people inside talking about a bunch of cars racing last night." She buckled her seat belt and pulled the gun out of her waistband, tucking it under her leg for easy access.

"I heard. The guys were all talking about a bunch of drag racing that happened along this street. One of their friends got forced off the road." He barely glanced at her as he accelerated out of the drive and onto the road. He checked all the mirrors, peering maybe a bit too intently into the glass.

It wasn't a coincidence then.

"They're what? Scouting? Searching?"

"One of them must have tailed us at a distance and lost us around here. Probably trying to flush us out, make a lot of noise, get us to come out of hiding."

In other words, exactly what Emery and Tori were doing now. It wasn't what she'd have done. Her first move would have been to steal a car to blend in, get close and stay under the radar. If she had to guess, this was the Eleventh flexing their muscle.

"What did Smith tell you? Were you able to call him?"

"Yeah."

She waited for a moment, but he didn't share more.

"And?" she prompted him.

"He's arranged for us to stay at a hotel."

That wasn't bad news.

"What aren't you telling me, Emery?" She could sense his reticence.

"The cops are going to let Evers go in the morning. They appealed for bail and the judge granted it this time around."

"What? Why? That doesn't make sense."

There were miles of proof that Michael Evers was a violent, dangerous criminal with the means to flee outside extradition. And they were letting him go.

"He couldn't say a lot, but I think we're in agreement on this. Someone in the FBI is covering for Evers. Otherwise, why isn't he in federal custody? What do they want?" He slapped the steering wheel with his hand.

They'd spent hours speculating about the lack of movement on the Evers case. She couldn't remember who'd thrown out the idea of federal shielding, only that once the thought was voiced it had stayed in the back of her mind. From the way others had whispered about the possibility, it was likely it wasn't just her. And now they had something close to proof. In less than twenty-four hours they'd know for sure. Someone was playing a game with their lives, and that wasn't okay.

"I don't like this." She peered ahead of them at the cars on the road.

"Neither do I." Emery reached for her hand, wrapping his around hers for a moment. He pulled her hand toward his lips.

Her thoughts ceased as she watched him buzz her knuckles with a kiss. She felt the brief contact all the way to her core. She wanted to kiss him. She wanted to crawl over into his lap, wrap her body around his and kiss him. She wouldn't, but it was a nice thought.

"We'll beat this." He released her hand.

She wasn't certain. CJ, Kathy, Julian, and Emery—the FBI would pull them out. They'd be protected. The rest of their crew could easily become collateral damage in this mess.

"Look out," Tori blurted.

She gripped the door and planted her other hand on the dash as a bright yellow car with a tall spoiler swerved in front of them, coming off the side of the road. Emery braked hard, shifting and cursing. The high-pitched rev of several engines heralded companions of the yellow car, whereas the Tesla's electric engine was nearly silent.

"Go, go, go," Tori chanted.

Emery accelerated, but the yellow car veered with them, cutting the Tesla off. Someone honked, reminding her they weren't the only people on the road. Emery merged into the right lane and the yellow GT-R moved with them. They continued this dance, Emery jerking the car one way or the other, and the other driver mimicking his moves, forcing Emery to slow down in the process.

"Go faster." Tori twisted to look out through the back window. There was a familiar silver Scion and what looked to be a red Lancer she might have seen a time or two.

"I'm trying. Hold on."

She gripped the door and braced her feet on the floorboard.

Emery slowed the car even more, barely doing forty. Suddenly, he jerked the car into the left lane, except he pulled up halfway there. The GT-R didn't recover, sweeping almost all the way into the other lane. Emery punched the accelerator, shifting as the electric engine shuddered and the car shot forward, passing the yellow car. Ahead of them, an eighteen-wheeler and a pickup truck blocked the lanes.

"Emery. Emery!"

The right two tires bumped along the grooved side of the road. The shoulder was narrow. Not even a full car-width wide. He kept the left tires on the white line and blazed past the truck within inches of clipping off his mirror.

She twisted to watch their six. The GT-R didn't even attempt the maneuver, but she could see it bearing down, riding the truck's bumper.

"Hold on," Emery warned.

She sat her butt back in the seat not a moment too soon. He swerved and zigzagged through cars, using both feet on the pedals. Her heart beat in her throat, but not from fear. Never in her life had she imagined Emery handling a car like this. It was pretty damn hot—except for the whole *running for their life* part of it.

They broke past the pack of cars and the road stretched out ahead of them, with only a few cars in the distance. That would change. This was a busy highway into Miami. How many other Eleventh drivers would they run into? Last they'd checked, the Eleventh crew was around nine-teen drivers strong. Emery probably had a more accurate account, down to the make, model, and VIN numbers of the cars.

"What are we doing?" She leaned toward Emery, but her gaze snagged on the dash.

The charge bar was dipping below 25 percent. They couldn't go hundreds of miles on a 25 percent charge. What if they lost it on the road?

She needed to make sure that didn't happen.

"Twenty-five percent? Twenty-five fucking percent,

Emery? Goddamn it." Tori pulled the gun out from under her leg. The FBI hadn't hired her and Roni for their ability to handle cars. Their father might have been a first-class jackass and shit at being a dad, but he had ensured his girls knew how to protect themselves.

"Don't worry about it," Emery said.

The Tesla needed a particular hookup to charge. The car hadn't been on a charge since—when? The morning he'd taken her to IHOP?

"I'm going to worry about it." She glanced behind them. The GT-R was coming at them fast. "Drive straight. Don't swerve. Let him catch us."

She popped her seat belt and rolled the window down.

"Tori—what are—? Don't." He seemed to realize what she was doing about halfway through the sentence.

Didn't matter.

She was already hanging out of the passenger-side window, the wind whisking the hat off her head. Tendrils of her hair whipped her face, lashing her cheeks. She stared down the sights and exhaled, squeezing the trigger, visualizing the path of her bullet. The blast of the shot was lost almost immediately. Emery was driving too fast.

It was stupid.

It was reckless.

But hell, they were desperate.

Emery grabbed the waistband of her jeans and pulled her back inside. She sat down hard and flipped the safety back on. She glanced behind them at the now-smoking GT-R. A radiator shot if she wasn't mistaken.

"Are you crazy? You could have shot a civilian," Emery yelled.

It was a risk. One she felt guilty about, but not enough to wish she hadn't done it.

"I hit the car, nothing else."

"But you could have shot someone else."

She didn't deny it.

"Drive faster and I won't have to do it again." Because she would. If Emery was in danger she'd protect him just like he'd protected her. It was a new feeling. Sure, the crew always had her back, but she didn't think Gabriel or John would go to the lengths Emery had for her. She also wasn't madly in love with the two mechanics, and now that she knew Emery liked her back—it was a whole new obsession.

Chapter Twelve

The swanky South Beach hotel was a definite upgrade from the grimy shack in the middle of nowhere. Emery squinted into the light pouring in from the wall of floor-to-ceiling windows that gave an amazing view of the beach.

"Remind me to always pretend to be newlyweds. This suite is sick." Tori squeezed past him, the little rolling bag thumping over the grooves in the tile as she took a quick turn around the room.

"I've got some IDs for you guys." Matt Smith closed the suite door and flipped the lock behind Emery.

"Thanks." He wouldn't bother to tell the detective he wasn't going to use any IDs he hadn't made himself.

Emery strode around the room, surveying it for weaknesses. He poked his head out onto the balcony. There was a partition wall between them and the rooms next door. It would take a daredevil to sneak over this high up, but he wouldn't put it out of the realm of possibility. Truth was, none of it would be good enough for him. He didn't like being in a hotel. There was no way to control the comings and goings of other people. There were too many access points, not enough security required for people to pass between floors. But he could hack into the hotel security and keep an eye on things.

"I got you a laptop. It's nothing fancy. I had to take what wouldn't be missed. Also, burner phones, like you asked for." Matt placed the items on the four-seater dining table in the far left corner of the room opposite the galley kitchen.

"Why are the cops letting Evers go?" Tori asked. Since meeting up in the hotel garage, they hadn't said much to each other. Matt had arrived with suitcases to help them appear a bit more like tourist newlyweds, and that was it.

"His lawyers argued he wasn't a flight risk. That he was forced to shoot those guys out of self-defense. There's got to be more, because those same arguments didn't work last time." Matt placed his hands on his hips and scowled at the carpet. "Hell, they just released a woman on bail who shot and killed a cop, and all they did to her was slap an ankle monitor on her and take away her passport. I imagine they'll do the same to Evers."

Michael Evers made enemies wherever he went. Over a year before, the Miami-Dade PD had been building a case against Evers. Except they hadn't counted on someone else taking the fall for Evers when they sprung the trap. The resulting shit storm had landed mostly on Matt's mentor, sending the decorated detective out to pasture in a small sheriff's office.

"That's bullshit. Did they even admit Aiden and Julian's testimony?" she asked.

"No. I think the Feds pulled it," Matt replied.

"Shit."

That was news to Emery. Who would pull evidence on a criminal they'd invested so much money and man-hours into arresting, and why? There had to be something they weren't seeing. A bigger picture.

Tori walked the room, seemingly admiring the small

touches. Emery doubted even Matt realized what she was doing. She trailed her fingers along the underside of a table, or felt around for the switch on a lamp. All good places to hide a bug.

The Russians wouldn't bother with a bug. It wasn't information they were after. They'd just walk in and shoot them all. Emery didn't think they were that far ahead of the hit team. They'd spent an uneventful night right under the Eleventh's nose, which was incredibly good luck to have remained hidden so well. He'd been a lot more careful this time around when he drove to the hotel.

"What are you going to do now?" Matt turned toward him. He'd taken off the badge that was normally clipped to his belt, but he still wore the mantle of cop.

"Eat something. Shower. Probably catch a little sleep." Emery shrugged.

Matt's lips compressed into a tight line.

"What?" Emery asked.

"I don't know if you know this already but . . ."

"But what?" Tori prompted.

"Gabriel is in the hospital. He said he was racing and someone forced him off the road. He spun out, tapped a concrete barricade and crunched his car. Pretty sure it was the Eleventh."

Tori gasped.

For a second, Emery didn't breathe. He scrubbed his hand over his mouth.

"How do you know it was the Eleventh?" Emery asked.

"Who was hurt?" Tori demanded over him.

Matt held up his hands. "Part of it was caught on a security camera. No plates, but I recognize the car. Gabriel got knocked around a bit, fractured rib and some bruising. They want to hold him for observation one more night. He knocked his head pretty hard. I just thought you would either know or want to know." Tori's gaze landed on Emery.

He could feel the weight of it. His fingers itched to reach out and touch her. He could almost count the minutes since he'd last kissed her. Could still remember the way it felt when she brushed against him in the elevator.

"We have cut communication with our team for safety," Emery said.

"Okay." Matt's frown clearly showed disapproval, but whatever. That wasn't Matt's call. "What can I do to help?"

Emery drew a deep breath. Help would be nice, but they also didn't want to end up making Matt collateral damage. The cop already had a target on his back for being the arresting officer on scene when Evers was taken into custody.

"Not a lot. Focus on the Eleventh. Nothing official, really, just encourage the patrol officers to pull over any and all street rides. Other than that, stay away from us. You've done more than enough right now. It's probably safer if you don't get involved more than you are."

Matt glanced at Tori. "And your sister?"

Tori's gaze narrowed. In the last three months, Matt had pulled Roni over four times. She was the only person on their crew the detective had made contact with, and Emery doubted it was for business reasons. Emery had kept tabs of the interactions, but that was it. Roni could take care of herself.

"She's safe," Tori replied.

Matt stared at her a moment, as if he could will more information out of her, but he was out of luck. Tori wasn't about to tell him shit.

"Guess I'll leave you two to it then. Need anything, just holler." He nodded and glanced at the door. He paused, but when neither Tori nor Emery told him to stay, he made his exit.

Tori followed him, flipping the locks and sliding the chain into place after him. She put her back against the door and stared at Emery. He could hear her unspoken question. *What do we do?*

He didn't know what they should do at this point. His best-laid plans had been dashed to pieces.

Tomorrow Roni would be back in Miami and in the crosshairs of the hit team. The Eleventh Street gang was flexing their muscle. And very soon their crew would have to worry about Evers again. Fracturing their team with a few people scattered around was a bad idea. He didn't like it, but it was the truth.

"We need to call CJ and get a status report," he said.

"Are you sure?"

"Yes. I'll use one of the burners. Keep it short." He nodded at the bag of things Matt had left for them.

Tori grabbed one of the packaged phones and they met by wordless agreement at the bar stools in front of the galley kitchen. He pulled out a pocket knife and sliced the plastic. The phone was simple. No frills. He plugged it in and the screen lit up, then he dialed the number for the Classic Rides landline. He could call CJ's cell, but it would be easier to trace.

Emery pressed the phone to his ear and looked at Tori. She reached over and placed her hand on his knee. The line rang several times with no answer. What if they'd closed the shop due to damages?

"Hello?" The gruff voice was familiar.

"CJ. It's Emery."

Silence.

"Is Gabriel okay?" Emery asked.

"He'll be fine. What the hell were you thinking disappearing like that? I'm assuming Tori is with you." A door closed. It made sense. CJ must have been out front in the shop area.

"I was thinking I needed to protect my team."

"Fuck it. I didn't know it was Matvei. The guy's worse

than a damn urban legend. If you'd have told me that I would have made a different call."

"Because that matters?"

"Hell yes, it does. We could have quietly paid off any other hit man, maybe gotten them arrested, but Matvei lives for this shit. Look, we need to pool our resources. Fast. Aiden and the others are heading back this way tonight. Canales wasn't at the races. Together, we can make a plan. The Russians and Cubans have been at it lately over all kinds of things up north. We do not need to be caught up between them if that fight comes to Miami."

CJ hadn't known the details, at least not all of it. Emery didn't agree with CJ's supposed plan, but it was in the past. He wasn't ready to outright trust the agent, but at least Emery had just confirmed they were all on the same side. Whoever was jerking them around, it wasn't the people they'd come to trust.

"What about Evers? Do you know?" Emery asked.

"Know what?"

"He's being released."

"Yeah. I heard."

Tori's jaw dropped. Clearly the burner phone also functioned as a loudspeaker.

"You knew?" What else had CJ kept from them?

"Only because I was paying the judge's assistant to keep me up-to-date."

"What?"

"Someone is keeping us in the dark. All of us. Me. You. The whole crew. It's like we're bait. We need to address this."

"Past time."

"Where are you? We've got to be business as usual here, but tonight me, you, Kathy, and Tori—if she's still with you—should put our heads together."

"Maybe." Emery wasn't about to agree to making Tori

a target again, and letting anyone know where she was meant more opportunities for just that kind of thing to happen.

"She probably thinks we don't have her back. That's why I didn't want to tell her. I wanted to handle it before she ever knew it was an issue. This isn't the way I thought this would go down."

"I told you."

"That there was a hit team? Yeah. I assumed it was related to Evers. You never told me everything. Matvei wouldn't work for Evers, not in a million years. Goddamn it, Emery. You're our tech. You've got fingers in every pie and feelers out everywhere. I've got to keep tabs on all of you. I can't double up and do your job when you already do it so well."

"Then why not tell me what you knew?"

"Again, I thought I'd handle it before it was an issue, but we've been chasing shadows lately. I made a bad call. I would never put Tori or Roni in this kind of danger." Honesty rang in CJ's voice. Damn it, Emery wanted to trust him. CJ had never given them reason to question him like this before. He might not be the friendliest guy to work with, but he was a good agent.

"I'll think about it." Emery hung up the phone and Tori blew out a breath.

"Well?"

"You heard all of that?"

"Yeah, but what do you think?" She crossed her arms over her chest, lines creasing her brow.

"My gut says he's telling the truth, but I'm not willing to bet your safety on a hunch." She was too important for that kind of gambling. Letting more people know where she was, hell, even meeting up somewhere with the others, might be too dangerous.

She studied him for a moment. Her features softened,

and damn it, he wanted to kiss her. Maybe whisking her away and taking on new aliases was a good idea. If the twins separated, they'd be less obvious. But Emery seriously doubted Tori would give up her sister. They were far too close.

"We can't do this alone." She uncrossed her arms and sighed. "There're too many things up in the air. We need backup. Besides, Roni's still with the crew and they won't hang us out to dry. Aiden, Julian, and Roni won't let them"

He took her hand in his and squeezed. Yesterday she'd wanted to run away from all of them. Today, she was willing to once more trust the very people she'd feared had betrayed her.

"You sure you want to do this?"

"No. I want to hide." She stared at his chest.

"There's nothing wrong in that."

"Maybe not, but I can't do that."

He remained quiet, letting her parse through her thoughts, sorting her options. He'd grown accustomed to the way she could talk almost all the time, but he also knew her quiet moments. The way she'd study a car, puzzling out the options, turning them this way and that until the pieces fit. She had a brilliant way of finding solutions under most circumstances.

"This hit team scares me." She chewed her lip for a moment. "Have we been able to find out why they were sent?"

"I only heard it was about a grudge."

She let go of his hand, paced to the overstuffed leather sofa, and dropped down, staring at the windows.

"They want something my sister and I don't have."

"What is that?" Emery followed her, walking softly and sitting on the coffee table, his every nerve on alert. If it was a grudge, it was very likely attached to her and her sister's old lives and maybe even her father. She'd never talked about those before, and didn't know he knew.

Tori turned her head toward him, her gaze unreadable.

"You already know," she said.

"I do?" Guilt gnawed at him. He had a good feeling he did.

"I'm guessing you do. You know everything about all of us."

"Not everything." But he knew a lot. Things the others would prefer no one knew. But it was his job to know everything. To keep tabs, to make sure the crew stayed on task and no one went off the rails. Well, no one except Julian. He'd jumped the tracks long ago and was someone else's problem. So long as he played the game close to the rules in Miami, Emery didn't have to mention it.

"You know my dad was KGB."

Not a question.

Emery nodded.

"Then you probably also know he turned informant in exchange for asylum for himself, my sister, and me." She paused.

"I do."

She went back to staring out of the windows. "He did that after our mother was killed. We were toddlers. He'd only seen us a few times after we were born. I don't think he really cared about us, but he didn't like people thinking they had leverage on him. There had to be more going on than we've ever known about." She fingered the charm at her throat. The one that had a picture of her mother in it. "I'm also pretty sure he took us and came here."

"You mean—he kidnapped you?"

Tori nodded.

"How do you know?"

"We don't. It's just what we think from how he behaved. All the moving around. Never allowing us to have a phone. He didn't want to be contacted or traced. Anyway, I remember men in suits coming to wherever we were living through the years and asking him things. The FBI is convinced we know secrets he never shared, and the Russians want to stop us before we tell them—something. I don't know what. The truth is he never told us anything. He was a cold son of a bitch who provided the necessities and that was it."

Emery could understand unfeeling parents. He'd grown up with two of them.

Tori's gaze landed on him once more. "What else do you know?"

Normally, he wouldn't reply. He'd make up another answer. But what was the point?

"I know your mother's name was Olga. I know that Tori Chazov isn't your real name. You're naturally a blonde."

"I think I like Tori the best." She chuckled and shook her head.

"Why red hair?"

"Because it was the last color we hadn't tried." She kicked off her shoes and curled her legs under her. "Like it?"

"I can't imagine you any other way."

"What? There aren't pictures in your files?"

"No."

"Oh my gosh, something you don't know." She grinned at him and the guilt disappeared.

He watched her a moment, not on the same amused wavelength as she.

"You don't mind?" he asked.

"What?"

"That I know?"

"It's your job. I don't really like the idea, but if it's just you who knows, I can be okay. It's just . . . there are secrets

in my past. Things I can't tell even you, and that's a lot
to ask."

"I don't have to know everything." He might want to,
but he understood that with her history, it might never be
open for discussion.

She held out her hand and he obliged by taking it.

"What do you want to do about tonight?" she asked.

Tonight. Right.

"It would be good to meet with CJ and Kathy, get us
all on the same page."

"Then we do that. Where? Here?"

"No, not here. I'd like to keep this place safe, if we can."

"Maybe Matt could help?"

"Perhaps. I'm not sure we want him knowing when
and where we do things. Not because I don't trust him,
but because it makes him a liability."

"I'm proud of you. Look at you using all these sentences. We're actually having a conversation, in case you
hadn't noticed."

"I've always been able to."

"Then why haven't you ever talked to me before?"

"Too busy admiring the view."

Her cheeks tinged pink. He stared in wonder—had he
ever seen Tori blush before? Was this a thing that happened?

"Where do we want to meet them tonight?" Tori's lips
curled into a smile and she shifted.

"There's a place." He had a few in mind, but he was far
more fascinated by the color of Tori's cheeks.

A day ago he might have packed away this moment to
replay in his mind, but that was before he'd known why her
cheeks blushed. A lot of things made sense now. The
reasons she called him, the little problems. She'd been
looking for as many ways to get close to him as he had her.
Except his ways weren't direct. He'd never been very good
with puzzling out women, because no two followed the

same set of rules. Tori had granted him the key to her code. There was no turning back. They'd accepted that this morning in the car.

"What do we need to accomplish between now and then?"

Damn her for being responsible.

"I'm going to get on that laptop and see what I'm working with. If I can get into my network, I'd like to do some research on Greenworks and look into the Eleventh's activity. I also want to know how the hell they followed us."

"A tail we didn't notice?"

"Possibly. We didn't expect them because we were so focused on the hit team."

"What can I do?"

"I downloaded the paper trail to the tablet. I want you to flip through the documents. See if you can spot anything that might tell us what they're doing in there."

"I can do that."

He wanted her to do other things, but she was right. They had to address the threat first. But damn, he wanted her. Again. Now, if possible, but it wasn't. Later, she would be his again.

Chapter Thirteen

Tori's eyes started to cross. Again. She'd gone through the PDF files at least twice. She hadn't been able to identify anything that appeared remotely useful, though she'd tagged and made notes on what stuck out to her. But who knew if even that would make a difference? This was all new to her. She glanced at Emery, but he had that look on his face, the one that said nothing else existed except the laptop in front of him. She'd come to recognize this single-minded work mode and knew better than to distract him.

She set the tablet down on the dining table and rubbed her eyes. Emery frowned at the laptop, but he'd been doing that for hours. Give her an engine to work on and she'd be set for a day. That tablet? Her brain was fried after a couple hours. There was no way she could keep doing that. She stood and stretched, peering out of the corner of her eye at Emery, but he never once glanced her way.

If he were a normal man and she a normal woman, she might take offense to the lack of attention, but they were nothing like a typical couple. What they did saved lives, and she wasn't about to intentionally distract Emery from what he was doing, even if all she wanted was to see him smile at her again.

She strolled to the windows and studied the beach. The sands were nearly covered with people sunbathing, swimming, or playing. She'd gone to the beach some with her sister, but usually they made use of the apartment pool. It was just easier that way. But a carefree day just hanging out? That she could get behind, not that they'd had many of those lately. Would Emery ever step away from work long enough for that? She doubted it, but then again, she was happiest in the garage anyway. Cars made sense to her when the rest of the world was too messed up.

Whenever Dad had something to work on he didn't want Roni or her to see or hear, he'd sent them to the garage. They'd tinkered with junk and parts, building make-believe spaceships, box cars, and their ride out of the hell that was their home life. Sure, their father had taught them the basics of how to fix cars, rig things so they'd work in a pinch, but from there it was trial and error, and reading a lot of manuals.

Tori walked along the window, admiring the view. Chances were she wouldn't get digs like this again. Detective Smith had to know someone with connections to get them the suite. She stepped through the open archway into the bedroom. It sat against the only solid wall in the space and was bordered on three sides by floor-to-ceiling windows.

There was only one bed.

She backed up and glanced around the suite. Okay, so it wasn't really a suite. More like a lavish room with some elbow space. The bathroom was easily a quarter of the space, and fancy. She was looking forward to the rain shower and soaking tub later. But right now her brain was hung up on one little fact.

One bed.

Only one.

For two people.

Sure, they'd had sex, but they hadn't slept together.

What if he didn't like the way she sprawled in her sleep? Or what if he ground his teeth at night?

She grabbed her suitcase and dug through it, looking at what she had to wear. As hot as it had been to feel Emery rip her underwear off yesterday, cotton granny panties were not sexy. Everything at her disposal was utilitarian and boring. Not that she hadn't picked out the clothes herself, but she'd been hoping to surprise herself somehow. Tori might not be style conscious like Roni, but neither did she want to look as sloppy as she felt. The right clothes could change a girl. Make her feel a bit more confident or desirable.

They'd passed a couple boutiques on the lobby level of the hotel, but it probably wasn't prudent to be out and about. Her style needs would have to take a backseat to impressing Emery. Besides, she had no idea where to start with picking out new lingerie. Her perception of him had been turned upside down and spun around. He was—and wasn't—anything like what she'd expected him to be, which was fine by her. She liked the man she was coming to know.

Since her infatuation began, she'd painted Emery as a quiet computer geek with passable social skills, a brilliant mind, and maybe a tad bit shy. The real Emery had far more kick-ass ability than she'd realized. He was every bit as intelligent, but she'd taken his single-minded focus on the task at hand to mean more than it did. She'd fallen for the wrong version of him, and in the process, fallen for the real him, too.

Come to think of it, she hadn't had any one-sided conversations with him in her head for a while now. Which was probably a good thing for her sanity.

She zipped her bag up, lamenting the lack of a hidden silk-panty stash, and turned away from the bed.

A figure filled the archway.

Tori sucked in a breath and drew up short.

"Shit."

"Sorry," Emery muttered, holding up his hands, but his gaze wasn't apologetic at all.

Once more she felt like the prey being stalked. Instinctively she wanted to take a step back, but she held her ground, dropping her arms to her sides. She didn't mind being stalked by Emery. In fact, she could get used to it. Those arms, the way he held her, how he moved inside of her. Yeah, she was good with this.

"Found anything?" Her voice sounded dry. She cleared her throat and tried to think past the way she could feel her heartbeat flutter at the base of her throat, as if it were trying to burst through her soft tissue and launch itself at him. It was a gory thought in reality, but damn, all of her wanted him.

"Gabriel appears to be doing well. They are keeping him overnight for observation."

"He's got to love that." She set her bag down next to the others.

"I can't find any connection between the hit team and Evers's people. I need my own equipment to dig further."

The hit team wouldn't be connected to Evers. She already knew that, but it wasn't exactly something she could tell Emery.

Right now it wasn't laptops and wires she was thinking about. She had to get herself under control. They had important things to do. Not that she could think of a single damn one with him staring at her.

"Okay. What do we need to do next?" Her palms were sweating. She rubbed them on her jeans, hyperaware of his clean linen scent mixed with citrus, the wrinkles in Emery's shirt, and the stubble lining his jaw.

The moment drew out. It wasn't unusual for Emery to take a second or two longer than most people to respond to questions, but his lips remained pressed tightly together, bracketed by the thought lines she liked so much.

"Emery, what should we do next?" she said again, hoping to prompt him into distracting her with some sort of purpose.

It was the shed all over again. Any second one of them would move and no matter where Tori stepped, Emery was going to pounce on her. Her body always reacted when he was near, but this was ridiculous. Her damn panties were getting damp and all they were doing was talking work. Clearly sex had not been the answer to her obsession issue. It was worse now than before.

Emery took two steps toward her, his ground-eating stride crossing the space until he almost barreled over her. He stared down at her, his gaze searching her face for something. Yesterday they'd acted on passion. Today, he knew all her secrets. Would it matter? For the first time, she didn't have to worry about hiding her history from someone. She didn't think Aiden or Julian knew the full story, but Emery did.

It was hard for her to breathe. She balled her hands into fists, unable to move or react until he did something. She'd never been shy when it came to men and what she wanted, but this was different. It was Emery, and he mattered. He was part of her crew; he knew what her life was like. Boyfriends came and went, getting the boot as soon as they started picking up that Tori's job wasn't exactly normal. But he wouldn't go anywhere. If they were going forward, it was serious.

What if it didn't work with Emery? Or what if it did?

She'd never know if he didn't kiss her.

Emery cradled the back of her head in his hand. She lost all ability to breathe in the seconds he stared at her mouth. If he didn't kiss her she was going to have to kiss him. It was quickly becoming the most important thing she needed to do.

He applied the barest pressure to the back of her head and she rose up on the balls of her feet the same moment he leaned down. Their mouths met in an eager kiss. She curled her hands over his shoulders, pulling him closer. Emery wrapped his arm around her waist, bending her backward slightly while he devoured her mouth. There was a rough, bruising quality to his kiss she reveled in. He thrust his tongue into her mouth and she squeezed her thighs together.

Oh God, why had she waited so long to jump him?

He stepped toward her, shoving his knee between her legs. The mattress hit the back of her thighs. She gasped when he tipped her backward just a bit more, but she needn't worry. The man had arms like tree trunks and her weight was nothing to him. Emery laid her on the bed, following her down, his mouth never leaving hers. She wrapped her left leg around his and wiggled her hips just a bit.

Tori pushed her arms under his until she could get her hands in his shirt. She ran her palms up his back. The scars felt different under her fingers, but they were still part of him and his story. He'd known so much pain, he'd been just as unwanted as she, until now.

His kiss gentled. He sucked at her lips, her face cradled in his hands.

This big, strong man wanted her. With no effort, he could have any girl he wanted, and still it was her he desired. There was a freedom in knowing that. It wasn't opportunity. It wasn't taking what was readily available. They wanted each other. And only each other.

Emery's hand settled on her breast, gently squeezing the mound in his palm. She gasped and arched into the touch. Her bra was chafing her hardened nipples.

Fuck it.

She grabbed the hem of her shirt and tugged it up, but the fabric was caught between their bodies.

"Emery," she muttered against his mouth.

"Hm?" He pressed his lips against hers in a gentle kiss.

"Up."

"No."

He sealed his lips over hers in a toe-curling kiss. His tongue flirted with hers and he drew her lower lip into his mouth, sucking the bit of flesh. Her clit throbbed with the added suction he applied.

She let go of her shirt and pushed her hand lower, until she could grasp the tab of his jeans. They were old and worn, so the button slid easily through the slit. Success. She slipped her fingers past the band of his underwear.

Emery sat up suddenly, pushing her hand away.

"No, I didn't mean that." He buttoned his jeans again, which only drew attention to the erection straining at his fly.

"Uh—what?" She sat up, trying to wrestle her lust-crazed thoughts under control.

"I only meant to kiss you."

"Okay." She stared at him. Was he serious? Because, damn, that was the cruelest kind of torture.

"I mean . . ."

"You mean you don't want sex." There was probably a good reason, like work and having people who wanted to kill them prowling around, but it still stung. She wanted him so bad it was her every other thought. Clearly their desire was mismatched. Never a good place to be. How long until he didn't want her at all?

"No, that's not what I mean. I think about sex with you all the time. Shit." He pressed his hand to his face.

Oh really?

Now that was something she liked to hear.

"I'm okay with that. It's kind of hot that you think about me that much." She smiled. All the time was more than every other thought.

"It's distracting." He dropped his hand to his side.

"Then . . . what's the problem?" Was it her? Or work? For work, she could suck up her disappointment and see the bigger picture, even if she didn't want to.

"I don't have condoms."

That was it?

It was her turn to stare at him.

Was he serious? That was the big problem?

"I probably broke some cardinal guy rule, but—I didn't expect things to turn out this way." His gaze heated and she felt the whisper of his remembered kiss on her neck.

Yeah, neither of them had expected for things to get quite so hot and sweaty between them.

She pushed to her feet, biting her bottom lip, feeling Emery's gaze on her. She took three steps to the general store bag with her purchases from that morning. She grabbed the little square box out of the bag and turned.

"I won't tell you broke a rule." She grinned and her stomach flip-flopped.

Emery snatched the package out of her hands and kept coming. He pressed her back up to the wall and kissed her with the same intensity as before. She reached for him, but he captured her wrists and pressed them to the glass. She didn't even try to break free—why would she? He was where she wanted him. Well, almost. Inside of her would be better, but they were getting there.

He kissed her cheek, down her throat and licked the pulse point at her neck.

"Keep your hands right there." His voice was lower, raspier than she'd ever heard him.

"Or what?"

"I'll put them there again."

She spread her fingers until they were each against the wall and watched her lover.

Emery stepped back a pace and tossed the condoms on the bed within easy reach. He tugged his shirt up and off, treating her to the view of his heavily muscled chest and arms. He was built like a god, and now she knew why. He put his body through strenuous activity just like he did his mind. He wasn't just the Walking Brain, he was so much more.

He grasped the bottom of her tank top and pulled it up. He bumped her elbows with his hands, but she kept them where they were.

"You said keep my hands where they were." She grinned harder at his deepening frown.

Emery didn't reply. He grabbed her wrist and yanked her arm up so high she stood on tiptoe. He wrestled her other arm up and held them in one hand while he jerked the tank top up and off.

"Turn around. Hands on the glass."

Someone had a bossy side.

Tori didn't ask questions and she didn't mind his orders. She faced the wall, all of South Beach laid out in front of her, and planted her hands on the glass. She could feel Emery's heat at her back. She thrust her hips backward and met his pelvis. The hard line of his erection pressed against her ass. So it wasn't just her who had a sexual interest.

He reached around her and grabbed the band of her sports bra and pulled it up under her arms, freeing her breasts. She sucked in a breath and fought the urge to cover herself. They were so far up no one could see her, but it didn't stop her knee-jerk reaction. He palmed her breasts, covering them from view. She could feel his breath on the left side of her neck. His chest pressed to her back, their bodies fitting together. Would he do her like this? It wasn't a bad thought, it was hot even, but—she wanted to see him.

His lips coasted down her neck to the ticklish spot at her shoulder. She could see his reflection in the glass, knew he was a hairbreadth from touching her there. She shuddered, all the humor leeching out of her. She wanted him so badly. He massaged her breasts, pushing them up, rubbing his palms across the stiffened nipples.

She groaned and let her head drop back against his shoulder.

"Emery." She said his name as a plea, surrendering herself to him. They were equals. Another time, she'd do what she wanted, but for now, she knew without words that he needed to be in control and call the shots.

He captured her nipples between his fingers, applying gentle pressure, but even that was too much. She moaned and turned her head toward him, but he was already kissing her shoulders and the line of her spine. He released her breasts and slid his hands down her stomach while his lips reached the skin above her jeans.

She closed her eyes, focusing on the way his hands and lips felt on her. There was no doubt he'd turned every bit of that powerful brain on her. She didn't stand a chance.

The loudest sound in the room besides her heartbeat was that of the snap coming undone on her cheap jeans and the zipper lowering. She held her breath. He slid his hands down her hips and into her panties. He pushed the fabric, taking both jeans and the cotton underwear down her legs. He kissed the dimples above her ass as he shoved her clothes to the floor. She didn't dare move, not even to step out of the clothing for fear she'd break the spell of the moment.

He ran his palms up and down the outside of her legs and cupped her ass. Her breasts might be on the small side, but she'd always had a nice ass. Or at least she thought so. She'd never had someone get close and personal with it like this.

Emery stood, keeping his hands on her at all times. He pressed his body against her, bracing her. She wished he'd say something, but he struck her as a silent lover. He splayed one hand over her stomach. The other cupped her mound.

She gasped, unprepared for the bold touch.

He didn't stop there. He slid his fingers through her folds. She cringed a little. She'd been wet before, so now she had to be dripping. Emery made a little, almost growling sound behind her and thrust a finger into her. Her jaw dropped at the intrusion. He pushed his knee between her legs, forcing her to widen her stance.

"Hm." The rumble of his voice vibrated through her body.

He pumped her slowly, slicking her arousal over her clit and rubbing the erect nub with his finger.

"Oh God, Emery." If she could dig her nails into glass, she would have.

She opened her eyes and found it hard to focus on anything except the vague reflection of his face over her shoulder. His hand slid up and grasped her breast. She wanted him to touch her everywhere, but more than anything she wanted him inside of her. More than just his fingers. Still, her body shuddered as he touched her just right.

No matter what she wanted, her body did what he commanded. Her muscles tightened low in her belly and almost screamed in protest, but what he was doing felt too good. He curled his fingers as he stroked her, hitting all her nerve endings and ratcheting up her desire.

Her body felt as though it burst apart. She squealed, but Emery held her, stroking her through the orgasm and into bliss. She let her face press against the glass, not entirely spent, but her world was definitely rocked.

Emery slid his hand out of her, but she still felt his

nearness. She heard the rustle of his clothes, the rasp of a zipper and the thud of his shoes hitting the floor.

Round two?

Yes, please.

She turned, taking in the sight of a completely nude Emery. She'd glimpsed him shirtless—what? Two days ago? Yesterday he'd barely removed any clothing. Today, there was nothing between them except air. He stood at the foot of the bed, condom in one hand, his erect cock in the other.

"I didn't tell you to turn around." He held her gaze, rolling the latex on.

"My hands are where they're supposed to be." She flattened her hands against the glass.

He crossed the distance between them in two strides and covered her hands with his. His erection pressed against her belly.

"I want to see you." She said it to his lips because she couldn't quite look at him when she admitted it. Sex could be great with anyone; what made this special was because it was Emery with her.

"I'm right here." He kissed her, forcing her up against the window with enough force their cells might merge.

He grasped her ass and before she could react, hoisted her up, pinning her to the glass with his body. She gasped and held on to his shoulders. He rocked his hips against hers, his gaze on her face. He hooked one arm then the other under her knees and her heart leapt to her throat.

He pressed his cock at her entrance, his gaze never wavering from her face. It was the same as yesterday. He penetrated not just her body, but her heart. She gasped and shifted her hips, seeking a better angle to accommodate him. Gravity worked in her favor. He sank all the way in. Her body stretched around him. There was a touch of soreness from yesterday, but the sheer pleasure of it was more than worth it.

Emery rested his forehead against hers, but he didn't kiss her, and he didn't close his eyes. Somehow, despite the lack of touch, she felt closer, more in tune with him.

He moved slowly at first. In and out. She held on to his shoulders, unable to look away. He grasped her ass with both hands and moved her, as if she weighed nothing at all. He thrust, harder, stroking deeper into her body. She gasped and dug her nails into his shoulders. Again, he thrust deep and hard, rocking her body. Liquid gathered at the corners of her eyes and her heart pulsed in her chest, stretching and growing. Their breath mingled, and never once did he glance away from her.

It felt as though her soul and heart twined together, coiling tight inside of her until she thought she'd burst. Her breathing hitched and she dug a hand into Emery's hair, yanking him closer. She kissed him the moment her body broke and the orgasm washed through her, leaving her breathless and boneless. But Emery wasn't through. He kissed her, thrusting his tongue into her even as he invaded the rest of her with his cock. She held on, denying him nothing until the moment he shoved deep and his breathing shuddered. She clutched him to her chest, hugging her legs around him. His body twitched within hers.

They stayed like that for several moments, utterly spent. She smoothed his hair down and kissed him, scared to speak for fear she'd break this tender connection tying them together.

Emery hoisted her higher, clutching her to him, and carried her to the bed. She mourned the loss of his cock, but he didn't leave her to clean up. Not yet. He cradled her to his chest, holding her just as tight as he had in the midst of orgasm. She blinked away the moisture clinging to her lashes. She was not crying. She didn't cry. But damn, he made her feel all the way to her toes.

Emery stared at the ceiling, his mind completely silent. He'd lived inside himself for so long that it was strange to not listen to himself. Tori shifted a bit, but her head nestled right back under his chin, arms around him. They hadn't spoken since the mind-blowing orgasm, which was probably why his head was so quiet. He didn't know what to think or feel about her. It was so new, he was half afraid that if he concentrated on it, she'd vanish. Not literally, but that everything that happened between them would fade.

Except they'd agreed to see where this thing went. But what did that look like? Was there a set of rules for this kind of situation? It wasn't like the magazines at the grocery checkout covered how to woo your woman and prepare for an urban siege attack.

"What are you thinking about? It's like I can hear the wheels turning up there." Tori stroked his back.

He was keenly aware of her leg over his knee. It didn't hurt in the least. For a moment, he struggled with the idea of answering her, but the truth was, he could deny her nothing.

"I was thinking about us."

"I like the sound of that." She smiled and shifted to look him in the face.

Emery stroked her loose hair, reveling in the feel of it against his palm.

"I want to do this right, but I don't know what that is," he said.

"That's okay. Neither do I. How much time until we meet up with CJ?"

"Couple hours."

Tori hid her yawn behind her hand.

"Let's get some sleep. I'll wake you." He kissed her brow again. She wasn't delicate, but she was the most precious thing in his life.

Emery hadn't given much thought to his life outside the FBI. Before, he'd dated with the assumption that he'd eventually marry someone, maybe have kids, but it hadn't been a priority. Now, things were different. The way they lived wasn't conducive to dating. Look at Madison: She went everywhere with a shadow or some kind of protection. It wasn't the right environment to date in. But that was before Tori.

What kind of a future did they have? Could they have one?

He'd never felt strongly about marrying and love, but that was changing. It was a slow shift he was aware of the longer Tori was in his arms.

A life with her in it. Could he dare to hope for such a thing?

Chapter Fourteen

Tori found comfort in silence. No one could be that quiet if they were sneaking up on her. Not even Emery. The temperature-controlled storage units seemed more like tombs where people brought their possessions to die than anything else. It was a great place for a meet, in theory. Public. With the facility's security cameras rolling so there could be no funny business. But not public enough they would be bothered. Especially at this odd hour of the afternoon. Most people would be headed home, not checking their storage. If the hit team wanted to come after them now, they were risking more than what her life was worth. The body count would be far too high. She appreciated CJ's forethought in arranging the location, but she didn't like how it would leave them blind during the meet.

"They're here." Emery's voice was low, for her ears alone.

After arriving early, they'd set up at one side of the building, where the shadows were thickest, to wait and watch for their team. Emery had tried to make her stay outside of the building until he gave her the all-clear sign, but she wanted to see CJ face-to-face. Hear him tell her himself just how much he'd fucked up.

So here they were, lurking in shadows on the second floor of the building, watching cars come and go.

Neither moved from their position.

The unit they'd do the meet in was closer to the back of the building. The plan was to allow CJ and Kathy to arrive there first so they took the position farther into the unit, allowing Emery and Tori the means to escape if necessary.

"Can I ask you a question?" The question had been on the tip of her tongue for hours, since she'd lain in bed stroking his back.

"Hm?" He turned his head just a bit, but never took his gaze off the parking lot below.

"How did you get the scars?" If he got those because of his parents or his brother's crap, she might have to hunt them down herself.

"Like I said, they took their payment from my hide." There was no emotion in his voice. No pain, no betrayal, nothing.

She understood complicated family relations. Her father kidnapped her and her sister, and her mother died so some asswipe could make a point. She'd never heard the words *I love you* until she was a preteen and Roni said it to her on their birthday. They hadn't understood, until they nearly lost each other thanks to CPS, but their father had snatched them up and moved in the blink of an eye. What Emery lived through, that was something else entirely. She wanted to hug him, to let him know that she cared. She wouldn't do that to her worst enemy, and she had a few.

The air conditioner kicked in and suddenly she could smell—pizza?

"Come on. They're here." Emery turned to face her. The thought lines bracketed his mouth and the way he looked at her—there was feeling there. She couldn't name it, and didn't think he could either, but there really was something between them. She didn't need her imaginary Emery voice to tell her that.

She pivoted, holding her breath. Emery's hand flattened against the small of her back, just above the gun tucked in her waistband. She'd never relied on a man for much after her father's death. They usually wanted something, or to hold their support over her head. But not Emery. He was just there. Next to her. Not in front of her or pushing her toward something; he was beside her. Walking into it with her.

They turned down another identical white-and-orange hall. The scent of pizza grease intensified. If she wasn't mistaken, she could also smell double pepperoni with extra cheese.

Her stomach growled.

Emery held his hand up in front of her and she hung back, allowing him to step into the unit first, hand at his hip on the obvious bulge of a gun. They didn't want to come off too aggressive to Kathy and CJ, but they had been facing more than their fair share of danger lately.

"Was wondering where you were." CJ's voice was the same low, gravelly tone she'd come to love. It pulled at her heart. She liked him, and it had broken part of her to think he'd betrayed her. "Tori with you?"

"Yeah," Emery replied.

Her cue.

She stepped into the doorway. The only furniture in the unit was a metal desk and a couple folding chairs. According to Emery, he'd used it a time or two to do undercover deals or broker information they needed. Now, Kathy sat at one end of the desk, a slice of pizza held delicately in her fingers.

Kathy smiled when she saw her, and CJ's whole body seemed to relax. He exhaled and stepped toward her. He didn't shake her hand. As they met, he pulled her in for a hug. Her breath caught in her throat and the hurt that had buried itself in her chest at the thought of his betrayal eased, healing itself. She didn't know if it was the truth, or if he was trying to reel them back in. But right now, it still made her feel better. She hadn't made an epic mistake staying in Florida.

"How you been?" CJ asked.

"Good." She stepped back, glancing from Kathy to Emery. They'd discussed what they would and would not say. Despite the show of good faith, they couldn't trust the couple enough to tell them everything. Like where they were staying.

Kathy slid between her husband and Tori, pulling her in for a quick squeeze. Kathy might be the mother hen, but she wasn't one for superfluous signs of affection. Her hug caught Tori by surprise more than CJ's. Tori blinked at Emery over Kathy's shoulder. She could count on both hands the number of times Kathy had initiated contact, and still have fingers left over.

"We were so worried when we found your car." Kathy stepped back, hands clasped in front of her.

"Hungry?" CJ gestured to the pizza.

"No, thanks," Tori said automatically. Hugging people she couldn't entirely trust was bad enough. Either Kathy or CJ could have grabbed her weapon if they wanted to. That was quite enough skirting danger for her tonight.

"Gabriel?" Emery leaned up against the wall, thumbs hooked in his jeans.

"He's good. Going stir-crazy, but I think the nurses like him." Kathy sat back in the chair and picked up her piece of pizza.

Tori wanted that slice so bad her mouth watered. "What did the Eleventh want?" she asked.

CJ blew out a breath.

Kathy answered first, gesturing to a file she slid out

from under the pizza box. "The driver was a new Eleventh recruit. We think it was his entrance test."

"Looks like the Eleventh is actively seeking out new drivers. No connection to the mob hit though. I hacked Greenworks and everything, but nothing." CJ shook his head.

Because the two were not connected. Only in Tori's fucked-up life would this craptastic series of events happen.

"I don't like it. Nothing adds up," CJ said.

"There's got to be a reason." There was a thread of frustration in Kathy's voice.

"A reason for a federal investigation to come to a screeching halt the minute its objective is cleared? Huh. Can't think of a single reason." Tori rolled her eyes, willfully diverting the conversation from the hit team. Yes, there was something seriously fucked up going on, but it was nice to know even their FBI partners were as in the dark as they were.

"Why would the Feds not take Evers into custody?" Emery asked.

Silence.

"Because that wasn't what they wanted," Tori answered.

"Then what do they want?" Emery stared at her.

Neither Kathy nor CJ scoffed at her statement. That alone made her wonder what they knew.

"That's what we've been trying to find out," Kathy said quietly.

"Whatever is really going on, it's not just the crew who is being kept in the dark. It's us as well." CJ gestured to Kathy and himself.

Kathy wiped her fingers on a napkin, lines of worry creasing her brow.

CJ's gaze went back and forth between Tori and Emery. "Our best guess is that there's someone else the Feds want worse than Evers. We never knew about the import-export business. We thought he had a supplier. What if there's more we don't know? What if they're in bed with the Russians?"

"It's highly unlikely the two are working together," Emery said. "Evers, though? We could never get a tap on Evers's phone. We all know he only does business verbally, no paper trail."

"Damn," CJ muttered.

Tori put her back against the wall. These were the kinds of chats Aiden and Julian were part of. Not her. She did what she was told and didn't worry about making the hard calls. Now, Aiden and Julian weren't here, and it was her life that was in the crosshairs.

"What do we do?" she asked.

"Try to figure out who it is they want." CJ shrugged.

It was easy, and impossible. How were they supposed to do that?

Emery wasn't surprised by CJ's statement. It was the same thing Emery had suspected. Figuring out the *who* was the hard part. They had a functioning database of all the people Evers was connected to, and a majority of them could be picked up on small crimes. Evers liked disposable people, which meant no one was ever around long enough to challenge him. It was all very controlled and intentional. Whoever the force behind him was, they went to great lengths to be invisible.

There was a subtle shift in the air, as if someone had opened a door. Emery might not have noticed it had he been engaged in conversation. He took a step toward the door and tilted his head, listening for some source of the pressure change.

"What is it?" Tori asked.

CJ and Kathy stopped talking, which only made the change more pronounced.

"Not sure. Stay here." He drew the gun at his waist and approached the door. The exterior facing rooms might have given him the ability to see what was coming in the reflection of the glass, but the interior rooms like the one they were in left him blind.

He paused at the door, but there was no sound, no other change that put him on edge.

It could be his imagination, the stress, or any number of reasons that triggered his paranoia, but he wasn't willing to chance Tori's life on anything.

There was always the possibility of being followed or found out during a meet. It was why meeting—even with allies—was dangerous in the field. You might be able to trust your friends, but what about the people following them? The Russians were good. They'd found Emery and Tori's safe house in record time, something that frustrated Emery to no end.

He glanced down either side of the hall, but nothing unexpected broke up the pristine white walls. They were alone. And yet, it didn't feel that way.

"Anything?" Tori asked.

"No. Going to look around. We leave in less than five."

They'd met. They'd talked. They'd found out what they needed to know. There was no use sitting around shooting the bull for the rest of the night when he could have Tori safely locked away in a South Beach luxury tower. They couldn't find all the answers tonight, but they were one step closer, and being able to trust their crew was a major move in the right direction.

Emery headed away from the main stairwell and the bank of elevators, toward the front of the building. He glanced behind him every couple of strides. Tori—or one of the others—had closed the door to their unit and he couldn't hear a sound coming from them.

It could just be his nerves, but they weren't in a position to brush off anything.

He kept his gaze on the growing reflection in the glass windows—but nothing showed itself. As he reached the front of the building, he glanced right and left. It might have been the way the light hit the windows, but he thought there might have been a flash of movement to his left.

He stared at the point for a moment, but the reflection was distorted.

They needed to leave.

There was no concrete reason, except he just knew. It was an ache in his knee that didn't actually hurt, only reminded him that he'd had a bad feeling before that he hadn't listened to.

Emery backed up, gun pointed at the ground, until he reached the door.

"We're going. Now," he said, keeping his voice low.

There was no argument from inside.

Tori stepped into the hall first. Emery knew without having to ask that he and CJ would keep the women between them. Sure, Kathy and Tori were more than capable of taking care of themselves, and he would rather have them at his back than half a dozen men. Still, no one was hurting Tori while Emery was still breathing. He held out his arm, pushing her back against the wall. Kathy followed them out, gun in hand.

A shot boomed, the sound ricocheting through the concrete-and-metal structure. Kathy cried out, stepping back, even as Emery shoved Tori into the unit. CJ went to the ground, shielding his wife with his body, and squeezed off a return shot, but the shooter must have taken cover around the corner.

"Get her inside," Emery snapped.

To CJ's credit, he didn't pause. They grabbed Kathy, one on either side, and lifted her. Blood dripped down from her stomach. She drew short, uneven breaths.

"Stay on the door," CJ ordered.

Tori took up position on one side of the door, gun in hand. Her face was pale, her lips tightly compressed and eyes wide. This was her nightmare. The thing she and Roni had skipped all over the states trying to avoid.

They pushed the pizza off onto the floor and laid Kathy on the metal surface of the desk. Her eyes were large and her teeth clenched so tight he could hear her molars grinding.

"Come out!" a man yelled, his voice accented slightly.

Emery left CJ to tend to his wife and went to stand opposite Tori. She stared at him, as if she could not bring herself to look at the desk. A trail of blood split the room in half. Kathy's breathing and helpless groans were the loudest sounds.

"Hell no," Emery yelled back.

The accent. It was all wrong for Miami. Which meant the Russians had found them. They had a four-man team if they'd brought the whole contingent. If Emery were in their position, he'd place two at either end of the hall, cutting off any escape. Emery's crew would take shots from the front and rear trying to escape. Holing up in the unit was fine and all, but they were sitting ducks if the Russians decided to close in and finish the job, though this wasn't their style. They were quiet, efficient, and wiped their prey off the face of the planet. The whole situation was shit.

"We want the girl. She is our prize," a different voice called out.

"Too bad you aren't getting her." Emery wasn't giving up Tori unless he was dead, and that wasn't happening. Not now that he knew he had a chance with her. It couldn't end so soon.

"Your friend won't last long with a gut wound. Nasty business." It had to be Matvei talking to them. He had an easy manner of speaking, heavy on the accent. He sounded bored.

"The clerk?" Tori whispered.

Emery shook his head. If the hit team was making such a bold move against them, they wouldn't leave witnesses to call the cops. They were on their own.

"Call Smith." She mouthed more than whispered.

The detective was good, but this was over his pay grade. Emery shook his head. They were better in this alone than with more casualties and an hours-long siege. If they didn't get Kathy to a hospital soon, she'd die. No amount of field training could save her. She needed help.

The whisper of footsteps drew nearer.

If he reached out to shoot, they'd pull the trigger before he could.

They were fucked. No two ways about it. The door wouldn't save them, and the walls weren't reinforced. Maybe if they were in a cinder-block outdoor unit it might offer them some protection, but they were sitting ducks in here with just a few sheets of drywall to protect them.

Kathy groaned again. CJ muttered to her while he pressed his hands to the seeping wound at her stomach. Her sounds of pain sliced Emery to the bone. He loved these people better than family, and now he had to choose.

"What do we do?" Tori asked.

There was a chance these people only wanted Tori. The one thing he cared about. The one person he couldn't give up. For Kathy to survive, they needed to stand down, but he couldn't.

Movement in the hall grabbed his attention. Emery lifted his gun, but a hand knocked it away. A male figure filled the door, dark hair and eyes, the heavy Russian brow. In that split second, he sneered. Tori stumbled back, lifting her gun. CJ yelled. Emery dropped his shoulder and rammed the figure into the door frame. The smaller man grunted as Emery lifted him off his feet. Something cracked against his back. Pain licked up and down his spine. A fist connected with his temple and the world flashed black for a moment and his limbs felt heavy.

"Don't! Don't hurt him. You want me, not him." Tori backed up, her hands in the air.

Another hard object smashed into his head and he dropped to the ground. Before he could push up, the muzzle of a gun pressed to the back of his head.

"Do. Not. Move." The accent was thick. Matvei.

For a few seconds, no one moved. The only sound was Kathy's whimpers and labored breathing. Emery tilted his head to the side, just enough so he could see Tori. She'd been forced to drop her gun. She stood, her face into the wall, one arm twisted up behind her by the youngest member of the hit team. The one that was active on social media. Emery was tempted to tell him thank you for the tip-offs, but now wasn't the time. The bastard had a gun to Tori's head

He was going to die. Emery had never pulled the trigger hoping to kill someone, but this time, he wanted the son of a bitch to die for threatening Tori.

Matvei was average. His height, build, coloring, all of it. He was a man who faded into the background, unnoticed until it was too late. It was one of the reasons why he was so deadly. And now that deadly gaze was focused on Emery.

"Our job was only her, but you are a problem." Matvei gestured with the gun in his hand at Emery and CJ. "Tie them up. Call that Canales and tell him we have something he wants."

"If you're going to kill us, why not do it now?" CJ snarled as his hands were wrenched away from Kathy.

The hit men offered no answer. Why would they? They had all the power—right now. But not for long. The anger moved lower, deeper in Emery's chest, turning into a white-hot burn. This wasn't over. Tori wasn't dead. He couldn't let that happen.

Tori paced the length of their cell, which any other time might be called a pitch-black storage container on a cargo ship. This whole thing was out of a bad action flick.

The hit team hadn't killed them. Instead, they'd taken the four of them in a van out to the big marina in Miami, onto a ship, and locked them up. The hit team had gagged and bound them, but hadn't worried about blindfolds. Probably because they anticipated killing Tori and the others before too long, but they wanted something from her first. Something she wouldn't give them.

Kathy groaned, louder. In the darkness it was easy to forget the others were there, but not for long. The Russians were giving Emery, CJ, and Kathy to the Eleventh as a favor so they'd look the other way about trespassing on their turf. The others didn't know. They didn't speak Russian. But Tori did.

"What were they saying earlier?" Emery's whisper was barely audible.

She hugged her arms around her and blinked into the darkness.

"How bad is it?" he asked.

"Bad." Her voice cracked. "They're giving you three to the Eleventh and Evers. They talk about Evers and Canales interchangeably. They're all in on it, somehow."

"And you?"

"What do you think?"

Tori glanced over her shoulder in the direction of the labored breathing and murmurs.

The last time she'd gotten a glimpse of Kathy, the woman was almost entirely covered in her own blood. A gut wound wasn't an instant death shot like in TV or the movies. It was a slow, painful end if the blood loss didn't kill her first. Without immediate medical care infection would set in. Busted intestines would turn septic. Without a doctor, Kathy would die. It might already be too late.

Tori turned toward the couple and her heart hurt. She could hear the scuff of CJ on the ground next to Kathy and the soft, whispered words for her ears alone. CJ hadn't cried or begged the hit team for help. He'd held her hand, muttering to his wife, keeping his focus on her.

If Tori thought that giving Matvei what he wanted would stop this nightmare, she'd consider it. The truth was, if she did, she would be putting their deaths in the fast lane. The longer she held out, the more chance they had to survive.

They all knew the outcome of this situation was grim. Unless the FBI stormed the building with every agent on the East Coast, there was a very good chance they weren't all coming out of this situation alive. Matvei's team was brought in to efficiently take people out of the way as if they'd simply stopped being and vanished.

Tears sprang to Tori's eyes. God, this was so unfair. All CJ and Kathy had been trying to do was help her, and now Kathy was dying. Tori reached out blindly, feeling for Emery. Her palm met the hard wall of his chest. His hand covered hers and she edged closer. She wanted to hug him, to bury her face in his chest, but it wasn't the time for that. Besides, if the Russians thought he was anything but someone she worked with, they might hurt him for the fun of making her beg.

"Can we do anything?" she whispered.

"No." His answer was quiet.

"Emery, I need to ask you to do something." Tori turned her back on CJ and Kathy, hoping against hope that nothing she said would be overheard. Chances were, she was about to die, and if the last thing she did was get a message to her sister, that would have to be good enough.

"What is it?" Emery asked after a moment.

She wanted to crawl inside his head, figure out what he was thinking. She only knew Matvei's reputation. Emery had no doubt studied the man if he thought he was a threat. She wanted to know what he knew. But she couldn't.

"Evers, the Eleventh, they won't kill you immediately. They'll want information, right? You can get away. Get away. And . . . Tell Roni to pass the ketchup. I know it sounds weird, but I need you to do this, please?" She leaned her head toward Emery in an effort to make as little noise as possible.

"Why?" Emery's voice was more of a rumble she felt than heard.

"I can't tell you. Please, please trust me."

"I don't know what you're doing, but we need to focus on how to get out of here."

"Emery, please?" Tori didn't want to die, but if that was going to happen, she didn't want anyone else to die with her. This was the only way.

"Then tell me what it means."

"I can't."

Kathy's whimper turned into a pained whine. CJ's voice rose, continuing to try to calm her, but damn. They were running out of time in a bad way.

"We've got to do something." Tori couldn't stand here and watch Kathy die.

"They're waiting on something or someone," Emery said.

"We force their hand."

"How?"

"I don't know. Help me think of something."

"Step back," someone yelled through the door.

Tori held her hands out to her sides as the door opened, casting a long rectangle of light into their prison. The hammer of a gun clicked.

"Bitch. Step out here or I'll put a bullet between pretty boy's eyes." The man's voice was cold, lifeless, and she had no doubt he'd do it.

"No," Emery growled.

"What do you want?" She sidestepped Emery, hands up.

"Out here. Now." The man holding the gun spoke. There was another behind the swinging door and two others, including Matvei, a dozen paces away.

She could refuse. It wasn't like she didn't already know what they wanted—and that she would not be playing ball with them. But she needed confirmation. To know the truth.

"Okay. I'm cooperating." She took a step out of the cargo container and onto the deck of the ship.

"Stand back," the man holding the gun said to Emery.

Tori winced as the door swung shut behind her. She dropped her hands, keenly aware of the gun and the fact that she knew what they wanted. They couldn't get it if she died. At least not easily. If she were killed, Roni would run. She'd go to ground, hide, change her identity; she'd survive, and these bastards wouldn't get what they wanted. As long as Emery passed her message on. If he didn't, well, she had no idea what would erupt, but she'd still be dead.

"Viktoriya Iradokovia." Matvei strolled toward her, thumbs in his belt.

Tori resisted the urge to shiver. She hadn't been called Viktoriya in ages. So long that it felt foreign to think of herself with that name.

She concentrated on keeping her breathing even, body loose. Matvei couldn't know he scared the piss out of her.

He came to a stop directly in front of her, hands at his sides. The dim lighting cast his face in shadow, but she could fill in the holes from the pictures Emery had shown her. Lifeless eyes. Short hair. A nose that had been broken a few too many times.

"Where is your father, Viktoriya?"

"Dead," she replied with a shrug.

"We know that is a lie. Where is he?"

"I can tell you where we buried him if you want to go visit."

Matvei laughed, a rusty sound that spoke of little use.

"I've been there. I know that isn't him in the ground." Matvei's mocking grin was terrifying. He looked more like an animal baring teeth than a human smiling. What was worse was that he was right. Whoever was in the grave wasn't her father. "I'll cut you a deal. We only care about your *otets*. Tell us where he is and you can go free."

"Right, and you didn't just sell us out to a car gang or anything?"

"We can handle them."

"My dad is dead."

"We both know you're lying. He's alive and working for Cuba. Where is he?"

Shit. She had no way to confirm if Matvei was right or not. Even if she could, all she would do is cement her death and those of the people she loved.

"I'm not going to tell you anything," Tori said, drawing

on every drop of bravado in her body. Roni was better at bluffing than she was.

"Then it looks like we have a transaction to make." Matvei nodded to his companions. "We will chat later."

She glared daggers at the man. He still wore a holster over his shoulders. If she could get the gun, she'd put a bullet through his skull and not even feel remorse. He'd shot Kathy, and he'd kill them all given the opportunity.

Chapter Fifteen

"What did he want?" Emery stared at the bit of space Tori had occupied. She was there, but he couldn't see her, though he could recall every feature of her face, the tiny mole by her temple, the freckles that were too often covered with dirt. He hadn't been able to hear everything Matvei had said to Tori. Hell, most of it didn't make sense. He was hoping Tori could shed some light on what they were facing.

He felt Tori's breath on his neck. She'd stepped in close without him realizing it.

"They're probably going to keep me. Torture me." She pitched her voice quieter, for his ears alone. "They're still selling you guys to Evers's people, I think. You could probably get away once you're out of here. Somewhere between the cargo container and the parking lot. I don't know if you could do it with Kathy though."

"We're going to get out of this." He didn't know how, not really. Not yet. But he would make sure they did.

"Emery, I need you to please give that message to my sister. Please." Her voice was barely audible.

"Not unless you tell me why."

She sighed. Her hands pressed against his chest and her head came to rest on his shoulder.

"My father is alive."

For a second he had to ask himself if he'd heard her barely there admission, or if he'd made it up.

"What?" He canted his head toward hers.

"He's alive and if Roni doesn't tell him to stay away, he'll die, too. I don't want them to get me and him. Please?"

"Yeah." What else was he supposed to say?

Nothing he'd read or heard indicated anyone suspected Alexander Iradokovia to still be among the living. It was a shocking admission.

Voices from outside the container broke the moment. Tori squeezed him tight as several loud people approached their position.

Tori squeezed him tight. Like she was saying good-bye.

Hell no.

They would get through this.

Metal scraped against metal as the door once more swung open. He blinked and shoved Tori behind him. Several people aimed high-powered flashlights in his eyes.

"Hands against the wall," a new voice ordered. It was an older, seasoned speaker.

"Emery . . ."

He turned toward the wall and flattened his hands against the cool metal.

"I'm coming back for you," he promised Tori. White dots swam in his vision from the LED flashlights.

"Who the hell is he?"

Emery knew that voice. Canales. The street thug stepped into the container and peered at Emery's face.

Emery kept his gaze forward. Raibel Canales wouldn't know him on sight, and that was exactly the way Emery liked things.

"This is the guy that was at the plant a few days ago. The one we followed." That voice. Emery remembered it. It was the punk kid who'd made him at Greenworks.

"He matters. Bring him and the other two," the faceless man in charge said.

Canales kept his gun pointed at Emery while the kid patted him down fast.

"You sure I can't convince you to part with the girl?"

"*Nyet*." Matvei chuckled.

"Can't blame me for trying. Come on. Get them."

Hands grasped Emery's bicep, pulling him out of the container. He swung his head, searching for Tori, and found her with her back against the opposite wall, one of the Russians standing guard with a gun to her temple. Beyond her, CJ had Kathy in his arms. She groaned when she should be screaming. That wasn't a good sign.

"Move." Canales shoved Emery out of the container.

His feet landed on the cargo ship's deck and he glanced around, taking in the new additions. Besides Matvei and his two other companions not holding a gun on Tori, there were maybe five Eleventh drivers Emery knew on sight, four thugs he'd make sure to acquaint himself with later, and an older man in slacks and a polo shirt who appeared as though they'd ruined his golf game.

Emery didn't recognize him at all, which worried him.

"Pleasure doing business with you." The Geezer shook Matvei's hand before gesturing at the security detail. "Bring them."

Canales walked at Emery's back, shoving him every couple of strides. They were still on the cargo ship, but it was easily two football fields long, stacked two and three high with containers in neat rows, which meant the ship must be in the middle of unloading or loading since they would eventually go four and five high.

Emery couldn't get off this ship without Tori. If he let

Canales march him onto the dock, he'd never see her again. From the marina, the hit team could take her anywhere, alive or dead.

He let his pace lag. CJ was easily a dozen yards or so behind them, and that was before they made a right and a left. Darkness had closed in and even the starlight above couldn't provide much illumination.

The old man's detail marched onward without a backward glance.

Now or never.

It was Emery—a trained FBI operative—against three assholes who couldn't keep their pants above their knees. Canales was the only one that worried Emery. Not horrible odds, but he was unarmed. All it would take was a ricochet, not even a lucky shot.

Tori was worth it.

He slowed a bit more until he felt the press of Canales's gun against his lower back. The others didn't even have weapons drawn, probably expecting their presence to be enough to keep him cowed. They had no idea he was an actual threat.

Emery stepped with his right and pivoted to his left, whipping his hand back to grab Canales's wrist and shoved the gun aside. The gun went off, the bang reverberating off the metal with a deafening boom. The other two flinched and ducked their heads while Emery delivered a hard right punch to Canales's jaw. The gang leader staggered back, releasing the weapon into Emery's hand.

"Yo, get him," the youngest thug yelled.

The third, closest gang member brought his gun up.

Emery didn't flinch or think, he shot the guy in the shoulder. He couldn't spare another bullet if he was going to take Tori back.

He turned and sprinted back the way they'd come, diving

left at the first opportunity. The cargo containers were stacked and organized in rows. It wouldn't be hard to figure out where he was going, so he had to use the shadows and momentary confusion to his benefit.

"Daniel, he's coming for you," Canales bellowed, closer than before.

"He shot me," the downed driver said over and over again.

Too many of these kids got involved with the Eleventh out of some misguided sense of community, never giving consideration to the danger. The kid was lucky. Emery could have killed him, but chose not to. Besides, they'd be more distracted dealing with an injured friend than a dead one.

So much for the element of surprise.

The containers formed horizontal rows, with enough space for a forklift on either side. He crept from the shadows of one to the next, watching for CJ's group.

"Where is he?" a voice Emery didn't recognize yelled from what sounded like the next row.

Emery slowed his pace, pressing his back against the end of the container, and peered around.

"He's close," Canales replied.

CJ crouched on the ground, shrouded in darkness, with Kathy laid across his thighs. He had an Eleventh driver on either side, both looking in the direction Canales had taken him. They weren't looking behind them.

Emery blew out a breath. The odds were stacked against them. It didn't take a complex program to calculate that. They were outmanned with no supplies or backup. He emptied his lungs, inhaled deeply and took a half step away from the container, lifting his gun.

He aimed, blew out a breath, and squeezed the trigger.

The first guy arched his back, blood gurgling as he fell forward.

Emery adjusted and fired while the second stared at his downed friend. CJ reached for the man's gun as he hit his knees, falling across the dead man. Coldness settled over Emery. Death was not normally his department, but for his crew and their lives, he'd go there.

"Stop right there." CJ aimed the gun at someone Emery couldn't see.

He jogged toward CJ, close to the opposite shipping container, until he could see who they were facing.

It was Raibel Canales.

Emery aimed at the leader of the Eleventh Street gang.

"Where's your friends?" he asked.

"I've got you covered," CJ said.

Emery stepped out into the open and jerked a second gun out of Canales's hand.

"Got a new boss now? Give me your keys." Emery held out his hand. They'd need a ride out of here. He wanted Canales dead, but he couldn't shoot him without cause.

"I ain't answerin' to nobody, punk." Canales sneered.

"Yeah. I see that. Keys. Now."

Canales unsnapped the hook that held the keys on his belt and tossed them over, glaring daggers at Emery. He'd have to watch his back from now on. The Eleventh would have him in their crosshairs for this.

"On your knees. Now." Emery glanced over Canales's shoulder, but it appeared the Geezer and his security detail had cut and run.

"If you're going to do me, do me." Canales spread his arms.

"Get. On. Your. Knees."

Canales tipped his chin up, managing to keep his sneer in place. He lowered to one knee, then the other.

Emery could kill Canales and solve several of their problems all at once. But that wasn't his way. He believed in justice, and right now killing Canales would be an assassination.

He grabbed the man's shoulder and brought the butt of the gun down on the back of his head. Canales slumped forward and Emery didn't ease his fall.

"CJ—"

"Go. I've got a gun and this guy's keys. Find Tori." CJ gathered Kathy to his chest.

She wasn't making a sound. Dread settled in the pit of Emery's stomach. Were they too late? Maybe for Kathy, but hopefully not for Tori.

He tucked the second gun in his waistband while keeping the first at the ready, and jogged back the way they'd come, keeping his eyes peeled for Matvei and his boys. There was no way they hadn't heard the gunfire, so either they were setting up to take Emery and the others out, or they were making their exit.

The container that had been their prison waited for Emery, open and empty.

"Fuck," he muttered, turning in place, scanning the possible avenues of escape.

They could be anywhere.

A distant, metallic bang—in the opposite direction from where he'd come—grabbed his attention. Emery's whole body went on alert. He jogged ahead, winding his way through the containers, listening for more clues to where they'd taken Tori.

"*Poluchit' yeye!*"

He sprinted toward the voices. Footsteps thundered toward him.

Emery stopped, listening to the disorienting thumps, trying to figure out which direction they were coming from.

"*Idi syuda!*"

Emery dodged to his left, striking off down a path that led to a right angle turn. The only light was from the moon and stars. Shadows seemed to move in the corners of his eyes, but he only focused on the deck ahead of him.

A female voice cried out.

Tori.

The sound was close.

Emery slowed, edging around a corner.

Tori was on her knees, Matvei's hand tangled in her hair, pulling her head back.

Hell no.

Emery squeezed the trigger, once, twice, pouring his rage into those bullets.

Matvei's arms windmilled backward, his jaw dropped, and his body went slack. He glanced down at the crimson splotches of color blossoming on his shirt and dropped to his knees. "Center mass" shots. The bullets probably clipped his lungs or heart. He'd die, suffocating in his own blood within moments. It wasn't long enough. The bastard deserved to feel every bit of pain he'd caused others.

Tori scrambled to her feet and backed up. Emery rushed to her side and grabbed her arm.

"Oh my God," Tori said.

The chill that had wrapped around Emery's body intensified. Killing was a necessary evil. It didn't mean he liked it, but if it was Tori or Matvei, Tori would win out every single time.

Matvei picked his head up, staring around him in the sightless way of a man facing death.

Tori strode to Matvei and knelt next to him. Death rattled his lungs. She lifted his shoulder and drew his second gun from the shoulder holster, wiping it off on the dead man's shirt.

Someone close by yelled, "Matvei?"

"Come on. Now." Emery gestured back the way he'd come.

"CJ?" She started jogging, keeping just a hair behind him, allowing Emery to lead the way.

"They should be off the boat now." At least he hoped so.

He took a right and a left, pushing them faster. His stride faltered. Someone yelled in the distance.

"Do you know where we're going?" Tori swung her head left and right as they came to another intersection.

"Off this boat."

"Great. Glad we have a plan. What happened?"

"The old guy's security detail hustled him out of here, left Canales and two boys with me. I gave them the slip, got CJ and Kathy free and came after you." Those were the only details that mattered.

"I didn't know you could shoot."

"They did teach me how at Quantico."

Any second, what was left of the hit team would sort themselves out and come after them. They needed to be gone before then.

"What's our plan?" Tori asked.

They had to be nearing the side of the ship. From there, they could find a way off, and hopefully CJ.

"Find a ride, maybe two, and get out of here," Emery said, collecting his thoughts.

"What then? Kathy needs a doctor."

God, she was amazing. This was the most stressful situation of her life, and she hadn't broken under the pressure.

They turned and surveyed the marina.

"There." Emery pointed to their left.

A set of stairs led from the deck down to the dock on their left. They had an open shot, but it would also leave them vulnerable. Except a car idled below. A man got out, a man who looked an awful lot like CJ.

"Oh, thank God." Tori took off for the stairs, Emery close behind her.

"One of us needs to go for Gabriel. He's too vulnerable at a hospital by himself. Shit is about to hit the fan. You drop Kathy at a hospital, make sure CJ keeps pressure on that wound. I'll get Gabriel, then we meet at the Shop." He wanted to believe that the Shop was safe and secure, but with the hit team and Eleventh after them, he had to operate as if they could expect an attack at any moment. Besides, it was still their safest and best-stocked location to meet up.

"Sounds good," Tori said.

They took the stairs two and three at a time. The skin on the back of Emery's neck prickled.

A blast broke the stillness, pinging off metal above them.

"Hurry up, you two," CJ yelled. His voice sounded strained. The man had to be close to his breaking point.

Their feet hit the dock running. Emery hated to see Tori sprinting away from him, but they had a job to do and Kathy's life depended on it.

He unlocked Canales's cherry-red monstrosity and dropped into the driver's seat. The cab light briefly illuminated what he had to work with. No backseat and the passenger seat was gone, to make way for a rig of NOS tanks, plus row upon row of switches. He had no idea what each of them did.

The red car revved to life.

Tori's silver car reversed. He hoped they got out of there fast.

Three men leapt and sprinted down the stairs, followed by a fourth. Canales.

Emery stomped on the accelerator as he shifted into reverse. The car shot backward and he twisted, following Tori's taillights. The report of gunfire blasted over the distant sound of sirens. He cranked the hand brake and shifted into drive the moment his wheels touched the street. There were still three cars in the lot, plus the injured guy and the kid he hadn't seen. Soon, they'd all be on their tail.

A third car swerved into Emery's rearview mirror. The kid? Maybe.

Behind them, Canales took to the wheel of another car while Emery peeled down the street. Tori's lights were gone. They couldn't go to the same hospital. It would just paint a target on Kathy.

What hospital was Gabriel at? Emery had a good idea, but he couldn't be sure. Smith hadn't told him that detail, had he?

A phone blared from a slot in the dash.

Emery reached for it, glancing at the screen.

Canales.

He ignored the call and dialed. Headlights lit up his rearview mirror.

The phone rang once, twice.

"Miami-Dade Police Department. How may I—"

"Detective Matt Smith. This is FBI Special Agent Emery Martin. I need Matt. Now." He didn't often utter FBI and his name in the same sentence. It was a jarring reality compared to the way his life had played out.

"Yes—uh—one moment."

Pop. Pop. Pop.

Emery winced, ducking his head and swerving. Bullets hit the street and the back of the car. He dropped the phone into his lap and shifted.

Shit.

He took a right and gunned the engine, speeding toward the highway.

"Emery?"

Emery jabbed the speaker icon.

"Matt, it's Emery. Where is Gabriel?"

"Kindred Hospital on Eighth. Is someone shooting at you?"

"Yes, damn it."

"Where are you?"

"Almost to ninety-five." But he couldn't get on the highway with shooters on his tail. Then again, Kindred Hospital was in a busy area near Classic Rides, and if he couldn't shake the Eleventh, they'd do some damage.

"Get me dispatch and nine-one-one." Matt's voice was muffled.

Emery was going to get canned so fast, but at this point, what were his options? He couldn't trust the FBI to not use him as bait for whatever grand scheme was going on. They were spread too thin. The cops were the only backup they had, and they just weren't ready to take on a hit team out for blood and a well-organized criminal organization barreling down on them at full force. And tomorrow Evers would be back at the helm.

He turned the wheel, tires screeching. He narrowly made it through an intersection at the entrance to the marina. The highway was just a few short blocks away. He punched the switch he hoped was NOS. What he needed was distance, space to get away from the other cars. Or Tori next to him. He hated this, but she could put those cars out of commission with a couple bullets. He'd have to rethink her methods in the future if he was ever in a situation where driving and shooting were involved.

The car shot forward as the NOS hit the system. His body was pressed back into the seat and the speedometer topped out, rattling against the pin, leaving him with no clue how fast he was going. He zipped past slower-moving cars. His pulse pounded in his throat. His focus narrowed to the obstacles in his path and stretches of uninterrupted road.

He glanced in his rearview mirror. Damn. He didn't

have anywhere near as much of a head start on the others as he wanted. The Eleventh cars were maybe fifty yards back and closing. The NOS was wearing off. Did he hit it again? It wasn't like he was concerned about maintaining his ride.

"What are you driving?" Matt's voice was a yell, probably trying to be heard over the roaring engine.

"Raibel Canales's car." He rattled off the license plate.

"What the—?"

Emery blew out a breath he'd been holding, only to suck in deep again.

The silver Scion Tori had taken was ahead of him now.

Emery laid on the horn. If Tori didn't pull out some fancy driving, they'd be overtaken by the Eleventh.

The silver car merged into the HOV lane and shot forward. Had she been waiting for some sign of him? He couldn't be sure, but damn her for not getting her ass out of Dodge.

"Tori is with an injured agent who needs a doctor stat." While every fiber in his body resisted revealing information, he knew they needed help. And who could they trust if not Matt Smith? The man was turning out to be an asset they hadn't expected.

"Fuck," Matt growled. "I've got units coming to you. They'll do what they can."

"That's all I'm asking for."

A black car with a custom swirl pattern on the side was the closest to them. Emery jerked his ride between two cars, cutting it close. He prayed the civilians on the road would be okay. A figure leaned out of the black car, a gun in their hand.

"Shit."

Emery punched the NOS and swerved. The shooter didn't take the shot, which was a good sign, except for the gun. He ate up the ground between him and Tori, and she never once accelerated.

"Come on, Tori, go."

"What's going on?" Matt called.

"I've got a shooter and Tori's not driving fast enough."

What was going wrong in the car ahead of him for her to be that distracted?

Chapter Sixteen

"CJ. CJ. Hold on to her." Tori gripped the wheel in both hands, trying not to look at Kathy.

God, the sounds she was making, they weren't good, and she was bleeding heavily again. The blood already coated CJ, the seat, and the passenger window. How could one person bleed so much?

Canales's red car shot past her with Emery at the wheel.

"Oh fuck," she muttered, glancing in the rearview mirror.

"Kathy, listen to me." CJ's voice broke.

She whispered something that might have been, "It hurts."

"I know." He stroked her face. "I love you. Hang on."

"No, seriously, hang on." Tori hadn't wanted to flip any of the switches on the silver Scion. Who the hell knew what they did? She'd need to examine the system to determine how the upgrades were installed, but she didn't have that luxury. It was time to flip them all and see what happened.

"Hang on, Kathy, do you hear me?"

Tori opened the plastic case over the switches. What

had she seen this car do? There were hydraulics, NOS, and what else?

She'd expect NOS to be easy to activate.

There were two switches a little bit apart from the others. She toggled the first and heard a hiss from the canister behind her. That was somewhat good. She flipped the second. It clicked into place. For a moment, nothing happened. Then the NOS hit the fuel system. The car shuddered. Exactly how much had she sent to the fuel line?

The car leapt forward. She jerked them out of the HOV lane and swerved around slower-moving traffic. They drew even with Emery's car. She glanced over, but couldn't make out his profile in the tinted windows.

"Hold on, Kathy," CJ continued to chant.

They couldn't lose Kathy.

She shut out the sound of CJ's voice. Emery was going to Kindred, but there was no reason for them to go that far. They just needed a hospital with a doctor and enough bagged blood to pump back into Kathy.

Pop. Pop.

Tori hunched down in her seat, her focus on the road ahead.

"You hold on, Kathy," CJ yelled. "You hear me? Hold on." He was crying. She'd never seen CJ anything but calm or pissed off.

"We're almost there," she lied, but what else could she do?

A white H on a blue background was mounted to a light post.

Hospital.

Kathy's breath rattled in her lungs.

Oh God, Tori knew that sound.

"Almost there, Kathy." Hot tears bathed her cheeks.

She hit the off-ramp, easing off the accelerator, but it didn't make a lot of difference. The car was still too fast.

She pulled the hand brake and turned the wheel. They coasted through the intersection, going sideways. Two cars jerked away to avoid hitting her. She punched the gas, following close on the bumper of an ambulance with its lights on.

They pulled into the ER breezeway.

"No, no, no!" CJ's voice grew steadily louder.

She couldn't look. Kathy had to be alive. They'd just gotten to the hospital.

Tori jumped out of the car, her hands up. Two officers near the door were already reaching for their weapons.

"FBI, we need help, agent down."

That got their attention. The officers were there first, opening the doors while paramedics rushed out, wheeling a gurney after them. Tori backed up three steps.

CJ screamed.

"No." She bent her knees and held her head between her hands.

They'd gotten out. They were free. She should have been able to hold on a little longer. That's how these things went, right? The good guys got to be patched up. They lived. And yet, she knew CJ's sobs would haunt her nightmares.

A man like CJ only cried for two things. The birth of a baby, and the death of his heart.

Kathy was his heart.

She might have been an agent, but she'd treated them all like family, pulling them in and making this operation work on more than rules and regulations. She'd gotten them to function as a unit because you didn't say no to Kathy.

Tori straightened, pressing the back of her hand to her mouth. One of the officers glanced up at her, his expression grim.

"She's okay?" Tori asked, dreading the answer.

He didn't respond or even shake his head.

Tori covered her face with both hands. What was the point of this if the ones closest to her died?

Tires squealed on the road and a siren wailed.

She turned.

A car with neon running lights took the corner at a high speed.

The Eleventh.

"Get down," she yelled, the same moment the man in the passenger seat squeezed off several rounds.

Everyone at the ER entrance hit the ground, taking cover. Tori dove for the car, throwing herself behind the rear bumper. The shots hit the palm trees and the sign mounted on the corner, maybe fifteen feet from where they were. Two patrol cars were already in pursuit, either from the Eleventh's shoddy driving or maybe Emery had gotten a call out for help.

"Ma'am." One of the officers grabbed her arm.

She instinctively yanked out of his grip, stood and backed away.

"Detective Smith says you have to go." The officer appeared puzzled by the order, but he wasn't stopping Tori.

She nodded and glanced at the gurney. The paramedics had pulled it parallel to the ambulance. CJ leaned over, clutching Kathy.

They hadn't even tried CPR or paddles or anything, not that Tori knew a lot about medical care beyond stitching up gashes and what it took to keep going.

"She's gone, isn't she?" Tori needed an answer.

"Yeah," the officer said quietly.

"He's probably not going with me." She glanced at CJ. He deserved to be with Kathy for as long as he wanted. Tori was on her own. What did she do? They'd gone years without uttering the FBI connection and now they were throwing it around. "Can you have someone call the local FBI field office?"

"Detective Smith says he's taking care of it."

Tori nodded. Emery must have gotten through, then.

She was numb inside. Even though tears hit her cheeks, she didn't feel them, or anything. This wasn't why she'd agreed to join the FBI, so she could watch the people she'd grown to care about die. For once in her miserable life, she'd wanted to do something good. Something that made a difference.

The Eleventh and the hit team would pay for this. Tori didn't care who'd pulled the trigger. They were all guilty. And they were all dead.

Emery snagged the jacket and tablet from a table in the cafeteria of Kindred Hospital. For a Saturday night, close to midnight, it was doing steady business. He felt only a slight pang of guilt at taking the items. Head up, he strode out of the cafeteria, tugging the borrowed baseball cap lower on his face. He'd ducked into the cafeteria to miss Raibel Canales coming into the hospital with one of the hit team hot on his heels. The last thing Emery wanted was those two groups working together.

He had to get to Gabriel first, and fast.

"Hold the elevator," he called to a nurse stepping into the first elevator.

She reached for the button pad and he jogged into the car. The skin between his shoulder blades itched, as if he were being watched. He turned, and the Eleventh kid from the cargo ship stood at the end of a hallway, phone to his ear. He'd changed his shirt, but the dark splotches on his jeans were probably blood.

His stomach sank. The race was on.

"Thanks." He shrugged into the jacket, complete with a hospital tech name badge.

"Floor?" she asked.

"Uh . . ." He glanced at the tablet screen and clicked the button. It was locked, but she didn't have to know that. What had Smith said? "Seven, please."

"Are they still having problems down there?" Her nose scrunched up. Another time and place, he might have taken note of her sweet face, but not anymore. He'd had a taste of Tori, and there was no going back.

"Yeah. Always something." He sighed and shook his head.

She studied him, far too interested for his taste.

"I don't think we've met." The nurse spoke with a smile in her voice. Yeah, she was too sweet for him.

"I'm new. That's how I got the night shift. My girlfriend's not a fan, but what are you going to do?" He shrugged and urged the car to rise faster.

The nurse shook her head. "That's the way of things."

The elevator slowed.

"That's my floor." He nodded at the nurse before stepping out.

He glanced left, then right.

Emery followed the arrows to the left, counting down the digits.

There weren't many people out and about in the hall. He passed a nurse on rounds, but almost all of the rooms were dark.

The elevator dinged behind him.

Room 7358.

One glance at the empty bed told him everything he dreaded.

Gabriel wasn't there.

He ducked into the next room, cringing at the click it

made opening. The occupant snored, the whir and beep of the machines creating a sort of white noise.

Emery put his back against the wall and peered out through the smallest crack into the hall. For several seconds nothing happened. No one stirred.

He heard Canales's voice first, then the others. Two? Maybe three? He stepped into the shadows. It wasn't just his own safety he had to be concerned about. The patient asleep in the room was as likely to be hurt if the Eleventh burst in here wanting to grab him. He needed to find Gabriel, get to the Shop, and get ahold of Aiden and the others. God only knew where Julian was; even Emery didn't have that kind of clearance. At least he didn't have to be worried about Gabriel. The man could take care of himself probably better than the rest of them.

"He ain't here," the kid said.

"He must have gotten to him first," Canales said.

"How? We were right behind him."

"Split up. They've got to be on this floor still. You come with me. You two go that way."

Four street thugs wandering the halls—that was bound to get the nurses' attention any second. Either the situation would escalate, or security would be called in.

Emery listened to the retreating voices and the occasional squeak of sneaker tread on tile. At least the idiots made it easy to hear them retreat. When he was reasonably certain the Eleventh was out of sight, he opened the door and glanced both ways. A couple of nurses were clustered together at one end, but the coast was clear for the moment.

Had Smith called ahead to warn Gabriel or the nurses? Did Emery have time to do a room-by-room search for Gabriel? Too bad the cell phone Emery had used in the car was dead.

He kept his head down and walked away from the nurses, toward the central nurses' station on the seventh floor. This late, the lights were dim and there wasn't a lot of activity, but there were two nurses at their stations, typing away, their faces lit by the monitors.

"Can I help you?" an elegant African American woman asked without glancing up.

"I'm looking for the patient in room seven-three-five-eight."

To her credit, she didn't flinch, gasp, or make any obvious indication those numbers meant anything, but Emery had made a study of people's bodies. It was in the way her typing slowed and the curl of her lips.

"Now why would you want to bother a sleeping patient?" she asked.

"He's not sleeping, or if he is, he's not in his room." Emery leaned on the counter. She finally glanced up at him. He'd hate to play poker with her, because she was good, but he was better. "Two men passed by here a few moments ago. I'm willing to bet a detective by the name of Matt Smith called you maybe . . . thirty minutes ago? Where is Gabriel?"

"Sugar, you should have just said the magic words." She tilted her head to the side. "I'll buzz you in. He's giving me a headache with all his broody silence."

Emery glanced in the direction she indicated. The nurses' break room. It needed a keycard entry. Smart. Gabriel had to love that.

"Thank you. Have you called security yet?" He straightened.

"Your detective did one better. He's down on six. I already told him to come up once I saw those boys in the hall. They ain't going to hurt anybody, are they?"

"Not unless anyone gets in their way."

Emery crossed to the break room and the door buzzed, the locks disengaging. He stepped into the dim room and paused to let his eyes adjust. Fabric rustled to his left.

"Gabriel?" Emery ducked and spun.

A man hunched over where Emery had just stood.

"Fuck, why didn't you say it was you?"

"You didn't ask." He tossed the tablet down on a cot and focused on Gabriel, who'd changed from the patient gown into nurse scrubs. He didn't appear to be in too bad condition, except he seemed winded.

"What's going on?" Gabriel straightened and a bit of light fell on his face. He had a stitched-up gash along his cheekbone, a bandage across his nose, and a black eye. It wasn't the worst he'd seen Gabriel, but he'd hoped for better.

"A lot. Can you move?"

"Not fast. Whatever shit they gave me makes me dizzy." Emery frowned.

"Are there more scrubs?" he asked.

"In the closet," Gabriel replied.

"We're going to need a wheelchair and your gown. Roll your pants up. I'll wheel you out of here." He opened the closet and pulled out the first scrubs he found. They were too big, but that was a bonus. He didn't have to take off his clothes, just put the hospital getup on over them. He left the tech's jacket, keycard, and tablet in the break room. Hopefully they found their way back to the owner with no one the wiser.

Gabriel meanwhile kept watch through the glass window set into the door as he shrugged back into his hospital gown.

"There's a wheelchair to the right of the door," Gabriel said when Emery was almost done.

"Service elevator?"

"No clue."

"Okay, let's go now before Canales shows up."

Gabriel pushed the door open. Neither of the nurses glanced up at them. Emery grabbed the wheelchair and held it for Gabriel. They'd make a go for the main elevator.

He hadn't seen Smith yet. All he could do was hope the detective had Canales in handcuffs already. It would take a lot of the load off Emery's shoulders.

Emery wheeled the chair down the hall. It seemed so much farther to the elevators than what he remembered. They passed a stairwell and a dozen or so rooms when two men stepped around the corner ahead of them at the end of the hall.

They were not cops. Or nurses.

It was two of Canales's boys. One of whom was the same one he'd seen outside the cafeteria earlier.

"You!" The man pointed at Emery, his voice booming down the tiled surface.

Now it didn't matter where Smith was.

"Stairs," Gabriel said. He lurched up, out of the chair.

"Stop right there," someone else yelled from the other end of the hall.

"Freeze! Police!" A third figure edged into view. A uniformed officer aimed his weapon at the driver.

"Emery." That voice was from behind them.

Emery turned and faced Detective Smith. The man wore stress like a second skin, but Emery was happy to see him.

"Shit." Gabriel sat back down in the chair, head cradled in his hands.

"Canales is still in the hospital." Emery glanced back at the other two—two less concerns for him.

"He's not on this floor." Smith put his hands on his hips. He seemed . . . thinner. More worn around the edges. Then again, the last few months hadn't exactly been a cakewalk.

"We have to go." Emery grabbed the chair and pushed Gabriel forward.

"We'll escort you out." Smith fell into step with Emery while the two arresting officers were still patting down the Eleventh gang members at the other end of the hall.

Emery led Smith and two uniforms into the elevator. He waited until the doors closed before asking, "Heard from the others?"

Smith didn't reply. It was as if he hadn't heard Emery speak.

Emery straightened, warning bells going off in his head.

"Have you heard from Tori?" he asked.

A muscle at Smith's jaw twitched.

"What happened?" Emery took a step toward Smith. If something had happened to Tori he would search this hospital for Canales himself and kill the bastard.

Smith's gaze dropped to Emery's face.

"She died before they got to the hospital." His voice was soft with a hard edge.

She . . . Emery paused . . . Not Tori. Kathy.

"She who?" Gabriel turned in the chair.

"Kathy?" Emery had to be sure.

"Yeah." Smith nodded. "She'd lost too much blood."

"Kathy's dead?" Gabriel's voice rose. He was usually the unflappable man, making calm, cool, and collected an art form so far above the rest of them, and yet, Kathy's death would shake him, too.

"Fuck." Emery put his back to the wall. He'd known it was bad—but he'd hoped that this one time, they'd catch a break.

"What the hell happened?" Gabriel stood, swaying slightly on his feet. They were about the same height, but where Emery had the build of a linebacker, Gabriel was lighter, quicker, and deadly.

"We got pinned down by a hit team who wanted to take out Tori and Roni. Kathy got shot." He'd known something was wrong. At the time, he'd suspected it was CJ and Kathy he couldn't trust. The hit team had probably followed CJ and Kathy to the meet as a way to find Emery and Tori, and while they worked through things, the hit team eliminated their audience and set up for an ambush.

"Is Roni okay?" Smith asked.

"Yeah, last time I checked her status." For now at least.

"Kathy—she's dead?" Gabriel glanced between Smith and Emery, his gaze begged for a different answer.

"Yes, I'm sorry," Smith said.

The unis shifted, doing their best to mesh into the wall.

The elevator dinged, hitting the first floor. The two cops were the first off, probably wanting away from the horrible news of death. Emery paused, letting the officers do the hard work for a moment.

"Is there anything I can do?" Smith asked.

"Stay away from us." Emery stared at him. "These guys don't care who they hit."

"Let me help."

"You're doing more than enough already."

Gabriel stripped the gown off, chucked it onto the wheelchair and stepped off the elevator. Emery followed, keeping an eye on the man.

"I don't know where CJ or Tori went after they left the hospital." Smith followed them while the two cops walked ahead, toward the nearest exit.

"Don't worry about that." The detective knew a lot about them, but some things only their crew could know. And right now, they needed to close ranks to protect their own. All others could only wind up as casualties of a war Michael Evers had started.

"Call me if there's anything I can do." Smith stopped at the glass doors, going no farther. The parking lot spread out on the other side of the door, and the obnoxious red monstrosity was illegally parked in a handicapped spot.

"You'll be my first call," Emery promised. And he meant it. They couldn't trust the FBI, but Matt Smith had proven to be a valuable friend. Emery just hoped it didn't cost the man his life or job.

"Canales is watching us," Gabriel said as they strode out into the night.

"Probably."

"I can feel him."

"Me too."

Chapter Seventeen

Tori paced in front of the monitors. The seat at the helm remained empty. The security cameras covered every angle of entry to the Shop and the side streets and rooftops. She'd always thought security here was a little over-the-top, but Emery's additions since the Evers arrest three months ago took it to a whole new level. Tonight she was grateful for it.

The warehouse was outfitted with equipment to service their less-than-legal rides, flip cars, store munitions, and other activities they wanted to keep secret. She'd never been to the Shop when it wasn't loud and buzzing with activity. Tonight it might as well be a tomb. CJ had retreated to the main office and locked her out. He needed time to grieve. And then there was reporting Kathy's death to the FBI, informing family, making arrangements.

Tori didn't want to even go there. She still couldn't believe Kathy was . . . gone.

She needed to hold Emery. To know he was okay. It could have easily been him that was shot. Or her. That it was Kathy was just—wrong.

"Pick up. Pick up. Pick up," she chanted into the burner phone.

Normally she wouldn't dream of making this call with the crew so close, but these were desperate times.

The call went to voice mail. Figured.

A mechanical voice rattled off the default message, then the line beeped.

"Pass the ketchup." Her voice trembled. "I don't like ketchup anymore. Leaves a funny taste."

Tori ended the call and quickly broke the phone down into its pieces. Once a month either Roni or Tori made the same call to check in with their old man as a way of telling him they were alive. If they didn't make the call, or if they used a different phrase, he'd come. And then the bloodshed happened. She didn't know what the Russians wanted her father for, but she wouldn't help them find him.

A red two-door car pulled up to the fence on one of the monitors. She held her breath. The driver punched in a code and the gate slid back.

Emery.

He'd made it.

She exhaled, shoved the pieces of the phone into her pockets and rushed to the rolling door. He didn't honk as was their custom, but she heard the engine idling. She pulled the chain, raising the door so the car could clear. Once the car was in, she lowered it again.

The doors opened and Emery and Gabriel emerged, wearing scrubs of all things. She wasn't sure she wanted to know why.

Her eyes burned and suddenly she couldn't speak. She took three steps and wrapped her arms around Emery, burying her face in his chest. The scrubs smelled of clean linen, but under that, she could smell him. He wrapped her in his arms and for a moment, she felt his lips on the top of her head.

"Where's CJ?" he asked.

He knew. She didn't know how, but from his voice she could tell he already knew about Kathy.

"In the office. He locked me out when we got here."

She could see Gabriel in her peripheral vision. There wasn't a lot of light in the warehouse, but she could make out the bruising on his face.

"What about Kathy, is she—is she really . . ." Gabriel leaned on the top of the car, one arm extended toward her.

Tori nodded.

It was hard to believe. An ugly truth she didn't want to be real. But it was.

"She couldn't hold on any longer." Tori let Emery go and took a step back. If it wasn't for her, for the enemies her father had made, none of this would have happened. She wouldn't be part of this crew, she'd never have met Emery, and Kathy would still be alive.

Emery pulled her to his side and wrapped an arm around her. She'd only ever relied on Roni, and yet she was quickly wondering how she'd survive without this man in her life. Even when she wasn't aware of what he did, he was looking out for her.

"How is he?" Emery asked.

"He won't talk. He wouldn't even stay with her. Said she was gone and we had shit to do. He's been locked up in the office since we got here."

"Let's give him some space," Gabriel said. He closed his door to the Scion and walked toward the block of offices they'd repurposed into a variety of uses.

Emery and Tori followed. She hooked her fingers in his, needing some form of contact. A reassurance he was real. And there. Gabriel led them into a long rectangular room with cots, a wardrobe, mini fridge and microwave. Their irregular schedules, odd operations, and covert dealings often left them at loose ends for a while. Like now.

"What are we going to do?" Gabriel sank onto the edge of a cot.

It was rather amazing the two quietest members of their crew were essentially the summation of their defensive strategy planning.

"Get some rest," Emery said. "Tori and I can watch things for now. We can switch later."

"Yeah. Okay." Gabriel stretched out on the cot nearest the door.

Emery grabbed some energy bars from a cupboard and water from the fridge before ushering her out of the room. The light under the small office CJ and Kathy had used on occasion was still on. She bet the door was also locked.

"I'm worried about him," Tori said as they entered the security room.

"Me too, but we don't have time to mourn Kathy right now unless we want to join her."

Her imaginary Emery would have never said something like that, but it was the truth. The real Emery was far more pragmatic and less romantic than she'd dreamed him to be, but that was probably for the best. What would she have done with her made-up version anyway? He totally wouldn't have done her in a garage, while the real Emery had.

"Something wrong?" Emery paused, studying her from across the L-shaped desk.

"No, just thinking."

"About?"

"Nothing related to the conversation."

He shrugged and sat down at the monitors. With a few keystrokes he took control of the cameras, swiveling them around before returning them to their programmed positions.

"Who was that man? The old guy?" Tori asked.

"I don't know. I'm guessing he's Evers's replacement, or maybe his stand-in."

Emery sat back and blew out a breath.

"What do you want to do?" she asked.

"You." He swung the rolling chair around to face her.

It was all too easy to imagine herself crawling onto Emery's lap, straddling him . . .

Her cheeks heated and she glanced away. A pang of guilt stabbed her. She should not have those kinds of thoughts now.

"I think it would benefit us to have a lookout on top of the building. With Matvei gone, we don't know who will take control of the situation." He rubbed his brow. They were all exhausted, but the bulk of the burden was falling on his shoulders.

"Evers gets out in the morning."

"Yeah, but what if this new guy has developed a liking for being in charge? How does the hit team factor into this? Even with Matvei gone, those other three guys are no joke. The little one? I'd bet money he's a Spetsnaz."

"There's no such thing as a Spetsnaz anymore." She rolled her eyes. Sure, during the Cold War, the USSR had super soldiers called Spetsnaz, but they'd been disbanded.

"If that's what you want to believe. Remember Pasha?"

"Evers's old bodyguard?"

"No one ever picked him up, so I did some digging. He was a soldier, but there are entire years where it's like he didn't even exist. Aiden said he fought like a Spetsnaz."

"Okay, so let's say Shorty is a Spetsnaz soldier turned hit man." That was a terrifying thought, especially considering what she knew of the training from her father. The things men were forced to do to prepare for war were . . . inhumane.

"So I guess I'll go up to the roof." She scrubbed her face with her hand. This day would never end.

"We'll both go."

She wasn't going to argue with him. They gathered a few guns from their cache and climbed the stairs up to the catwalk and used a ladder to access the roof. She'd come up here a handful of times in the beginning when Emery was doing the security install. At the time she'd been suspicious of the whole team and wanted to know what he was about. Maybe that was where the seed of attraction had taken root?

Unlike the others who rebuffed her questions, Emery had answered. They'd been short replies, but he hadn't begrudged her wanting to know who the hell he was and why she should trust him.

They sat on the roof, backs against an AC unit, and tore into the protein bars.

"Your father is alive." Emery didn't ask. He wasn't questioning her.

"Yes." She stared down the street that ran parallel to the building on the north side. It would be easy to jump in a car, hit the road, and never look back.

"Give me a reason to forget that."

She blew out a breath.

"I can try." Tori glanced at him, then away.

"So try."

"When Roni and I were seventeen he faked his death. It was so thorough we believed it. He had been set on fire and burned to death behind the house we were squatting in. His screams, they gave me nightmares for weeks. I have no idea who that really was. Knowing Dad, it was probably some guy who wouldn't be missed. We buried the body. We were so damn happy he was gone, at first we didn't question that he was dead. Then we began to notice little things. A couple missing documents, running low on some supplies, and everything just ended far too neatly."

Emery squeezed her hand.

She glanced at him, but couldn't bring herself to smile. "The files I read omitted large chunks of information."

"He prepared us to survive. In his mind, we needed to be ready for anything, and that meant wilderness survival, shooting, hunting, living in the elements. We lived in a constant state of dread whenever he'd put us in his truck and start driving. I can't tell you how many times he'd take us somewhere, make us get out, and leave. If we were smart, we'd have gone to some house or found a cop to pick us up, but he'd brainwashed us, made us think everyone was out to get us. We hated him back then, but he was all we had. One thing he taught us was how to place a classified ad in code. Roni and I started jumping at our own shadows, so we placed an ad to see if anything happened."

"Did he answer?"

"Not at first. We put a different ad in each week. There's an art to it. You want it to stick out enough so your intended recipient picks up on it, but not be too obvious. About two months after we placed the first one, we spotted his ad. It essentially told us to stop contacting him. A couple weeks later we were in this dive bar hustling the pool tables and he walks in. Except he didn't look like himself anymore. I've seen him once since that meeting, but he made it clear his debt to us was paid and he was out."

"But you still contact him?"

She bit her lip. What the hell? He could already sink this ship if he wanted.

"Yes. It's more like we check in. Give the all-clear sign, and move on."

"Why do that?"

"I think . . . I don't know if he knows how to love. He was a crazy asshole, but he did the best with what he had and took care of us the only way he knew how. Now, it's like his only way of showing us he might have ever cared. If we really needed him, if it was life or death, he'd be here."

"Is that what you wanted me to tell Roni? To bring him in?"

"No. I wanted her to tell him to stay away. We have a strict do-not-communicate policy."

"Tori—"

"Bringing him here is what the hit team wants. They were going to kill me no matter what, so why give them what they want? Better to deny them and get Roni out safe than all of us end up dead."

Emery studied her for a few moments, holding her hand.

"How you doing?" he asked.

She chuckled, but his own reference seemed to go over his head.

"What?" He frowned.

"You never watched *Friends*, did you?"

"No."

"Then you wouldn't get it."

"Okay." He continued to stare at her while she scanned the rooftops for movement.

This was some date. Looking for covert urban operations happening around them. On the other hand, it was nice that he knew, that Emery was aware—and accepted—this part of her life because it was his as well.

"I'm okay. Just . . . sad."

"Yeah."

"Part of me feels guilty. CJ and Kathy were there for me, so why wasn't it me they shot?"

"The world isn't wired that way."

"Are you going to tell the FBI about my dad?"

"Depends."

"On what?" She pulled her hand from his.

"What's he doing now?"

"I can't tell you that." Her heart rate kicked up. Damn it all. She'd told him almost everything.

"Tori, is he actively endangering people?"

"No." She shook her head. Last she knew, he'd gone to work for the Cuban government dealing in intelligence, mostly to do with people already living in Cuba.

"Then no. He's dangerous, and rooting him out from wherever he is could get a lot of people killed, but I'm trusting you."

She didn't think Emery would lie to her.

"Did you know Kathy and CJ worked together for years before they dated?" Emery tipped his head back, resting it against the air duct.

"No, but she did say it was a gradual falling in love." Tori leaned her head on his shoulder. "How long were they married?"

"I don't know. Years before they were assigned to this. The FBI tried to break them up, but they refused to let them." Emery's hand covered hers.

"I always appreciated how Kathy could laugh at me, stitch me up and tell me where I went wrong without sounding like a bitch. It wasn't mom-like, but I appreciated it. She was always looking out for me.

"She dropped off food for me and would leave these notes. *Don't forget to mask the cell signals* or *watch for that next shipment of coke*. I'd never forget to do those things, but . . ."

But Kathy wasn't the kind of woman who told you she loved you. It was in what she did for their crew without being asked, how she gave them everything she had—even her life.

Tori wrapped her arms around him, resting her head against his chest. A few tears leaked out the corner of her eyes. Emery slung his arm around her and stroked his other hand over her hair. She felt his lips on the top of her head and squeezed him.

"She lived the kind of life she wanted to live, doing what she loved to do." Emery's voice was quiet, soothing, but it would be a long time before the place where Kathy lived in Tori's heart healed.

"I'm going to miss her."

"Me too. We had her for far too short a time."

"I like it when you actually talk to me."

"Complete sentences?"

"You're a fast learner."

She felt more than heard his chuckle.

What if she lost Emery tomorrow? They'd only had a few days of really knowing each other. She was just now beginning to peel back the layers of what made him tick and learning to love the real Emery. What if she lost him tomorrow? Tonight?

Her heart clenched at the thought.

"Emery?"

"Hm?"

She opened her mouth to reply, but what did she say? I love you, don't die?

"We're going to get through this, aren't we?" she asked instead.

"We are." His answer was quick, certain and assured. The arm around her pulled her in closer.

"How do you think this is going to end?"

"I thought it would wrap up when Evers was arrested, but now I'm not so sure."

Would it ever end? The last three months proved that when Evers was down, someone else just took his place. Tori didn't care who they eliminated so long as the bad guys were put in prison. She wasn't like Julian or Aiden, who had personal beefs with the bastard. For her, it was the job. The knowledge that she was doing something good with her life. Racing fast cars was a serious perk. Emery though? He was the icing on top.

"What are . . . what are *we* going to do?" she asked.

For a moment he didn't reply or even move. Did he

get what she was asking him? What she couldn't outright tell him?

"We're going to stand watch. The others will get here. We'll make a plan and some bad guys will go to jail. After that, I don't know, but I'm looking forward to it."

"I don't want to lose you." There. She said it. Or as close as she could come to saying what she felt.

"You won't."

Could she hold him to it? How long did a promise like that last?

Chapter Eighteen

The hours wore thin through the night. The clear sky grew overcast and thunder rumbled in the distance. Emery kept one eye on the streets while the other strayed back to Tori while they made their rounds. With the hit team out there, they couldn't be too careful. Now more than ever he wanted to lock her up somewhere safe, but she'd likely shoot him for trying. She was amazing.

Her secret didn't bother him like it should. Then again, so long as Alexander Iradokovia remained a shadow, he didn't care what the man did.

Emery strolled another lap around the building, but in the early morning hours the streets were quiet. Tori was waiting for him back at the air duct where they'd stashed their water and extra ammunition.

"There's nothing going on." She frowned, gaze on the buildings. Thanks to all the streetlights, there was plenty of illumination to see by, but once it started raining it could leave them blind. Of course, it could make their attackers blind. "Do you ever worry that someone might find this place?"

"Sure. That's why I'm always working on security here. For all we know, they might already know about it." He was fairly confident their location was still safe, but it was always smart to behave as though the enemy was out there. Which was why the entire building was reinforced. From cinder blocks stacked up inside the walls to the cameras and bulletproof windows, the Shop was as safe as he could make it.

"Do you think they'll come after us?"

"Maybe."

Matvei had been the brains of the operation. The other three might need to call home for instructions. Their team was a valuable resource to the Russian mob network, and expending them on Tori and Roni, might be a poor expense of manpower. Hell, the girls weren't even a threat to the organized crime unit, but the Russians didn't know that. And the mob had just lost one of their best assets.

Tori edged closer. He hooked his arm around her waist and pulled her in until their bodies pressed together. Her hands splayed over his chest and she stared up at him. He couldn't make out her features in the dim light, but he knew them from countless hours spent watching her. Poor thing had no idea he wasn't going to let her go.

He lowered his head and brushed his lips across hers, savoring the way she sucked in a breath at the first touch. Her hands curled into fists, bunching his shirt in her grasp. He swept his tongue along the seam of her lips, still cool from the bottled water.

A hundred thoughts, urges, and desires ran through his brain. He wanted to plug into her, show them all to her, but that wasn't how she worked. She needed his words. Complete sentences.

"I can't stop thinking about you." She was his every other thought. His obsession. Worse now that Kathy was gone. Their lives were too short to spend waiting.

"What part of me?" She leaned into him and he loved the smile that tugged at her lips.

"All of you." It was completely unnatural to speak his thoughts, but for her, he'd learn.

An engine revved, breaking the stillness of the night. Tori stepped away from him and grabbed the rifle on the air duct. He drew the Glock he'd tucked in his waistband and together they crept toward the edge of the building.

"See anything?" he asked Tori.

"Nothing yet." She peered through the sights on the rifle, sweeping the streets for a sign of the car. The first light drops of rain began to fall.

With all the concrete and brick, it was hard to pinpoint the location of the car.

"There." Tori pivoted. Headlights slashed across a building and the car turned down the road that ran parallel to the Shop. She dropped the rifle into the cradle of her arms. "It's Julian."

Julian.

Emery exhaled, but it wasn't in relief.

This was going to be a bitch.

"Come on, we need to update him." He gathered up the trash from their protein bars and followed Tori to the ladder.

By the time they reached the warehouse floor, Gabriel was rolling the door up for Julian. Emery glanced at the office where CJ was ensconced, but the lights were off. He could only hope CJ had passed out. He might have an easygoing, disarming appearance, but the man underneath was a skilled agent who'd outlasted and outshot his enemies to survive this long.

"Gabriel, you look like shit." Julian got out of the sleek, black car and stretched.

Gabriel grunted and lowered the gate.

"Emery." Julian's brows rose, no doubt surprised to see Emery at the Shop without an obvious reason. "Going to kill someone? What did I miss?"

"A lot." Emery nodded toward the security office. They needed to be inside where they could keep their eyes on the cameras.

"Shit. At least let me grab something to wake me up." Julian strode to the bunk room and within moments the scent of coffee wafted toward them.

"Where do you think he's been?" Tori asked as they entered the security office.

"No clue." Usually Emery tried to keep tabs on Julian's assignments though it wasn't his job, but he'd been distracted.

"How much are we telling him?" She kept her voice low and she settled into one of the chairs lining the wall.

Emery resisted glaring at Gabriel, who settled into the seat next to Tori. The swift kick of jealousy was something he'd need to deal with. Tori worked alongside Gabriel every day. If there was anything between them, Emery would have known by now. That knowledge didn't appease his desire to shove Gabriel aside.

"I don't know." Emery sat in the rolling chair and glanced at the monitors.

Julian was on a hair trigger these days. If they'd thought it was bad before Evers was arrested, he was nearly unbearable since the arrest. They had to tell Julian that Evers was being released tomorrow, yet another thing going wrong for them. Then what? The news of Kathy's death needed to be broken carefully, and they should be prepared for an outburst. Everything else was small fry compared to those two details.

He scrubbed his face. The couple hours of sleep last night and the post-sex nap that afternoon weren't enough to keep him going. They needed a better plan, that was for sure.

"Okay, so what shit storm have you stirred up while I

was gone?" Julian leaned against the door frame, stirring his coffee.

"Where's mine?" Tori asked.

"Where I left it." One side of Julian's mouth hiked up. A good sign. Wherever he'd been, the job must have gone well.

"Jackass." Tori grinned and set the rifle on the desk.

"Why are you packing a sniper rifle?" Julian's good humor faded.

For a moment none of them spoke.

"A lot has happened." Emery sat back in the chair. Where to start?

"Okay." Julian sipped the coffee and stared at Emery. There was an edge there, one Emery wasn't sure wouldn't cut him.

"Short version?" Tori twisted to face Julian. "The Eleventh is working for Evers. They have a compound facility north of here. The Russian mob sent a hit team here to kill Roni and me. They shot Kathy instead."

"Is she okay?" Julian asked before Tori could continue. Tori cringed.

"No, she's not." Emery put his elbows on the desk and stared up at Julian. "She died earlier."

Julian's tanned skin went pale and the coffee cup crinkled, spilling a little of the liquid on his hand and the floor.

"She's dead?" he asked.

"Yes. She died at the hospital. There was nothing they could do," Tori replied softly.

Julian sank into a chair and Tori moved into the one next to him. She took the coffee from his grip before he crushed it, and put her other hand on his shoulder.

"What about the others? Do they know?" Julian lifted his head and glanced around to take them all in. His gaze landed on Gabriel. "What happened to you?"

"Fender bender." Gabriel leaned against the wall behind his chair.

Emery answered Julian's first question. "CJ was the last person to reach out to Aiden's group. They're on their way here, but they don't know everything that's happened in the last twelve hours." Emery glanced at the clock. "I would have expected them here already."

"How's CJ?" Julian asked.

"He's been locked in the office since we got here." Tori rubbed her hands on her jeans. There were a few bloodstains on her jeans and tank top, but he hadn't pointed them out.

"I'm calling Aiden." Julian grabbed his phone out of his pocket and cursed. "Got a charger?"

Emery held out his hand and grabbed a charging cable with the other. Julian hesitated before handing it over. What didn't Julian want him to see? Emery made a note to check Julian's phone later. He stole a quick glance at it as he plugged it in. Three missed calls from Lily? *Lily*, as in Madison's best friend? The same friend Julian had rescued? That was interesting.

"Here." Gabriel handed over one of the extra phones he must have picked up earlier.

Julian grabbed it and stepped out into the warehouse to make the call.

"That went better than I'd have thought." Tori sank down in her chair and closed her eyes.

"It hasn't really hit me, ya know, that she's gone?" Gabriel stared at the floor.

Gabriel was right. It would sink in over time. Kathy wouldn't answer the phones at Classic Rides anymore. There would be no more notes. A hundred little things she'd done for them would be missed and the ache would persist until they'd all learned to move on.

All at once the rain let loose, pelting the warehouse and drowning out Julian's voice.

"Where have you two been?" Gabriel asked, lifting his gaze to Emery.

"I heard about the hit team, then I made the call to go to ground. Hoped it would protect the rest of the crew," Emery replied.

Gabriel glanced at Tori, then back to Emery. Gabriel was observant, but what was between Tori and Emery was none of his fucking business.

Julian stepped back into view and leaned on the door frame. "They should be here in two hours, maybe less. A couple Eleventh guys ran John off the road, so they had to stop to make a few repairs, farted around. I gave them the highlights."

"Emery and Tori need some downtime," Gabriel said.

"Why don't you and I take watch? You guys can get some rest. When the others get here we can make a plan." Julian was incredibly calm considering the mess their operation was in. He was almost like the old Julian. The one who had passion, determination, and a streak of goodness in him.

"Don't have to tell me twice." Tori stood and stretched. Emery didn't look at her, but he was aware of her every movement. "I'm going to go find a spot to nap." She left the office without a backward glance.

"Emery. Stay a moment." Gabriel leaned forward, elbows on his knees.

Julian propped himself on the door frame once more, blocking the exit and any chance Emery had to see where she'd gone.

"What's up?" Julian asked.

Emery glanced at Julian, then Gabriel.

"You and Tori?" Gabriel tilted his head to the side.

Julian's eyes widened, but he said nothing.

"Yeah?" Emery curled his hands into fists.

"The suits won't like it."

"And?"

"Be careful. If not for you, for her."

"Shit." Julian sat down in the seat he'd vacated and stared at Emery. "How long?"

Emery forced his hands to relax and folded his arms over his chest. He'd followed the rules, done everything they'd asked of him, but this might be too much.

"Not long," he replied.

"Is it fuck buddies or—"

"Julian." Emery's vision hazed red.

"I had to ask." Julian held up his hands. "Gabriel's right. Be careful. Tell him."

Gabriel blew out a breath and glanced at the door.

"She's gone to her car, man." Julian leaned back, peering out of the door.

"You know I used to be FBI." Gabriel stared at Emery. It wasn't a question.

Emery knew every member of their crew's history, but with Julian and Gabriel, there were huge chunks missing. He'd filled in most of it by looking up other reports and connecting the dots, but they'd never outright talked about it. Gabriel, like most of their crew, was a contracted employee for the FBI. He might work for them, but he wasn't an agent. Which was how their superiors liked it. If shit went to hell, they could cut ties and pretend to be blameless.

"I was . . . in a relationship with my handler. I'd been deep cover since joining the agency and she was the only constant in my life. The last operation, it was messy. Bad stuff. When shit hit the fan and everything came out, I couldn't stomach the bullshit anymore. I had words with our superiors. They cut me, kept her, and I've been floating since then."

"That was fucked up." Julian shook his head, but didn't say anything else.

"I like Tori. I don't want to see her or her sister burned. Especially not now." Gabriel's stare was honest, a real been-there-done-that vibe.

Anger boiled in Emery's veins, but even he recognized that it was misplaced. It wasn't Gabriel he should be angry with, and just because that was what happened to Gabriel didn't mean it would happen to Tori. But when the chips fell, and Kathy's death factored into the FBI's plans, would they determine Tori was too much of a liability to keep?

If it came to that, he'd leave. Pack up and go with her. Roni could stay, and he'd watch Tori's back.

"When did this happen?" Julian asked.

"I was wondering if one of you'd ever make a damn move," Gabriel drawled. "Be careful, man. I don't want to see what happened to me happen again to the two of you."

"You ever talk to Gage again?" Julian peered at Gabriel, but the other man stared at the floor.

"No, man. She wouldn't speak to me. Sent my stuff over in a box with a *don't ever contact me again* note."

Gage? Emery couldn't remember anyone by that name, but he'd have to make himself acquainted with her file. Later. Right now he needed to clean himself up before he went to find Tori. He wanted to touch her. To hold on to her. If today had taught him anything, it was that every moment mattered.

Chapter Nineteen

Tori stretched out in the front seat of her 1957 Chevrolet Bel Air. In a perfect world she'd be looking out at the stars above Miami, but her life was a shit storm. Instead, she ignored the roof of the warehouse above her and brainstormed how she'd restore the Bel Air. The car needed a lot of work and she wasn't flush with cash to get the job done yet, so here it sat. At the Shop, in a far corner behind a couple unmarked vehicles they used from time to time. The engine couldn't even turn over, but that didn't stop her from visiting it and sitting behind the wheel from time to time.

She needed space from the others, and this was the best she could do. Except she didn't really want to be alone. There was only one person who could soothe the rawness, who grounded her. But he was probably passed out in the bunk room or talking security with the guys.

This was stupid. She should have waited for him. Made it obvious. A few days ago, he hadn't realized she was into him. More than into him. Her chest ached, as if there was too much emotion knotted up inside of her, stretching her ribs to accommodate this new feeling. Why should his oblivious nature change in a few days? But maybe he wasn't oblivious. She hadn't realized he liked her, too. Maybe it was willful ignorance, or they'd each been too circumspect.

She leaned her head against the window and closed her eyes.

Love sucked sometimes.

She loved Emery.

And tonight she could have lost him instead of Kathy.

She toyed with the necklace at her throat and opened her eyes, too restless to try to sleep yet.

Movement at the front of the Bel Air caught her eye. A dark figure stepped into view at the front of the car and stopped. The light was behind him, but she knew those shoulders, his shape. She blew out her breath and waited. The moments dragged on, and she swore she could feel his gaze all over her body. She was exhausted, and yet too amped up to sleep.

Emery stepped between the Bel Air and a white van. He opened the passenger door and leaned in. His shirt was different and she could smell soap. So that's where he'd been. Cleaning up. They didn't call him the Walking Brain for nothing.

"You okay?" he asked.

"Yeah." God, her stomach did that flip-flopping thing she hated. They'd had sex, maybe even made love, they'd agreed to see where this attraction went, and yet—with the crew coming back together, could they do it? Would things change? She loved him, but was it the same for him? "Want to join me?"

"Sure."

She sat up, putting her back against the driver's door and drawing her legs up to make room for him. She curled her toes against the leather, nerves rattling her. He settled into the passenger side and twisted around to get a look at the car.

"This yours?" he asked.

"Yeah. It needs a lot of work, but the frame and engine are still good."

"Seat's comfortable."

She chuckled. "That's because the guy who owned it before me replaced the seats. He started to restore it but couldn't afford it."

The seats weren't vintage, but the gray-and-black-flecked leather was luxurious and comfortable. Way more cushioned than the cots in the bunk room. Emery put his hand on her knee and slid it up and down her thigh. It was a casual gesture, except things between them were far from casual. Fissures of heat went through her body and her breasts felt heavy.

Neither spoke, and for the first time in ages, she didn't sense the need to fill the silence. She covered Emery's hand with hers, lacing their fingers together, and squeezed. He turned his head and stared at her. Another man might give her comforting words, tell her everything was going to be okay, but not Emery. He'd been honest with her even when the truth made her bolt. The difference was, he'd have her back.

Bolting hadn't solved her problems. It had made them worse. Maybe in the past running was the answer, because Roni was all she'd had. Now, the crew had her back. She should have called CJ, talked to him herself when the shit hit the fan. If she had, would they still be in this position? Perhaps, but it might have had a different outcome.

Her arms broke out in goose bumps. The air was cool, almost chilly with the rain setting in.

Screw this.

She crawled across the bench seat and sat in Emery's lap. He didn't protest the action or miss a beat. His arms wrapped around hers and he shifted, settling her more comfortably until she could lay her head against his shoulder. She closed her eyes and soaked him in.

"Things will get worse before they get better." He pressed a kiss to her brow and stroked her back.

"Yeah."

"The FBI might try to put pressure on you."

"Wait—what?" She lifted her head and stared at Emery. There was just enough light for her to make out the shape of his face. She lifted her hand and trailed her fingers down his cheek, feeling the thought lines around his mouth.

"The FBI doesn't have a policy about interdepartmental relationships. That's how Kathy and CJ could be married. But it doesn't mean they like it."

"They'll try to make me go away."

"Maybe. I don't know."

There were a lot of ways the FBI could leverage the safety they'd provided for her and Roni. Being with her could hinder Emery's future, his career. She wasn't a bad person, but life and necessity had forced her to make some choices that crossed the line.

"Emery, I don't want you to make sacrifices for me." He'd already had a rough go of it. She wouldn't stand between him and a better life.

"It's a job, Tori. A job I like. A job I'm good at. But this isn't my life. I'll be okay. But they might try to bully you, and if it should come down to it, and you want to go back to how things were, I'd—"

"Please do not say *I'll understand*."

They stared at each other. He had a lot to lose. A reputable career that meant something, showing his worthless family just how great he really was. Of course, right now with the way they'd spun things, Emery looked like a money launderer, so probably not as great in the eyes of the public.

"I would. I'd understand. If they threatened you or Roni, I'd get it."

"Has something happened? Do they know already?"

"No."

"Then why are we creating problems? Don't we already have enough crap to handle?"

"I want to be prepared."

"That's great, but right now I don't want to think about it all. It's been a shitty night." She was done crying and being angry, if only for a little bit.

He nodded and pulled her closer, until her breasts pressed against his chest. She slid her arms around his neck. Thank goodness the real Emery was nothing like what she'd made up. She'd have walked all over that man. This one? Well, he'd already proven he could put her on her ass and walk next to her into trouble. What more could she ask for?

She tilted her head to the right a bit and he mimicked the movement. At least they were on the same page. She pressed her mouth to his in a chaste kiss, simply wanting to savor this connection between them. There'd been a lot of men in her life, and very few had ever put her needs above theirs. Emery had not only endangered his career for her, he was ready to stand up to the agency for what he wanted. If that wasn't the foundation for love, for something better, she didn't know what was.

Emery's mouth softened and he licked her lower lip. His right hand slid down to her ass and squeezed, forcing her to rock into him.

There was a much better way to do this.

Tori grabbed the back of the seat, ducked her head and straddled Emery's lap.

Who needed sleep?

He cupped the back of her head and pulled her down for a toe-curling kiss. His tongue tangled with hers. She wanted to get closer, under the skin, until nothing separated them. He sucked her lower lip, gently biting down before releasing her. The rain redoubled, drowning out the sound of their breathing.

She could tell him now. He'd never hear it. But Emery would want to know what she'd said. Unless he could read lips. She wouldn't put it past him.

His hands smoothed over her hips and cupped her bottom. He pulled her closer. She gasped and flattened her palm against the roof of the car as pleasure cascaded through her. She rolled her hips, rubbing against him. It was too dark to make out his expression in detail, but she could imagine it: Emery's face tightening, his features becoming sharper. His cheeks sinking in and his lips thinning. He had this ferocious look when he was aroused. If she didn't know him, it might scare her.

He made that growling noise in the back of his throat again and yanked her forward. His mouth grazed her neck, then he started kissing down her throat. She arched her back. Her nipples tightened, sending a jolt of awareness to her pussy.

Tori smacked her head against the top of the car, not too hard, but the impact and thud surprised her. Emery cupped her skull, his passionate exploration of her chest forgotten.

"I'm okay, I'm okay." Heat crawled up her chest. *Great. Awesome move there.*

Her voice was barely audible above the din.

Emery gently pressed at the spot, urging her to bend her head.

"I'm fine." Just horny.

He kissed the spot and she chuckled. She stole a glance at him and an invisible hand gripped her throat. God, he was handsome when he smiled.

Tori pushed his shoulder and shifted her body. He went with it, stretching out along the seat. It wasn't long enough for him and he wound up with his knees raised, but that could work for her. It wasn't dark enough that she missed his smile. Despite all the crazy shit going on in their lives, they'd found each other. She bent and kissed him, pouring everything she couldn't say into the kiss, praying he'd figure it out for now. If things ever settled down, if they made it through this, she could find a way to tell him. But not until she knew he'd be okay. That he wouldn't lose everything he'd worked for because of her. He mattered to her that much.

His hands pushed up under her shirt. He hooked his thumbs in the bottom of her sports bra and pulled it up under her armpits and freed her breasts. She sucked in a breath. His rough fingertips rubbed her tight nipples. He grasped the tight peaks and pulled. She hissed and bent lower, until his mouth was next to her ear.

He spoke, but his words were covered up by the storm. She tilted her head closer, but his voice was pitched too low to hear. If he was trying to be bossy, well, too bad. There were things she hadn't done yet that she wanted to do. And where better to do them than the front seat of her Bel Air?

Tori wiggled out of his grasp and knelt on the floorboard. She grabbed the waistband of his jeans and slipped the button through the hole. They had a finite amount of time together before the inevitable crashed into them, and if it was she who died today, she wanted to know she had taken every possible opportunity to love Emery.

She lowered the zipper, her brows rising when she didn't encounter underwear. Well, that was one less thing to worry about. He propped himself up on his elbows and lifted his hips and she tugged his jeans down around his knees. She wanted to get all kinds of naked with him, but the facts of their life remained the same. They needed to be ready for anything at a moment's notice. So she'd leave is jeans around his knees and her shirt on. Besides, she didn't want to show her tits to anyone other than him.

His cock jutted up from the dark patch of hair. She hadn't had an opportunity to really take him in before. Their first time was too fast, the second was born of need. Now, she wanted him, but not like the other times. Not in a frenzy of desire.

She wrapped one hand around the base of his erection and stroked his length. Out of the corner of her eye she saw his head drop back against the door. Her focus remained on his cock, the way the tip glistened with a drop of moisture, the thick vein she didn't need light to trace. Being with him was different. He wasn't selfish; it wasn't about getting him off and shuffling off to the bathroom to finish herself off. Even when they'd fucked that first time, he'd shown more concern for her pleasure than his own.

Emery was not a selfish man. She was growing to learn that, from the way he talked about his history to the way he spoke about the future—it wasn't about him. It was the crew, or her, or his family—never himself. She wanted to be the woman who cared for him. Who saw to his pleasure, his well-being, and his happiness.

Tori leaned forward and licked the moisture seeping from the slit. The salty flavor went down smooth and his sharp intake of breath sliced through the noise from the rain.

Oh, she was going to enjoy this.

She stroked his cock from the base up as she kissed the crown, flicking her tongue over the sensitive cap. She sucked lightly, then she continued her investigation, tracing the underside of the mushroom head. His hips lifted a little, pushing his length farther into her mouth. He seemed to realize what he was doing and stopped. She cupped his balls, rolling them in her palm, and lowered her head, taking more of him in her mouth. She rubbed the flat of her tongue against him while she pumped the base with her other hand.

His fingers grazed the top of her head before sliding down over her cheek. She opened her mouth, taking as much of him in as she could. His hips bucked and he uttered a curse she couldn't make out. She chuckled around his girth while she lifted her head and eased back down concentrating on relaxing her jaw muscles.

He planted a hand on the window above his head and a foot on the passenger door. There was a steady stream of words. Curses? Dirty talk maybe? What she wouldn't give to hear buttoned-up Emery say something so out of character. Did he like her mouth? Her tongue? His enjoyment only got her more into the act. Just watching him, feeling the way his body reacted, turned her on. With every pass up and down his cock, her breasts rubbed his thigh. It wasn't much, but in her aroused state she'd take what she could get. Now if only she had another hand to rub her throbbing clit.

Emery grabbed her by the arm and pulled her forward. She rocked up on her knees, inhaling and taking him all the way to the back of her throat.

"No." This time she heard Emery's hoarse cry above the rain.

He rose, picking her up and dragging her across his body until he took her mouth in a bruising kiss. His hands held her face and he kissed her as if it were his life's mission. He nipped her lip, soothed it with his tongue. She leaned into him, denying him nothing. Anything he wanted, she'd give him.

She'd known her attraction to Emery was a dangerous thing, but loving him was worse and better all at once. He could destroy her, and yet, he was the kind of man who would go down with a sinking ship. She didn't deserve that

ind of loyalty—or dare she call it love? Could he love her
ack already?

Tori wrapped her hand around his still erect cock press-
ng against her hip. His slick skin slid easily through her
ist.

"No," Emery said again, though this time she felt it
ore than heard it.

He pulled her hand away from his stiff flesh while the
ther yanked at the cheap snap holding her jeans together.
)esire burned in her belly. There was something about a
an ripping clothes off her body that made her crazy.
he'd wanted to please him, but now she needed him
nside of her.

She planted a hand on the dash and a hand on the back
f the seat to steady herself. Her thighs shook when she
ose. Emery did the rest. He yanked her jeans and panties
own, bending almost double as they twisted and shifted
ntil the only thing she wore was her tank top and the
unched-up sports bra.

She straddled his thighs and scooted her way up. His
and splayed on her belly and she arched her back.

"Condom." He sat up, reaching around her and into his
eans. This close she could feel the passion in his gaze, the
vay it felt as though he invaded her body without actually
ouching her.

Fuck a condom. She wrapped her arms around his neck
nd kissed him. He continued to fumble with his clothes,
erking on something until he got it free.

He was right. In their line of work it was dangerous
nough to care about people. A kid was out of the question
nd downright cruel.

She heard the crinkle first, then a thump. His wallet hit
he floorboard. He leaned back, ripping the condom open
nd holding it to the light for a second before he reached
etween them and rolled it on. He hooked his arm around

her, yanking her forward until his erection was trappe
between their bodies.

The roar of the rain lessened. The sound of their breatl
the occasional creak of the car, normal sounds, drifte
back into her awareness.

"Say something dirty." She lifted up until her head h
the top of the car.

He leaned back, guiding his penis until the head notche
against her opening.

"You have the best goddamned pussy I've ever felt."

Her muscles turned to mush and she fell more tha
lowered herself onto him. They both gasped and Emery
spine came off the seat. Her body burned deliciously. Sh
shifted, giving herself a moment to relearn the feel of hir
inside of her. She splayed her hands on his chest, archin
her back and wiggling her hips.

"You feel so good inside of me." She groaned, letting he
eyes close while she contracted her muscles around him

He palmed her breasts through the thin tank top, curl
ing his fingers around the mounds. She pulled her shirt up
until they were skin to skin. Her breasts might not be fu
or round, but damn they were sensitive and she loved th
rough sensation of his fingers on her.

Tori grasped the seat and steering wheel with eac
hand. Maybe it was the level of desire or just exhaustio
weighing her down, but it was hard to make herself move
She rose slowly, sucking down breath.

"I want you to fuck me." Emery's voice dropped to th
deep notes she was beginning to learn meant he was ridin
the edge of control. She'd broken that tenuous hold onc
and loved it. Making him lose it might be her new favorit
hobby.

"Like this?" She rose and fell, groaning as his coc
stroked her internal walls. Leveraging herself on the ca
she picked up the pace.

"Yes," he growled out.

She let her head drop forward, allowing her more room to move. He began to shift under her, lifting his hips to meet her, working in tandem.

"Oh God," she muttered, closing her eyes.

She couldn't look at him. If she did, if she stared into the maelstrom, she'd tell him. She'd lay herself bare and he'd know. He'd know she loved him because she was barely holding herself back from saying it now.

His hand slid down her body. She inhaled, tensing the muscles in her stomach, but he passed them by.

"I'm going to come so hard." He spoke as though he were clenching his teeth, trying to hold back.

"Come on. I want to feel you."

The hand at her stomach splayed over her mound. His thumb swiped over her clit, applying pressure, but it was the rough quality of his skin abrading the sensitized nub that made her gasp. Again and again he massaged the bundle of nerves in time with his thrusts. Her jellied muscles couldn't keep up and she hung suspended over him while he thrust in and out of her body as cascading colors lit up the back side of her eyes.

"Look at me," he said in that deep, dark voice.

His eyes seemed to glitter in the semidarkness.

"Come. Come on," he chanted at her.

He'd hold back until she came. Even when she tried to make it about him, he turned it around. God, he was amazing. Her heart and body were so full of him. The need for release coiled low and tight in her belly. She rolled her hips and he thrust up to meet her. He reached up and cupped the back of her head, bringing her down on top of him until their tongues tangled in a kiss so deep she didn't know where one ended and the other began.

This was love. How could it not be?

Her body must have sensed the revelation. Pleasure so

deep she wanted to scream unfolded within her, spreading
into every cell of her body. He thrust again, the motion
rougher, the hand between them clenching at her hip. H
groaned his release. Emery stilled and she collapsed on to
of him, wholly spent.

He wrapped his arms around her and she smiled befor
she ever felt the kiss to the top of her head. Such little
sweet gestures from a man so used to being cast aside. I
the FBI ever did pressure her into leaving him, she'd hav
to. She couldn't ask him to go down with the proverbia
sinking ship.

"You hugged my penis with your pussy."

The statement was so unexpected it made her giggle.

"I did." She peered up at him and her heart clenched a
the look of utter completion on his face. Had she ever see
Emery happy? How could she leave him?

"I liked it."

She grinned and tightened her lower muscles. H
groaned.

"Don't do that or I'll get hard again."

"Oh really?" She chuckled and kissed his frowning lips
"Fine. I'm sleepy anyway."

"Next time we can use a bed. It'll be a novelty and the
you can do that as much as you want."

She liked the sound of *next time*. Of making plans wit
him. They'd agreed to see where the attraction went
Maybe she wasn't strong enough to walk away from thi
She laid her head on his chest and hugged him with he
arms this time. They'd become entwined sometime in th
last few days. It could be the situation they'd found them
selves in, or just maybe it was meant to be.

Tori kissed his chest, above his heart. She didn't know
what the future held, what the FBI would do or if the h
team would attack again. There was no point in makin

promises to herself without knowing the future. She'd love Emery while she could.

"I'm going to put my pants back on. I'd like to keep my ass a private matter." She pushed herself up and he hissed as his cock slid from her body. The physical connection she missed immediately, but the truth was they had something deeper, something that went beyond touch or feel.

She grabbed her clothes and opened the passenger door. The warehouse was still silent, save for the lessening rain. The calm before the storm? Maybe. But their lives were in a constant state of upheaval these days.

Clothed once more, she crawled back into the car. Emery had cleaned up and his jeans once more sat low on his hips. Had she ever noticed the dips of muscle along either hip bone, pointing toward his crotch? Another time she'd have to appreciate them more, but now she was too tired.

Emery grabbed her hand and pulled her back on top of him. The Bel Air had a big front seat, and they covered every inch of it.

"I turned the cameras away from the car. They can still see the windows above us in one shot, but not the car."

She rolled the statement around in her head. On one hand, his attention to detail was sweet. On the other, he'd totally planned on coming here and banging her lights out. She chuckled and squeezed him tighter.

"Wait . . . does that mean . . ." The guys knew? That they were together? A little panic went through her . . . but what were they hiding?

"Julian and Gabriel know." He went still under her, maybe a little tense.

"Roni is going to chew me out." She winced.

"Why?"

"She didn't know first." She thumped his chest. "Thanks

a lot for getting me in trouble. You could have at least waited an hour."

"They figured it out on their own." He sounded almost guilty.

"I'm not mad, but Roni might be. She'll get over it."

"You're okay with people knowing?"

"You'd keep me a secret?"

"No."

"Then why hide it?"

"I don't know."

"Neither do I." She smiled at him. "I like talking to you."

"I'm tired of talking. It takes effort."

"Okay." She kissed his lips. "Go to sleep."

She settled back against his chest and smiled when he rubbed her back. Yeah, because she could so walk away from this. She was a goner.

Chapter Twenty

Emery stabbed the computer keys with his fingers. The screen could barely hold his attention. Tori had followed him into the security office after a couple hours of deep sleep in the Bel Air and promptly curled up in a bed made of two office chairs situated seat-to-seat. It was beyond him how she could possibly be comfortable enough to sleep contorted into a pretzel, but if he were her size, maybe it wouldn't be so bad. More than anything, her presence calmed him. Even if all he wanted to do was watch her breathe.

He could watch her sleep for hours if he had the time. Instead, he had hundreds of video files from Greenworks to slog through. His transmitter worked beautifully. Even now he could get a real-time feed if he wanted to watch a bunch of dark rooms. He'd tabbed through the current time stamps to see what, if any, activity was going on at Greenworks, but the factory was quiet.

There were far too many files to go through, so he focused on the cameras covering the gates, writing down license plate numbers of cars in three columns: Eleventh, Staff, and Unknown. On another piece of paper, he kept tally marks in an attempt to figure out how many people might be in the facility at a given time.

He was determined to find out who the old man with the security detail was and how he fit into the picture.

It didn't take a genius to figure out that CJ would be out for blood. Julian just wanted to cause havoc and knock heads together. Aiden would want to hold back, make a plan, and evaluate the situation. When those three got together, it would explode. CJ had always been somewhere in the middle of things, but now it was hard to tell.

CJ had emerged from the office for a few moments to grab something to drink and use the bathroom. He'd still worn blood-soaked clothing, but the most telling thing of all was his eyes. CJ had always been reserved, but now his gaze was dead. Lifeless. He didn't care. Whatever happened today, it wouldn't be good.

A black town car with heavily tinted windows rolled across the frame in triple time. Emery jabbed the pause button and scrolled it back until he could see the license plate—except the digits were obscured. There were a number of tricks, from special covers to clear grip tape, that could do that. Who would want to hide their license plate number, besides a drag racer? Could it be the Geezer?

He let the footage roll in real time. As the car left the frame, he switched feeds, tabbing to the corresponding time code. The car stopped and the driver got out, but before he could open the back door a man pushed it open.

"Who are you?" Emery peered at the image.

He was older, with white hair and a thin build. The Geezer. Unlike most of Evers's people who moved in and out of the building, he was dressed in a black suit and his eyes were shielded by sunglasses. He scanned the roads once before walking toward the building. Emery scrambled to change cameras, tracking the man and a few of Evers's people through the building. Who was he? The way people

moved out of his way, he was clearly someone important.
There were gaps in the coverage, but he didn't lose them
until the group of six men entered something that looked
like a set of offices or maybe a conference room.

What was in there?

Emery pushed back, rummaging in the stack of papers
and things he'd dumped on the desk until he came up with a
tablet. He pulled down a couple files from his cloud storage
and opened the blueprints to the Greenworks building.

"What are you doing?" Tori groaned and stretched,
sticking one leg straight up in the air.

Huh. He'd have to remember she bent that far.

"Nothing. Go back to sleep." He zoomed in on the doors
where he'd lost them. Beyond there was a whole section of
rooms, like a honeycomb, that weren't covered by cameras.
Whatever was back there was a mystery.

Evers's operation was predominantly drug-based. This
could be the new warehouse for the merchandise the street
thugs would sell. Having the expendable Eleventh on the
payroll meant a direct line to customers and a highly
mobile fleet of deliverymen. It could be a perfect reason
for the perceived lack of activity on the part of Evers's
people during his incarceration. Once more Emery kicked
himself for letting the Eleventh fall through the cracks.

"What's this?" Tori wrapped her arms around his neck
from behind. Her breasts pressed against his shoulders and
she rested her cheek on his head.

"You're supposed to be sleeping."

"So are you."

"I slept. I'm good."

"What? Two hours?"

"It's enough."

"Whatever. What's this?"

"Blueprints for the Greenworks building."

"Is there anything you can't get your hands on?" She kissed his temple and splayed her hands over his chest.

Her heart. He couldn't touch that. There was no way to make her love him back, though right now knowing she wanted him was enough.

"I have a theory. Tell me how this sounds." He detailed his thoughts on Evers's use of the Eleventh. Tori remained quiet while he detailed each reason he thought it was a sound idea.

"That sounds good, except I don't see Raibel Canales working for Michael Evers, you know?" She pivoted and sat on the desk. "Think about it. Evers took Canales down a few pegs, so Canales retaliated and got Evers busted. They aren't going to work together by choice."

He blew out a breath.

"They're working for someone else. Maybe the guy we met at the docks. What if he's the real boss behind them all?" He clasped his hands together behind his head and stared at the ceiling.

"I don't know." She shrugged.

"What do you think?"

"I think he's someone important, but he's not Evers. He doesn't have the presence to intimidate people. Do you have Evers's friends on file or a list or something?"

"Yeah. I've got files on anyone Evers has ever spoken to. His associates, friends, buyers, suppliers, even the guy who cuts his lawn." He brought up a digital corkboard where he'd pinned the information of a couple dozen people of interest.

"Okay." She peered at the screen. "Wait, he was already here?" She pointed at the grainy image of the Geezer he'd just imported to the program.

"No. I just added him."

"From what?"

"He's on the tapes from Greenworks." He pulled the

camera footage up on another screen and backed it up so she could get the full impact of the man in the suit with Evers's people.

"He dresses like Evers does, but not as flashy." She squinted at the image. "Evers always stuck out because he was so well dressed. This guy's . . . old. Old money? Mob? Could that be the Russian connection?"

"Maybe."

"What if he's a buyer? Or some port official?"

"They take officials out to fancy meals; they don't show them their stock."

"Is that what they're doing?"

"No idea. No cameras in that area."

"Damn."

"Yeah."

"Okay, so he's clearly someone important, but would the boss come count beans?"

"Probably not."

"Then this guy isn't *the* boss, but maybe he's Evers's boss? The person over him? Do we know who has been paying for Evers's defense?"

"His on-again, off-again socialite girlfriend, Fiona Gonzalez. They've been off since January, but she showed up with his lawyers the day he was arrested. Hasn't been around since, but phone records show he's gotten a couple of calls from her." He clicked on the image of an artificially beautiful woman. He also had a list of the nips and tucks she'd had, to obtain such a flawless appearance.

"What's their connection?"

"Not much. Parties mostly. Some vacations. But she's not leaning on him for cash."

"Is he paying her back? Where's her money come from?"

"Someone might be giving her cash to cover the lawyer fees. Hers comes from family. Rich people stuff. All aboveboard and clean. Believe me, I've been all over her life back when we started."

Tori sighed and massaged her temples. "This is crazy. Why are we doing this?"

"Because we were hired to."

"I might have liked you better when you didn't talk so much." She smiled and that damn invisible hand gripped his heart. She nudged him with her toe. "Kidding. Keep talking. What should we do?"

He'd thought about that. There were options, but they all hinged on CJ, Julian, and Aiden coming to an agreement. Something he wasn't sure would happen once they were all in a room together.

"Yo," Julian yelled from across the warehouse.

A car horn blared three short bursts.

Aiden and the rest of the crew had arrived.

Tori pushed off the desk and scampered around, shoving her feet into shoes. He followed at a slower pace. He was glad everyone else was here safe and sound, but the circus was about to start.

The rolling door rose and one after another, three barely legal street rides rolled into the warehouse. Their engines drowned out all other noise and the music pumping in Roni's car alone was enough to deafen them all.

Tori jogged to her sister's Lancer and opened the driver's door. Roni stood, wrapping her sister in a tight hug. John and Aiden killed their engines and slowly got out of their cars. They didn't appear the worse for wear, though they had taken twice as much time to get home as they should have.

Julian got to Aiden first. The two men clasped hands and slapped each other on the shoulder. Emery approached slowly. Madison was already tucked under Aiden's arm by the time he reached the two other men. Gabriel and John stood off to one side, their heads together. Roni and Tori weren't paying attention to the rest of them, and from what he could make out by watching their lips, neither was even speaking English. Looked like he needed to brush up on his Russian.

"Emery, what happened?" Aiden asked him.

"Julian get you caught up?" Emery nodded at the other man.

"Yeah, but where were you? What went down? Where's CJ?"

Emery glanced over his shoulder at the office. The light was back on. Sooner or later, they were going to have to do something about the agent. He gave Aiden the short version while the others gathered round.

"I'm going to go talk to CJ." Aiden let go of Madison and took a step toward the office. "Emery, walk with me."

Together they strode away from the group and through the bays they used for a variety of automotive purposes.

"How bad was it?" Aiden asked.

"Bad."

"How is he?"

"Don't know."

"What about Tori?"

"What about her?"

Aiden glanced at him and frowned.

"You've been into her for a while now. Just wondering."

Emery didn't reply immediately. He'd tried to hide his obsession, but Aiden was one of the people he spent the most time with. If anyone would have known, it would be him.

"Tori is good. Upset. But we all are."

"And CJ hasn't come out at all?"

"Not for anything besides water, coffee, and some food. He hasn't spoken to us."

They crossed the last few yards in silence. Aiden stepped up to the door and knocked on the metal.

"CJ? It's Aiden and Emery. Can we come in?" He tilted his head toward the door, but there was no sound from within.

Emery shrugged and twisted the doorknob. Unlike before, it gave under his grip and swung inward.

CJ sat at the desk Kathy had used. It faced away from the door, was devoid of anything personal, and carried no mark of her presence. Yet, it had been hers. The monitor was off and the remains of the food and drink CJ had consumed lay scattered on the surface along with the firearm he'd taken from their captors. Kathy's killers.

"CJ?" Aiden said.

"What?" CJ's voice was gruff and raw.

"Wanted to check on you, man." Aiden stepped into the room. Emery followed, at a loss for what to say or do.

How did they ease the pain of Kathy's passing? The loss wasn't real to Emery, not yet.

"Everyone here?" CJ asked.

"Yeah, we're all here." Aiden stood beside the desk, hands on his hips, but CJ didn't glance at either of them. He just stared straight ahead at the dark screen.

"Good. I want everyone together in ten minutes." CJ stood and the chair rolled back. "I know you've been on the road, but we've got work to do."

"You sure that's what you want?"

CJ turned toward Aiden. His face was gaunt and his eyes rimmed with red.

"We're going to kill those bastards. Get the crew."

Aiden glanced at Emery. This wasn't going to go well. From Aiden's frown, it didn't take a lot to figure out that he didn't like the plan, and they all knew Julian would back up anything to do with going balls to the wall.

Emery tilted his head toward the door.

"I'll get the crew." Aiden turned on his heel and left the office.

CJ stared after him, gaze narrowed.

"If it was Madison—"

Emery held up his hands. They'd stormed Evers's mansion for Madison. For one of their own? He wasn't ruling out homicide. Look at what he'd done for Tori. Matvei's death didn't even weigh on his conscience.

CJ scrubbed his face with his hand.

"Want a change of clothes?" Emery asked.

"Sure." CJ glanced down at himself.

Emery crossed to the bunk room and grabbed a set of CJ's clothes. Kathy's hung next to his in the lockers-turned-wardrobe. He grabbed her clothes and stashed them on top of the lockers out of sight. Later, once things settled, he'd make sure her things got packed up. For now, he returned to the office and handed the polo and jeans to CJ before turning his back on the other agent.

"Thanks. Aiden's not going to be on board with this, but I need you to convince him. You've always been better at getting in his head than I am." Clothing rustled as CJ shed his ruined garments.

"What do you have in mind?" Emery listened to Aiden, that's what the difference was. Unlike Julian, Aiden thought things through.

"Kill them."

"How?"

"With a gun. My bare hands if I have to."

Shit. Not good.

"Who do we want to kill?"

"All of them. The hit team. The Eleventh. That fucking bastard who ran off. They all need to die."

"Did you call it in?" Emery asked. His only hope now was an FBI intervention.

"Why should I? They didn't warn us and they fucking knew what was going on. They fucking knew." His voice rose until he yelled the last words at Emery.

"Who told you that?"

"Come on."

Emery glanced over his shoulder. CJ tucked the gun into his waistband. Great. Bereft and loaded. Emery didn't for a second believe CJ had called anyone at the FBI field offices. He was operating on assumption, grief, and the desire to strike back.

The crew was in the bunk room, cups of coffee handed out as they were brewed. These were not the conditions under which they should be planning an urban battle. They should relocate, regroup, and then make a plan, but that wasn't going to happen. Something was going down in the next few hours and it wouldn't be pretty.

"CJ." Tori took a few steps toward them when they entered the bunk room, but stopped a couple of feet short. Anguish twisted her features into a pained expression.

CJ reached for her, squeezing her arm and muttering something only for her ears. She nodded and glanced at Emery. The others stopped speaking, all eyes on CJ. The silence stretched on. He walked to the other end of the bunk room. A whiteboard took up most of the surface and provided a stark background. Despite the change of clothes, Emery could almost see Kathy's blood still clinging to him.

He crossed his arms and hung back near the door while everyone turned to face CJ. Tori came to stand by Emery's side, so close she even leaned her head on his shoulder. He curled his hand into a fist and for a second didn't dare to breathe. Julian and Gabriel knew. Roni would know if she didn't already. Were they at this point already? Was he allowed to touch her?

Madison sat next to Aiden on a cot in front of Emery.

Aiden hooked his thumb in the waistband of her shorts. A possessive action, when Aiden hadn't exactly been the possessive type in the last few years. Emery had watched the growing familiarity between the two, so he'd seen the gradual change, how they touched without being aware of it. Was that what it might be like with Tori? If they ever got the chance.

"Thank you all for your support." CJ cleared his throat. "We're lucky more of us weren't hurt. It's still early, but today's going to be a long one. Evers's people haven't hit us yet, but they're going to. We need to hit them first."

Silence greeted this statement.

"What does the home office say?" Aiden asked.

"Does it matter?" CJ planted his hands on his hips and leaned forward.

"Look, man, I'm right there with you, but is this the best plan? Maybe we should get backup." Aiden leaned forward, planting his elbows on his knees. It was Madison's turn to stroke his back in a show of support.

"We've called for backup—how many times, Emery?" CJ pointed at Emery and suddenly all eyes were on him.

Emery shrugged and CJ went on without his input.

Six times they'd called in requests for support, to tip off any number of the alphabet soup of agencies, yet nothing had happened. It was frustrating to have everything lined up exactly as they were supposed to and yet be told it wasn't good enough. Why were they here then? To be bait? Act as a decoy? *Frustrating* wasn't a strong enough word. They'd been betrayed by the very organization they'd fought to support, but Emery wasn't on board with taking the crew rogue. It didn't look like he was going to get a choice in the matter.

Aiden was the conservative left. Julian and CJ the extremists on the right. Everyone else fell somewhere in the middle. Tori had seen everything, and he wouldn't fault her for wanting to ease her conscience and help CJ. Where Tori went, he expected Roni would as well. With Gabriel's history, Emery expected the former agent to hold very little value in adhering to the rules their superiors were breaking. John, well, he was probably closer to Aiden's stance, but Emery didn't really know.

The key was going to be keeping them all alive no matter what happened. He glanced at Tori, his new reason for breathing. For her sake, he needed to come up with a plan before CJ and Julian led them in a fatal frontal assault.

Chapter Twenty-One

The room was so loud with CJ, Julian, and Aiden yelling at each other that Tori covered her ears. She totally understood what CJ wanted. To some degree, she wanted an eye for an eye, but they'd already killed Matvei. Or Emery had. Her tummy twisted at the memory. She hadn't even asked him about that or how he was doing.

"What would you have us do? Stick our thumbs up our asses and sit around, waiting for a hit team to come through the doors or the Eleventh to wreck us on the road?" Julian bent forward at the waist, his bloodshot gaze on Aiden.

"No, that's not what I'm saying. I just don't want anyone else to die because you go off half-cocked." To Aiden's credit, he was trying to keep his calm, something that hadn't happened very often before Madison entered his life.

"So we call the FBI?" Julian straightened and crossed his arms.

"Yeah, you know, the people who write your paycheck? Fuck knows you don't do enough around the shop to earn shit." Aiden glared.

"The FBI is using all of us," CJ interjected before Julian could get worked up over that little bomb.

Aiden and Julian were co-owners of Classic Rides, but it was no question who ran it. Aiden kept it going and operating as a business while Julian showed up for a couple hours a week to put in an appearance before going to play spy. It was a point of contention, and Tori fell on Aiden's side. It was usually her responsibility to pick up Julian's slack. No one could argue with the FBI, who practically owned Julian.

"No one's arguing that." Gabriel leaned against the far wall. He'd perked up quite a bit since his nap. Sure, the bruises looked bad, but he seemed to be back to himself, which was good if they were going to go storm anything.

"I'm not saying we don't attack them. Can we just have a goddamn plan?" Aiden blew out a breath and the room seemed to exhale with him.

"We're wasting time here." Emery's voice skated across her skin and her body took notice. "We don't know where the hit team is, and the Greenworks building is built like a compound. We can't just drive up and shoot it. Aiden's right." He held up a hand to stave off an argument from CJ and Julian. "If you'll pull your heads out of your asses you'll realize we're all saying the same thing. Give me ten minutes. I'll see what I can find out. Get us inside Greenworks."

"What's the point of getting inside?" Aiden asked.

"We want to accomplish something. Well, let's do that. Our mission from the beginning was to shut Evers's operation down. Today he gets out of jail at eight o' clock. That's just a couple of hours from now and he's back at the head of this thing. If we take it down before he's out—he's done. He'll have no structure, no product, nothing. We cut the legs out from under him the only way we can. From the inside of Greenworks. And if the FBI won't back us up, call in the cops. Once we have the Eleventh and this new leader in custody, we can flush out the hit team, if they're even still in Florida. For all we know, they're already headed back up north."

She stared at Emery, still fascinated he could put that many sentences together. That, and he was basically telling their leadership to grow the fuck up. It was pretty damn hot.

"We are in a no-win situation." He swept the room with his gaze, all eyes on him. "We sit here, we're targets. We call the FBI, they tie our hands. We launch an offensive against them, well, we'd be on everyone's shit list, but we could do it. The only option to color inside the lines is to run away. We've never run, and if we do, we ruin all the work we've done over the last three years. So we have to protect ourselves. But we don't have to throw away our lives to do it."

For several seconds, no one else spoke. Emery was a quiet power within their crew. He'd never really flexed his muscle until now, and man, did he have muscle to flex.

"Okay, what do we need to do to make that happen?" Aiden asked.

"Ten minutes." Emery held up his hands. "Don't do anything for ten minutes."

"You got it," Julian said, slanting his gaze toward Aiden. The two had pulled each other out of situations worse than this. The least they could do was avoid murdering the other for a little bit longer.

Emery jerked his head in a nod and turned, striding out of the door and no doubt back to the security room. Curious gazes slid toward her. Screw it. Her sister knew; Julian, Gabriel, and CJ could all fill them in. She followed Emery, jogging to catch up with his long strides as he entered the security office.

He rounded the desk and glanced at her.

"What are you going to do?" she blurted.

"Don't know." He sank into the desk chair and turned toward the monitors.

"What can I do?" She clasped her hands together, unsure where to start. She was good with action, doing things, but Emery's specialty was in an area she couldn't begin to help with.

Aiden stepped into the office, glancing between the two of them before settling his gaze on Emery.

"We need to talk." He grabbed the door and swung it shut, blocking out the low hum of conversation while the others dispersed from the bunk room.

Emery merely glanced up at Aiden before returning to tap at the keys.

"This is a suicide mission to CJ. He doesn't even care who we hit, so long as someone dies," Aiden said.

"Then we can't do this," Tori blurted.

Tori sat down hard. The thought had come to her, but she'd shied away from the idea of losing both CJ and Kathy. What was worse, Emery didn't deny it.

"We either go with him, or he goes by himself." Aiden stared at the desk. "There's no best way to handle this. There's just—doing it."

"That's what I'm trying to figure out—a way to do it. What do you want?" Emery's tone was brusque. There was too much to do and she wanted to shield him from having to shoulder more.

"Two things." Aiden's lips were thin, hard lines, his posture tense. "Madison recognized the surveillance picture of the older man."

"The Geezer?" Emery paused his typing.

"Yeah, said she knew him as the owner of that company that Evers used to ship those cars. Mr. White."

"Well, that's an alias." Tori rolled her eyes. There were a few names so incredibly common that they stuck out.

"I want to talk to her. See what she can remember. Maybe we can get some additional records from the FBI. He could be the link we need to figure all of this out." A break. That's all they needed. One break to solve this thing. There was no way Evers was the boss. The evidence, the continued success of his operation, that couldn't have happened without someone directly in charge of things while Evers was in custody. Emery grabbed a pen and jotted down a list of questions on the back of an envelope.

"Also, do you think we can use Detective Smith?" Aiden asked. "If we're going off the rails here, we need someone to make the arrests."

Emery's fingers paused on the keys for a moment.

"Yes," he replied.

"Okay. Good. I don't think—"

"I will call Smith. Julian will just start a fight if you're involved. Get some sleep, try not to get in a pissing match with Julian." Emery examined the blueprints for Greenworks.

"You got a plan?" Aiden asked.

"I will if you and everyone else will leave me the hell alone for a minute."

"Sorry, man." One side of Aiden's mouth hitched up and he glanced at Tori. Seems she wasn't the only one to notice the change in Emery's behavior. "Let me know when you've got something."

She glanced away from Aiden. Was this change her fault? She didn't think it was a bad thing. Emery was smart. He should have more of a say in what they did, especially because they all leaned on him so much.

Aiden left without another word and Emery didn't deign to speak. She had nothing to offer in the planning department. Instead, she gathered the mess of wrappers and cups from the desk and tiptoed out of the office. If they were going to survive on just a few hours of sleep, they were both going to need a little liquid stimulation.

She dumped the trash in one of the garbage cans scattered through the warehouse. Roni, Gabriel, and John had their heads together looking at John's truck, the same one that had been forced off the road. From where she stood, Tori couldn't spy any damage done to the exterior. CJ and Julian stood in the doorway to the office. There was no sign of Madison or Aiden, which was probably for the best. The boys couldn't start anything if they weren't rubbing each other the wrong way. She went back to the bunk room and brewed two cups of coffee.

"What about Emery?" Roni's voice startled Tori. She jumped, turning toward the door, poised to throw the cup of scalding liquid at her sister.

"Shit. Don't do that." Tori shook her head and pressed her hand to her chest.

"Sorry." Roni chuckled and selected one of the coffee pods for herself.

Tori glanced around before grabbing her sister's arm and pulling her deeper into the bunk room.

"We need to talk about—Papa."

"Sh." Roni glanced over her shoulder at the door.

"Emery knows. CJ does, too. It's a matter of time until the others find out. We need to contact him. To tell him not to come here, that he might need to burn his identity."

"Goddamn it." Roni stared at the ceiling. "I like this life."

"I do, too." Tori had Emery now. She wasn't going to give that up. "I can't make contact with Emery around me all the time. Can you put out an ad?"

"Yeah. Yeah, I'll handle it. Plus, we can't ask Emery to turn a blind eye if he never sees it happening. Consider it done."

"Thanks, and I'm sorry."

"For what?"

"This. All of it."

"If I was in town, they'd have been after me, too. The only reason they were after your ass is because you were here. And thank God Emery had your back."

"Yeah, yeah, I know." It didn't make her feel any less responsible.

"You owe me details."

"I don't know where to start." Tori blew out a breath. Three days and her life was in a completely different place.

"I'm not interrupting, am I?" Madison paused in the doorway, one hand gripping the frame.

"Nope. Just asking my sister when she's going to tell me about whatever it is she's been doing with the Walking Brain." Roni leaned against the cinder-block wall, grinning.

Tori frowned, unable to shake the sudden irritation. *Doing with him?* Of course Roni would take the boiled-down version of the last few days and assume it was a fling, a simple fuck she needed to get out of her system. As if she could—or wanted—to forget Emery.

"You've woken him up, that's for sure." Madison picked through the basket of coffee choices. "I dig Emery. I think someone like you could be good for him. Shake him up, ya know?"

Tori smiled. Yeah, she felt the same way. Look what she'd accomplished so far. The man was a conversational prodigy in just a couple of days.

"Please. He's a computer geek." Roni shook her head.

"He is not just a computer geek." Tori turned on her sister and jabbed Roni's shoulder with her finger. "I'm sick of you talking about him that way."

"Wow, I didn't—" Roni held up her hand, eyes going round.

"No, that's exactly what you meant. Do you realize he does more for us than fart around on computers and shit?

Do you have any idea what he goes through for us?" Anger simmered just under Tori's skin.

"Dude, I—"

"You don't care that I like him. That maybe he might be more than a screw to me. I'm sick of hearing that from you."

Roni stared at her. Between them, Tori usually took a backseat to Roni's more vocal nature, but sometimes a girl had to stand up for herself. They might be twins, but they weren't identical in every regard. Tori was in love with Emery, and while she wasn't ready to admit that much, she was taking a stand for what they might have together, so long as other people kept their opinions to themselves.

"Okay. My bad. Sorry." They stared at each other for a moment. Roni shifted from foot to foot and Tori balled her free hand into a fist. It wasn't a good idea to punch her sister, but right now she wanted to. "It's not that I don't like him. I do. I just want the best for you, and with how we work, that's someone who's got your back."

"I think Emery proved that." Tori glanced down at the second cup of coffee that was finished brewing, but it wasn't coffee she saw. It was Matvei in those last seconds. Emery hadn't even hesitated when he shot the man.

"He did, didn't he? You still owe me details about that." Roni nudged her aside and dropped her coffee in the machine.

"You two done with the sister act? Or should I go?" Madison stared at them, and with good reason. It wouldn't be the first time Roni and Tori duked it out to blow off some steam. Sometimes they were as bad as the guys.

"Nah, we're good." Roni grinned. "I think he fucked some spunk into you."

Tori's jaw dropped.

"Uh, that could be taken two different ways," Madison said.

"Shit. The good way!" Roni slapped her forehead and Tori laughed.

Madison tossed her head back, and that was it. All three were lost in a fit of giggles; Tori's side ached she laughed so hard. They leaned on each other, and even Madison was overcome to the point of tears. Gabriel stuck his head in, frowning at them.

"You girls high or something?" he asked.

"No, nothing, go away." Madison waved him off.

"I cannot believe you said that." Tori wiped her tears away and grabbed the coffee.

"Hold on. What exactly are you wearing?" Roni asked, holding her at arm's length.

"I'm not sure. They're jeans. It's a tank top. They cover me." Tori wasn't about to mention the cheap quality of her panties and where that had gone.

"Before we go anywhere, you need a change of clothes, because that is so not acceptable." Roni's nose wrinkled. Only one of them could have fashion sense, and it wasn't Tori.

"Thanks."

"Hey, what are sisters for?"

Tori grinned at her sister. They always had each other's back.

Madison grabbed a napkin and swiped at her cheeks, reminding Tori there were other things in the works.

"Madison, when you have a second, Emery has some questions for you about Mr. White." Tori picked up the coffee, one in each hand.

"Oh. Right. Aiden told him." Madison blew out a breath.

"I missed something, didn't I?" Roni glanced between them.

"I recognized the old guy from the surveillance footage.

I've met him. It's all so crazy." Madison poured a cup of coffee. "Just tell Emery to text me when he wants to ask me the questions. I don't know a lot."

"It's more than we knew earlier."

Tori left the bunk room, feeling lighter. She didn't like butting heads with her sister, but she didn't mind standing up for herself either. Roni didn't have to understand why Tori was falling for Emery, she just wanted her sister to support her. Maybe now she would. Emery deserved better than her, but she wasn't about to let him go. The man had made the choice when he'd left IHOP with her instead of just letting her bolt.

Emery was still intently staring at the screens when she returned. She placed the coffee and sugar in easy reach before taking up a spot near the door. He patted the sugar packets, finding them by touch and selected two of them. He prepared the cup without ever looking at it.

This wasn't the first time she'd watched him work. Usually it was in small doses amidst the heat of a crazy operation. This was different. She was a fly on the wall, soaking up exactly what it must be like to be him every day. It was amazing what one person could do with the right tools. How many things did Emery take care of in the background while they went on about their lives? What threats did he head off before they ever knew about them? He really was more than the amazing Walking Brain.

"There's only one approach," he said into the silence. He tapped at the screen, as if she could see what he was talking about. She didn't dare move for fear of breaking his concentration or train of thought. "It was built for semis to drive into the plant. It's the most vulnerable access point to the whole facility. The docks go all the way to the side of the building. We could ram the gates if they're closed, drive through the lot, up the ramp, and into the building. We'd want to get into the main chamber before getting

ut of the cars. Then it's a thirty-yard dash to these rooms
where they've got—whatever it is they're holding in there."

"When?" she asked.

"Let's see what's going on there. It's only"—he glanced
at the clock on the wall—"four in the morning."

She rose, creeping around behind Emery to see what
he saw.

He flipped through several camera feeds, but the Greenworks building was quiet. Most of the lights were off.

"You think they packed up shop?" she asked.

"No—there." Emery stopped on a screen. It was the
docks. Canales and six of his crew were gathered together
while he talked. Or more likely yelled, talking smack, if
he had to guess from his liberal use of gestures. "They
must be staying at the plant."

"Where's the hit team?"

"No idea. I haven't been able to track them anywhere."

"They could be gone, right?"

"Maybe. Best to assume they're still out there."

"We could go now. Grab the Eleventh. Smith would
love to arrest them."

"CJ wants blood. He'll push for going later."

"Well, it's Sunday. The place probably doesn't run at
full capacity if at all. They said they weren't producing
anything yet, right? Wasn't that what you said?"

"Yeah, it was more like they were getting ready to do
something."

"So not a lot of workers there today." And how were
they supposed to get the hit team to go where they wanted
them to?

"Let's call Smith. Get him up to speed." Emery grabbed
a cell phone sitting on the desk and jabbed in a string of
numbers.

"Do you remember *everything*?" she asked.

"No, but his number seemed important at the time."
Emery tilted his head to the side.

She could hear the call ringing in the quiet office.

A groggy masculine voice answered. "Who is this?"

"Detective Smith, it's Emery Martin."

"What happened this time?"

Emery glanced at her, brows pulling down. She shrugged
only a little guilty at her not-so-subtle attempt to eaves
drop. He shook his head and jabbed the speaker key.

"Emery? You there?" Matt asked.

"Yeah, sorry, you're on speaker with me and Tori. You
know Kathy died. Our crew is back from Orlando. Things
are looking pretty dicey here. I was hoping you would like
to make a few arrests today."

"Who?"

"Raibel Canales."

"When? Where?"

"The Greenworks plant. I'll send you the address. It's in
Fort Lauderdale. Think you can find a reason to be around?
Not sure of the when yet."

"What do you guys have planned?"

"Not much right now, but things are getting kinda
hairy."

"What exactly is going on? I was able to put people off
yesterday by saying it was a federal case, but that's not
going to last long, especially with two departments involved."

"Take down this number. Ready?" Emery rattled off a
string of digits. "You need anything to cover your ass, call
that number. It's the director in charge of this operation.
The hit team was better than I expected. Last night they
shot Kathy, grabbed us, and we had to shoot our way out
of where they were holding us. The hours since then have
been tense. We're okay, but either they find us or we find
them. Things aren't running exactly to code right now,
which is why I want you there to make any arrests so i

an't be argued in court that we were rogue. If you do it, there's no question. And if you have to arrest us at the same time, do it."

The line was silent for a moment. Emery glanced at her and she had to wonder what else was going on with Detective Matt Smith.

"You're asking a lot of me." Matt's voice was gruff, a little beat down.

"I know that," Emery replied.

"My ass is already on the line over Evers."

"Well, if someone should report gunfire at the Greenworks building and you should just happen to be nearby when the call comes in, who could fault you for showing up? Like I said, arrest us if you have to."

"And put you in jail with the people you've put there? No, thanks. I'd like to keep the inmate death rate at zero if possible."

"Your call."

"Don't be anywhere that I'd need to arrest you and we'll be good."

"We appreciate the backup, man. You ever need anything, give me a call."

"I could get used to this. The Feds owing me favors."

"It's not all it's cracked up to be. Don't get used to it."

The two bantered a moment longer before Emery hung up the phone. He leaned his head back in the chair and closed his eyes. She sat in his lap and laid her head on his shoulder. He wrapped his arms around her, hugging her close. Being with him felt right. As if it was where she was meant to be.

"Do we have a plan now?" she asked.

"Yeah, but I don't like it."

"Think about all that's changed in the last six months. Did you ever think we'd get here?" Their operation had excelled at blending in. They'd gathered data, evidence, and had had a constant rotation of surveillance on Evers for close to three years. It had become more sophisticated over time, but they'd never stepped out of the shadows. I was a completely different game now.

"It was bound to happen eventually, but I think we al expected it to go down in one bust and be over. None of u: expected—this."

"Is it going to end?"

"I don't know."

"It has to at some point, doesn't it?"

"I suppose."

But would any of them be alive to see that ending?

Chapter Twenty-Two

Tori held her hands up, finally giving in and letting Emery go over the straps on her Kevlar vest himself. The thing was uncomfortable, not intended for a woman even with small breasts, but it would protect her from most center-mass shots. Of course, if the asshats shooting at her had body-armor-piercing rounds, she was toast anyway.

"It's good, Emery," she said, keeping her voice low.

His lips curled, as if he was holding back his real thoughts, and instead gripped her by the shoulders, his fingers curling under the vest.

"Be careful. Keep your head down. Get out of there if anything goes wrong. I don't like this." His gaze bored into her skull. He seemed to vibrate with intensity, but under that there was feeling, an emotion she could see, and if she stared deeply enough she could feel it, taste it, even smell it.

"I'll be okay. Promise."

She lifted up on tiptoes and pressed her mouth to his.

Truth was she might not survive the hour. Fifteen minutes after six, the same mysterious older gentleman had arrived at the Greenworks building at the same time as the remaining three Russian hit men. There was clearly something up, maybe something really bad. They also couldn't ask for a better opening. All the fish were in a single barrel. They just had to show up, hit them while they didn't expect anyone, and hope the cops showed up before they had multiple homicides on their hands.

Emery hadn't been able to tell what was being said between the three parties on the video feed. Hell, Tori could barely see their lips much less read them. The tension between the old guy, the Russians, and the Eleventh already at the building had telegraphed clearly, though. Something was happening at Greenworks and if their crew wanted a piece of the action they needed to get their wheels spinning.

Of course, they didn't know why the hit team after Tori and Roni were suddenly in bed with the Greenworks operation. It smelled fishy to Tori, but that didn't seem to matter to CJ. What were they doing? Were the remaining three assassins going rogue?

"I'll be watching you. Headsets won't be live until you exit the highway, but if you need me, buzz me." Emery backed away. There was a discordant vibration in the air that made her skin itch. They were separating. Emery wasn't going to be by her side, and that felt wrong.

"Ready?" Roni asked from the other side of the Lancer.

Tori glanced at her sister. The only other person to never fail her. Emery had to stay here and serve as their support. Without him they were blind. Gabriel's busted ribs and injuries were too much of a liability if they got into a jam. And Madison was only just learning how to hit what she aimed at. It sucked to leave them behind, but the purpose of this hit was to be quick.

"Yeah." The weight of extra ammunition hung on her hips. Two holsters were strapped to her legs. This kind of tactical gear was foreign to her, but the need was real.

She settled into the passenger side of Roni's Lancer and

blew out a breath. John and Aiden were in another car, with CJ and Julian in a third. The other two cars were tactical vehicles. Reinforced cars that ran a little heavy, but could be used for ramming things like gates and doors without taking too much of a beating or deploying airbags. They hadn't used them more than once or twice before for small, unrelated gigs the FBI had assigned them in the beginning.

"I put in an ad earlier, by the way," Roni said.

"Already?"

"The wonders of the Internet. He's going to know about all of this."

"Think he'll reply?"

"Nah. He'll be too pissed. I'd reckon we've got six to eight months before he makes contact."

"Does it hurt?"

"What?"

"Knowing that he's aware we're in trouble and he won't help? I mean, I don't know what he'd do, but he's our dad."

"And he was a coldhearted bastard who taught us how to fend for ourselves." Roni sighed. "But yeah, it does suck. I guess that's why Mom had us, so we'd be there for each other when they couldn't."

Julian's car whipped out of the warehouse and Roni gunned the engine to keep up. The force of the acceleration pressed Tori back into the seat as they peeled out and into the fenced-in lot, leaving any and all concern for their father behind.

The plan was to travel in a convoy, with Roni and Tori in the middle, right up until they went through the Greenworks gates. At that point, Aiden and Julian would take the lead to ram through anything in their way and clear a path straight to the heart of the building. They could drive up almost to the doors behind which the mysterious man and his entourage of criminals had disappeared.

"I'm going to have to scrap this car when this is over," Roni said mournfully.

"We can get you a new one," Tori replied.

"Yeah, but it won't be the same."

The streets of Miami passed in a blur. They broke more laws than they followed. Lights, stop signs, even pedestrian rights-of-way didn't register as they sped toward their target.

"What do you think happens after this?" Roni asked, raising her voice over the roaring engine.

"I don't know."

"We could leave. Right now." Roni glanced at her. She wasn't joking.

Tori shook her head. Friday, if Roni had asked her that she'd have yelled at her sister for not already being on the road out of town. Today things were different.

"If we leave it doesn't end, for them or for us. Besides, it wasn't us they wanted. It was Dad."

"Did you call him?"

"I left a message, told him to stay away."

"Good. We won't give these assholes what they want." Roni switched the radio off. They were both too tightly wound to listen to music.

"Emery knows, by the way. I had to tell him," Tori said in a rush, before Roni could cut her off.

"Why?"

"Because if I didn't make it off that ship, he had to be ready to make the call to you, and he wouldn't unless I told him why."

"Will he tell?"

"I don't think so."

"We should leave now. Get on the road while everyone is distracted."

"Then what? Where would we be?"

"We don't need the FBI," Roni said.

"You sure about that?" Tori glanced at her sister. The day they'd accepted the government contract that dumped them in Miami was the day several of their problems just went away. She wasn't stupid, and neither was Roni. For all the FBI's shortcomings, their protection went a long way in making their lives comfortable. The bad guys out in the world had to really want to mess with the twins if they were also going to tangle with the Feds. Sure, they could survive on their own, but would that be a life?

"Fine." Roni smacked the steering wheel with her palm. For a moment, neither spoke. "I just don't see this ending. This mission or the shit with Dad."

"I don't either."

The exit loomed ahead. Tori pulled one of the twin Glocks out of the holsters and checked the chamber to give herself something to do.

If tonight taught Tori anything, it was that they'd been living in a daydream where they got to keep their daddy's secret and pretend to be the good guys.

"Gabriel said you did Emery in the Bel Air." Roni grinned.

Tori stared at her sister, heat crawling up her neck.

"You did!" Roni thrust her finger at Tori.

"You said Gabriel already told you."

"I lied. But you did it! In the Bel Air? Nice."

"Shut up. I am not talking about that to you."

"If you can't talk to me, who can you talk to? And what if you die? What if I die?"

"Don't say that." Tori didn't like the flippant way Roni spoke, or even putting those ideas out there.

"I'm just saying if you're going to talk to anyone about it, it might as well be me." Roni glanced at her out of the corner of her eye. "Well? Did the shocks hold out at least?"

"Yes. Oh my God, yes!" Tori buried her face in her hands, the gun cradled between her thighs. Of course her sister would want to talk about sex right before they went in guns blazing.

"You really like him." Roni's nose scrunched up as they took the exit.

"I do."

"Okay, I won't knock it. He hurts you, though, I'm breaking his kneecaps."

Tori laughed and shook her head. Sisters. They were good for bodily threats, making inappropriate comments and being a shoulder to lean on. What more could she ask for?

The Bluetooth headset beeped in Tori's ear, the comms going live early.

"Power just flickered at Greenworks. Half the cameras are off-line." Emery's voice was all business, focused and devoid of emotion.

Tori glanced at her sister. They turned right, heading away from the highway. It was too late to abort. They were almost there. The sky was streaked with yellow and orange while the rising sun painted the clouds a myriad of colors. The tall smokestacks of the Greenworks building stuck out against that backdrop, growing steadily bigger.

"We are not deviating from the plan," CJ said through the headset.

Tori double-tapped her headset, activating the mute function. She could hear everything her team said, but they couldn't hear her. Roni followed suit, glancing at her.

"This is all too convenient," Tori said.

"What do we do?" Roni asked.

"We can't let them go in there without us." There'd been half a dozen people on the camera feeds, and she didn't know how many more might have arrived or were lying in wait.

"Tell me what we're doing, sis." Roni turned and the

entrance to the Greenworks facility came into view, maybe seventy-five yards ahead of them.

The other armored car passed Roni. She dropped back, following the plan.

"Stay with them. We might have to pull their asses out of the fire." Tori cursed under her breath and sat forward. She jabbed the automatic window button and the humid air whipped in, bringing with it the salty tang of the ocean and the scent of freshly cut grass.

Ahead of them, the first armored car made the ninety-degree turn, smashing through the security arm. Several tricked-out street rides sat at the ready, without drivers, in front of the docks.

She glanced at the security shack when they passed it.

The empty security shack.

"Something's not right." She slapped at the Bluetooth, activating the line. "This is wrong. There isn't anyone here."

The first car zoomed up the ramp, never once tapping its brakes.

"I can't see you," Emery replied.

The lead car hit the rolling metal gate. The car reversed, revealing a huge dent. The second car hit it. Metal screeched so loud Tori heard it over the roar of the engine. The first car rammed the door the instant the second reversed. The sound of metal things popping grated across Tori's nerves.

"Fuck, couldn't they just open the damn door?" Roni yelled over the noise.

The rolling door bent inward, the housing hanging from the roof. There was a car-shaped hole where the first armored car passed through. The second gunned the engine and shot through the same space, sparks flying from where it scraped by.

"Oh God, don't let the airbags deploy." Roni didn't punch the accelerator. She carefully maneuvered the Lancer through the space. Both girls cringed. The sagging door scraped the top of the car.

They made it safely through the open space, no worse for wear save a few scratches to the exterior. An overturned cart and a few flattened boxes were all that was left in the wake of the other two cars.

"Where are they?" Roni asked.

"I don't know."

Tori leaned forward, gun gripped in her right hand. She could hear the sounds of brakes, a metallic ping, but no yells, no security, no other sign of human life.

It was wrong. All of it. So why were they still going?

"Eleventh is in sight," Julian said. A second later brakes squealed down the hall.

Tori accelerated through the first chamberlike room, into the second, then the third.

"Fuck!"

Roni yanked on the emergency brake and turned the wheel. The car slid sideways, coming to a full stop parallel to the door. The two armored cars sat nose to nose, the four men crouched behind the hoods.

Tori dove out the passenger door, keeping low until she reached Aiden's side.

"What the hell?" she demanded as a shot went over their heads.

"Eleventh," he said.

"Anyone else?" She took a knee, hunching to stay below the car.

"Not that I see." Aiden's gaze remained locked on a target on the other side of the room.

Too easy.

She glanced behind them, but nothing moved.

"Something's wrong. This isn't right," she said, hoping the headset picked up her voice.

"Shoot, goddamn it!" CJ yelled at her.

The Eleventh had become street thugs. Raibel Canales was a sociopath, of that she had no doubt. But was that enough to kill them in a shootout? Was it worth risking her crew if she didn't take a shot?

Tori held the Glock in both hands, stretching her arms out along the hood of the car, lining up the sights.

The Eleventh had taken cover behind a couple of metal barrels.

A flash of movement slightly to the right caught her eye. The open doorway was dark, which made the neon quality of Raibel Canales's hoodie stand out more.

She exhaled and squeezed the trigger. The recoil reverberated up her arms. A blast of bullets followed, the sound so loud in the concrete space that her ears rang.

One of the Eleventh drivers held up his hands, then another.

Raibel Canales lay on the ground. As the gunfire ceased, she could hear his groan of pain. She couldn't bring herself to feel sorry for the bastard.

"Don't shoot," a young Cuban yelled. He made her think of the guy Emery had encountered at the bodega.

"What are you doing?" Canales groped around. Even from across the cavernous room she could see his face contorted in pain.

"Call Smith," she said, despite not being quite able to hear the headset from the residual deafness.

CJ and Aiden leapt over the hoods of the cars, crossing the distance in ground-eating strides. Julian was hot on their heels, while John, Roni, and Tori held their positions, guns aimed to cover their companions. She didn't take her gaze off the Eleventh, despite the skin between her shoulder blades crawling.

"Can you hear me?" The voice was masculine, much like Emery's, but her ears wouldn't stop ringing.

"Emery?" She shook her head. She circled the front of

one car, crossing with John and Roni toward the others. She kicked guns out of the way, taking mental stock of how many men, the guns, and injuries.

Where the hell were the Russian hit team and the Geezer?

Aiden, Julian, and CJ slipped restraints onto the wrists of each member of the Eleventh, even Canales and the other injured guy she'd never seen before.

"Where are the Russians?" CJ yelled in Canales's face.

Tori glanced over her shoulder, unable to ignore the sinking suspicion they'd fallen into a trap, yet there was nothing behind them. No one, save their team. There should at least have been weekend workers, someone to hear the racket. A janitor even.

"They left." Canales spat at CJ. Blood bathed the man's right arm from a wound to the meaty part of his shoulder. Raibel would live, but if there was any justice in this world, he was going to jail for a long time.

"Emery? You there?" She held her finger to the headset, pushing it farther into her ear.

"They're gone." Emery's voice was loud and he spoke slowly.

"They're what?" she asked.

CJ's spine straightened and Aiden glanced toward her.

"They're in a car headed west. Smith's got them," Emery said.

Tori blew out a breath. It was over. CJ wasn't getting blood, but it was over. No one else died. It would be okay.

Emery toggled between the cameras available to him at the Greenworks building. It would take time and too many hours to hack the various networks that controlled all of the red-light, teller, and security cameras up and down the streets around the compound. While there was a good chance the mystery man and hit team's escape was getting caught on a dozen different streams, it meant nothing to Emery without the man-hours to get the video. Hell, a court order might be faster in the long run, but wouldn't help him right now.

"Suspect vehicle is in sight."

The hit team was going down.

Emery glanced at the digital stream that represented the police scanner he'd hacked after a tip from Matt. The detective really was on their side. Emery just hoped it wasn't career suicide for the man.

"Proceed with caution." Matt's voice was louder, and from the echoing quality, Emery guessed he was inside the Greenworks building.

"Can you see them?" Gabriel hovered over Emery's shoulder, while Madison practically perched on his armrest. It made Emery's skin crawl. He was not used to working under anyone's eye save Kathy's and CJ's. Even Tori wasn't as intrusive with her constant stream of discourse.

"Hold on."

Emery muted his headset, changed the feeds again on the main display, and saw a dozen or more officers advance down the corridor toward where Tori and the others still held what was left of the Eleventh at gunpoint. Half a dozen had been picked up since their highway shootout last night. He might be wrong, but the Eleventh was on the verge of being wiped off the streets by the looks of it.

The crew was silent over the headsets.

"Is Aid—everyone okay?" Madison was holding it together. The woman had a knack for rolling with the punches, but the last couple of months were a lot for a civilian to take in.

"Aiden's okay," he replied.

His gaze dipped to the slender figure of Tori, her back to the camera, gun trained on one of the several unfortunate young men who had tossed their keys in with the Eleventh. Emery knew what a felony could do to a twenty-something like these guys. If it weren't for the FBI, he'd have lost everything. He'd never have met Tori. Things were different for him. For the Eleventh drivers and thugs? There weren't going to be many options.

The minutes dragged on. The police stepped in, making the arrests, and the EMTs rushed in to see to the two injured toughs, one of whom he recognized as the young man who had confronted him outside Greenworks a few days ago. Most of Emery's crew had their headsets muted, so it was hard to tell where they were in the process of Mirandizing the gang members. He could catch bits and pieces through one or two live mics, like Tori's from where she stood in the middle of it all.

"What's going on?" Gabriel pointed at CJ, who thrust his finger, poking John in the chest.

Emery blew out a breath.

"CJ's pissed. He wants to go after the hit team." Aiden pushed CJ's hand aside. "Aiden's telling CJ he called for the cop backup."

"Shit, this isn't good," Madison muttered.

"What about the cruisers arresting the hit team? Did they catch them?" Gabriel asked.

Emery glanced at the police scanner. There was plenty of chatter from the officers on the scene at Greenworks, but nothing from the cruisers in pursuit of the other vehicle.

He grabbed his phone and punched Dial on the last number called. It rang. He watched Detective Smith's figure on the security camera, but the man never once reached for his phone. The call went to voice mail after half a dozen rings.

Emery dialed it again, switching it to speaker while he

brought up a new browser window. He needed to see inside that cop car. They should have heard something from it by now. All cruisers were equipped with dash cams that fed video back in a slightly delayed feed. The Miami-Dade PD didn't have the dollars to spend like Evers's organization did on a top-notch security system. Regardless, Emery wanted to see the old guy's mug on his screen.

After a couple rings, the detective snatched the phone from his hip. They really were getting real-time video, which was damn impressive.

"What?" Matt asked.

"What's the number of the cruiser that was following the other car?"

"Fifty-one-S-two. Why?"

"I want to know what's going on with our suspects."

Matt turned his back and pitched his voice low. "This was too easy."

"I know."

"I want to know what's going on. Those are my men out there."

"I know."

Emery had a sick feeling. They'd been waiting for the other shoe to drop. Had they by chance fallen into a trap? Not one that would spring shut on them, just distract them long enough for the real players to escape? But what sense did it make to lure them to the Greenworks building if the others were going to simply slip off? What was their target?

He glanced at the clock.

"Where is Evers being released?" Emery asked.

"Don't know. It was being kept secret," Matt replied.

It only took a few keystrokes to hack into the police network. When this was over, Emery might have to repay his debt in some man-hours beefing up their system. He muttered to himself as he bounced from page to page, getting closer to the information he wanted.

"Emery, what are you doing?" Madison asked.

"Who's that?" Matt asked.

"Madison and Gabriel," Emery replied.

"Madison?" Matt repeated.

For a brief while, Emery had suspected Detective Matt Smith of harboring feelings for Madison. At least, that was how it appeared from the attention he paid her, and the police patrol he assigned to shadow her, at least until Aiden stepped in and cut the cops off from who they'd hoped would be their star witness. For all Madison knew, she was no star witness to hang a case on. Just a woman caught up at the wrong time and place.

"Hi, Matt." Madison's voice was tense.

"Hey, your man's here. He treating you okay?" Matt turned toward Aiden, still embroiled in a heated one-on-one with CJ.

"Yeah."

"Good. Good. I'd hate to have to kick his ass."

"Please don't." Madison chuckled.

Emery withheld his thoughts on that matter. He'd had his ass handed to him a number of times before he could ever hold his own against Aiden or Julian. The kind of training those men had beaten into them was the stuff that kept them alive when the shit got real. He didn't think Matt Smith had ever faced anything that bad, even on the streets of Miami.

"I'm not hearing anything from those cruisers," Gabriel said, keeping his voice low.

Yeah, Emery had noticed that. Not a peep. That couldn't be good.

"Got it," Emery said.

"What did you get?" Matt asked before anyone else.

"Where they're releasing Evers."

They'd known Michael Evers was being housed at the Dade Correctional Institution south of Miami, but thanks to the news coverage, not to mention enemies, he couldn't just be released from custody. He would be released at a different location, probably into the arms of friends, security, and lawyers who would keep his nose clean until trial.

"What's that got to do with anything?" Matt asked.

Emery didn't bother to reply, not when he was on a hunt. He sliced through the layers of police security, hacking his way without finesse. The dash cam videos were kept on an external server. Once he had the IP address, he didn't need the police access point. He dropped out of their system and after a few short seconds and one password-breaking program later he was into hundreds of files.

It took another couple of valuable seconds to orient himself to the way the files were stored. He skipped through the years to the current date, down into the unit until he found the fifty-one-S-two car. A supervisor? Smith must have pulled anyone and everyone he could get his hands on.

The feed blipped once before filling a bottom monitor.

"Oh my God." Madison turned.

"Fuck," Gabriel muttered.

Emery's stomach rolled.

"What? What is it?" Matt asked.

"This was a setup. We were supposed to focus all our attention on the Greenworks site. They're either about to hit you, or I bet they're going after Evers." Emery skipped through the other cars in the unit, discarding those that showed cops on patrol or that were off the clock.

"How? Where are they going?"

"Does dispatch monitor the dash cam feeds?" Emery asked.

"No. What is going on?" Smith demanded.

"Shit." Gabriel slapped the back of Emery's chair. "The guys in that car were done hitman-style."

"What?" Matt's voice cracked, rising at the end, from shock no doubt.

Emery pulled up another dash cam. This car didn't have officers in the front seats. Two men in navy button-up shirts that could never pass for police uniforms navigated the car. Only two? There should be three.

"I'm sorry, man, it looks like what's left of the hit team and this old guy took out the officers." Gabriel narrated the feeds as Emery searched for the other two Russians. Matt got on the horn with dispatch and radioed in the missing cruiser. Chances were, the officers were already dead, but maybe they'd get lucky and someone was still alive.

"There." Gabriel hunched lower over Emery's shoulder.

The older man was still in his black suit, while the third hit man drove another cruiser. The GPS feed of the vehicle was easy enough to skim and place on a map in real time.

"They're headed for Evers." Emery glanced at the clock. "He's being released in twenty-three minutes. At a private residence. Madison, I need you to sit here and watch the feeds. If anything changes, if they do anything, tell me."

He jerked open a drawer, thrusting the Bluetooth head-sets at Gabriel and Madison.

To Madison's credit, she didn't balk or shy away from the responsibility. She sat down in the seat he vacated and blew out a breath, staring at the screens. He reached over her and killed the feed on the dead cops. They were going to have enough on their hands without the weight of the dead on their shoulders.

"What the hell is going on?" CJ's voice roared over the channel.

"Update him," Emery said to Madison. He ushered Gabriel out of the security office. "Get some guns. I'll get us a ride."

He swept the available cars in the warehouse. None of

them were his. He considered and discarded most of them until he came back to Julian's GT-R. It had the speed, but if he took it, Julian was going to murder them. They had to survive the day, first.

Emery ducked into CJ's office and approached Kathy's desk, a knot in his throat. CJ might not even know, but Kathy had quietly convinced him to make keys of everyone's current rides—just in case. He knelt and felt along the inside panel to the right of the desk. He'd created a key box that, to his knowledge, was their secret.

The panel slid off, revealing tiny hooks with dozens of different keys. Each one was color-coded and had a paper tag attached to it with their names. There were even notations about modifications and switches. She'd thought of everything. Emery snagged the key to the GT-R and replaced the panel. Kathy had contingency plans for her contingency plans. What were they going to do without her?

Gabriel was waiting for Emery next to the black sports car, several guns in hand. His expression was stony, impassive. He'd had a long career with the FBI before they cut him loose. For some people, the agency was in their blood. Gabriel was one of those. No matter how far he went, he'd always carry the mark of a covert agent if you knew how to look for it. But then again, Emery was surrounded by people just like Gabriel, so what did Emery know?

"Ready?" He unlocked the GT-R and sank into the driver's seat.

"Yeah." Gabriel handed over two 9mm Beretta handguns with silencers already in place. "Know where we're going?"

"Evers's girlfriend's place."

They paused only to make sure the warehouse was locked up tight for Madison's protection before hitting the road. It was a calculated risk to leave her unprotected, but they had to take it. All hell had broken loose when she relayed their plan to the rest of the team. Even now, CJ and Julian barked demands at Emery, which he ignored. The facts were simple. The rest of the crew were a good thirty to forty-five minutes out if they pulled out all the stops and if they ran full speed behind the cops with lights on. Emery was maybe ten minutes away. And the armored cars would make the guys run slow, so it was a no-brainer tactical decision on his part to move without bothering for permission from the others.

The GT-R ate up the road as they navigated the city streets. He could totally understand the Nissan's appeal, but the roar of the engine was deafening compared to his Tesla. He could barely think over the sound, much less hear Madison or the others over the headset.

Chapter Twenty-Three

"Why is the hit team going to Evers? Are they going after him?" Gabriel asked. Since his voice didn't also echo through the headset Emery double-tapped his to cut the feed.

"You tell me." They were both smart, and this wasn't their first operation.

"Spitballing here, a trained hit team in town at loose ends, they can't go back to the mob because they'll be held accountable for Matvei's death. This Geezer guy wants to keep hold of the power."

"And?"

"The FBI thinks someone else is in power. One theory is that Geezer is the boss and the hit team is his way of taking out a liability. But that doesn't add up. Yeah, Evers is a problem to whoever could be pulling the strings. Maybe Evers's operation wants to off him to prevent making themselves weak?" Gabriel's tone went from certain to unsure.

"Someone else *is* pulling Evers's strings." They didn't have proof, but all things pointed that way.

"They could have a jail hit done on him for less than the Russians cost, so now it's personal."

"Maybe. Don't know."

"What if Geezer is organizing a coup? It makes a lot more sense that way. We know he's their import and export guy, how Evers got the drugs in and out of the country. What if Geezer's not happy playing the delivery boy role anymore and wants more power? What if he's offered the hit team sanctuary in exchange for helping put him on top?"

Everything sounded crazy at this point. They were burning rubber to save a piece of shit criminal from an execution squad—why? Because they wanted to see justice served? Because they might get answers someday? There were too many questions. If the FBI wouldn't answer them, well, maybe they could learn something if they had Evers in their custody.

"Emery. Emery!" Madison's panicked voice rose above the snatches of conversation the now-mobile crew was having in the background.

Emery activated his headset with a quick double tap.

"What?" He prayed Madison took a breath and calmed the fuck down.

"They've stopped. It looks like a bunch of houses. Nice ones. With gates and landscaping." Her voice lowered, leveling out into the focused Madison he'd come to know. The one who knew roller derby strategy and numbers. Good.

"The girlfriend's house?" Gabriel asked.

"Yeah. What else do you see?" Emery asked Madison while he focused on the road, sliding between two cars, using the shoulder illegally. Tori would be proud.

The way the dash cam was positioned, they'd only get to see the interior of the car. He should have brought up the feed showing the exterior, but he'd been of a single mind when leaving the Shop.

"They're in the car." Madison paused. The line was

quiet. The others must have muted so they could all hear what she was saying. "I think . . . I think they're watching the rearview mirror."

"Which *they*?" he asked.

"The two younger guys. The car with the man in the suit is still moving. I don't think they're there yet."

"Can you see anything out the back of the car?"

"A really big house. There are stone columns, but the gate is open. There's a white car, looks like a Bentley, maybe?"

"Is anyone there?"

"I don't see anyone besides the hit team. Oh, the other car just stopped. These guys are looking out the right side."

Gabriel stared at him. "The two hit men on one side of the gate, the others across from it, that's a good setup to hit the drop car. They could tap Evers and get out of there before anyone calls the cops. Hell, before we get there if Evers's police escort is on time. Floor it."

Emery downshifted and he took a turn into the ritzy development. Granted, most of Miami was blanketed in homes that cost a fortune, but some were more outrageous than others. This particular one was one at the top.

"Gates. Gates!" Gabriel yelled. He braced a hand on the top of the car and his feet on the floorboard.

Emery accelerated, the car roared, and they hit the fancy wrought-iron gate at full speed. It was a calculated risk. If it was a solid system, they were toast. However, the electric gate whined and popped as it bounced open, not even strong enough to trigger the airbag deployment. The metal on metal squealed and he no doubt lost a lot of paint. Yeah, Julian was going to hate him.

"They're getting out of the car. Emery! They're out. I can see Evers. He's there. Oh my God, Emery!" Madison's panicked voice rose to a shrill note. "Holy shit!"

He could hear the *pop pop pop* of gunfire now. Gabriel rolled his window down, guns in each hand.

"There are others," she continued, speaking in a rush. "Men. Three, no, four of them. They're all shooting."

Emery rounded a turn. Luxurious mansions lined the intercoastal waterway. Three months ago they'd picked up Evers in a similar situation at a more modest house. Coincidence? Not so much. The waterways and abundance of boats made trafficking hard to combat and easy to hide. Was it time they looked into the girlfriend? After this, she was sure as hell going to get more scrutiny.

"I see them," he said over Madison's narration.

The scene was more chaotic than Madison had related to him.

The mansion was on a slightly larger plot than its neighbors, with ten-foot brick walls surrounding the property. The house itself was a three-story, white-and-peach construction reaching for grandeur. The men in black with guns ruined the image.

A beat-up blue sedan sat halfway through the front gate, abandoned. The two stolen cop cars were exactly where he'd envisioned them outside the fenced and gated property. One was a dozen or so yards on the other side of the gate and empty, while the other was across from it. The old man and two hit men were poised around the entry to the property, exchanging gunfire with whoever was inside guarding Evers.

"We want Evers," Emery said.

"Good luck getting him," Gabriel replied. He stared down the barrel of his gun.

Emery shifted, pulled the handbrake, and the car pivoted a neat ninety degrees, blocking the street while also providing cover. This wasn't the kind of neighborhood where people just parked along the curb, either.

One of the Russians crouched and fired at their car.

Emery took aim and returned fire, but the three dove inside the perimeter. Chunks of masonry exploded where his bullet hit, sending shards of stone flying.

Emery left the vehicle and jogged to the wall, Gabriel close on his heels. It had to grate Gabriel to not be in the lead, but his injuries were a detriment to their goal. Emery slowed as they neared the entrance. For the span of several seconds, no one fired, but he did hear a man yelling inside the house.

"One down," Emery said. He visually swept the scene. The poor driver of the sedan never had a chance. The man slumped over the wheel, missing a very important part of his skull. The hit team probably got him first, thinking to disarm the car and snatch Evers for an execution-style job.

Madison muttered something too low to hear.

"Where is everyone?" Gabriel demanded.

"They're almost there. Just, maybe, ten more minutes?" Madison replied, somewhat calmer, but still on edge.

"That's not fast enough," Gabriel said, frustration lacing his tone.

"We're more like fifteen out," Julian said over the line, a muted roar in the background.

Tori and Roni would be faster. Not that he wanted them anywhere near this place. They weren't traveling in a vehicle weighed down by armored panels, but still were too far away. He and Gabriel were doing this rescue on their own.

Emery reached the edge of the gate, or where the gate would be if it were closed. It stood open for anyone to enter. Either Evers had a security team here to meet him, or his people were prepared for this kind of attack. Either way, Emery saw their chance to grab him slipping away.

"I don't see anyone," Emery said, more for Gabriel than the others.

He pivoted, stepping into the entrance, guns raised.

"FBI, ma'am, go back into your home," Gabriel yelled at someone across the street.

Emery didn't pay the woman any mind. His focus was ahead of them. Where was the third Russian? They'd only seen the two with the man in the suit. Was the third dead? Or was he ahead of them?

The thick foliage made it difficult to tell who might be hiding on the edge of the property. If the hit team's focus was Evers, and since they were outmanned, he doubted they'd leave even one valuable member to guard their back. If the Russians had still had Matvei, Emery would be willing to bet they could take the whole situation easily in hand, but Matvei had likely been the brains behind the bunch. Without him, they were just men with a few kills under their belt.

Voices farther back on the property rose, yelling at one another. The fronds of a large-leafed plant were broken by the passing of others along a narrow path leading around the house. Emery crossed the circle drive, Gabriel walking almost backward to cover their six.

"I can't see you anymore," Madison said.

Emery ignored her statement, straining to make out what was being said.

"Shh," Gabriel whispered.

They progressed along the side of the house. A patio and pool stretched along the side, bordered by hedges that would provide a green shield to keep anyone on the outside from looking in. It was a home designed to hide the activities of the inhabitants. What did Evers's on-again, off-again girlfriend have to hide?

A gunshot rang out, followed by two more, breaking the eerie silence. Emery dove forward, dodging behind the hedges. There were neat breaks every six feet. He took a knee, peering through one as a boat motor revved to life. A speedboat shoved off from the docks at the rear of the

house. It was weighted down with six men, one of whom
stuck out in dull, blue scrubs.

Evers.

The others had to be his protective detail. They were too
far away for Emery to ID them on sight alone. This must
have been the plan all along, to have Evers delivered here,
then use the water to get somewhere else. In Miami, a guy
could get almost anywhere out on the water.

The remaining three hit men, plus the man in the suit,
stood behind whatever they could for cover near the
water's edge, firing at the boat. At least one of the people
guarding Evers was injured, judging by the red streaks
over the white fiberglass sides of the boat.

Damn it.

Evers was the key to whatever the hell was going on.

"Get down." Gabriel shoved Emery to the side and they
rolled on the hard flagstones. A bullet ripped through the
bushes where they'd been moments ago.

"There!" one of the hit team yelled.

"Through the house," another called.

Bullets peppered the bushes, pool, and low retaining
wall in front of them. Emery and Gabriel crawled for their
lives to the relative safety of a poolside bar, built out of
heavy stone with a wooden counter. They tumbled over
each other getting behind the makeshift cover.

"Fuck." Gabriel sprawled on the floor of the bar, gripping his ribs.

At a glance, there didn't appear to be any blood on him
save a few scratches.

"Stay there." Emery crouched, ducking his head under
the teak bar, listening—but there were no sounds.

He lifted his head, images of the poor sedan driver
sticking in his mind. Near the house, someone moved. He
ducked reflexively and the stone bar exploded, sending
chunks of rock flying in every direction.

"Shit." Gabriel kneeled, watching the front of the house. A gash on his head dripped blood down the side of his face.

"Think they're going through the house?" Emery asked.

"Fuck if I know."

Glass broke somewhere in the vicinity of the house. Both Emery and Gabriel pressed themselves to the stone as three shots hit the side of the bar.

"That answers that question." Gabriel swiped the blood off his brow.

"Gabriel? Emery? Are you okay?" Madison's voice was calmer, but there was still strain there. With Kathy gone, the roller derby queen was going to have some big shoes to fill.

"Still breathing," Gabriel replied.

"Keep an eye on the dash cams. Where is everyone?" Emery peered around the corner but the hit team was gone.

"They're in the car. They're in the car!" Madison chanted.

"Which car?" Emery hunched, keeping low, and stepped out from the bar. He kept his gaze on the front of the house, finger on the trigger and gun pointed at the ground.

"The . . . uh . . . all three of them are in the—oh my God!"

A loud crash, scrape of metal, and tinkle of shattering glass made Emery's stomach drop.

"Oh my God," Madison said over and over again.

Maybe she wasn't the best for the gig, but she was all they had.

"What happened?" Gabriel snapped.

"They—oh my God—" Another crash and the sound of tires peeling drowned her out. "They hit Julian's car."

That's what Emery was afraid of.

He jogged around the house in time to see the back of the cruiser turn the corner at the end of the street.

"Damn it," Emery growled.

Gabriel headed for the other cruiser and jumped in the driver's seat.

Julian was going to kill them. He loved that damn car.

The second cruiser screeched to a stop next to him. Emery grabbed the door and slid in, Gabriel accelerating the moment most of Emery's body was inside. The door banged his leg, but they were gone. The beaten-up shell of Julian's sleek, black GT-R sat to the side of the road.

"They turned left, right, then left, and they're going straight," Madison said in a rush.

"Take a deep breath and slow down," Emery said, one hand braced on the dash.

"They've got to be almost out of ammo now, don't you think?" Gabriel asked. He followed Madison's sketchy directions back to the main drag.

"Maybe. They probably expected to run into some trouble, but not this much. We grab the old guy, get him to talk, cut a deal, we'll know something then. Kill the hit team." Whoever the man in the suit was, he knew more than they did. If they could hold on to him long enough to squeeze some answers out of him, they might learn something. They could finally figure out what the hell they were caught up in. The hit team, well, they were a liability to Tori's safety. Besides, Emery didn't think they'd get away.

"There's a marina. They're getting out." This time Madison spoke slower, the shrill notes in her voice gone.

"They're either trying to escape or going after Evers," Gabriel said as they skidded through a red light, barely missing a convertible.

"Evers. If they don't get him, they're all dead. Evers will make sure they go down."

"Do we follow them or get them?"

"We won't get Evers, but if we get the Geezer we might find out who Evers is working for."

"Or with."

Emery didn't acknowledge Gabriel's point. Right now, it didn't matter if Evers was the front man, the brains, or the money. He was on a boat getting away from them.

"I see it." Gabriel rattled off the address of a marina ahead of them. He pulled into a fast-food joint next to the upscale docking site and killed the engine. By the look of the place, not just anyone moored their boat here. It was dock-to-dock yachts and expensive toys for the rich.

"Where are you, Aiden? Julian? Roni?" Usually Emery knew the exact location of his entire team during an operation. It was weird and out of synch to be boots on the ground instead of manning the comm and relaying vital information.

"We're five minutes out." That was Tori's voice. He'd know her anywhere.

"Shit. We're seven, maybe ten away." Julian continued to curse.

"Where's Matt?" Emery jumped a white wooden fence and jogged between cars parked nearest the road at the marina.

"Behind us, maybe a minute or two?" Tori replied.

Gabriel shadowed his movements, one car to his left.

The abandoned cruiser sat blocking the way to the docks. A cluster of men in dark clothing stood around the slip of a medium-sized yacht. Not exactly a speedboat.

Were they trying to chase Evers? Or get away?

They crept closer, weaving between cars and SUVs. Emery crouched behind a luxury Hummer, peering around the tailgate to see the old guy's muscle circling the yacht's owner.

"We're almost there," Tori said over the headset.

"I can swim that distance. Can you get overboard or jam the propeller?" Gabriel handed his Desert Eagle over. The handgun wouldn't do shit underwater.

"I'll see what I can do." Emery shoved the guns into his waistband.

Gabriel slipped out of his boots, tied the laces together, and looped them over his shoulder. Emery waited until the other man crossed to the water and slipped in, disappearing under the gently lapping waves before making his move. Emery wasn't certain Gabriel could make the swim. He was still beat up pretty badly and the water was choppy after last night's storm.

Emery could boat-skip down the dock, jumping from slip to slip, but that would take too much time and the Geezer and assassins were boarding now. The yacht owner stood on the docks, a bag in hand, staring at the crew taking over his ship. It was remarkable they'd left the guy alive. They probably didn't want to deal with dumping a body.

The crew was likely to pull out of port any second.

This was going to hurt. Hopefully this encounter didn't take a pound of flesh out of his hide.

"What are you guys doing?" Madison asked.

"Gabriel and I are getting on board." He blew out a breath, visions of Tori doing exactly that filling his mind. Her habits were rubbing off on him. He'd always picked up other people's quirks and discarded them after a while. He might keep hers though.

"No, we're almost there," Tori said, as if thinking of her conjured her voice.

"Get the cops here." He rattled off the name and description of the boat. "Tori, stay on the dock, wait for the others."

It would be just like her to run after him.

He straightened, his knee twinging in remembered discomfort, and strode down the dock. His feet thudded on the wood.

"We're pulling in right now. Damn it, Emery, wait." Tori's voice was rising.

He could do this so long as she was safe on land, which meant he acted now or risked her putting her neck on the line.

Emery picked up the pace. He kept one hand wrapped around the handle of his gun, tucked behind his leg. Waiting for Tori meant putting her in danger. She'd already been in the crosshairs enough, and the hit team was likely to shoot her on sight to cover their ass. Emery couldn't just let them go. He had to stay close to them. No matter what that meant.

"Remember, the headsets are traceable." He'd built them himself and the functionality was easy enough that someone should be able to figure it out if the need arose. He pulled the headset off and shoved it in his pocket, still transmitting.

Two of the Russian muscle stood aft, releasing the lines mooring the boat to the dock. The one poised as lookout saw Emery almost immediately.

Emery held up his hands, Beretta hooked on his thumb.

Yeah, this was going to hurt.

"Stop right there," the smallest man said. He was the one Emery thought might be a Spetsnaz. He aimed a Kel-Tec gun at Emery, probably something he'd taken off a body. The gun was too average for the likes of him. Hell, the guns were made in Florida, so it wasn't like they had to go far to get one.

"Not shooting. I just want to talk this out." Emery took another slow step forward. He needed on that boat.

The second man got the yacht free of the mooring lines while keeping one eye on Emery. He was bigger, a little soggy around the middle.

"I said stop right there," Spetsnaz said a second time. He seemed shaken, which was weird. What would spook a special forces guy?

And was that splashing sound normal? Or Gabriel? Emery couldn't be sure, so he took another step toward the boat. The second guy drew his gun.

"I said, stop—right—there," Spetsnaz said again. He edged his way off the boat, stepping onto the dock.

"All right." Emery inhaled and the skin across his shoulders tightened.

Tori.

If he turned around, would he see her?

Probably not. She was a hell of a lot better than that.

Soggy snatched at the gun hanging in Emery's grasp.

"What the hell is taking so long?" Geezer descended from the helm on the second level of the yacht.

"This one followed us." Spetsnaz edged around Emery, divesting him of Gabriel's gun and stashing it in his waistband.

"Fuck. Bring him on board." Geezer grimaced.

What? Plans not going according to schedule?

Emery tensed, not daring to turn his head to keep an eye on Spetsnaz as the guy circled him. Pain exploded from the back of his head forward, his vision hazed to black. A hand shoved him forward. He stumbled and blinked, staggering onto the boat.

"Let's go," Geezer yelled up to whoever was manning the helm. He reached the deck and strode with purpose toward the front of the vessel, gaze sweeping everything in sight.

The yacht vibrated as the engine came to life.

Spetsnaz shoved him toward the stairs. The boat lurched away from the dock. Emery turned. He couldn't help it.

A figure clung to the support beams under the docks.

Gabriel.

He hadn't made it on board the boat.

Two black cars pulled into the lot. The rest of the crew. But no sign of Tori. Where the hell was she?

"Watch out for that boat," a man yelled from above.

A scream rent the air and there was no mistaking the sound of splintering wood. The yacht lurched and he had a sick feeling in the pit of his stomach.

"Dumb bitch." That was Geezer. The old man leaned over the side, gun in hand.

Fucking—Tori!

Chapter Twenty-Four

Tori hung from the bottom deck rail of the yacht, staring up at the muzzle of a Kel-Tec. If she was going to take a bullet today it was not going to be from a fucking Kel-Tec.

"Why couldn't you just die?" Geezer yelled at her.

Where was Roni? She didn't dare look around for her sister, not when her grip was slipping on the cool chrome railing. They hadn't expected the yacht to launch so fast. She'd hoped for a second to get on board after she'd shed her heavy gear, and instead the stolen boat was floating in pieces in the yacht's wake.

Tori blew out a breath, pushing thoughts of her sister from her mind, and focused on the screaming muscles in her shoulder and back. The breeze hitting her as the boat picked up speed swept her hair into her face. She had to get another hand on the rail or she was going to slip off and into the water. She was too close to the prow. There was no way she'd fall free with enough distance to not get hit by the boat, and then there was the propeller to worry about, not to mention the Geezer might still shoot her.

Okay, so this was a shitty place to be.

Someone grunted and the rail reverberated with an impact she couldn't see.

Geezer glanced over his shoulder and the gun swung off its mark—her.

This might be the only chance she got.

Tori swung her body, using the boat's momentum, and wrapped her hand around the man's wrist. She yanked down and he lurched forward, bending over the rail. His eyes opened wide and he yelled. She yanked a second time, keeping him off balance.

He grunted and one foot came up off the deck in front of her. She let go of his wrist and swung, using the momentum of the boat to grab the next highest rail.

A body tumbled into Geezer's back, pinning him to the rail. It was one of the hit team. The painfully average-looking guy with the seriously jacked-up nose. She kneed the old man in the face as she got her feet on the deck, still clinging to the rail, and wrestled the gun out of Geezer's clammy hand.

Emery grappled with the Spetsnaz, holding his own for now.

She hauled back, bending her arm, and smashed her elbow into the soft portion of Jack Nose's neck while throwing all her weight onto Geezer. Jack Nose shoved at her. She vaulted the railing, over-rotating and hitting the deck on her side. The impact drove all the air out of her lungs, but she kept moving. She rolled, barely missing a heavy boot to the head, and crouched on her feet.

Two assassins and one old guy. The only unaccounted-for hit man had to be driving the boat. Three on two weren't bad odds.

She dodged left, away from the prow on instinct. Jack Nose dove through the space she'd just occupied. He drew his gun. She'd lost hold of hers when the yacht accelerated, but she'd make do with Geezer's Kel-Tec.

Tori brought the gun up and fired before she'd really aimed, and the shot went wild. A fist hit her in the side, bruising her kidney. She grunted in pain.

The damn Geezer.

She pivoted, putting the cabin to her back, and swung her gun toward Geezer. The hit team had nothing left to lose. Geezer, he was the moneymaker. The one pulling the strings.

"Drop it or I shoot him," she said.

Jack Nose lifted his arm, gun in hand, the same moment Geezer drew a second weapon.

Shit.

Tori dove, shoving the cabin doors open. Bullets blasted through the expensive wood paneling and shattered glass inside.

Two more blasts, *thump thump*, softer than the others. Suppressors?

"Hands up."

That low, stony voice stopped her in her tracks. Her heart rose in her throat and it took everything in her power not to rush blindly back onto the prow.

She turned, keeping low, until she spied Emery's profile. He held his gun aimed directly at Geezer.

Geezer dropped his second gun.

"Tell the driver to stop the boat."

Tori edged toward the prow, taking in the space that was usually used for sunbathing passengers. Jack Nose lay facedown on the deck.

"Where are the others?" she asked.

"Out of commission." Emery spoke without looking at her. His tone, his expression, it was completely robotic, cold.

"Stop the boat," Geezer barked to the helm without taking his gaze off them.

"Move." Emery shoved the Geezer back to the stairs.

Tori followed, taking in the difference a few moments

made. What? Five minutes ago she'd been hanging for her life off the prow of the yacht and now two men were dead. It was the kind of results she'd expect from Julian or Aiden, not Emery. Not her quiet Walking Brain with the deep thought lines bracketing his mouth.

It wasn't that he could kill that gnawed at her. It was that he had to. The few times she'd shot to take a life, it had been in self-defense. Emery had killed Matvei, now the two men on the boat, all for her. It was a weight she didn't want him to have to carry.

"Take it back to the dock." Emery held the muzzle of the gun to Geezer's head while the fifth man stared at the blood they'd tracked up the luxurious stairs into the helm. How many people were on the damn boat?

"Do it. Now," Geezer snapped at the man. He pivoted to study Emery, tilting his nose up.

"Who do you work for?" Emery asked. It was the only question that mattered. The one they all wanted to know the answer to.

"If you don't know already, you'll never know." Geezer's gaze slid to her. "If you would have just died it would have all been easier."

"Why the hit team?" she asked.

Geezer shrugged.

Emery jerked Geezer toward him, pressing the muzzle to the man's temple.

"You look at her again and I will kill you, understand?"

"She's something you want worse." Geezer grinned.

The ride back to the dock was made in tense silence. Emery emptied out Geezer's pockets, passing his phone and other tidbits to her. The phone was a burner, not even password-protected, with nothing on it except a few calls. It would, no doubt, be useless, but she kept it anyway.

The boat slowly drifted back into the slip they'd left. Footsteps below and on the stairs heralded the others. Tor

urned, and Roni almost tackled her, dripping wet, followed
by Gabriel and Aiden.

"Matt is right behind us," Aiden warned. He leveled his
glare at Geezer. "You want to deal with the cops or us?"

Geezer glanced at the open water. He'd just been involved
in killing several officers. Chances were, he wouldn't get
top-notch treatment behind bars. If their guess was right,
he'd just tried—and failed—to start a coup with the very
organization he worked for.

"Who do you work for?" Emery grabbed a fistful of the
man's shirt and shook him.

The cops, led by Detective Smith, thundered up the
stairs. They pried Emery off Geezer, shoving Emery back.
Tori reached for him, wrapping her hand around his arm,
and tugged him to her. This ice that had formed around
him, it had to thaw. If the Miami heat wouldn't do it, she
would, but this wasn't him.

An officer she didn't recognize said something to her
she couldn't hear. Emery thrust his firearm at the uniformed
man, his gaze never leaving her. Right. The weapons. They
would need them for ballistics and evidence.

She handed over the Kel-Tec, perfectly happy to never
see that particular gun again.

Emery closed the distance between them and everything else faded away.

He could have died. The moment she'd seen him striding down the dock, his gun lowered, she knew what he was
doing. Because in his position, she'd have done the same
thing. They couldn't let their only lead get away, so the
only alternatives were to sneak aboard, follow, or be taken
prisoner. The fastest and surest way was the prisoner route.

She wrapped her arms around his neck, all the talking
and noise fading away. She sucked in a deep breath, clutching him to her. He was alive. They'd survived. She dug her
fingers into his shirt, yanking him down to her level, and

kissed him. He tasted of saltwater, lip balm, and heaven. H
held her, squeezing her so tight it was hard to inhale, bu
she didn't care. He was there.

"Come on, you two, for fuck's sake, this is a crim
scene now." Matt's grousing went mostly unheeded. Th
only reason it was a crime scene was because they'd tol
him about it.

Emery broke the kiss and clutched her face in bot
hands. The ice was gone, and in its place, his brow crease
in worry.

"God, I saw you there and—don't ever do that again.
His frown might have quelled a lesser woman.

"Me? You didn't wait for backup." She jabbed at hi
chest with her finger. God, her heart hurt. What if he'
been slower to act? What if the bodyguard had shot first o
the docks instead of taking Emery prisoner? It could b
Emery's blood they were tracking everywhere.

"Unless you want to be arrested—move." Matt's frow
marred the Golden Boy expression. He was also soppin
wet, as if he, too, had taken a swim for some unknow
reason.

Almost everyone had cleared the helm save for two of
ficers and Matt. Roni, Aiden, and the rest were already o
the docks.

Emery wrapped his hand around hers and led her dow
the stairs, past the carnage. Her stomach rolled. Deat
would never be an easy thing to take in, but now she knew
just how far Emery was willing to go for her. He had he
back, and he'd protect her no matter what. The sentimen
went both ways. If it was the other way around and she ha
an opening, she'd kill for him, too.

"What happened out there?" Aiden asked as soon a
their boots hit the dock.

"He was about to shoot Tori," Emery said.

Aiden nodded as if that answer made any damn sense. It wasn't the first time she'd been nearly shot at, but it was the first time someone had killed, not once but multiple times, to keep her safe.

"Emery." She pulled him back a step, away from the others and the boat.

He turned, blocking her view with his wide shoulders. She placed her hands on his chest. His features were still hard, but his eyes—that's where the difference was.

"You okay?" It was such a ridiculous thing to ask, but how did she fold all her concerns into one question?

He closed his eyes, sucking in a deep breath through his mouth. Some of the tension in his face eased.

"I was so scared when I heard you scream," he said so low she could barely hear him.

"That wasn't me, it was Roni."

"Didn't matter. It sounded like you."

"I do not scream."

He frowned at her for a second before one side of his mouth hitched up.

"Yes, you do," he said.

She opened and closed her mouth, the sudden heat rushing up her neck making it hard to speak.

"That's different!" she protested.

Emery bent his head until their noses almost touched. Warmth spread through her body and she curled her toes inside her shoes. That was the kind of love this was—the toe-curling kind.

"I will do anything to keep you safe." His tone was soft, different, and she completely understood what he was really saying.

The same reason he'd acted to protect her was the same thing that drove her to jumping in a boat and trying to rescue him. It's what made him willing to risk his job with the FBI.

Love.

She loved him, and she was pretty damn sure he loved her too, now more than ever. It was too soon for declarations like that, but the feeling was there.

"Sir, ma'am, please put your hands up." A very polite young officer stood a few feet away, hand on his holstered firearm. He seemed almost apologetic about it.

"What the hell?" Emery let his hands drop to her shoulders, but didn't release her.

Matt strode toward him, the rest of the crew standing in a cluster near a couple of police SUVs, everyone handcuffed.

"Emery Martin, Tori Chazov, I'm placing you under arrest," Detective Smith said.

"What?" Tori snapped.

"You have got to be kidding me," Emery growled.

"I'm not. Go along with it." Matt placed his hands on his hips and stopped at the side of the abashed officer.

"Fucking hell." Emery thrust his hands forward.

Chapter Twenty-Five

"Like I said, nothing personal." Detective Smith sliced through the plastic restraints binding Emery's hands. The whole crew stood in two holding cells in the downtown Miami station.

"What the hell is this supposed to accomplish?" Tori leaned on the bars separating their cells. The boys on one side, ladies on the other.

"You guys don't exactly travel with *paper*." Matt's gaze slid toward Emery.

Most of their crew had probably lost or hidden the badges that labeled them FBI to deepen their cover. Smart, since they had enemies that would love to use that bit against them. Unfortunately, it made proving their status problematic.

"What do you want from us?" Emery asked. Matt wasn't protecting them.

"The old man's name is Victor Sleigh."

Emery's memories flipped like a mental Rolodex, pulling the bits of knowledge from the recesses of his brain. "His name was on invoices from Greenworks. The name's fake."

Smith's frown deepened. "He's real, he's just not American. Cuban. Any second the FBI field office is going to descend on this place, and the moment I go into interrogation Sleigh is going to ask for a lawyer."

"You want one of us to go in there and question him?" CJ paced toward them. "All right, let's do this."

Matt held up his hand. "I'm not letting you anywhere near my suspect."

CJ growled something, hands curling into fists, and lunged at Matt. Aiden grabbed one of CJ's arms, Julian the other, and together they held CJ back.

"Think about it," Aiden barked.

The agent tried to yank his arms from their grasp.

"You need someone with credibility." Emery glanced back at Matt. With Kathy gone and CJ ready to blow a fuse, that left Emery or Julian. Between them, Julian's interrogation tactics relied more on intimidation and fear, which wouldn't go over well in a law-abiding environment. Emery had actually excelled at the more diplomatic study of interrogation, which was a lot less exciting than popular media pretended it was.

"Yeah. Needs to be now." Matt thumbed over his shoulder. "I've got clothes and a shower."

"Tori comes, too."

She might not be as legally FBI as he was, but this whole mess was wrapped around her.

"Shit." Matt glanced at Tori and scowled. "I'll have to find clothes. You can't go in there looking like extras from *Dexter*."

Smith motioned to someone they couldn't see. A double buzz and both cells slid open.

"The rest of you are being released. We'll work out a cover with the field office." Matt gestured for Tori and

Emery to follow him. Most officers they passed found somewhere else to look.

"I heard things here have been rough," Emery said, keeping his voice low. They crossed from holding into the offices used by officers.

"Rough is an understatement," Matt muttered.

"Let me know if I can help."

Matt paused outside of a set of men's locker rooms, his gaze bouncing from Tori to Emery. "I only arranged for one of the locker rooms to be empty."

"We'll be fine." Tori shoved Emery through the swinging door and flipped the lock before Matt could follow them in.

He knocked on the door. "I'll be back."

Emery pulled Tori toward him, needing to touch her, feel her lips against his. She lifted up and kissed him. He felt the shock of that touch all the way to his feet. God, she was amazing, and he could have lost her today. He pushed his fingers into her hair, tipping her head back and deepening the kiss. She groaned and pressed closer.

"Damn." He tore his mouth from hers. He wanted long hours to spend going over her body, showing her just how well she screamed, but they had a suspect to interrogate.

"Get cleaned up. Now."

They descended on the row of sinks, stripping off articles of bloody, saltwater-stained clothing.

She finger-combed her hair under the spray and wiped away streaks of dirt and dried blood. He barely paid attention to his own cleaning routine, too fascinated by Tori, the way she moved, how she breathed.

"Got any plans for next weekend?" He used soap from a wall dispenser to scrub his hands and forearms, trying to ignore the magnetic pull between them. There just wasn't time for anything of that nature right now.

Tori glanced at him. One brow arched.

"What do you have in mind?" she asked.

"A bed. A damn big bed." No more of this doing it in the heat of the moment in a garage or up against a fucking wall. A bed, with pillows and sheets, and takeout only a call away. They might have to make do with his place or a safe house if things got hairy, but he was willing to bet they could make it work.

"Really? I was thinking about working on the Bel Air. You never even got to see the backseat or that trunk. You could fit a body or two back there." She grinned and her nose wrinkled.

"Come here, you." He grabbed her hand and pulled her to him.

One kiss wouldn't delay them much.

"What about tonight?" she asked between the moments their lips were touching.

"What about it?"

"I don't know, just curious."

Tonight, tomorrow, everything was still up in the air, but they had each other. But for how long? CJ had Kathy, and now she was gone.

"Emery." She pushed at his shoulders.

"I'm in love with you." His voice was lower, rougher, but damn, he loved her. All the time. Now she was inside him. He didn't have to think about it. That was just a truth that was. He loved her. Had for a long time.

Tori stared at him, her lips parted and eyes wide. Red hair clung to her face, her lips were swollen and damp. Her chest heaved and she blinked rapidly. Yes, he loved all of her.

"A-are you serious?" she asked.

"Yeah." He swallowed around a knot in his throat and stepped back, out of reach. This was not the time for emotional declarations, but if he didn't tell her now, when should he tell her? When they weren't in danger? Because that was never going to happen. "We need to get going. Now."

"Emery, no, stop." She grabbed his arm. "Just hold on. I wasn't ready for that."

Tori slid her hand down to clasp his.

"Matt will be back any second," he said.

He grabbed a paper towel and scrubbed it over his face. Clothes hung on a hook he could only assume Matt had left for him. He was right, they couldn't walk into an inter-rogation covered in blood. Emery turned the water off, but remained rooted to the spot.

He dressed in the borrowed clothing. There was every-thing from socks and shoes to a belt, besides the slacks and dress shirt. He hated the silence and awkward tension res-onating from Tori. He should have waited. Now wasn't the time to focus on them; they needed their heads in the game, not each other. It didn't change how he felt though.

He was halfway ready when someone pounded on the door.

"Stay here," he told Tori.

He'd hate to have to kill Matt for seeing Tori in nothing but jeans and a sports bra, though from the way the man was acting, Emery didn't think it was Tori Matt was inter-ested in. Between the man leaping into the ocean and his numerous instances of pulling Roni over, Emery was going to have to keep a closer eye on them. Matt knew how to pick a challenge. Tori and Roni might be twins, but there was a world of difference between them.

Emery paused before unlocking the door.

"Who is it?" he asked.

"The Muffin Man. Open the fucking door."

Emery snorted and flipped the lock, pulling the door open. Matt shoved a plastic bag at him, still scowling.

"It might not fit her," Matt warned.

"Haven't dried out yet?" Emery noted the water still weighing down the man's trousers, the darker color of his cuffs and collar.

"Yeah, I smell like a damn sewer." Matt swiped his hand down his chest, lips twisted into a frown.

Emery glanced at Tori, softly padding toward him along the wall and out of sight. He stepped between her and the detective, shielding her from view, and held out the proffered clothing. She took the bag, winked at him, and scurried back to the relative safety of the showers to change.

Matt still stood in the hall, staring at the wall.

"Let me guess. You jumped in the water as Roni was climbing out?" Emery asked.

Roni had never struck Emery as the kind of woman to accept help. It was half the reason she didn't work in the garage as much as her sister, and instead manned the front desk. *Does not play nice with others* was an understatement.

"Maybe? Hell if I know." Matt shrugged and stuck his hands in his pockets.

"A bit of advice?" Emery set his shoulder against the door frame. Water trickled down the back of his neck, but he ignored it and the throbbing of various body parts, not all of which hurt. "Find someone else to rescue."

Matt's gaze narrowed.

"You've got a hell of a picker, man." Emery shook his head. If the detective wouldn't be deterred, well, that was his business.

"Can we get one more moment, Matt?" Tori spoke from right behind him.

Emery turned a bit to catch a glimpse of her.

She'd slicked her hair back into a wet bun high on her head, elongating her neck. Damn, she was beautiful. The clothes didn't work for her at all. The skirt suit and white shirt were too big, but the shoes appeared to fit. They were, however, black-and-white. A staple of the Fed wardrobe. Ill-fitting would work in their favor. Agents weren't exactly fashion plates, not that he was one to judge.

"Sure, but make it quick." Matt's glare said they didn't have time, but he wasn't pushing them.

Emery let the door close, though he really wanted to flee after the detective. He'd never told anyone he loved them before.

Tori stared up at him, her hands clasped in front of her. She seemed just as off balance as he felt.

"You don't have to say anything back," he said. He hadn't expected her to, but perhaps he should have added that to his earlier declaration.

"That's not it. It's just . . . I've liked you for a long time, but I liked this imaginary version of you in my head that was quiet, a doormat, and obedient. You're not anything like what I thought, and I don't really know where or why I assumed those things about you, because they aren't traits I like in a man. You're different. You're you. You're better. You're . . . You make me feel—things." She shrugged. "I don't know what to call how I feel. I think it's love, but it's new, and with everything else going on, it's a little scary."

The hand holding on to his throat loosened its grip and he took an easier breath.

"I'll take that." He held out his hand. She was right; a lot had changed and would continue to shift in the coming days and weeks.

Tori's hesitant smile spread into a grin. She took a step toward him and wrapped her arms around his neck, pulling him down for a quick kiss.

"We can figure it out later?" she said.

"Later."

He opened the locker room door and almost ran into Matt.

"Let's go." Emery gestured for Matt to lead the way.

Once more, the few officers and staff found somewhere else to look when they passed. A show of solidarity? Support? By all rights Emery and the others should be treated like the rest of the Feds, or maybe worse considering they barely obeyed the laws, but it appeared the Miami-Dade officers were on their side. He wanted to know who at the local field office had pissed off the cops, the better to keep his distance.

"Something happen?" Tori asked, pitching her voice low.

"Yeah. Guy killed three cops, fourth might still die, and we all know the Feds will bury this just like what they're doing with Evers. You think he'd be out if the Feds hadn't taken evidence we needed for the case against him?" Matt shook his head, fury radiating from him. "You're the best damn hope we have of getting any answers or justice."

Emery glanced at a clock as they reached a room situated in a back corner. They weren't going to have much time.

"Here's everything we could pull up on him. You've got a couple minutes. When the Feds get to the front doors I'll pull you out, sneak you out the back—unless you want to join the fun?"

Tori scowled. She flipped through the folder of information Matt had for them.

"Hell no." Emery knew the hammer was going to come down hard on him once they reported in detail the recent events. He wasn't trying to hasten his professional suicide.

"Okay. I'm not recording this because this technically never happened, but I'll be watching. Just me." Matt gestured to a TV mounted to the wall. The station was a bit more high tech than he'd realized. Good for them.

"Do we have a plan?" Tori asked.

"Not really." Emery shrugged.

"Great." She rolled her eyes. "Has he asked for a lawyer yet?"

"Haven't given him the opportunity," Matt replied.

"Let's do this." Tori tugged the jacket into place and nodded.

Emery pulled the door open and they walked into what might as well have been a human freezer. Tori strode ahead of him and set the folder down on the table between her and Sleigh.

"It's kind of cold in here, don't you think?" She glanced at Emery, but kept her question aimed at Victor. "Would you like a coffee? Anything to drink?"

Victor merely snorted.

"I think I'd like some coffee. Could you see if they could get us some?" She gestured to Victor. "Black, no cream or sugar, right?"

That made Victor pause. His fingers stopped tapping on the desk and he actually looked at her. Tori simply smiled back, radiating warmth.

Good girl.

One of the first tactics of real interrogation was to put the interviewee at ease. He'd let her take point on this. Victor would probably see Emery as a threat, considering he'd held the man at gunpoint. Of the two of them, Tori was the less intimidating.

Emery stuck his head out of the interrogation room door. Matt was already pouring cups of coffee from a rolling cart that hadn't been there a few minutes before.

Go team.

* * *

Tori pulled out one of the rolling chairs provided for officer use. Victor sat in a heavy, uncomfortable metal seat. Both were intentional. Everything about interrogation was done with purpose. It wasn't the yelling, throwing, or abusing the suspect often portrayed on TV. True interrogation was far less overt. Now, if only she could get her head into the mind-set and not think about the locker-room chat.

Emery loved her? It was fast, but it felt right.

She pushed the jittery feelings away and focused on the man handcuffed to the table.

"Victor, may I call you Victor?"

He curled his lips downward and flicked his fingers, as if to say it didn't matter to him. There was something off about him. She'd seen a number of interviews over the years. Suspects in his shoes were nervous and jittery, or sneering and overly confident. Not him. He was . . . waiting. On what? A rescue? A plea bargain? What?

Sweat broke out along her hairline.

There was a ticking time bomb in the room and she had no idea what the trigger was.

"The last address I have for you is a couple of years old, but you don't live there anymore, do you? Uniforms had been there, and according to the current residents, they purchased it a little over two years ago. Where do you live now?" She wiped her palms on her thighs and counted to ten, willing herself to be calm.

Emery returned, sliding one coffee to Victor, the other toward her, before taking a seat at her side.

"Around," Victor replied.

She kept her smile firmly in place. Emery remained quiet, but his body language was anything but passive. Even pretending to be relaxed, he was still in motion.

She could feel his mind at work. Had he picked up on the impending doom in the room? What else were they going to face next?

"Do you live with your daughter?" Tori tugged a photograph of a charming young woman from the folder and slid it across to Victor.

He refused to even look at the snapshot. Either he didn't care about her, or he wanted to protect her. She'd come back to the young woman.

"You're originally from Cuba? Sleigh, that's not a Cuban name, is it?"

Again, Victor deigned to reply.

"Isn't that more of an Anglo name? I think I read somewhere that it means crafty. Cunning. You're a smart man, Victor. What is your daughter going to tell us about you? You know officers have been dispatched to her home to question her?"

There.

His brows lifted slightly. The lines around his mouth deepened.

"What do you think Evers's people will do to your daughter when they can't get their hands on you?" She sat back and glanced at Emery. "We've seen some of their work. They can get pretty—creative."

He turned his head, gazing out of the narrow windows, clinging to the disengaged act.

Victor Sleigh was a smart man, she had no doubt of that, who made unfortunate choices. Had his little coup gone off without a hitch, well, she might be looking at the next kingpin of Miami instead of the lockup's star prisoner.

"Have it your way, Mr. Sleigh." Tori flipped the folder closed, but left the photograph on the table.

"You're not Feds or cops." Victor glanced at Emery. "Who are you?"

"People who can help." Emery reached out and put a hand on her arm, as if he were insisting she stay.

"You can't help me. No one can help me." Victor reached out and straightened the image of his daughter. His face softened, and for a moment he was just a father.

"We could help her." Tori leaned forward.

"You won't be able to find her." A challenge.

"Are you sure about that?" She and her sister had lived their lives being hidden and on the run. If anyone could find Victor Sleigh's daughter, Tori and Roni were it.

"Positive."

"You think they're going to kill you. Don't you?" She rested her elbow on the table. He wasn't stalling them. He was waiting. "You know how they'll do it, too, don't you?"

Victor glanced up at her. He'd known the risks, calculated his odds of winning and made a gamble. Too bad he'd lost.

"Why not help us? Stick it to the people you want brought down? We could make it worth your while. Maybe even protect you. You're not dead yet. She's not dead."

For several moments they stared at each other, but he wasn't budging.

They had to find the daughter.

Whoever she was, she was important. Tori felt it in her gut.

Victor's silent challenge. His refusal to speak about anything else. It had to tie back to the daughter. She was key.

"Okay, if you don't want to talk, at least tell us what happened out there. Who hired the hit team? Why try and kill your business partner?" This might be Tori's only chance of getting information straight from the source. She wanted to reach across the table and shake it out of him.

"Michael Evers is not my business partner." Victor's voice dripped with disdain.

Okay, no love lost there.

"Then what is he?"

"A means to an end." Victor shrugged.

He was talking.

"And the hit team?"

"None of my doing."

"But you had them try to kill Evers."

No answer.

Damn it.

"I think you and Evers work for the same person. You clearly don't like Evers, which means this person you work for has to be bad enough and scary enough to keep everyone in line. But you saw an opportunity to merge Evers's operation with yours and you took it. Right?"

"You're very perceptive. No doubt from your father's genes."

A chill seeped into Tori's body. Yes, people knew her secret. Dangerous ones. But they hadn't killed her yet.

"Tell me I'm right." She had to know.

Someone knocked on the door. Emery unfolded himself from the chair and crossed to the door. She could pick out Matt's voice, but not what they were saying.

"Tori?" Emery straightened and glanced over his shoulder at her. He nodded toward the hall.

Damn. Their time was up already.

"Am I right, Victor?"

"Close enough." Victor shrugged.

This was all the confirmation they were going to get. It killed her to get up without more answers. Maybe they could find the girl. She had to know more.

Tori took the file with her. It had little more than a precursory background check. She knew he was from

Cuba, a couple places of residence there and previous charges, but that was about it. Chances were, the file would get a whole lot thicker before the day ended.

The door shut behind her, and Matt hustled them back the way they'd come.

"Shit, they're already in the building," he muttered, glancing at his phone. "This way."

"What do we know about the daughter?" Tori asked.

"Not a lot," Matt said. "Sofia Sleigh. Twenty-nine. No record. Worked as a tech analyst up until a year ago. Patrol said the house listed as her latest residence is boarded up. No one's been there for years."

"We need to find her. Was it just me, or was he telling us she was a clue? Or a key? Or something?"

"Sounded to me like he wanted us to leave her alone." Matt waved his key card in front of a pad and let them out into a wide hallway.

"She has to mean something." Tori glanced at Emery's impassive face. Was she reading into things because of her father?

"Where's everyone else?" Emery asked.

"Taqueria around the corner." Matt led them downstairs through doors and finally out a side exit into a little fenced-off yard with benches and tables. He gestured at a break in the fence. No sooner had the door closed behind them than his phone began to buzz. "Out here, across the lot, to your left, around the corner."

"Thanks," Tori said over her shoulder as she strode, or more accurately tried to not limp, her way along. The shoes were a size too small, but they covered her feet.

"I'll try to update you later." He swiped his key card and disappeared back inside the building.

Emery fell into step beside her, managing to make the borrowed clothes look as good as he did.

"Am I crazy? Or is the daughter involved somehow?"

"She could be, but that's something to worry about later. I doubt she's even in Miami."

"How much trouble do you think we'll be in?" she asked.

"CJ and me—a lot. You and the others? Not so bad. I think they expect trouble from you guys, but someone has to get it."

"I'm sorry." She winced. All of this—because of her.

"Hey." He wrapped his hand around hers. "I wanted to be with you. Nothing anyone could have said or done would have changed that."

She nodded. It might be the truth, but she didn't want Emery to make sacrifices on account of her. But when you loved someone, well, the rules changed. There wasn't much besides Roni's safety that Tori would be willing to part with for him.

By the time they reached the open-air taqueria they were both drenched in sweat. The crew had taken over one corner of the patio with the other patrons giving them a wide berth. That was no surprise. Between Roni looking like a drowned rat, Gabriel nearly dead on his feet, and their overall greasy appearance, they were a rough group. They'd at least taken advantage of the opportunity to grab food and a drink. At least half had already been served while the others were polishing off the first basket of chips and salsa.

"Where's CJ?" Emery asked, surveying the group.

For a moment, no one answered.

"He was called into work," Gabriel said, his brows lifted.

The Feds.

Had they known CJ was here? Or were they aware of his involvement? Either way, a weight settled in Tori's stomach. They weren't finished yet. Emery squeezed her hand and led her to where Roni sat.

"What's our plan?" she asked.

The day was far from over.

Chapter Twenty-Six

Tori felt only marginally better after a shower at her apartment and a meal she didn't have to make. She'd have felt a lot better if she were with Emery, but it made no sense to go with him when all of her stuff was in the apartment she shared with Roni. It didn't stop her from thinking about him every second they were apart.

How would a relationship work? Until this weekend, the crew had been very careful to not be seen with Emery in public. Could they keep a relationship a secret? How would she deal with that? What were they going to do?

A lot of Emery's value to the team was his ability to move covertly in circles the rest of them were unconnected to. This weekend might have blown that cover. Hell, everyone in Miami might know they were FBI now if the wrong people talked. Their whole operation could be blown wide open. Things were changing, but all she wanted was Emery.

"Are you going to speak to me at all?" Roni asked. She drove them the longest way possible back to the Shop.

"Sorry, just thinking."

"You're making my head hurt with all the thinking. Talk to me."

"I can't believe Kathy's gone." That loss still hurt. Sh
didn't quite accept it, either.

Roni was quiet a moment before she whispered, "
know."

"That and . . . what's going to happen next?"

"We've been holding our breath, waiting for the shoe t
drop for months. I don't know if I'm glad something fi
nally happened or what."

"Exactly." Tori sighed. Having a sister who knew her s
well was a relief. There were many thoughts she didn
have to enunciate because Roni already knew what sh
was thinking. At least, in all areas but one. "And Emery.'

"What about him?"

"How's this going to work? Can it?"

"*Lapochka*, I think that man is motivated to make
work." Roni chuckled.

"You think?" Tori grinned, warm fuzzies permeatin
her hard shell of worry.

"You jumped on a boat to save his ass. He'd be stupid t
not keep a woman like you, but I'm biased."

"Yeah, well, keep being biased. I need to hear that.
Emery had told her he loved her and she'd said wha
amounted to nothing. She loved him, but why was it s
hard to tell him? Was it because she couldn't shake th
feeling that he deserved better than her?

"What is it with you and the silence? Has he bee
giving you lessons or something? Gah."

"Sorry!" Tori chuckled. "I'm just—I think . . ."

"What?"

"He told me he loves me."

"Shut up! When?"

"At the station." Tori covered her face with her hands.

"What did you say?"

"I didn't know what to say! I just . . . stood there.
mean, I tried to tell him that I think I love him but—wha

everything dies down and it changes? You know what it's
e when everything is crazy and you get hot for some-
e?"

"Yeah, but we're talking about the Walking Brain, here.
u've been hot for him."

"Yeah." Her cheeks flushed at the truth of it. "I just . . .
want what's best for him."

"That's when you know you really love someone. Take
e and you. I dogged Emery, but it was only because I
ant someone who will be there for you like I am. Who'd
ke a bullet for you. I'll admit, I was skeptical, but he's
on me over. I owe him one for looking out for you."

"I'm not sure I'm good enough for him," Tori blurted out.

"What?" Roni stared at Tori, face twisted up in a grimace.

"I know, that sounds crazy but . . . you don't understand.
is family, they might have been worse to him than Dad
as to us." At least their father had looked out for them in
s own way, right up until the end.

"All the more reason to love him back. I'm not going to
gue this with you. You either love him or you don't."

"I think I do."

"Then what's the big deal? Enjoy it."

"I don't know."

"Tell me more about his family. What kind of fucked up
e we talking about?"

"The turn-on-you kind."

"Damn."

"Part of me wants to go find them."

"Don't. Don't go there. We'd never have allowed anyone
mess with Dad, and Emery won't appreciate you trying
fix his family."

"You're right." She slumped in her seat. "I just . . . I
ther want to make them pay for turning their backs on
m, or make them realize how awesome he really is."

"In our line of work, you can't do that. Okay, so you

could probably torch their place and get away with it, b
it would be a bitch move. So don't. It's not like any of
have great home lives right now. We lean on each other. I
what makes us tight. It also protects his family. Don
knock the distance. It's probably saved their lives already

Tori mulled that point over. She hadn't thought of it li
that, but she could understand it.

Roni sped down the final stretch toward the Sho
The massive warehouse sat dark, by all appearances. S
pulled through the gate and into the lot before easir
through the open door into the warehouse. Inside it was
up and full of the most important people in their live
Their chosen family.

From the looks of things, they were the last to arriv
She glanced over the cars, her heart aching a bit whe
she saw Emery's Tesla plugged in and charging. A han
ful of hours apart and she felt like she'd lost an arm,
part of her heart. Everyone else was clustered arour
one of the main bays, chowing down on pizza, but Emer
was missing.

She slid out of Roni's Lancer and headed for the sec
rity office. She didn't take an easy breath until she sa
him. Emery stared at the screens, deep lines bracketing h
mouth. He didn't even appear to notice her, which was
completely normal.

Tori circled the desk and wrapped her arms around h
neck and laid her cheek against the top of his head. For
second his muscles tensed, as if he really hadn't notice
her until she touched him, then relaxed and his hand covere
hers, squeezing it. So much for big, bad, super-spy sens
He was still her oblivious techie.

"You smell good," he said.

"You noticed?"

"I always notice, but complete sentences, remember?
He twisted his head and smiled at her.

She kissed him, breathing in his scent, the feel of his skin, everything she'd missed in just a couple of hours.

"I'm here," he said against her lips.

"I know, I just . . ." She rested her head against his. She needed to feel him. Touch him. Reassure herself she wasn't dreaming.

Losing Kathy still wasn't real, but she was beginning to feel the ache.

A car horn blasted and Aiden's classic Charger rolled in.

"CJ's here." Emery squeezed her hand before standing.

They walked out to join the others, hand in hand. A few of them glanced their way, but for the most part no one commented on the sudden relationship.

CJ, Aiden, and Madison climbed out of his Charger, none of them looking too happy. The crew circled around, tension making her fidget. Tori could barely breathe.

"I'm off the case," CJ said without preamble.

"What?" Tori gasped.

"No way." Julian straightened.

Similar statements came from the others, completely caught off guard by such a drastic action.

"I expected it. After—after Kathy died, they were going to do it. Observation, evaluation, and all that bullshit." CJ tossed a weak smile Julian's way.

"You'll come back, right?" Gabriel asked.

"No idea. They're telling me to report to the shrink in Quantico by Thursday. I'll keep you up-to-date, but don't expect for me to find out much. They're pissed, no surprise there, but I'm not being told shit."

The coarse language surprised Tori. Usually CJ stayed pretty professional, but losing his wife and partner had probably unhinged him a bit. She couldn't imagine what it must be like for him. The loss wasn't just now, it would continue in a hundred little ways for a very long time.

"I'm sure more than ever that we were bait. I don't

know who Victor Sleigh works for or how he fits into this but find out." CJ stared around the bay, as if willing them to all promise to take on the order.

Julian rested his hand on CJ's shoulder. Aiden joined them and the three men put their heads together, planning and scheming even now.

"What does this mean?" she asked Emery.

He merely shrugged and studied the two groups talking in hushed tones. His silence irked her, but she let him think.

"Hopefully CJ takes a vacation and comes back, right? Tori knew that wasn't the case. She'd been around the FBI long enough to know that when an agent screwed up badly she never saw them again. It was more likely those poor souls were relegated to desk work than canned, but it was all about the same to her. Without movement, action, she'd go crazy.

Emery didn't bother answering her naive question. His phone began vibrating so loud she could hear it. She watched him frown at the display before answering it with a curt, "Hello." Emery glanced at the others, his brow rising at whatever the person on the other end of the line was saying. Finally, his gaze landed on her, and the frown had nothing to do with thinking.

"It's for you." He didn't sound pleased about that.

She took the phone and pressed it to her ear.

"Hello?"

"Tori, it's Matt."

"Don't say anything," Emery whispered.

"I need you to listen very closely to me. Sleigh wants to talk, but he's only going to talk to you. The Feds are leaving him here overnight in lockup until they can transport him. I can get you in to talk with him in an hour, just after mealtime. Got it?"

"O-okay." She didn't know what she might have said

Victor that would convince him to talk to her rather than anyone else. The actual FBI could help protect him far better than she, but if he would part with valuable information, she wasn't about to argue the hows or whys.

"Let me speak to Emery," Matt said.

Tori handed the phone to her boyfriend. Boyfriend? Was that what they were? Or was this something else?

Emery listened for a moment, nodding or making sounds of agreement. "Got it. See you then." He ended the call, glancing over at the others, who were too involved in their conversations to pay them any mind.

"What's the plan?" Tori kept her voice low.

"We need to go, now. My car should be charged."

They circled the group, a few people giving them the side-eye for leaving, but no one stopped them. Let them think they were leaving to go make out or something.

It felt like a month since she'd last sat in the Tesla Roadster. In reality, a day? She closed her eyes, feeling all the bruises, bumps, and soreness as she settled in.

"What do we tell the others?" she asked. He steered the car out of the warehouse.

"Nothing until we know what he wants to tell us."

She didn't like that answer, but she also knew the FBI might pull the rug out from under them in a split second. With CJ leaving, everything was going to change. They drove in relative silence through Miami. It seemed wrong that the sun should shine and the sky be so clear on such an awful day. Rain and storms would be far more appropriate.

Emery parked a couple miles from the downtown police station where Victor Sleigh was being held. He stashed the Roadster in the back of a lot behind a Dumpster, but made no move to get out. At least not until a familiar, unmarked police SUV eased up behind them.

"What the hell is going on?" She twisted in her seat,

peering at the car. Matt. "You couldn't have told me he wa
picking us up?" For that, she smacked Emery's arm. H
merely frowned at her, not the least bit bothered.

"Come on. It's the easiest way into the station."

They got out of the Tesla and met the detective betwee
the two vehicles. There wasn't another uniform in sight.

"Thanks for coming." Matt shook their hands.

"Thanks for the ride." Emery strode to the back of th
truck.

"Should you handcuff us first?" Tori had an aversion t
cop vehicles of any nature. She'd had her fill already.

"Easiest and fastest way in. Sorry. We've got a tigh
window to make." Matt held the door for her while sh
climbed inside and strapped in. Unlike the marked car
Matt's SUV was comfortable and clean, a lot like the ma
behind the wheel.

"Won't the on-duty officers, or, I don't know, the secu
rity cameras see us?" This didn't make any sense to Tor
There were too many holes. Just how were they suppose
to do any sneaking in or out?

"Well, it just so happens that our security cameras ar
unreliable since an incident with a hacker." Matt twisted i
his seat, grinning at them as he reversed.

"I didn't touch that part of the system." Emery scowle

"You know that. I know that. But the Feds? They don
know that." Matt straightened and accelerated, mergin
into traffic.

"I think we're a bad influence on you." Tori slumpe
down in her seat, amused by the officer's shenanigans. Sh
just hoped it didn't come back to bite him in the ass.

"You know whatever he tells us we might not be able t
tell you?" Emery said.

"Sure, but you guys will do something with it. Thes
assholes just want to shove paper and insults around. He

nly spoken to his lawyer since you guys left." Matt slapped
ne steering wheel.

She wasn't sure she wanted to know what the FBI
gents had done or said to earn the proverbial middle
inger from the detective.

Tori and Emery kept their heads down while Matt drove
nem around behind the building and in through an auto-
natic rolling gate. It locked them in a large garage that
ould hold maybe a half dozen cop cars two abreast and
hree deep. To their right was a door and two panels
f bulletproof glass. If they were actually being processed
s they had been earlier, there would be mug shots taken,
 pat-down search, among other boring bits of paperwork.
 his time Matt hustled them past officers too busy shuffling
 aper to notice them beyond buzzing them through the
 oors and gates.

"We'll get maybe fifteen minutes before they bring the
 risoners back from the showers," Matt said. They strode
 own a cinder-block hall.

They entered a large, square space. An empty desk sat
 gainst the left wall. Cell doors were set into the cinder
 lock. These were more secluded and secure than the gen-
 ral holding cells Tori and their crew had hung out in. Matt
 vent straight to the desk while Emery and Tori approached
 he only closed cell.

"Victor Sleigh?" Emery stopped in his tracks.

Tori almost ran into his broad back. She peered around
 im and gasped, her stomach rolling in violent protest. The
 uzzer rang and the locks on the cell disengaged.

Emery rushed through first, shoving the bars back, but
 e pulled up at the edge of the blood pool. Tori was right
 ehind him. The silence was absolute. There wasn't even a
 eath rattle.

"What? What happened?" Matt crowded into the small
 pace behind them.

Victor Sleigh lay awkwardly on his side, his nec
slashed. His chest didn't move. His eyes didn't blink. Th
only thing moving was the blood pool as it slowly draine
from his body. Emery even scooted back to avoid contac

They could never have been here.

Matt whirled and called out for an officer by name.

"We have to go," Emery said, grabbing her arm.

"But—what was he going to tell us?" Tori glance
around the cell, but there was nothing. The man hadn'
been in lockup long enough to accumulate keepsake
Everything he'd had with him would have gone into ev
dence.

"I don't know, but we've got to get out of here befor
they decide we were involved."

Tori spied a crumpled-up bit of trash under the bun
bed. She cleared the blood pool and body in a single leap
going to her knees and grabbing the balled-up paper.

"Tori, come on." Emery scowled at her from the cel
door.

"You have to leave," Matt said.

"We know," Emery replied.

Tori edged around the body and slipped out afte
Emery, keeping her hands to herself. The last thing sh
needed was her prints in the cell.

"Go back the way you came. They'll let you out." Ma
grabbed a radio on the desk. "Go."

Emery took her hand. This was bad. Very, very bad. Ma
had organized for everyone to look the other way for a ver
narrow bit of time. Someone knew that. And at the perfec
moment they'd managed to kill the only person willing t
talk. Hell, the death had to have occurred the instar
the cameras went down, to have killed him so fast.

Officers rushed past them, turning a blind eye on thei
presence. They made it back out of the precinct withou

nyone stopping them. It was a minor miracle. Someone
vas going to take the fall for Sleigh's death; she just hoped
t wasn't Matt. The guy had helped them so much, but that
probably made him an easier target.

"What did you get?" Emery asked. They strolled down
he sidewalk almost a mile from the car.

"I don't know." She dug the paper out of her pocket.
"They would have cleaned out the cell of everything, even
rash, before putting him in there. So whatever this is, it
vas dropped while he was in the cell. Where do you think
he got it from?"

They paused, Emery peering over her shoulder. She
moothed the thick piece of paper out, studying it.

It was a ticket. Like, something handed out at concerts
or sporting events.

"Jupiter Hammerheads?" Emery muttered.

Tori turned the ticket over and over, looking for any-
hing unusual about it other than that it had shared space
vith Victor at the time of his death.

Tickets.

Why did that sound so—familiar?

"That's a two-week-old ticket. It's just trash," Emery said.

"No, wait." She spun, placing her hand against his
chest. "That spy ring in New York the FBI broke up."

"The Russian one?" The thought lines around his mouth
deepened.

"Yes. They used hats, umbrellas, and tickets—*tickets*—
o communicate with each other. What if he got this from
his lawyer, or someone, to leave us a trail?"

The case was still ongoing. She wasn't sure how they'd
used the tickets or why, but it was a chance.

"I think . . . I'm not sure that's applicable here."

"Okay, hang with me for a second." She turned and
started walking toward the car, faster now. "Victor knew
my background. He knows I was born in Russia. Let's say

he also knew that trying to turn on Evers and getting picke
up by the cops meant he'd just risen to the most-wanted
dead list. He could be trying to tell us where to pick up th
information. A drop site."

Emery's frown wasn't the greatest vote of confidence
but he wasn't stopping her. And maybe she was graspin
at straws, but it was something when before they'd ha
nothing.

Emery crept down the concrete stairs by feel more tha
sight. The almost full moon shed enough light on the smal
stadium that he could see across the field easily enough
but there were still too many shadows and places to hide
Sleigh might be dead, but Emery was highly skeptical tha
they weren't being watched. What if Sleigh's final act wa
to ensure Tori died? Of course Tori wouldn't wait at hom
or in the car while he did the pickup.

They'd chosen to wait for the cover of night to jump th
fence into Roger Dean Stadium. This way there were fewe
questions, and more importantly no one knew where the
were. He was still skeptical that anything waited for them
Why would Sleigh refuse to help them, then change hi
mind? It didn't make any sense. He didn't have the hear
to tell Tori she was grasping at straws, that the
were probably not going to find anything, that the ticke
was just what it appeared to be: trash.

"This is the row." Tori pointed ahead of him, two row
down.

"I see it."

He kept his gaze moving, searching the shadows, read
to throw Tori behind him if someone should take a sho
There were too many places to hide. This close to the field
they were completely exposed. It would be a great setu

r a sniper hit. Of course, Tori hadn't wanted to hear any
f that. He could have tried locking her up, but he had no
ubt she'd escape and come here by herself. Which was
w he wound up agreeing to this idiotic plan. If it came
wn to it, he'd be her human shield. He'd done stupider
ings in his life, but none of them were better motivated.

Where Tori went, he went also. It was the way of things
w.

He edged sideways down the row while she counted the
ats out loud until they got to number forty-three. This
as it. If someone wanted to hit them, this would be where
would happen. He crouched and pulled out a flashlight,
ining it on the bottom of the seat.

"There's nothing here," he said, part relieved and part
sappointed.

"Let me look."

"Hold on, just give me a second."

He pushed the seat down, searching under the armrests,
d got down on his hands and knees. Still nothing except
icky residue. He was about to tell her they'd wasted their
me when something glinted gold near the base of one of
e legs. Stretching, he reached back, brushing God-only-
new what, until he could get his nails behind a plastic
sing.

"Damn it," he grumbled.

Tori had been right.

He pried the plastic case of an SD card out from the
etal support, gripping it in his hand. He'd have felt better
they didn't find anything. What bomb had Victor Sleigh
st dropped in their laps?

"What is it?" Tori whispered.

Emery straightened and glanced around the empty
adium. It wasn't empty. Whatever was on this SD card
as worth killing for. That meant it was valuable enough

for someone to hang around, waiting to see if it would [
picked up.

"Go." He pushed Tori back the way they'd come.

"What is it?" She was excited, like a kid on Christma
but he wasn't about to open her casket. There was still
chance this could be a setup.

"Go now," he snapped.

Tori's spine straightened and she whirled around, n
arguments passing her lips. She'd left her hair down, so
bounced and shimmered down her back as she took th
stairs two at a time. He stayed right behind her, nev
letting her get more than a step or two ahead of him. The
didn't speak all the way back to the gate they'd left ope
until they were back in his Tesla. Even then he could st
feel eyes on him.

"Emery?"

He glanced around the empty lot, seeing movement
shadows everywhere. It was his mind playing trick
but he felt better punching the accelerator. Didn't eve
mind the squeal of tires as they shot forward, out onto th
main drag and away from whatever danger lurked.

"Here." He handed the SD card to her.

She took it, turning it over in her hands.

"There's a tablet under your seat." He'd stashed sever
things in the car after their latest round of excitement, ju
in case. He would never be caught unprepared again.

Tori dug the cheap tablet out and plugged the SD ca
into the side slot. It took her a moment to pull up the file
He itched to grab it from her, do it himself, but there we
only so many things he could multitask and do well behi
the wheel.

"You're going to have to look at this. It's gibberish
me," Tori said.

He eased to a stop at a red light and took the tablet from
er, flipping to the details view.

"What the heck are those?" Tori asked, peering over his
houlder.

"Holy shit . . . FTP connections. A lot of them." He
crolled through them, noting the numeric categorization.
. meant nothing to him right now, but it couldn't be a dif-
icult code to break.

"FTP I get, but—what are these?"

He didn't answer. Instead he tapped one and an Internet
rowser popped up. More files filled the screen. Emery se-
:cted one and opened it. Each FTP file would connect to
new server. A new batch of files. And God only knew
hat they would contain.

"I'll be damned," Emery muttered.

The file tried and failed to load, but he knew the exten-
ion type. It only loaded in a popular accounting software
rogram.

Victor Sleigh had given them hundreds of accounting
les. For what? Or who?

The light changed green and he shifted, driving nowhere
s fast as he could, his brain working a mile a minute. He
ould feel Tori's impatience across the car. He took her
and and kissed her knuckles, thankful for the moments of
uiet to focus.

"Some file transfer systems use a downloadable packet
 connect a machine, our tablet for example, to the server.
'hese give us automatic access to whatever's inside the
:rver." And it could be anything. Anything at all.

"Are you serious?" She clutched the tablet to her chest.
1formation was gold. They lived and died by it.

"Yes."

"Well, what do we do with it? Julian and Aiden—"

"Can't know."

"What?" She stared at him, jaw dropped. He'd neve
point out to her just how much she and Roni had come t
rely on the group. They might fancy themselves two boat
adrift on the ocean, but the truth was they'd banded to
gether with the rest of the crew to make something bigge
Better.

"CJ's leaving," he said quietly. That truth still hurt, bu
he had to think carefully about what they did next. "Th
FBI will send a new case agent down to oversee us. Julia
and Aiden will have to tell them everything they know. I
they don't know about it, they can't tell the FBI."

"So, we keep it a secret?"

"Maybe. Gabriel has a lot of contacts. Maybe we coul
use one of his sources to analyze everything once I down
load it." He reached over and squeezed her hand. Onc
their new FBI overlord arrived, things were going to g
dicey. He'd have to keep his nose clean to protect not onl
himself, but Tori.

"Okay. I'm sure Roni and I might know someone, too
But is this the best plan? I'm not arguing, but really?"

He pulled into an empty lot and shifted into park. H
twisted to face her, draping one arm along the back o
her seat.

"Things are going to get messier. I don't know why th
FBI has kept us in the dark, but I can't bring myself to trus
them when they chose to put the people I care about a
risk." He pushed a tendril of hair behind her ear.

Right now, nothing mattered more to him than Tori.

She stared at him for several seconds, as if weighin
him and the crew. She was loyal to a fault, even if she didn
realize it. He'd show her that they were protecting thos
they cared about, that he had her back.

"Okay. I'm in then." She squeezed his hand, one sid

of her mouth kicking up. "And, I'm pretty sure I love you, too."

Those words took the breath right out of his lungs. He stared at her, replaying that moment again in his mind. Tori leaned toward him and he met her halfway, sealing his mouth over hers, drinking her in. Emery could spend a lifetime with her, and it wouldn't be enough. He'd never seen this one coming.

Epilogue

Six weeks later . . .

Tori watched the second hand make yet another full pass around the clock on the wall above Emery's desk. He hadn't glanced up once in five minutes from whatever he was doing. He might be able to kick ass and take names, but a five-year-old could take him out if he was this concentrated on something. She loved his single-minded focus at times, but the man needed some serious situational awareness.

She blew out a breath and grabbed the back of his chair. He blinked back at the screen as she rolled him away from the desk he'd practically chained himself to.

"How long have you been there?" he asked, staring at her. He had the most adorable, boyish look on his face when he got that entrenched in his work. Of course she'd never tell him that.

"Just walked in."

Lie.

He probably realized it, but she wasn't going to call him on the lapse in awareness just like he wouldn't willingly dig himself a deeper hole. It was no wonder the man worked in a bunker. When he was focused, nothing in the world got through to him. Well, she had gone to some pretty creative lengths to get his attention, and succeeded, but it was always for his own good.

She plopped down on his lap, letting her legs drape over the arm of the chair, and rested her head on his shoulder. He cradled her closer, shifting until she fit perfectly against him. There was something to be said for having a man with some serious strength in his arms.

"You're wet." He frowned at her bikini.

She grinned. How nice of him to notice.

"Want to find out how wet I really am?"

His gaze narrowed and he frowned. She laughed. Teasing him was her new favorite pastime.

"Oh, come on. Give it a rest for a bit, okay?" Tori tipped her chin up and batted her eyelashes at him. She tried her best to not take up too much of his time, but she was no saint.

He held out for a count of three.

"Fine." He stroked her leg in an absentminded gesture she adored.

"What are you working on?"

"I thought you said to give work a rest."

"I'm curious, okay?"

Emery swiveled the chair, glancing at the door. They'd brought Gabriel in on the secret after downloading all of the files. Victor Sleigh had given them the accounting ledgers. All of them. To every single front business he supplied drugs for. It was a mountain of information, and buried in it were the puzzle pieces to figure out who he'd been working for. Who Evers worked for. But it wasn't a fast process.

"Nothing new," he said, referencing their secret. "But we're getting there."

"We are." She drew little circles on his shoulder. There

was another reason she'd found it worthwhile to distract Emery from his work. "Roni and I got a notice today our lease is up soon."

"I was thinking about that, actually. I put together a list somewhere of rental properties that have better security that would be more of a fit for you guys. It's around here somewhere." Emery swung the chair around, glancing at the desks that formed a U around his computers.

"You did?" She stared at him. Well, that wasn't exactly what she'd wanted to hear.

"Yeah." He reached for a tablet that was just a few inches too far away.

She snatched the tablet before he could grab it and thumped his shoulder with it.

"You are so damn oblivious." She smacked his chest with her fist for good measure, but not too hard.

"What?" He held up his hand, fending off her weak attack.

She dropped the tablet onto her lap and shoved her hand through his hair. It was getting a tad bit too long, even for him. Tomorrow she'd have to remind him to go get it cut or she'd snip the front part herself.

"Don't you realize most of my stuff is already here?" She'd taken over part of his closet, an entire dresser, and completely personalized all the photographs in the house. Little things that changed it from being a front to a true home. Hints he'd totally missed. It boggled her mind how someone so sharp and smart could be utterly clueless.

"No, I didn't know that." He frowned. In his defense, the house was large, but not that big.

"It is." She paused, but he only continued to stare at her, not saying anything. Was she really going to have to point out the obvious solution to him? Was that where they were? "What I'm getting at is, what would you think about living together? Roni and I talked about it. It was actually

ter suggestion, which surprised me. I figured it would
be—"

"Okay," he blurted over her.

It was her turn to stare at him a moment. Was he serious? No talking about it? Lists of pros and cons? Just,
okay?

"Yeah? You think you'll be okay with it?" Excitement
bubbled up inside of her. She'd never lived with a
boyfriend before, and Emery was so much more.

"Yeah." A slow smile spread across his lips. "I'd like
that."

"Me too." He scooped her up and straightened, a pur-
poseful glint in his eye.

"Mm, what are you thinking?"

"That I should be done working for the day. We've got
serious house stuff to discuss." He stepped sideways past
the racks of servers and equipment.

"Yeah? Like what?"

"Like where to christen this new step in our relationship."

She tossed her head back and laughed. Tori had never
thought being with Emery would be this much fun, but he
continued to surprise her every day. She was, quite frankly,
the luckiest spy girl in the world.

Emery, relaxed into the armchair, watched the moonlight bathe Tori's body in a molten pattern of shadow and
darkness. She snored softly, a secret he'd never tell her. It
was kind of cute, actually. He still hadn't figured out the
trick of sleeping through a whole night, but he was learning, if for no other reason than to lie next to her for a while
longer.

He rubbed at the ache in his chest. He hadn't loved
anyone in years. For a long time, he didn't think it was

possible anymore. And then Tori walked into his life. She's
gone from a pleasant interruption to his worst obsession.
He loved her. And there was nothing that would stop him.

The FBI had made a weak attempt to thwart their relationship, but it hadn't amounted to much. Either they had
bigger fish to fry or their operation was right where the
Feds wanted it. Rocking the boat too much wouldn't be in
their best interest. The crew had closed ranks around them,
showing Emery and Tori their full support.

Somehow, Julian even managed to spin the whole take-
down of Sleigh and the arrests into a story even the most
streetwise crook was believing. As far as anyone knew,
Classic Rides was home to the new gang in town. Aiden
wasn't thrilled since it meant business for the Shop was
down, but otherwise it was working out well. Even for
Emery. No one questioned why a money launderer would
date a mechanic. There was a power grab going on in
Miami for control of the crime scene, and their crew was
poised to at least appear to take over.

A lot rested on what strings the FBI pulled next. Who
they sent in to work with them. Since CJ's exit, they'd
heard very little except for a few nastygrams from the local
field office. But they were always on the crew's bad side.

His phone vibrated off the armrest and into his lap. He
opened the text message from Special Agent Tony Cardno,
the one he'd been waiting for.

Some guy shanked him in the showers. He's dead.

One last threat to Tori was taken care of. Tony had kept
Emery in the loop on the remaining hit team member,
who was quickly transferred into Tony's jurisdiction.
Emery wasn't responsible for the man's death, but he'd
known it was coming. It was hard to contain the mob's
wrath over the botched job with the twins and Evers. The

it had been announced as publicly as any hit might be,
so it was only a matter of time until the assassin was assas-
inated himself.

Emery would spend the rest of his life eliminating the
dangers to Tori, making her as happy as she made him.

He hadn't told her yet, but he planned to keep her.

Forever.

Don't miss the first book in the Hot Rides series,
Drive,
available now!

And keep reading for a sneak preview of
Chase,
coming in December!

The Classic Rides crew takes on top secret at top speed—
and chases the same thrills between the sheets . . .

For Gabriel, the FBI is just a painful memory. His new
team of motorheads may work for the Feds undercover,
but they're nothing like the backstabbers and bureaucrats
he left behind. Hunting drug dealers and smugglers in
Miami gets him the adrenaline rush he wants
and the justice he needs. All that's missing is the seal on
the badge—and Nikki, his sexy ex-partner.

Until she shows up at his garage, wearing short shorts
and a look that spells trouble. Nikki has never forgotten
the heartbreak Gabriel left her with last time. Even if she
can't have him, she still has to work with him. There's a
homegrown terrorist recruiting military vets into a cult of
fear and deception, and they all have roots in Miami.

It will take Gabriel and all the Classic Rides crew to stop
a catastrophe. But in close quarters with sparks flying,
it's only a matter of time before the old flame ignites . . .

Identities were like T-shirts, easy to change out until you found one that fit.

Gabriel Ortiz had worn so many identities in his life, sometimes he wasn't sure who he was anymore. At least until he got behind the wheel of a car. It was easier to tap into the parts of himself that were Gabriel, and not a made-up persona for a job. When it was just him, his car, and the road, things made sense. Lately he'd spent almost all his spare time behind the wheel of his new ride, a bad little Nissan Skyline he'd rebuilt piece by piece.

"I cannot believe how badly you smoked them." Roni Chazov, one of his fellow mechanics at Classic Rides, smacked him on the shoulder. She grinned at him, a rare thing these days, and flipped her long, red hair over her shoulder. Men fell over themselves for Roni's attention, but she'd always been one of the guys to him.

"Yeah." He nodded.

"You could at least act like you're having a good time." Roni crossed her arms over her chest and turned to face the line of cars across the street.

Hip-hop thumped from a chrome-plated lowrider. Half a dozen other cars had their hoods popped while drivers and onlookers kicked tires, talked shop, or bragged about their fastest time. Several of them were Gabriel's friends and coworkers, people he'd bled with. People he'd die for.

"They're watching us," Roni said, pitching her voice low.

"I know."

Their crew's reputation had always been solid on the streets, but now people were scared of them. Fear didn't sit well with Gabriel. At least not while he was himself. He'd pretended to be men who thrived on that kind of attention, but that was not Gabriel. Not his real self. He didn't like it at all.

"What do you think they're saying?" she asked.

"Probably wondering where we hid the bodies."

"That's not funny." Roni shot him a glare.

"Hey, you asked what they were saying. I just answered." He shrugged. It wasn't an understatement. Rumors were all over Miami about what their crew had done to a couple of hit men out for the Chazov twins.

"Yeah. I miss the days when they just wanted to know what was under the hood." Roni tapped the Skyline's tire with the toe of her boot.

Gabriel nodded. They'd all known the day was coming when their undercover FBI operation would change the street game. But none of them had anticipated this. Thanks to a friend at the Miami-Dade PD keeping the details of the arrests under wraps, they'd been able to put a spin on the latest exploits to paint themselves as the new street bosses. With their biggest rivals out of the picture, Gabriel and his crew were it. Which was the biggest joke there was. They were the crime kings who didn't do crime.

"Where's your twin?" Gabriel asked.

"Where do you think?" Ice laced Roni's tone.

"Things okay between you two?"

"Yeah."

"Okay." He shrugged.

Unlike most of his crew, Gabriel had experience with ong-term, deep-cover missions. They were hell on the ody and the soul. That they were three years into the peration without any real problems with their people was emarkable. In his book, Roni's sister shacking up with heir field tech wasn't all that bad. He was even happy for hem, if he could be happy about anything.

Roni leaned toward him. "I was thinking—"

Gabriel's pocket chimed, and an echoing noise emanated rom Roni's pocket.

That couldn't be good.

He dug his phone out of his pocket, unlocked the screen, and tapped the message notification from—speak of the devil—their field tech, Emery. In Gabriel's periph-eral vision he could see the others doing the same thing.

Alarm at Classic Rides. Security off-line.

"Shit," Roni said. She glared at him. "Get driving. You're fastest."

Classic Rides was the business they all worked out of, restoring classic muscle cars, and after hours was when they did their FBI gigs. They didn't keep anything at the garage except tools and cars, but thanks to current events, they had a huge target on their backs. If someone wanted to fuck with them, the Shop was a prime opportunity.

Roni jogged toward her new V10 Viper while Gabriel pulled the door open to his Skyline and dropped into the driver's seat. The onlooking pedestrians scattered, jump-ing onto the sidewalk as Gabriel peeled out in a plume of exhaust and squealing tires. He glanced in his rearview mirror. The closest headlights were over a car length away. Aiden's if he had to guess. Their fearless leader was the shop owner, and had wrapped up his life's savings in the Shop.

The fastest route to Classic Rides this time of nigh was via I-95. Gabriel ignored a red traffic light, barrelin through before the oncoming traffic had even let off thei accelerators. Another car turned onto the old two-lan street ahead of him, blocking him. He jerked the Skylin into the left lane, stomped on the accelerator, and shifted The car lurched forward, the engine barely even working Yet. There was a discernible lack of vibration as the ca coasted over the road as if the tires never really touched the asphalt. This really was the fastest car he'd ever had.

And right now, he needed every second it could buy him.

Being part of the crew at Classic Rides had given him a purpose when he had nothing. After his world crumbled and everything he thought he had, walked out the door, the crew had put him back together. They'd given him a mission. Something to live for. The garage might just be a building, but it was more to him.

"*Ándale, ándale,*" he chanted.

He coasted through another intersection, weaving between cars, and passed under the overpass, cutting a sedan off as he changed lanes, ignoring the angry blare of the horn. The speakers began to ring and Emery's name flashed across the display mounted into the dash.

Gabriel pressed a button on his steering wheel, activating the call.

"Talk to me."

"You're the closest. I have no eyes on the facility. Someone had to have taken the security out at the power source." Normally Emery was quiet and rather mild-mannered. That was a well-constructed front. Right now, Emery cursed and growled with the best of them.

"I should go in hot, you mean?" Gabriel maneuvered around the slower traffic, making liberal use of the shoulder.

There were only two exits to go. He couldn't see Aiden in his rearview mirror. He pushed the car faster, his focus narrowing to the vehicles around him and the way the Skyline handled.

"Yes, but hold up a second and wait for backup. We don't know what's in there yet, and I want them alive."

He could hear the frustration in Emery's voice. Classic Rides had remained as secure a location as they could make it. No doubt Emery would take it personally should the facility ever be breached. Like now.

"No can do, Brain."

He flipped on his blinker as he coasted over the white line, cutting off a red van. The Shop was a few streets over from the highway, still a couple lights to go.

"That's not a good idea. Wait for backup."

Emery's voice drifted into the background. Gabriel pulled the hand brake and let the car whip around at a ninety-degree angle. Cars honked and their tires screeched as drivers swerved to avoid him. He gunned the engine and shot forward, the familiar storefronts a blur as he focused on the retro sign of Classic Rides ahead, with the purple and indigo night sky behind it. Palm trees waved in a stronger than normal breeze.

A single bay door was open and all the lights were on. The parking lot was empty, save for the cars for sale, lined up along the perimeter. Hell, the gate and chain were down, too, almost as if someone had opened the Shop for business. It wasn't exactly a covert setup.

Screw it.

Gabriel steered the Skyline into the parking lot and shifted hard into park. He grabbed his primary weapon out of the center console, while keeping his gaze on the open door. His 1967 Pontiac GTO was inside. If whoever thought about hitting them tonight touched the car, he was

likely to ignore the directive to take any and all adversarie
alive.

He got out of his car and crept toward the bay doo
keeping his eyes on the storefront windows.

Nothing moved.

In the distance he could hear the rumble and whine c
engines. The others would be here any moment. The sma
thing to do would be to wait, but this shop, these peopl
they were his safe haven. His family. When it came t
those things, he'd face down a dozen thugs for them.

He took a deep breath and peered around the open doo
into the garage.

Four cars sat ready for the morning. A tune-up, an o
change, Gabriel's other ride, and a complete restore jot
All the familiar smells filled the air: oil, rubber, an
lemon-scented cleaner. Nothing was out of place, excep
the woman with dark hair wearing a suit, standing with he
back to him. She appeared to be looking at something o
the workbench surface.

Suits meant Feds.

He took another step, gun trained on the woman.

"Turn around," he barked.

The woman straightened and for a moment neithe
moved. Did she have a partner? Someone hiding as he
backup? There were easily a dozen places in the garage t
take cover. They'd designed it that way for exactly thi
reason.

She pivoted to face him and everything stopped. H
didn't breathe or blink. The world could have stoppe
moving for all he cared.

The hair was different and he'd never seen her in dra
black before, but the face was still the same. Or simila
She'd always smiled when he'd seen her, but that wa

efore. Now, her lips were compressed in a tight line. Pity,
ae was rather stunning when she smiled.

"Hello, Gabriel."

"Nikki?" He lowered his gun, frowning. Lights slashed
cross the garage as one and then another car turned into
ae parking lot. He stalked toward her, needing to know it
as really *his* Nikki before the others arrived and all hell
roke loose.